DEFIANT

He leaned forward, his lips brushing her skin. The touch was surprisingly gentle considering how captive he held her body. Her hands, still held above her head, relaxed.

His mouth lingered on hers. There was no bruising demand for domination, just a slow, gentle conquest. She felt her body slacken, allowing him to explore, allowing herself to feel the sensation of lips touching lips, breath touching breath.

Heat pooled between her thighs.

His tongue licked the seam of her lips and tightness formed in her belly. For an instant the world stood still as he tasted her mouth. He did not hurry and she felt herself being sucked under his spell. . . .

Books by Jessica Trapp

MASTER OF DESIRE

MASTER OF PLEASURE

THE PLEASURES OF SIN

DEFIANT

Published by Kensington Publishing Corporation

DEFIANT

JESSICA TRAPP

ZEBRA BOOKS
KENSINGTON PUBLISHING CORP.
http://www.kensingtonbooks.com

ZEBRA BOOKS are published by

Kensington Publishing Corp.
119 West 40th Street
New York, NY 10018

All Kensington titles, imprints, and distributed lines are
available at special quantity discounts for bulk purchases
for sales promotion, premiums, fund-raising, educational or
institutional use.

Special book excerpts or customized printings can also be cre-
ated to fit specific needs. For details, write or phone the office
of the Kensington Special Sales Manager: Attn. Special Sales
Department. Kensington Publishing Corp., 119 West 40th
Street, New York, NY 10018. Phone: 1-800-221-2647.

Zebra and the Z logo Reg. U.S. Pat. & TM Off.

ISBN-13: 978-1-4201-0095-2
ISBN-10: 1-4201-0095-5

First Printing: December 2010
10 9 8 7 6 5 4 3 2 1

Printed in the United States of America

To Bet Pichardo
You are a true friend

Chapter 1

Jared St. John thumbed the engraving on his staff as he contemplated the best way to steal a lock of Lady Gwyneth's hair. Monastery life was notoriously bland and perhaps having a small token of the world he would be missing when he took his vows would appease his longing for a home and land—things a common falconer would never have—especially one with a heart as black as his own.

He drew the knife from his rope belt. Gwyneth's shiny hair was tempting as treasure to a pirate. It was not blond, nor white, but intermingled strands of gold and silver—as if she were not quite human but something otherworldly—fey or elvin. The luminous mass hung in a glittering cascade past her hips, the ends curling and skimming midway down her thighs.

The majestic black-and-white hawk on his shoulder dug her talons into the leather padding Jared wore beneath his clothing as if to protest his immoral desire.

"Peace, Aeliana," he cooed to the goshawk. "I only

want a tiny curl. There is a loose one hanging by her shoulder. She will not even notice."

Skillfully, he concealed the blade in the folds of the brown monk's robe that he wore.

The bird ruffled her feathers at the motion.

"We will hunt later, my friend," he murmured to soothe her as he strained his neck to watch his prey wander through the crowds that had gathered here at Windrose Castle. "One small curl will not be missed."

Aeliana's feathers fanned against his cheek as if she understood every word and clearly disapproved.

"Perhaps I could gift her with something as an even exchange," he mused. Most of his possessions had been given into the church treasury. He only had his hawk, his staff, and, in his pouch, a small book. Yes, the book would be a perfect gift. It was valuable and gilded like Gwyneth's hair. The original leather cover had become worn with age and he had crafted a wooden cover for it that he had carved himself and covered with gold leaf. Surely something like that would satisfy anyone's sense of fairness.

Whistles and cheers rose from the crowd as if applauding his decision, although he knew no one paid any attention to him. Silken banners waved, acrobats performed on the lawn, and toward the back of the large bailey, an area had been set aside for a tournament. Merchants pushed carts filled with flowers and apples and trinkets. Children, limbs flailing, kicked a ball this way and that followed by a rowdy pack of small dogs.

Lady Gwyneth turned slightly. Jared's breath caught in his throat. Many women at the festival were beautiful, but she was glorious.

Her skin was alabaster, her eyes a brilliant blue.

She had a slightly pointed chin and delicate ears. A sapphire ring twinkled on her finger.

Never in his life had he seen a woman like her.

Bewitching.

His heart pounded and he tightened his grip on the staff. He tried to tear his gaze away, but could not.

Damn. More reason he must get to the monastery—never be near a female again. One woman had nearly ruined his life—torn apart his family and his heart. Monkhood offered salvation for his sins.

Gwyneth's left cheek dimpled as she smiled at a child. She spoke softly to an elderly hag, then she reached and patted a dog on the head as she passed.

Everything about her bespoke kindness, caring. Qualities he knew that he himself did not possess. Not after what he'd done to his brother.

He closed his eyes.

He would never deserve a woman like her.

He thought of his mother for a moment. With her coiffed hair, shiny jewels, and glittering gowns, she glistened like a cathedral alcove. And like the icons at the church, she always looked at him with blank eyes. He knew little about her except for catching glimpses of her across the bailey when she happened to be out for a walk while he worked with the castle's falcons. He was an embarrassment, her bastard child—proof of her indiscretions.

He slammed his thoughts against the memory.

The crowd was thick and loud and people bumped into each other at every step. If he was quick, he could reach forward, lop off a single lock of hair without her noticing as she passed by. He would braid it and keep it nearby to remind him that there was more to life than kneeling on cold stone floors and endlessly reciting Latin chants: a future he deserved, but one he looked forward to not at all. It was his duty to mend the strife he had caused between him and his brother. His duty to pay penitence for the woman and babe he'd killed.

"I thought you were done with women." Rafe, his half brother—the noble-born son who had grown up in the keep rather than in the falconer's mews— sidled up to him. He punched Jared on the arm, nearly dropping the two steaming meat pies and the loaf of bread that he was holding.

Blast him! Quickly Jared hid the sharp knife within the folds of his robe, adjusted his staff to hold it in the crook of his elbow, and took one of the pies.

"Watch your clumsiness," he snarled.

They stared at each other for a moment. Aeliana fluttered.

Rafe was shorter than Jared, but slightly stockier. In sharp contrast to Jared's plain robe, he wore fancy green boots with silver buckles and a finely embroidered surcoat. He tucked his thumb into his belt and braced his legs wide apart.

So much bad blood between them.

"You nearly dropped our food," Jared groused, but did not bring up the past between them. Rafe's betrothed. A beautiful woman. A passionate affair. The accusation of rape. And then her death. And the unborn babe's as well. 'Twas the reason he must enter the monastery—set himself away. He could ne'er trust his own flesh again.

A tinge of lavender wafted into the air. The luscious curves of Lady Gwyneth's hips swayed side to side as she sashayed past.

Curse Rafe and his timing! The opportunity for stealing her hair was gone! Guilt touched him, but he let it go: 'twas only hair and not her virginity or her soul or her life that he planned to steal. Unlike Colette. Unlike the baby daughter who had been inside her.

The crowd parted for Lady Gwyneth as though she were a princess. She wore finery—silver and blue silks, sapphire jewels, and ermine trim. Small satin slippers graced her feet. Her ethereal beauty set her apart—made her seem to float rather than walk as other humans did. She had delicate brows and generous lips.

"Close your hole, Jared." Rafe sipped ale from his drinking horn. "You are acting as though you have ne'er seen a woman afore. And after what you did with—"

Giving his brother a withering glower, Jared took a step forward and allowed himself the guilty pleasure of admiring the way Gwyneth's neck swiveled as she greeted the horde of young men who had come to this feast to vie for her hand. Her hair glistened like a gold-and-silver cloud.

"She's glorious," he whispered.

She was an angel. The most picturesque sight he had ever seen. Light and sparkle compared to the darkness and cold inside his own being. He longed to run his tongue over the skin of her shoulder, tease her to pleasure.

Rafe rolled his eyes. "Bah. We will head to the brothel later. One woman is the same as the next."

Anger flashed inside Jared.

"I have no use for whores," he said with a piety he didn't feel. He latched onto the wooden cross hanging from a cord about his neck for good measure. Guilt wound through him that he had just imagined the fey Lady Gwyneth in an unclean manner, that he had considered stealing a piece of her hair. He would take his vows soon—become a man of peace and live only for heavenly treasure. There would be no more tasting of women for him.

He tucked his knife into the rope belt.

Aeliana twitched restlessly, her wing brushing against her face.

Lady Gwyneth stopped. Ignoring the scores of admirers, she swooped up a small girl, placed the youngster on her hip, and tickled her toes.

Jared's pulse leapt as she laughed in response to the child's giggle. Her white-gold hair mingled with the girl's brown locks.

What a wonderful wife she would make.

If only he could rip the novice robe from his back and use his staff to fight for her hand as others at the faire would do this day.

He looked down at his plain brown robe and simple leather sandals. Even if he could be free of the guilt that regaled him to be in a monastery, he could not support a wife such as Gwyneth on the meager income of a falconer. He was not of noble blood; it would take a castle with strong walls to keep her safe from men who wanted to steal her.

Asides, she had not so much as glanced at him.

She was far above his station.

Her father—at least Jared supposed it was her father—frowned and cleared his throat. He was an elderly man with a well-stitched tunic, a ceremonial sword, a gray beard, two deep lines betwixt his eyes, and a demeanor of disapproval.

The smile melted from his angel's face. She set the young girl on the ground and stared straight ahead. Utter misery clouded her sky-colored eyes.

Sadness washed over him. He flicked his fingers against his staff; the wood felt solid and smooth against his palm. Clearly she had no real desire to be here either—to be shown and displayed as a prize.

Likely she was a pawn in her family and, like himself, forced to a life path that suited not at all. Her shoulders slumped as she followed Graybeard toward the box above the field where she would watch the tournament. Banners waved above them.

Were those tears in her eyes? Surely he could not see such from this distance.

The longing to protect her flowed through his heart. If she were his, he would give her all the babies and children she wished to hold. He would never frown at her for tickling a girl's toe.

Her hips swayed as she climbed the steps. His groin tightened.

Rafe let out a raucous guffaw. "Oh, she's a fine vixen, that one. Just look at her arse. I could turn up her skirt and tup her right hard, I could."

Swiveling on his heels, Jared forgot his guilt, forgot all reason to become a man of God and live a life of celibacy and peace.

He punched his brother in the nose.

Gwyneth of Windrose gazed at the bowed head of the handsome novice who was saying grace and wished she, too, could join a monastery instead of parading about with her titties half hanging out. Being heiress to Windrose along with her own dower lands made her a sought-after prize, and her father's quest to marry her off to the highest bidder revolted her. Somehow she had to persuade him that 'twould be best to hold off just a little longer—that none of the young bucks here were quite rich enough, quite powerful enough.

She should be allowed to control her own lands, her own destiny—no need of a man at all. Her dower estate, given to her by her mother, was small but profitable—all she truly needed. Then Windrose could be given to one of her sisters and she could live a life of freedom rather than duty.

The prayer ended and the young novice lifted his head. Heavens, he was tall. And wide-shouldered. His green eyes locked with hers and she felt a bolt of attraction. Unlike the others, his eyes remained fixed on her face instead of her bosom. He had straight dark hair, chiseled features, and an enigmatic gaze.

Pushing her hair over one shoulder, she smiled at him. He seemed friendly. Safe. A welcome respite from the shamelessly lustful stares she had endured most of the day.

"A toast to Gwyneth's beauty," crowed a fat, drunken nobleman. The beginnings of his meal dripped down upon the patterns of his blue brocade doublet.

The scents of roasted game and cinnamon apples wafted through the great hall.

Ivan of Westland, a young lord wearing a prissy tunic with lace around the sleeves and shoes with points so long they were tied to his knees, yanked off his feathered cap and held it to his breast. "Gwyneth, my fair love," he sang chivalrously.

Another man raised his tankard, spilling drops

of brown ale as he leaned over to peer at the young mounds of flesh pouring over the top of her square-cut bodice. "To Gwyneth's breasts, er, beauty!" he echoed.

Raunchy laughter burst throughout the chamber.

A pox on them all!

She glanced at the young monk, wishing for a friendly face, someone who did not see her as an object of lust, but he had turned aside, apparently in disgust. At her?

Gritting her teeth, she glared at her father. 'Twas he who insisted she display her wares as fully as if she were a harlot in a brothel. She had done naught wrong! She never showed this much flesh. 'Twas unseemly! She wanted an apron, a needle, to do something useful. As her mother would have done.

Brenna, her sister, gave her a cutting look from across the trestle table. She wore a green gown of fine silk and her red hair was swept into an elegant updo with long, curling tendrils that concealed the scar on her cheek. "Slut," she muttered, not even trying to hide her animosity.

The unfairness of her sister's envy was a knife stab in the gut. Only a few months ago, the two of them had been stealing pies together and hiding beneath the North Tower's stairs.

But then their mother died.

Everything had changed. Their friendship. Their relationship. The love between them.

Shrinking in her chair to make herself as inconspicuous as possible, she stared down at her hands, at her mother's sapphire ring encircling her index finger, and wished she could go back in time.

Brenna pushed around the dish of stuffed salmon

on her trencher until it was piled and shaped like two pink breasts. She leered at them in mocking imitation of what the menfolk had been doing for most of the day.

Gwyneth felt her ears heat. "I'll tell father," she whispered, kicking her sister beneath the table. It was an empty threat. He would punish her severely for fighting at the feast instead of playing the part of hostess and lady of the keep. She forced herself to sit up straight and proper. The way her mother would have wanted her to do.

Brenna wagged her tongue vulgarly.

"Go rot," Gwyneth mouthed at her, careful to turn her face to one side so her father could not see the action.

From atop the gallery, a band of musicians warmed up their instruments. A minstrel started in on a warbling ode to the color and shine of her hair.

Faith! She'd heard every trite word of praise over and over until they all ran together: a mishmash of idiotic terminology.

"Ivory glowing in the dawn," the bard proclaimed. "The fair Gwyneth's hair outshines them all."

Out of the corner of her eye, she saw Ivan lick his lips and the young monk curl his in distaste.

Heat flooded her cheeks. She jabbed her eating dagger into a hunk of rosemary-roasted rabbit and staved off the urge to scream. Of a truth, she would cut the mass to her shoulders if she did not fear her papa's reaction. The way men reacted to her was dunderheaded!

Brenna glared at her. "You know you love the attention."

A tight ache banded Gwyneth's chest; surely her

sister knew she had no say in the bard's choice of songs.

"You preen like a peacock," Brenna snarled, "flirting and prissing about and wanting all the men to follow you."

"That's not true!"

"Bah. I saw you making eyes at that monk—"

"Your *jealousy* is pathetic."

"Your *vanity* is so great that you even want men of God to lust for you—"

"You go too far."

Twisting away from her sister's mocking face and the horrible pile of salmon that rounded up on her trencher, Gwyneth searched the sea of faces. If only she could find someone to ease her hurt. She told herself she was not looking for the monk.

Emily, a girl who had been her friend just this past summer, turned a shoulder away as Gwyneth offered a tentative smile.

Brenna coughed at the victory and Emily turned toward her, took notice of the mound of fish on Brenna's trencher, and giggled under her breath.

Stinging prickles crawled down Gwyneth's neck, flushing even the tops of her shoulders.

"Gwyneth will make an excellent wife," she heard her father say in a loud, booming voice as if this were an auction and not a meal. "She's got fine wide hips for bearing heirs."

The hundreds of flickering candles lighting the chamber whirled in a spectacular display of color, and it was as if his voice were far, far away.

She longed to cover her ears, to get up, to run, anything besides sit here and pretend this was normal. Twirling her mother's ring, she stiffened her back and squared her shoulders. *A lady should never slump,* her mother had instructed.

"And she has her mother's bosom."

"Father!" she admonished, but he gave her a sharp look that threatened violence if she interfered.

"And, here, even the bard sings of her beauty."

Because you paid him to, she longed to wail, but instead stared down at the table and prayed for the evening meal to end. At this point she would have agreed to marry even old man Blake, the gong farmer, to end the festivities.

"Look at those bones on her face, so fine, so feminine—"

"Fath—"

"And she knows how to embroider in the tiniest of stitches. Her delicate hands would tend a man's every need."

More guffaws echoed around the chamber.

Unable to bear any more of her father's comments, she stood.

"Where go you, daughter?" he blasted out. His gray beard fluttered.

She offered a shaky smile. "To . . . check on the kitchens. The ale runs low."

Her father frowned, working his jaw back and forth. "Tell Brenna to do it—"

"My lady?" Someone tapped her on the shoulder.

She whirled and gasped in surprise. The novice monk! Up close he was even more handsome. His eyes were a startling shade of green—spring grass ringed with the darker shades of summer. His lips sinfully lush. His tall, wide-shouldered body seemed woefully out of place in religious robes, and the plain garments did nothing to distract from his appeal. She wondered how his dark hair would look when it had been shorn and tonsured. It seemed a crime to do anything to mar such perfection.

"I wished to give you this, Lady Gwyneth."

In his hand, he held a small book. The front cover was made of thin wood that was elaborately carved around the edges and coated with gold.

Wide-eyed, she stared at the gift. "You wish to give me a book?" What on earth was a novice monk doing with something so valuable? Why would he give it to her?

He seemed suddenly self-conscious, flustered.

Brenna tsked. "Seducing a man of God is a sin," she whispered. "I saw how you were looking at him."

Oh, heavens.

"I can't read," she blurted, feeling her cheeks heating all the way up to her ears.

Her father cleared his throat. "Women have no need for reading."

At that, the novice straightened his shoulders. He was several inches taller than her father. He winked at her—not monklike at all! Her stomach fluttered. She had the clear impression that all his earlier frowns were for the others and that the two of them were somehow in a conspiracy with each other—that he had sensed her discomfiture, understood how embarrassed she felt about being displayed so improperly. She wished to be a stately lady, modest and regal, like her mother.

"The book contains instruction on the proper place of women," he said piously, but the twinkle in his green eyes belied the words.

Her heart warmed. She had a friend in this dreadful place after all.

Her father grunted. "For certes my daughter should learn some manners."

"Mayhap she should start by wearing more modest apparel."

"I did not choose—"

The monk pressed the book into her hand, giving her fingers a little squeeze. Her skin tingled at his touch and her protest died in her throat. Who was he? Was he on her side or not?

"Women should be tending to their duty, the needs of their husband and children, not reading," her father said, reaching for the book. "Thank you for the gift, monk. I will use it for her dowry."

"Nay!" She clutched the book to her chest. Likely he planned to sell it or try to buy a favor with it!

Her father moved forward. "Give that to me." His gray beard bristled and puffed around his lips.

She stepped back. The air in the great hall felt thick and murky despite the fact that she had instructed the maids to sweep it clean and put down new rushes just this past week.

His fingers touched the book's gilded wooden cover.

"'Tis mine."

"Daughter." His voice was a warning.

Abruptly she whirled and fled to the door in the side of the great hall.

"Gwyneth!" she heard him bellow behind her, but recklessly she rushed outside, away from them. She knew she would be beaten for her imprudence later—that her unruly behavior would spoil all his plans for a good marriage—but she did not care. He would not take the young monk's book from her.

"Good riddance," she heard Brenna say behind her in a loud whisper. "Mayhap the minstrels will play some decent music now without you whoring around with the priests."

Her eyes stung.

Blinking back tears, choking back the agony threatening to swallow her, she fled out the keep's door and down the steps. Her fingers squeezed the book painfully. Perhaps she could find Adele, her younger sister who had managed somehow to escape the festivities.

Later, she would choose a husband. She would submit to a life of duty—but her father would not take the book. And she would learn to read.

Chapter 2

Rain scented the air as Gwyneth hurried, heart pounding, for the copse of trees down by the river, her thoughts muddling together as she hopped her way across rocks and patches of grass so that her satin slippers would not get dirty.

It would be best to hide until her father calmed down.

Stopping for a moment to catch her breath, she leaned against a wide oak, laid a hand on her chest, and wished she could somehow thwart her father's plans to sell her off to the highest bidder.

As she waited for her heart to calm, she realized the book the young monk had given her was still in her hand. Curious about it, she turned it over and over, examining the binding. It was small and exquisite—only the size of her palm—and much too expensive a gift to give to a stranger. The front was made of thin wood that was covered in gold leaf. A dragon, meticulously carved, graced the surface.

Why would he give it to her?

Puzzled, she opened it, recalling the strange way he

had said it would instruct her on the place of women. The sly wink and grin he had given her—as if they shared some grand joke together and he was fully on her side—was vexing. 'Twas not at all monklike and she suspected the book had nothing to do with instructing women at all.

The writing was in clean, beautiful loops and lines of various lengths and heights, artistry all to itself. She squinted at the pages, flipping here and there and holding it this way and that, trying to understand what any of it said. She could make out an A on one page and three T's on another, but she did not know any other letters.

She ran her hand across the carved cover, wondering at the care that the craftsman had taken in fashioning it. It was a beautifully fashioned golden dragon with delicate scales and a long, curved tail. Its wings—open and lovely—seemed to beckon her to soar, too.

Why had the monk given her something so expensive? Why had he been so cryptic?

Questions with no answers.

Frustrated, she tapped the binding a few times with her palm.

Her father said that women didn't need to learn to read; the church and society preached that educating women wasted time and resources—a sin to be so lavish—but curiosity burned inside her. She wanted to know what it said! Surely learning to read was only a small indulgence in the pleasures of sin.

Stuffing it into her bodice, she determined that when she returned to the feast she would demand answers from the young monk.

She tugged at her dress, but the bodice was cut so

low the book's spine poked out the top no matter how much she tried to adjust it. She frowned, irritated once again with her father for insisting on displaying so much of her cleavage. She pressed her breasts down, wishing she could make them flat again as they had been only a year ago. Her body had changed so much in the past months it felt as though an animal lived under her skin—a lump here, a lump there.

A sense of deep loss chilled her inside. Her own body had betrayed her, growing in places that once were flat and trickling blood down her thighs each month. She wanted her dolls back, her sister back, her own clothing back—the plain kirtles and tough leather boots—garments she could kick a ball in unhindered. These huge fancy houppelandes with their immodest hems and delicate embroidery seemed too flimsy for any use but to make men leer and women jealous.

A woman's scream rent the air, interrupting her morose musings.

Gwyneth jumped, terrified it might be Adele, her younger sister. She had not been at the feast and often walked in the woods with her two dogs.

The sound, like that of a wounded animal, came again. She whirled. "Adele?"

A long stone's throw away, through the thick trees, a flash of colors—blues, reds, purples—sharply contrasted with the greens and browns of the forest. A large man with dark hair, a short beard, and cruel features was tackling a girl, pulling her to the ground. Not Adele. A peasant.

The girl fell, her skirt hiked to her waist, and the man reached to yank down his hose. She twisted to one side, scrambling for freedom. He slapped her across the face.

Gwyneth's body jerked in reaction. Her legs liquefied. She crumpled forward, clinging to a sapling for balance. She should run, go get help.

The man ripped down his hose and a sausage-shaped piece of flesh sprang out. His tunic slanted to one side. His clothes bespoke the noble class. He wore a fancy pair of green leather boots with silver buckles. "Lay still, wench."

There was another scream and another slap.

The girl ducked her head and put up her arms to guard her face.

Bile rose in Gwyneth's throat as the man lunged atop her. His hips thrust between her legs, forcing her thighs to part. She didn't scream again, but let out a yelp that sounded like a cow being impaled.

Nay.

Nay.

Nay.

Terror mixed with indignant rage gripped Gwyneth's mind and she wanted to kick herself for standing helplessly about while another woman was being brutalized. She had to do *something*.

She glanced back at Windrose. The turrets hung over the tops of the trees. Too far to go for help.

Heart pounding, she stooped to a crouching position and searched around frantically for something to use as a weapon.

"Blasted dress," she muttered as her legs tangled in yards of useless silk, then felt her heart jump against the book that rested in her bodice. She needed to be quiet, enormously silent, speechless—use her mind, not brute strength.

Her hand closed around a fallen limb. She lifted but it didn't move. A curse on being born female.

Carefully, she selected a smaller stick, one about four feet in length and only about the thickness of a woman's wrist. The wood scraped her palm, rough and dry. She would sneak behind him, wallop him over the head. Surely she could distract him long enough for the girl to get away.

And mayhap the brute would turn on her . . .

She tightened her grip on the limb.

Her stick, her wits, the element of surprise—those weapons would have to be enough.

Please, God, she started, wishing desperately that she had not neglected her prayers all this past week. *Dear Mother Mary,* she tried again. Perhaps Mary would be more generous than God with religious shortcoming.

She would attend Mass twice a day, confess how she'd watched a spider crawl across the tiles instead of listening to the prayers and hymns.

Holding her breath, she crept through the woods as quietly as she could, working her way behind the man. The brute twisted the girl's titties in his fingers so that they looked contorted. Pain laced her face, but she no longer fought him. The scent of sweat hung in the air.

"Un, uh, uh," he grunted, hips pumping in and out between the tangle of her skirts.

Determination flooded Gwyneth's mind and in that moment, she hated men. All men. This would be her lot as well if she were sold in marriage. Mayhap it would be on a soft, clean bed and not some dirty forest—but 'twas the same for all women. They were forced to open their bodies for a man's brutish lusts.

The girl's eyes rolled back in her head, her face pulled into a grimace.

A knot twisted in Gwyneth's stomach. Her satin slippers sank in the mud, making hideous sucking noises as she advanced, but the man did not turn.

He continued his onslaught.

She took another step. And then another. Only five steps more and she would be upon him. The stench of unwashed bodies and some sickly sweet toilet water assaulted her nostrils.

A bramble snagged the hem of her gown, pulling her up short with a lurch. The damn blasted gown. She would shred the thing when she got home, take out all her fury on the yards of lace and silk.

She twisted to pull her skirt loose but the movement caused another section of it to entangle in the thorns.

Curses!

She pulled harder and a ripping sound rent the air.

The man's piglike noises stopped abruptly and he turned, his eyes going wide.

Coldness burst in her chest and for an instant her lungs refused to breathe.

Too panic stricken to think, she tore her skirt free, raced forward and slammed him across the forehead with her weapon. The stick splintered into two pieces.

Gasping, she clenched her fingers around the remaining part of her weapon so tightly that her palms went numb.

The man began to rise; his hands reached for her. "You little wench." His dark brows were drawn together and his lips lifted in a snarl.

Oh, saints. Oh, Mary. He was going to kill her.

With a scream, she raised her shortened club and clobbered him across the face.

"Run! Run!" she yelled at the girl. At least one of them should get away.

Blind panic took hold of her mind and she beat him again with the stick.

A crunching noise sounded, red streaks appeared on his cheeks and blood splattered from his nostrils to his chin.

He yowled. His eyes glowed with fury. Greenish black. Like a dark, evil spirit dredged up from the bog.

"You'll pay for that, bitch." He lunged for her.

The numbness in her fingertips spread to her arms, to her legs, across her shoulders.

She hit him again. *Wap. Wap. Wap.* And *wap* again.

He staggered to his feet, but tripped on the hose that he had shoved down his legs. His eyes rolled back in his head and he melted atop the girl.

With a grunt, the girl pushed him off. His body landed with a *thuck* in the mud. Blood pooled beside him.

The girl began straightening out her garments—a dirty peasant skirt and a simple blouse—and rose to her feet.

Gwyneth heaved uneven breaths and pressed her palm to her chest; the book was still safe. Her shoulders ached and all she wanted to do was run back to Windrose. The feast that had been so awful only moments before seemed tame compared to this.

The man twitched, or maybe he just slid farther into the muck. Rivulets of blood ran down his face and his nose hung lopsidedly to one side.

"Um. I think 'e's quite down," the girl said, dusting

her hands back and forth on her skirt and pulling her blouse to cover her chest.

Gwyneth's spine seemed to crumple of its own accord. Sickness washed over her.

"Ain't ne'er seen a noblewoman do that." The girl cocked her head to one side and looked impassively from Gwyneth to the man lying among the leaves. Red blood and brown grime oozed together. "I do thank you, me lady."

Startled, Gwyneth stared at the girl, seeing her clearly for the first time since the ordeal began. The girl might have been two or three years older than herself. They were similar in height, but she wore a patched homespun dress and no jewelry whatsoever. Her tattered garments smelled of some sort of cheap toilet water and the stench of male sweat. She had mussed brown hair, a crooked nose, high cheekbones, and a large mole on her chin. Despite her common appearance, her chin lifted and her back was straight. A dark wisdom flashed in her brown eyes.

Unsure what to say, Gwyneth scrutinized her for signs of distress, for some indication that the girl was about to collapse into a sniveling heap. Perhaps she should take her back to the castle. At any moment, she would surely sink to the ground and start crying.

Instead, the girl stared back, a hand on her hip.

After a long pause, when no such fits of hysteria seemed to be forthcoming, Gwyneth asked, "Are you all right?"

"Better now." The girl gave a slight smile and the corners of her mouth quivered, the only tangible sign that she might have been upset by what she had just suffered. She plucked her yellow shawl from the ground and wrapped it around her shoulders.

Reaching forward, Gwyneth patted her awkwardly on the arm, wanting to give sympathy but confused about the best way to go about doing so. Having no female friends these past months since her mother had passed on left her feeling insecure about how to handle uncomfortable situations. She found herself retreating into formality, the mere crust of what she should do. She tried to think of what her mother, a grand lady of the keep, would have done.

Maybe she should hug the girl. But that did not seem quite right. She was a peasant after all, not a particularly well-off one based on the look of her. And she was dirty.

They both gazed down at the man. Mud splattered his tunic, which was flipped haphazardly to his waist showing his turned-down hose. His male member flopped against one thigh.

Bile rose in her throat. Gwyneth drew a hand over her mouth and averted her gaze.

Above, a lone hawk circled, black-and-white wings flashing in the lowering sun. An omen?

The man's eyes were still weirdly wide open. They were dark green, nearly black, but had a glazed, dull look about them.

He wasn't moving.

"Is 'e dead, you think?"

Chapter 3

Dead?

The question about death was asked so mildly that the girl could have been asking if soup was finished, but it struck Gwyneth like someone had punched her in the gut.

She stiffened, then shifted her body so she faced a nearby shrub. "Surely not. We'll just be on our way and when he wakes up, he'll wonder what happened." Her father would be livid and she needed to return to the feast. Every second she lingered, she would have more questions to answer. Likely he would take a belt to her for her disobedience. "I'd best be heading home."

Ale spilled from the man's drinking horn and the stench clung to his prone body. It would serve him right to awaken with a throbbing headache and with his hose entangled, undignified, around his legs. Mayhap his member would even become reddened and burned by the sun. Or a wild animal would come by and bite it off so he could ne'er again force a woman.

Whirling, she turned to leave.

"Nay, me lady. Methinks 'e really am dead." The girl stopped her with a light finger on Gwyneth's arm and peered closer at the man lying crumpled on the ground.

"Of course he's not." She would not even entertain the possibility. "I'll just be going now."

"Um."

Stomach churning, Gwyneth took two steps away. Of course the man wasn't dead. That was impossible. Unthinkable. She could not have just killed a man. She delicately lifted the hem of her houppelande to walk home, noticing that it had a few ripped places on one side and splotches of brown swirled with red around the bottom. Her father would be furious.

Behind her, she heard the girl shuffle as if she were tapping her foot a few times. "Me lady, why'd you rescue me if you weren't meanin' to save me? That seems downright selfish if you ask me."

Gwyneth spun, a flash of anger sparking inside her. Her enormous skirt swirled around her ankles. "I just saved your life, wench, and you dare call me selfish." Who knows what her father would do when he saw the state of her dress. She should have turned and run when she first heard the girl scream.

"Beggin' your pardon, me lady, you didn't save me life. You only stopped a man from tupping me."

Frowning at the fuzzy-headed girl, she put her hands on her hips. "He was hurting you."

"True enough. But 'twas only a tup after all and not much more. Asides, 'is cock were as soft and stubby as they come. If we leave the body 'ere I'll be ablamed for it and it will be worse than if you 'ad not interfered a'tall."

"He's not dead."

Shifting her yellow shawl on her shoulders, the girl looked from the open-eyed brute to Gwyneth and back again. "Beggin' your pardon again, me lady, I think that 'e is."

Ice ran up Gwyneth's spine. He was not dead. He could not be. That would just be wrong of him to up and die on her like that.

She stared at the man, at his carelessly flopped legs and arms, at the white patch of skin and lifeless member exposed between his turned-down hose and flipped-up tunic, at his dirty black hair . . . at all the blood on his face.

A red liquid pool was forming around his head. His sightless eyes were turned upward toward the tree canopy. Trying not to look at his nakedness, she bent slightly forward to determine if his chest was moving up and down at all.

Naught. Not even the tiniest of movement.

She bent down farther.

Still nothing.

The forest spun in a lazy circle as she straightened; the colors swirled as if she had drunk too much mead. Oh, heavens.

She clutched her throat. Why had she left the great hall? Why? How would she ever explain this to her father?

"Well, come on then"—the girl tapped Gwyneth on her shoulder—"let's move 'im, aye? We'll weight 'im down with stones and sink 'im in the river." She latched her hands around one of the man's legs and began to drag him. The body moved a few finger-lengths toward the water. Panting, the girl stopped. "You gonna 'elp or just watch, me lady?"

Startled, Gwyneth flinched.

Dead.

Completely dead.

Gone.

Not coming back.

Stinging acid rose in her throat. It burned her tongue, the back of her mouth. Clenching her stomach, she turned to one side and retched over a pile of leaves as a series of dry heaves overtook her.

Her mind whirled, the thoughts tangling one upon the other like balls of embroidery thread. She should not have left the keep. She should have paraded around exactly as her father had wanted, married the first man who offered. They would come for her, put her in prison. Shudders rocked her body. She would be branded a murderess.

"Me lady?" The girl slid next to her and put her arm around Gwyneth's shoulder. The wind seemed to kick up. Leaves swirled. Or maybe that was her own dizziness. She sank downward, but the girl held her upright. "Me lady, cease. 'e was a bad man and not deserving of your spewing, I swear. The earth's a better place now."

The earth was covered in blood.

Murderess.

How could she face the stares of others when they discovered this? No decent man would marry her, now that she had blood on her hands.

Her father might disown her . . .

She tried to suck in a breath, but her chest caught, making it impossible to take in a lungful. She coughed, then heaved again.

Reaching forward, the girl wiped beads of sweat

from Gwyneth's temple. How could she be so calm when it felt as though the world had gone mad?

She gazed at her, and her features—the chin mole, the wide eyes, the mussed hair—all seemed to meld together like wax.

"Me name is Irma, me lady. Wot's yours?"

"G-G-Gwyneth of Windrose," she stuttered, then out of habit added, "How do you do?"

The simple introduction brought a measure of familiarity into the scene. Gwyneth knew plenty about being introduced at faires and tournaments. She tried sucking in another deep breath and this time was able to do so.

"Well, grab a leg then, Lady Gwyneth." Irma wrapped her dusty hands around the man's ankle.

Choking back her revulsion, focusing on the task, Gwyneth took hold of the man's other ankle. The man's green leather boots were still warm from his body's heat.

She shuddered, and together, the two girls dragged him to the river.

How could she have killed a man? How could she—

"'e deserved it, me lady," said Irma, as if reading her mind.

Her voice calmed Gwyneth's spinning emotions. She clutched her chest, feeling the carved wooden cover of the book that the young monk had given to her. A book from an earlier time. A treasure. An anchor in a spinning world.

The man's body stretched out behind them on the ground. Leaves and sticks slid aside as his head thunked over tree roots and small sticks. A trail of crimson marked their path.

Shuddering, Gwyneth looked straight ahead, focusing on the sound of the babbling river, on the knotty tree branches, on the feel of the grass and leaves beneath her feet, on anything besides the horrible deed she had just committed.

When they neared the water, Irma gathered river rocks and began stuffing them into the man's tunic and breeches. She untied his pouch and pushed it into the bosom of her dress.

Gwyneth gasped at the girl's unemotional, mercenary action. She felt more blood drain from her cheeks as if it would flow down her body and pool on the ground to unite with the dead man's.

Irma stuffed another rock down the man's tunic. "Beggin' your pardon, me lady, but I didn't kill nobody—you did. Now hand me another stone."

Body trembling, Gwyneth mindlessly bent down to do as Irma had requested. She could see the book's spine poking out of her bodice and she forced herself to think about that—of how she would learn to read. Of how she would fly above the mundane world like the carved dragon on the cover.

The rock she picked up felt cold and solid in her hand, a little piece of reality in this turbulent world. The trail of blood merged with the mud, turning it a dark, murky color. They would have to cover it before they left. Her mind raced for excuses that she could give to her father for the amount of time she had been gone. Should she confess?

Nay.

She forced her mind to calm. Get rid of the body. Go back to the feast. Soothe her father. It would be simple. Easy.

At last the man's tunic and hose—Irma had pulled

them back up on his legs—were stuffed to overflowing with rocks. He looked like a bumpy, overfilled scarecrow.

Irma stripped off his boots with the same cold efficiency she had given to the pouch. They were unusual—green leather with fancy silver buckles—and would likely fetch a high price. She threw the man's drinking horn into the pile as well.

"Well, 'tis done," she said, tossing the boots beside a nearby sapling. "'elp me drag 'im to that rock and push 'im off. The water's deeper there. They won't ne'er find 'im and ifin they do, well, then we'll be long gone."

Horrified by her own actions, but knowing she had no choice, Gwyneth did as she was told.

"No one must ever know of this," she said, her voice sounded small. If anyone found out, she'd be imprisoned, ostracized. Her father would never forgive her for destroying his plans for a decent marriage.

"Of course not, dearie. No one will find out."

They stood on the rock watching the man drift downward and become covered by the swirling river. Bubbles flowed to the surface and popped. Even after he disappeared, they stood there for a long time. Not speaking.

"Wot were you doing here, me lady? Asides rescuing the likes of me, I mean," Irma finally asked.

Gwyneth blinked as if waking up from slumber. The day's events seemed foggy, unreal.

"There was a feast—lots of people—I felt crowded."

Irma cocked her head to one side, the same way she had done earlier. Her eyes were keen. "There's more to the story than that, ain't there?"

Gwyneth nodded, but her problems seemed so petty, so mundane in light of the rape and murder.

"My sister was mean to me." There was something of a release that came in her chest at admitting something so trivial. As if things were normal again and she only had to deal with adolescent problems and not the sin of killing a man.

Perhaps she could dedicate her life to the church like the young, handsome monk who had given her the book. "Ever since I started into womanhood, my father has been determined to use me for political gain. I have duty and responsibility to be the lady of the keep." She pulled the book out from her bodice, inspected the gilded dragon on its cover, and was pleased to realize it was unharmed. It was a token from the time before she was a murderess. "Even strangers are handing me instruction books on the place of women," she continued, but her thoughts drifted to how the monk had winked at her.

"Hmph," said Irma, crossing her arms. "I can tell you much about the place of women. But finish your story. You came out here to get away from the fancies?"

"I thought I could find my younger sister. Oft she roams in the forest with her pets."

Irma gave a pointed look at the bosom of Gwyneth's gown, at the swell of cleavage pushed up on the shelf. "Better the animals of the forest than the animals of the feast."

Gwyneth shrugged, feeling self-conscious that she had said anything at all, that it had even bothered her that Brenna and Emily disliked her. She had done nothing to harm them. Unlike what she had done to this man. Her hands shook with sudden nerves.

"Methinks you oughta be using your beauty," Irma continued. "With your looks you could have anything you want."

"Except friendship—"

"Bah. You do not need friends like those. Think about your own wants."

She longed to say that she wanted the love of her sister, the regard of her father, the respect of the servants, but out of a sense of camaraderie with Irma, she bit her tongue. "A noblewoman's life is about duty."

"Mayhap. But if I had your looks and position, I'd be the most sought-after woman in England. I'd command respect and wield power, make changes for good."

Gwyneth sniffed, appalled at the girl's cheek. A woman wielding power like a man? "A woman is to marry, care for a man's household. I need to get back to my father." She should go home, get away from these fanciful ideas.

"Just look how lovely your hair is. The color is magical and it's thick and long like a princess."

"I'd like to cut it off."

"Nay, me lady. Do not say such. With your beauty, your strength, you could learn to control men rather than be controlled by them."

The thought held such appeal that tears welled unbidden in Gwyneth's eyes. She wished she could be that sort of grand woman. But the men she knew horrified her, and now the thought of facing a wedding night, of experiencing what Irma had just gone through, sent a shot of repulsion up her throat.

"I—I'm not strong." An abrupt longing for her dolls burned into her mind, but she pushed it aside.

When she had first come here, she felt like a child, a girl, but things had changed.

"Mayhap not this instant after you jes killed off a man, but you could be a grand lady who sets things aright for justice in the world between men and women, jes as you did today."

The thought sounded positively sinful. And yet, she'd been setting things in order around the keep—structuring the maids, dusting the rugs, organizing the pantries—ever since her mother had passed on. Perhaps setting order in the world would be a mere extension of that.

She stopped sniffling and stared down at the rips on her houppelande, at the hands that had just gripped a stick and pounded in a man's head. "I'm not going to murder anyone else!"

"Of course not."

"Then whatever do you mean?"

Irma took her hand and the gesture startled Gwyneth. It had been so long since someone had made a play for friendship that her heart gave a little leap. Since her mother had died and she had been made to fill the role as lady of the keep, her child-hood playmates seemed to have all faded.

"There is a place I know, women who have been wronged by men—a noblewoman such as yourself could work to set things aright. You could use your dazzling beauty to charm your way into places that plain-faced peasants like me cannot go." Irma thumbed the mole on her chin.

A tear flowed down Gwyneth's cheek, but inside she felt a glimmer of hope that seemed to have been all but dead this past year. That her life could be more than an endless parade of silly feasts with gossiping matrons, leering men, and giggling, cruel girls held appeal. Her mother had been a grand lady—modest and kind. She'd made a difference where she could, but in the end it seemed that she did little more than mend her father's socks.

Gwyneth wanted . . . more.

Irma wiped away the moisture on Gwyneth's chin with her thumb. Another tender gesture. Something her mother would have done. But her mother was gone. Her only ally was dead.

Embarrassed by the way she craved the attention, Gwyneth remained perfectly still, neither moving backward nor leaning forward.

"You have lovely blue eyes and don't want to make them puffy with crying," Irma clucked. "But you could wear a little kohl, mayhap."

The young monk's cross came into view in her mind's eye. "Harlots wear kohl."

"So do queens. Like Cleopatra."

Gwyneth glanced from the blood trail in the trees to the river where the dead body was. It was nicer to think of herself as a queen than a murderess. She ran her finger along the edge of the pages. Surely queens would know how to read. She would find the young monk and ask him to teach her.

"You can't go back to the keep looking like you are. Your dress needs stitching and your hair is tangled."

Looking down at her disheveled form, Gwyneth tried to brush a spot of dirt off the blue silk of her dress. She pulled a leaf out of her hair.

"We'll hide the tracks and then you'll come with me an' I'll take you to put on a bit of kohl. Yer face is pale as a ghost—it'll give you some color." Irma's voice was firm, resolute, kind. "I'll tell you about the women you can 'elp. I want to be friends."

Friends. How nice it would be to have a friend again.

"Asides, you can meet me daughter."

Daughter? Irma was surely not old enough to have a daughter. "H-how old are you?"

"Don't know really. Wots it matter? How old are you?"

"Fifteen summers."

"Must be nice to know such things, I think."

They stared at each other for a moment, then, as if knowing exactly what to do, Irma took Gwyneth firmly by the hand and led her away from the bank of the river, away from the man sunk down in the bottom of the muck. Away from innocence and childhood and all the things that had seemed so important only hours before.

"'elp me wipe up the blood trail an' we'll be going."

Gwyneth found she had no will to resist. The temptation of a friend, of a life that promised more than being a pawn in her father's game, gave her hope. The least she could do was discover the possibilities this strange girl offered.

Curious, disconcerted by the day's events, she followed.

Chapter 4

Three years later

Water dripped.

Moonlight shone.

Rats scattered.

Three years. Three bloody years, and still no hope of release. Jared St. John slumped against the damp wall of the hellhole of a prison, forgotten and forsaken. Thick calluses and red bumpy scars surrounded his ankles and wrists where the iron manacles rubbed against his skin. Dirt caked his hands and feet.

Inside him, rage burned like an inferno. He was innocent, by God—had been on his way to a monastery—and was not responsible for the murder of his brother, Rafe. He thrust a finger through a threadbare place in his monk's robe.

They had no proof.

They had no reason to suspect him.

They had nothing.

Yet, here he was. Sleeping in rat piss with only moonlight for company.

His mind drifted to the facts he knew: his brother, the woman they had shared, his brother's death.

He growled. This was his own doing. If he had not been sucked into Colette's spell, he would never have been suspect to the murder. Colette was proof of the wicked entanglements of women—of the agony they caused, of how they snared a man's mind and soul by ensnaring his body. In his experience, women used their power—displaying a luscious shoulder here, a slim ankle there—to sway a man's mind, to think illogical thoughts until all his life was destroyed. Colette's glossy black hair, husky voice, and feathery fingers had been intoxicating. He had loved her passionately—until she had betrayed him.

Gwyneth's beautiful face with her slanted eyes and sharp chin floated into his mind. In sharp contrast to Colette's darkness, Gwyneth had been an angel of light. He shook his head, trying to shove aside the memory before the inevitable stab of pain came into his chest. She had been an innocent when he'd last seen her—picking up children and hating the low-cut gowns that her father had forced her to wear. A beacon of female goodness.

Forcing down his impotent fury, he reached into his threadbare and filthy monk's robe and pulled out a lock of white-gold hair. The strand he had deftly stolen from Gwyneth while she was distracted by the book he had given to her.

The ritual was the same: He brought the braided tendril to his nose—it had long since lost its lavender aroma—but he inhaled anyway and imagined his beautiful Gwyneth, unsullied by the world, living a life of happy contentment, then, carefully, he unbraided it, smoothed out the strands, and rebraided it with deft fingers. Even in the dim glow of the prison cell, it glistened.

The meticulously crafted ritual focused his mind, soothed him. Her memory had kept him alive, kept him sane. He saw her in his mind, holding a child on her hip. Had she learned to read?

A flutter sounded.

Aeliana the hawk pushed through the bars of the small window at the top of the cell. Her black-and-white feathers gleamed in the moonlight and her yellow eyes, always keen and knowing, observed him.

His heart swelled. 'Twas both odd and comforting that she had not deserted him. He had released her from her tether when he had first been taken, because he could not bear to see her harmed. Most hawks would have flown from their trainers at the first hint of trouble.

But not his Aeliana.

Wings beat the air as she flew into the cell. A pigeon was encased in her talons, and she dropped it at his feet.

"My dear friend," he murmured. Her loyalty warmed him, thrilled him. 'Twas her care that had kept his muscles from wasting to nothing on the thin gruel the guards gave him. Ripping the feathers and skin from the dead pigeon, he sank his teeth into the raw meat in rapt appreciation.

Keys jangled. The door to the cell creaked open with a weary rasp. The guard carrying the day's bowl of watery stew entered. He was a medium-size man with a broad, flat nose and stocky legs.

"Wot's this 'ere?"

Spooked—the guard had never entered while she was there before—Aeliana fluttered, lifted, and, talons extended, flew at the man as he rumbled into the cell.

"Aeliana!"

The guard screamed, startled.

The bowl lurched and was hurled into the air. Brown liquid splattered across the stone floor. The man's arms flew around like medusa's hair to defend his face and eyes as the hawk attacked. He staggered one direction, then another. His boots caught on the gruel. He careened backward. A loud *thunk* sounded as his head hit the stone.

Jared cringed in empathy.

Then, the man lay perfectly still, his keys beside his legs.

"Guard?" Jared ventured.

No movement.

"Guard?"

Had good fortune at last looked his direction?

Taking a breath of the tainted prison air, Jared stretched out his manacle-clad leg and reached for the ring of keys. His toe caught them. With a grunt, he forced himself to stretch farther. And farther. Until he was able to move the keys a hairbreath toward him.

Hope shot through his body. Three years, but no longer. Soon he would be free. Nay, not truly free until he had found his brother's murderer and cleared his own name.

A few moments later, Jared crept from the jail. Aeliana flew overheard.

Dogs barked in the background. Likely, a search party had been formed. He raced through the streets and alleyways, taking great gulps of freedom into his lungs and looking for a place to hide. The saltwater and fish from the nearby docks smelled like heaven.

He pumped his fists and sweat poured down his back. The scars on his legs pulled and twisted.

Rage melded into determination. They would not capture him. He would find his brother's murderer and make him pay.

Chapter 5

Lady Gwyneth covered her nose with a lavender-scented kerchief and swore under her breath as she gazed around at the wretches who moldered on the mildewed hay of the women's prison. The stench of rat dung and piss choked the air, making her lungs nearly burst.

She shuddered as she always did when she came to this place and forced herself to survey the women in the cells. Forced herself into numbness. Forced herself to focus on her mission of rescuing two of them rather than give in to the deep aching feelings of helpless rage that weighed on her chest over the hundreds who remained.

The baker's wife, Blythe, here because of her husband's drinking debts, lay against the damp stone wall, a thin shawl wrapped around her shoulders. She had been lying in nearly that same position for the last three months, eyes closed, face turned upward.

Elfreda, originally a stocky woman, grew thinner each time Lady Gwyneth returned. She had been taken here for her brother's treason on the trumped-up charges of "comforting the king's enemies," but it was clear she was simply being held against his return.

And then there was Elizabeth, a dark-haired child who had been brought last week. No one knew for certain where she had come from or even how old she was. A peasant couple found her on the steps of a church wearing naught but a small smock. It was possible that she had been at an orphanage, but there was no way to tell because she could not, or did not, speak. She had an aristocratic nose—likely the bastard daughter of a nobleman. To communicate, she made grunting noises and waved her hands around. She had been imprisoned because she had cut the strings of a man's purse.

Intense heat flowed from the base of her spine all the way up to her neck as anger coursed through Gwyneth in waves. She kept her facial features and posture as neutral as possible. All the women in this hellhole were here because of the misdeeds of irresponsible men!

Tucked inside her bodice was the small book that the handsome monk had given her three years ago. He had been different. He had wanted her to read, to use her intellect. She had never learned to read—these past years had been filled with late night after late night of embroidering sleeves and trim to earn enough money to release women. She had never seen him again, but all the same, the book with its carved dragon on the cover represented hope to her. Hope for women to learn and grow and make something of themselves—to fly like dragons in the clouds. She had sold all her jewels except for the sapphire ring, which had belonged to her mother.

A few months ago the storm that had surrounded her father's acts against the king had occurred—what a maze he had led their family into! Blasted man! Since he had been exiled she had been busier than ever. It was only by sheer luck that she and her sisters were not living at the brothel themselves. In any event, she had not even had a chance to see about her own dower lands.

The jailor, a bull-sized man with a large nose and one earlobe significantly larger than the other, gave her an uneasy glance. He must have been a new guard, because she had never seen him before. Still, she knew his type well: big, dunderheaded, and easily charmed with the slightest bit of female attention. Unused to noblewomen who paid him any heed.

"I've come for the two women who are to be shipped today." She smiled her best smile and blinked a few times.

His eyes widened and he looked slightly taken aback. It was a reaction she had come to count on with men and she tossed her head, allowing her mass of white-blond hair to fall over one eye and across her bosom. The ends curled past her hips.

He watched her; his mouth fell open as he drank in the way her locks framed her curves.

The fool!

She'd cut her hair to her nape if men weren't so bedazzled by it.

While he still seemed slightly smitten, she reached beneath her silken surcoat, pulled coins from the pouch dangling from her girdle, and handed them to him. A bribe. Not much, but if his eyes raking across her form were any indication, it would be enough.

"Well," she said, not shrinking from his indecent perusal. This was the most dangerous part of the transaction—the part where he decided if he would take the bribe or not.

"The magistrate—"

"—has given me leave to take them." She laid a hand on his forearm, silently willing him to give over to her.

He reached up and pulled on the short earlobe in obvious discomfiture.

"Prithee, Master Jailor," she pressed, not wanting to give him too much time to think through what she was asking. Likely he'd never been addressed as "master" before. Men seemed to respond well to little niceties of respect. Especially peasants who were clearly beneath her station.

He puffed his chest out a fraction.

She smiled at him, waiting.

It did not take long.

He slid the coins into his purse and nodded.

Victory! Inwardly she smiled. It was the combination of charm and imperiousness that the men responded to most of all. She smiled at them sweetly, then commanded them while showing a margin of respect and they simply did her bidding. It had worked time and time again and she wondered if all men were so shallow that they were taken in so easily by flattery and a comely face.

Your beauty is a gift from God, Irma had instructed. *Put it to good use. Learn to charm them.* It had seemed almost sacrilegious to think such at first, but the women she had rescued had erased her initial guilt.

"Up there, my lady," the jailor grunted. He pointed ominously down the dank hallway toward two shivering women who huddled, waiting to be taken onto the slave ship. The authorities didn't call them slave ships, of course, but that was what they were all the same.

A life of misery, backbreaking work, and a joyless existence would be their future. They would go to workhouses or brothels or (if they were pretty enough) a harem.

Turning numbly from the women in the cells, she moved toward the two she could rescue today. Tamsin, a harlot, and Norma, a nobleman's bastard, she had been told.

Two more. She had saved two more. But how many others would be gone, taken away, before she was able to stop the trade of human souls?

If only she had control of her dower lands in her own right, then perhaps she could set up a place to teach the women a trade of some sort!

She let out a breath of frustration. She had managed to stave off marriage to a slew of unsuitable men but had not been able to talk her father into allowing her to manage the properties herself.

So much had happened, her father had been exiled to Italy and her sister's husband, Montgomery, set up as overlord. More frustration! Montgomery disliked her, so there was no possibility of him giving her leave for her own properties and she had overheard talk of yet another marriage plan.

Elizabeth's large green eyes haunted Gwyneth as she walked out into the cold, foggy morning and headed down the cobbled streets of the city with the two women following her.

She should feel good for those she had saved, but a sickness settled in her stomach. For certes, the child would be next on the ship unless she could come up with the means to release her.

Of all things, she needed to solve the dilemma of her dower lands and gain control of them in her own right. She could not leave the child here alone with no hope of a future.

Chapter 6

"Getting married tomorrow is unthinkable!" Gwyneth yelled at her sister Brenna later that night as they sat across from each other at the chess table. Fire burned in the hearth, but a chill hung in the air.

"'Tis a noblewoman's duty to marry."

Gwyneth threw the white rook across the board, knocking over a pawn. "What has happened to you since meeting Montgomery?" Their relationship, which had gotten better for a time, had soured again.

"I have come to understand the importance of the duty of marriage," Brenna said.

Gwyneth snatched another pawn from the chessboard. She definitely had no time for silliness such as marriage. Not when women were daily being raped and killed in the prisons.

A husband would take her away. Far away from her work here and the wrongly imprisoned ladies who needed her.

"Tell that ogre you call husband to release my dower lands so that I can have full control of them myself! There is no need for me to be wed to any man!" And indeed every reason she should not.

Gwyneth stood so quickly that the chess table tipped, then righted itself. Pawns, knights, and rooks scattered into the rushes, but the two queens remained.

"That *ogre* is my husband and our new overlord," answered Brenna, taking hold of the black queen and turning it over and over in her fingers.

"He could be the devil's pet pig for all I care," Gwyneth hurled, punctuating her words by pointing and glaring down at her sister. Her mother's sapphire ring—a token of authority—encircled her index finger, but the bauble mattered little ever since Brenna had married James Vaughn of Montgomery a season ago.

Since that time, her freedom had been taken from her bit by bit. Her father had been sent to exile, and her sister Brenna had been established as lady of the keep. Now, worst of all, Montgomery was insisting that she marry—that her lands, the lands she wanted to use as a school for rescued women, be used as a prize.

Brenna's back was against the hearth and the fire cast a shadow that made the scar on her cheek dark and prominent. "You will obey his orders," she said sharply, taking hold of the black queen. She tapped the piece against the blue silk of her sleeve.

"I will marry no man! The lands were given to me by Mother for me alone to control."

There was an awkward silence. Brenna and she had only recently discovered that the two of them had different mothers. Another issue their father had inflicted upon them.

"'Tis unnatural for a woman not to marry," Brenna said. "The banns have been posted."

Gwyneth looked intensely at her sister, sudden understanding piercing her as sharp as any double-edged dagger. "This is *your* doing, not your husband's at all!"

Brenna at least had the grace to blush. The scar on her cheek darkened.

Pain lanced her chest at how quickly her sister had used her place as the overlord's wife to do such.

"Of all the spiteful things!" This development took things too far. "You envious little bitch!"

"Nay, sister, 'tis not jealousy, but concern. A woman with your beauty who is the heir to prized lands is like to be stolen or to cause a war—"

Gwyneth cut her off with a wave of her hand.

"'Tis bad enough that the kitchens and laundry have deteriorated into disorganization under your guidance. Now you order me about like a bloody queen," Gwyneth hissed. "You need not pretend concern for my welfare. I know you care nothing for our family. What of our father—have you forgotten him altogether in your new marriage?"

"Father is well cared for. We received a missive last week." Brenna stood and reached toward her, palms held out in a sisterly gesture. "Prithee, Gwyneth. We have done well for you with this match. 'Tis for your own good."

"For *your* good, you mean. You wish to be rid of me so that you can further allow your husband to rape our lands. Does he yet beat you as he did afore?"

Brenna might seem blissful now, but Gwyneth could never forgive her brother-in-law for how he had acted before he and her sister had married.

"Gwyneth—"

"Ah, there you are, wife," boomed a masculine voice near the entrance of the great hall.

Whirling, Gwyneth saw Montgomery pacing toward them. The bloody ogre. What Brenna saw in him was beyond her fathoming. He carried himself like an emperor. He was too tall. His shoulders were too wide. His voice was too commanding. He wore all black and could easily be mistaken for the devil.

Her gaze flicked disdainfully over Montgomery's form and she noted that her sister had painted— painted! What sort of woman painted instead of embroidering trim on a garment?—little green vines around the hem and collar of his tunic.

Revolting.

Brenna had never been able to stitch very well but was skilled with a paintbrush. That she had meticulously used her skill to make pretty little decorations for her atrocious husband's garment sent a shooting pain behind one of Gwyneth's eyes. Montgomery had caused the people much heartache. How dare she betray them all thus!

Enraged at her sister's disgusting devotion to her husband and her willingness to sell her own kin off in marriage, Gwyneth snatched Brenna's outstretched hand and spit in the palm.

"Eek!" Brenna squealed.

"Ha!" The small satisfaction, wasn't much but 'twas better than doing naught.

With a grin, Gwyneth tossed Brenna's hand aside, pushed past Montgomery, and scampered for the exit. She yanked open the heavy oak door and ran out into the bailey. Somehow she would find a way to get out of their plans for marriage.

"Gwyneth!" she heard both of them call in unison behind her but she did not turn around.

"A curse on both of you!" she tossed over her shoulder. "I will marry no man!"

"Come back, sister!" Brenna's voice carried across the yard.

"Should I go after her?" she heard Montgomery say.

"Nay, 'tis me she is angry with. I—"

Behind her Gwyneth heard shuffling and some discussion, but she could no longer discern individual words. Her hair floated like a flowing cloud as her cape's hood slid downward and she fled, panting, away from the keep at Windrose, running to speak with Irma, her only true friend in the world.

"Reconcile yourself, wench," Montgomery blasted just as she reached the cove of trees and the secret path that led into the town. "The wedding is at dawn."

The harsh fist of determination closed around Jared St. John like a cold iron clamp as he surveyed the Windrose lands and sensed that he was closer than ever to finding his brother's murderer. Bitter revenge at the injustice of losing his freedom for three years flowed inside him.

Rafe's drinking horn had been found and he had heard gossip that a man wearing his green boots with silver buckles had been seen down by the docks.

It had been two long months of hiding from the authorities, but somehow he had escaped their claws. Oft at night, he'd awoke to the sound of hounds howling and thought that soon he would be arrested again, but so far he had managed to remain free.

Jared gripped his staff—a new one that he had carved from a small sapling. It was nearly as tall as he was and sturdy in his hand. On the top of it, he had whittled a dragon into the wood. Its reptilian tail wrapped around the base. It was still somewhat crude, and Jared wanted to add other carvings to the stick, but he was pleased with how his creation had turned out. He had even found a small red rock for the dragon's eye. In three years he had not lost his skill with a knife.

Aeliana perched atop his shoulder. From his position on a hill above Windrose, he watched shadows grow long in the town surrounding the castle. Another day gone. Time seemed to be passing all too quickly. He gripped his walking stick, his every desire that he could clear his name. Get his honor back.

But he would not become a monk. God was dead to him—had died and left an empty coldness in his soul. Unlike Joseph of the Bible, Jared had not resisted the siren's call of a woman who belonged to another. His irresponsibility had caused her death—and that of an innocent child as well. He had wanted to pay penitence and had ended with his brother dead and him in prison instead. Proof that God had abandoned him.

The lowering sun bathed rooftops with orange fire. Frogs chirped. Birds roosted on the eaves of the church, their twittering a continuous hum as they settled for the night. Workmen walked the cobbled streets, the tools of their trades rolled into packs as they headed back to their huts and houses, the day's work completed. A queue formed outside the bakery— women purchasing meat pies and bread for the evening meal.

Somewhere, hidden amid the town and castle folk, he would find the truth, the answers he needed.

Restless, longing to rush forward to solve the mystery, he turned his staff over and over in his hands. The smooth wood slid against his palms and the engraved dragon at the top twisted this way and that.

Rafe's body had been found by a fisherman. His tunic had been loaded full of rocks and his boots stripped off. If only he could find the boots, then he would have a clear trail to the murderer, could clear his own name, and make him pay for the long nights spent in prison.

Aeliana fluttered her wings in agitation. Her feathers brushed his cheek and her soft, musky scent tickled his nostrils.

"Easy, my friend," he murmured, narrowing his eyes at the turrets of the castle and forcing his fingers to still. "We'll bring the killer to justice soon. Then you can stop wandering around the countryside sleeping in caves with me. You'll like that, won't you, girl?"

The hawk twitched her head as if in answer; her yellow eyes gazed at the sky. She ruffled. She wanted to fly more. But they had just returned from the hunt and it was time to settle for the night in the cave that had been their shelter the past while.

Knots ran from his lower back to beneath his shoulder blades, his body's protest against being disguised, pretending to have a limp and being smaller, weaker than he was. The restrained investigations he'd done these past months went against his preferred methods of straightforward conversation. He wore a hood most of the time and had grown a goatee and mustache to disguise his features—set himself apart from the smooth-shaven monk and the scruffy-bearded prisoner he had been—so that he would not be recognized.

How much easier it would be to charge in sword first; to slash, to slay. The only trail he had seemed to end at The Bald Cock, a brothel in the low-class area of town. Some of the women had seen a man wearing distinctive boots—green with silver buckles. Rafe's boots.

Jared rolled his shoulders.

Aeliana flapped her wings and dug her talons painfully through the leather padding and into his flesh. Clearly she neared the end of her patience with his musings. She wanted to hunt, and if not to hunt, then eat.

With a grimace, he relaxed his shoulders and turned toward the cave.

He would feed Aeliana and leave her so she would rest, then head toward the brothel where he'd been gathering information. He'd have that fuzzy-haired whore named Irma bathe him and rub the worst of the tension from his shoulders. She had gentle hands and a loose gossipy tongue, and didn't question his lack of desire for her sexually.

He had no interest in a whore or, indeed, any other woman. Love was an illusion and lust beguiled a man's soul.

His Aeliana, loyal and sagacious, was the only female he could trust. Even his own mother had not wanted him.

The unfairness of being imprisoned ate at him. All passion had been swallowed up by the thirst for revenge. The scars surrounding his wrists and ankles—red and bumpy—and the white ones on his legs drove him to that end.

Jared made his way into the cave, fed Aeliana, and decided to skip his own supper. He sighed. Mayhap Irma would have some interesting gossip to share tonight—something to lead him one step closer to clearing his name and bringing the murderer to justice.

Chapter 7

Gasping for breath, Gwyneth drew up her hood and pulled her cape—the homespun, tattered one she used when secrecy was required—around herself. With a shove, she entered the well-oiled back door of The Bald Cock, a tawdry brothel, to look for Irma— just as she always did when she needed consolation and advice.

Marriage was akin to death for a woman—first there was the wretched act of consummation, then being a broodmare, and if a woman survived that, she would live a meaningless life in complete subjugation to her husband.

She had much more important work to accomplish. Somehow she and Irma would come up with a plan to avoid tomorrow's wedding.

The acrid stench of ale, sweat, and lust bit at her nostrils as she walked inside the whorehouse. Balls of mud dotted the floor, and an oily film caked the sconces and walls.

The sheer dirtiness repulsed her. It proved the base nature of men, of how they cared for naught more than shoving themselves inside a woman's body until their vile lust was spent.

The back door opened to the kitchen area rather than the main chamber. Barrels of ale and dirty dishes were stacked along the cabinets. Harlots and a few kitchen boys ran back and forth through a swinging door. One girl, barely seven summers, stood on a stool and halfheartedly dunked tankards up and down in a pan of scummy water. Another child, not much older, dried them with a greasy cloth before one of the whores would rush in, yank it out of her hand, fill it with ale, and race back out through the swinging door.

The chaos set Gwyneth's nerves on edge. No one cared that tankards were not properly washed, that the linens were filthy, or that flies crawled across the cabinets. Haphazard piles lined the walls and she longed to wrap her hands around a broom.

In the corner, five smaller children played with wooden blocks, building some sort of tower. Kiera, Irma's daughter, was among them.

"Lady Gwyn!" she called, leaping to her feet. Her hair, the same mousy brown as her mother's, sprang in loose curls all around her head. Her wrinkled dress had two splotches of dirt where her knees were.

"Shhh!" Gwyneth admonished, gathering the child into her arms for a quick hug. "Where is your mum?"

The child pointed a thumb toward the door leading to the main chamber of the brothel. "Working," she said casually.

Gwyneth cringed at how indifferent the girl was toward her mother's career. The very idea of union with a man wrenched her stomach.

'Twas loathsome. Absolutely loathsome.

Likely the girl would be servicing men in a few years if Gwyneth could not come up with a plan to control her dower lands and take her away from this revolting place.

Through the door, she saw Lord Ashland and Master Baker standing by the wall. Even Lord Mallory was here.

Eventually, all men came and tasted the wares, or so Irma said.

"Did you bring me an apple, Lady Gwyn?"

"Not this time, child. I must speak with your mother," Gwyneth said, setting the child back down.

Kiera stuck out her bottom lip. "But you promised me."

"I know, sweetling, but this trip was urgent and I did not have time to plan. Go play with your blocks and I'll return on the morrow with two apples and a haircomb for you."

The child's eyes widened. "A haircomb? Will it be silver with jewels?"

A silver comb with jewels would ransom two women.

Gwyneth patted the girl on the head. "Nay, but it shall be well crafted, I promise." She'd steal Brenna's.

"All right, Lady Gwyn. I will dream all night about it." The child turned and flounced back to the other children.

Inside, Gwyneth felt her heart break. She wanted more for the child than merely a haircomb. An education. Some skills. Something to do so that she would not have to earn her keep with her legs in the air.

With a renewed purpose, Gwyneth pulled her hood firmly over her head to avoid being recognized and headed for the swinging door.

The stench in the brothel—sweat and sex and

cheap toilet water—grew more rank as she moved
into the main chamber. The vulgar way the men's
eyes roved over exposed skin and the degrading way
women's bodies were used for men's uncontrolled
brutality disgusted her.

Frequently, she had urged Irma to leave, but her
friend always smirked at the thought.

Through the haze, Gwyneth saw Irma, wild brown
hair curling around her face. She sat on a wobbly
three-legged stool holding a tankard. She was smiling, tittering, gazing with round eyes at a stoutly man
at least twenty-five years her elder who had a potbelly
and an expensive-looking pin clipped to the enormous lace kerchief at his neck.

"Psst! Irma!" Gwyneth whispered, staying near the
back of the chamber and praying her disguise would
hold so that none of the patrons would take notice of
her. She had not changed her clothing after the row
with her sister. Beneath her shabby cape, which she
had snatched from its secret hiding place in the sta-
bles, she still wore a finely stitched houppelande. The
dress would be noteworthy and the last thing she
wanted was male attention. If she was discovered
here, she would be ruined.

Turning, Irma took in Gwyneth in one full blink.
It was one of those looks that Gwyneth had come
to appreciate both for its worldly wisdom and for
its care.

Irma sidled off the stool, leaving her customer
gaping after her, his sentence half finished. Obviously
forgotten. She'd never cared a whit what he was
saying anyway, of that Gwyneth was sure.

Irma had shown her how to paint her eyes with
kohl. Irma had taught her how to roll her hips when

she walked. Irma had been her teacher in how to charm men, to pretend interest, to get what she wanted. The skills had served her well in releasing women from the prison.

"Wot's wrong, m'dear?" Irma wrapped her arms around Gwyneth.

"Ohhhhhh," Gwyneth moaned, hugging her friend tightly. "I'm to be married off."

"I see." The stench of toilet water permeated the yellow veil around Irma's shoulders that announced to the world she was a harlot. She wore a low-cut blue gown with droopy embroidered trim that was ripped in three places, likely torn by an overzealous customer.

Despite the inappropriateness, Gwyneth's fingers itched for a needle and thread. Such actions were useless—life for women came unstitched faster than anyone could sew up loose ends. Had not her mother proved that? All the mending in the world had not appeased Papa or kept him from stupidly getting himself exiled. Now that Montgomery was overlord, her own marriage seemed imminent.

Wending around tables and serving wenches, Irma steered Gwyneth to a private area in the corner. Girls sauntered back and forth, hips wiggling, breasts bobbing in display. Ale sloshed. Men laughed. A minstrel played a bawdy song. One girl, clad in gypsy garments, danced in an undulating rhythm while balancing a tray of flaming candles atop her head. Tallow smoke hung in the air.

"You've always got out of the proposals afore," Irma said once they had settled onto the bench. Crumbs and droplets of wine marred the worn tabletop.

"With Brenna's help," wailed Gwyneth. "Now that

she's married, she's sticking by her husband. 'Tis as if she's lost her spine. Damn the man."

"Humph. Stay 'ere, luv. I'll fetch a flask of wine and we'll conjure a plan, eh?"

A plan. Irma always had a plan. The two of them had never gotten themselves into a situation where they could not get out. Somehow working together they fooled magistrates and jailors. They had released woman after woman from the prison cells.

Taking in a steadying breath, Gwyneth resisted the urge to lay her head down on the table as she watched her friend saunter back into the brothel's chaos. Irma's hips rolled as she walked; she smiled easily at the other women. Despite her working conditions and the disgusting thing she did to earn her keep, her shoulders were as loose and carefree as a child's.

Irma could come and go as she pleased, she could spit and drink ale and ride horses bareback. She was never sequestered away, squeezed in houppelandes, or shoved into pointed, pinching shoes.

A pitcher of ale was set before her and Irma poured it into two tankards. "No wine tonight. Too watery."

An ache formed in Gwyneth's chest, and she wrapped her hand around her drinking vessel. As the daughter of a wealthy baron, she never lacked for wine. She should be grateful for her life, but she felt shattered and splintered inside.

The brothel's abbess, a tall, thin woman whose dour expression could have rivaled any convent nun's, shot her a glare. She was busy soothing the pride of Irma's jilted customer.

With a huff, Gwyneth dug into the purse tied to her girdle, pulled out two coins, and handed them to her friend. "Here. This should keep the abbess happy."

Irma smirked. "No' much'll keep that woman happy except the wenches 'ave their legs in the air several times a night, you know. But me customers pay me well, so she leaves me alone, she does. I'll take this, though, and give 'er 'alf. That'll leave me free for the night."

They sat there for a few moments in companionable silence.

"Why don' you jes refuse to marry the lout?" Irma asked, pulling the conversation back to the issue at hand.

Gwyneth drew circles on the table with her index finger. "It's not . . . that simple."

"Sure 'tis. Say nay and 'ave done with it."

If only she could. If only it were that easy. But Irma could never understand her life—the ties, the rules, the duty.

Tracing her fingers round and round the patterns of wood grain, Gwyneth stared at the remains of spilled ale encrusted into a knot of wood.

"The arrangement must be broken amicably," she answered at last. "I am bound by honor."

"Bah," said Irma, flicking a crumb off the table. "Honor is for men. Women have better ways."

Gwyneth sighed and gave a slight smile, amused by her friend's unorthodox outlook. Irma's life gave her freedom that Gwyneth would never know. "Even if I were able to get out of this marriage, there would be another proposal, and then another. 'Tis been thus for year—"

"—but you 'ave gotten free afore—"

"'Tis the lot of noblewomen to marry and bear a man's heirs," she said miserably, parroting the words of her sister. "We're to be chattel and broodmares."

Irma cocked her head to one side, getting that look

of possibilities in her eyes the way she did when she was coming up with something outrageous.

A moment passed. Tension built. In one corner, a bard sang a bawdy song. The titters of harlots reminded her of the London court. In many ways, it was not so much different—women being sold for money.

She thought fleetingly of the dark-haired Elizabeth in prison—likely the jailor was making arrangements to sell her as an indentured servant or slave. The child could not even speak for herself. Often she sat along the dank wall chewing the ends of her straight, dark hair and staring up at the cobwebs.

Irma drummed her fingernails on the tankard, a habit of hers, one that Gwyneth could never have— not *ladylike*, her tutor had chided when she had accidentally imitated her friend at sup one evening. The sting of the switch across her knuckles had made a lasting impression.

"Have out with it," Gwyneth said finally, unable to contain herself when Irma kept tapping her fingers and staring across the chamber, her eyes slightly up and to the left the way she did when she was deep in thought.

Gwyneth snapped her fingers.

Irma blinked as if coming back into the present. Her sharp eyes glittered with intensity. "You should marry."

Huffing out a breath, Gwyneth picked up her tankard and looked out into the busy room. Hundreds of tallow candles flickered and smoke swirled in the air. At the bar, a group of swarthy men, arms around each other's shoulders so that they formed a chain, toasted the air and sang along with the bard in loud, drunken voices.

"Have you not been listening? I am going to marry. Tomorrow morn."

"Nay, I mean you should marry tonight."

Gwyneth nearly choked on her ale and she had to cover her mouth and nose to keep from spewing on the table.

"Tonight?" she squeaked out when she recovered herself.

"Aye. But not to some silly lord. To a man of your own choosing—one you can command, control, even send away at will."

"I have tried. Papa never approved any of my choices and Montgomery, the new overlord, is even worse! At least I had some sway with Papa. I do not even know the name of the man that was chosen."

Irma didn't argue, she just sat up straight and looked around the brothel. "'ow about tha' one?" She pointed to a young blond man with a foppish hat.

Gwyneth grimaced. He was scarce more than a lad.

"We could steal 'im. Feed 'im a sleeping draught and 'aul him to a church. We'll find Brother Giffard and insist 'e marry the two of you. Then you can tup 'im for good measure and send 'im on 'is way with a purse full o' gold."

The plan was unthinkable.

Annoyed with Irma's absurdity, Gwyneth slammed her palms on the table in an uncharacteristic gesture. She should not have bothered even coming here. "Preposterous. And stupid."

Irma looked at her impassively, then they both started giggling. It was sheer freedom to be able to make unladylike gestures and have no sharp rebuke or switch across her palms for the action.

"It were the mention of the tupping you didn't like, eh?" Irma said.

Gwyneth cringed but said naught, pushing away the flood of bad memories from watching a man brutalize her friend.

Scratching her head, Irma scrutinized the brothel, thoughtfully taking in the immodestly dressed girls and their bedecked patrons.

"There's a good one." She pointed toward a tall man, sitting alone at a corner table, hunched over a tankard of ale. His crude brown cape was pulled up over his head so she could not discern his features. At his side, leaning against his stool, was a long wooden staff that had a dragon carved into the top of it. "'is name is Jared."

Gwyneth gave Irma an exasperated glare and began to rise, ready to head back to Windrose and spend the night crying across her bed. "I do not want a man."

Irma cocked her head to one side. "All noblewomen want a husband."

"Not me." Gwyneth shuddered, remembering Irma lying on the dirt beneath the grunting brute who pumped himself into her. She wanted none of that. And no babies either. The women she rescued from the prisons needed her more than some man needed heirs. "I do not wish to marry at all."

"'ear me out, now, I say." Irma latched onto Gwyneth's forearm in a tight grip. "'e comes in every week and pays me to bathe 'im and that is all. 'e's unmanned. It must 'ave something to do with the injury of 'is legs, because 'e never asks for a good tupping. 'e's got long scars from his groin to 'is knees, and even when I touch 'im 'e stays soft as a floppy carrot."

A giggle welled in Gwyneth's throat at Irma's description even despite the bleakness she felt in her heart.

"'e told me once all 'e wanted was a cottage in the woods and a place to raise 'is birds—'e's a falconer—and a kind one at that. 'e speaks to me as if I were a lady and 'as never tried to pinch me in any way. 'Tis almost as though there is a deep sadness in 'is 'eart. 'e comes 'ere, drinks ale, we a-go to a bedchamber, and I bathe 'im. You'd never 'ave to worry about the consummation."

Gwyneth pursed her lips; Irma's mad plan had more and more appeal as she kept talking. "I cannot believe I am listening to this," she muttered.

"'e's a peasant—jes marry 'im, give 'im a bag o' gold and send 'im on 'is way. It ain't like 'e's going to find some other woman, bein' unsexed and all."

Shifting on her stool, Gwyneth took in the man, trying to determine if Irma had spoken truth. He had turned slightly, and she could see a little beneath his hood. His face, still covered in shadows, was an interesting blend of darkness and light. He had straight, dark hair that hung past his shoulders, winged brows, and a mustache and goatee. She could not make out the color of his eyes, but his expression seemed pensive. He looked a little dangerous to her.

"Are you sure he's unmanned?" she asked warily.

Irma nodded. "For certes. 'e never even twitches down there during the whole bath. It's plain odd, it is. 'e's the kindest man I've ever known—not that any man is kind, because they all have black, dirty souls—but 'e never even tried to pinch me titties."

Gwyneth leaned forward, trying to peer deeper

beneath the man's cowl. Darkness shadowed his cheeks. He didn't look kind.

He looked lethal.

Still . . . Irma hated men, so if he'd been kind enough to win Irma's regard, he must be special. A man who didn't try to paw at women in a whorehouse was rare indeed. Irma knew a lot more about men than she did.

Mayhap the plan might have merit after all.

"Perhaps he's a half-wit," Gwyneth suggested.

"All the better. We don' need 'im's brains, only 'is hand in matrimony."

The reversal of roles, the thought of forcing a man to marriage rather than the other way around, made a small spark of power surge up Gwyneth's spine.

"We can't steal a man," she said rationally. But another part of herself wondered if the plan, addled as it seemed, might work. She would no longer be hounded and bothered by marriage proposals that she had to work her way out of.

"Why not?"

"It just . . . it just isn't done."

"Well, not yet. But we give 'im a pitcher with herbs then we can just walk 'im out of 'ere nice an' easy. 'e ain't got no friends, leastwise, I ain't never seen 'im with any, so it's no' like 'e'll go a-missin'. We'll take 'im to the church on the other side of the bridge and 'e'll be as docile as a lamb, happy to wed you and do your bidding for the rest o' your life."

Gwyneth lifted her hand to chew on one of her fingernails, then put her hand back down on the table. She'd been broken of that particular habit years ago—had been made to scrub the walls until her fingers bled as punishment—and had no intention of going back to it again.

"Do you really think he might?"

"O' course, luv! Wot could be easier?"

Gwyneth looked from the man to Irma and back again. "He's awfully large."

"'e's lame! 'is legs are all scarred up like Satan got ahold of 'em."

Without waiting for further comment, Irma stood. Her curly hair fanned around her face. "Come with me," she instructed. She strong-armed Gwyneth to her feet and forced her toward the back of the brothel where the kitchens and pantries were.

They passed the man in question and she could practically feel him watching her. She spared a glance at him, this time able to see farther into the shadow beneath his cowl.

His eyes were darker than anything she'd ever seen before. Darker than midnight.

Instinctively, she drew her hood farther over her face, hoping he had not caught a glimpse of her hair. Too many troubadours sang about that particular feature of hers and 'twas best to keep it covered or she'd be recognized for certes.

Once they were in the kitchens, Irma busied herself gathering dried herbs and dumping them into freshly poured ale.

Kiera ran up to her mother, hugged her legs, then turned to Gwyneth. "Lady Gwyn."

Gwyneth picked her up. The scent of the brothel, of ale and sweat and fornication, permeated the child's smock even though Irma kept her sheltered here in the back room as best she could. Gwyneth's heart squeezed. It wasn't right for children to grow up in brothels.

"Here," Irma said, taking Kiera and handing the tankard to Gwyneth. "Take this to 'is table and give 'im a smile. 'e'll be grogged up afore you know it."

"I cannot do that!" Gwyneth said, but she was looking into Kiera's large brown eyes, as innocent as a doe's.

The dower lands could provide shelter for this child and many others. Like the dark-haired one who never spoke.

"Sure you can. Easy as pie. Then you'll marry 'im and your worries will be done with."

Her fingers whitened on the ale. Was it possible?

"Go on!" urged Irma. "You'll be getting married one way or another; might as well be to a man of your own choosing."

A shot of boldness coursed through Gwyneth. Why should she not choose a man of her own? Make her own way in life? Not be so bound by duty and honor? Have a sanctuary for women.

Her sister and brother-in-law would be furious.

That thought made her take a step forward. What fun to see Brenna's face, to tell her she had taken care of the situation herself. It would serve Montgomery right to have to make excuses to the man he had arranged for her to marry. Likely it would even cost him to get out of the betrothal. Too damn bad.

"Out with you, then." Irma opened the door that led back into the main room of the brothel.

"Why me? Why can't *you* take him the herbed ale?"

"Because you're the one going to marry 'im. Might as well get a good look at 'im up close."

Gwyneth considered for a moment. "I need a disguise."

"Fine."

Moments later, Gwyneth wore a low-cut bright red dress, had her hair tucked under a red feathered headdress, and wore a cowl. Irma smeared white powder on her face while one of the other women painted her eyes with kohl. A patch was applied to her cheek along with two red spots of rouge.

Irma clucked her tongue. "Just right. You look stunning and not at all like the fresh-scrubbed lady you were when you came in. No' a customer in the place will recognize you."

Gathering her courage, Gwyneth rose and tried to imitate the way Irma walked. With measured steps, she sauntered, hips swaying, out the brothel's kitchen doors and over to Jared's table. How hard could this be? Go to the table, set the ale in front of him, then flee back to the kitchen to wait until he drank it. She was used to charming men into doing her bidding— not dressed as a harlot, but surely it would not be so difficult.

His head raised and he looked sharply at her. His eyes looked familiar, but she could not place his face. She filed quickly through her memories. He was not a nobleman, of this she was certain. Likely someone she had seen on one of her trips into the town.

"Who are you?" he asked.

Her legs turned to water, but she forced a smile. *Your bride.* "I'm new."

His dark brows drew together and he touched a finger to his goatee. "I've been waiting for Irma. Where is she?"

Irma? He was asking for Irma?

"I thought you might like a tankard of ale." She

made her voice sound flirtatious, slightly shy, just as Irma taught her.

He didn't reach for the cup. "I just want Irma and a bath."

Perhaps she should take the ale back to the kitchen. Nay, that would make her look dim-witted. She set the tankard on the table in front of him.

"Irma's coming," she assured him, changing her tactic slightly. "She was the one who wanted me to bring this to you because of the delay in her coming to you." There. That should set his mind at ease. "There is no charge for this tankard tonight."

His gaze flitted from her eyes to the patch on her cheek to her hood and back again. "Do I know you?"

Panic shot through her. If he had seen her before, recognized her, she could be ruined. "Of course not. I have just arrived." Too late, she realized that she'd let aristocratic haughtiness creep into her voice.

She turned her face away, thinking to head back into the kitchen.

He reached up as if to flip her hood down.

She gasped, jumping back and barely checking the urge to slap him for his impertinence. How dare he! But of course he would dare. He thought she was a harlot.

"I like to see who is serving me."

"It is unnecessary to remove my cowl." Gwyneth drew her hood even farther over her head.

He stared at her suspiciously. "Are you truly a whore? The way you speak . . ."

Fluttering nerves clustered in Gwyneth's stomach. Surely if he knew who she was, he would have said something by now. She licked her lips, determined to bravado through their encounter.

His eyes went wide at her motion. They were not black at all, she realized. Green. Moss green. An interesting green. The familiar male reaction brought her a measure of satisfaction, and she felt her confidence grow.

"I'll jes take this one," she said boldly, plucking the mostly empty tankard from his grip, "and go see about Irma." Careful to keep her hair covered, she let her cape slide open at the neck and stuck out her bosom in the manner she'd seen other girls do.

He released the tankard easily and relief poured through her.

Victory.

With what she hoped was a disarming look, she turned, gazed at him over her shoulder, and sauntered back toward Irma, who was standing, holding Kiera, and waiting for her near the door of the back room, only slightly out of sight.

He lifted the herb-laced tankard.

"Perfect," Irma cooed when Gwyneth reached her. "Give 'im some time and 'e'll be passed out cold."

Sheer giddiness settled on Gwyneth. Even with all her ploys at the jail, she had never done something so utterly shameful or bold. A lofty sense of female power flowed through her.

The abbess walked by and gave them both a good hard glare. Gwyneth pulled her hood back up so that her face was again in shadows and mulled over the possibility of marriage to a man she could control. She would be mistress of her own properties. She would have a place to take Kiera and Irma and Elizabeth and others as well. She would have gold of her own. She would have freedom.

At long last, the man's head began to droop.

Irma scrambled to her feet, pulling Gwyneth from

her thoughts. She sent Kiera over to play in a corner with two other children.

The abbess looked in his direction, a severe frown on her pinched face. Men were not allowed to sleep here; it was against brothel rules, bad for business.

They rounded on Jared, who let out a loud sigh.

"You'll 'ave to go," Irma coaxed him, "on yer feet." She swung her arm around his shoulders and tried to lift him.

He didn't budge.

With her eyes, Irma guided Gwyneth to take the other side of his large body.

Nervously, Gwyneth wrapped her arm around his waist and they lifted. The movement felt vaguely reminiscent of the last man they had carried together.

Jared was heavy, and her shoulders sagged under his weight. He smelled faintly of leather and the outdoors, an altogether masculine scent, one she was totally unused to. It was almost heady.

She shook off the silly thought. She did not wish to be attracted to him. Their relationship would be a business transaction—like buying a loaf of bread. Or a meat pie. She would marry him, give him a bit of gold, and send him on his way.

He lurched, his legs shaky with drug. "Huh? Oh. I dishn't mean to shrinks show—"

"Just come on, dearie. We'll show you to a nice bed to sleep it off, we will," Irma said, tugging him farther upright.

They dragged him, stumbling, through the kitchen. He kept moving one foot in front of the other in an artless stupor, half in, half out of slumber. He muttered unintelligible words. At last they got him, swaying this way and that as he went, to the back door.

Freedom was just one husband away.

Chapter 8

A pox on women!

Jared St. John, bound and gagged, knelt on the hard stone floor of a small church not far from the brothel and vowed that when he got free, the whore holding a dagger to his back would get her comeuppance.

He'd see her begging for a mercy that would not be forthcoming.

He'd have her thrown into prison.

He'd have her tried as a witch and burned at the stake.

"Move forward," she demanded. "Toward the altar. It's only a little farther."

His pride, a fierce barbarian that hammered war drums in his chest, yowled in outrage as the point of her dagger pricked him betwixt his shoulder blades and prompted him to shuffle in the direction she wished. The small pinprick of pain, intensified by the spinning of his head, nearly sent him toppling to the floor.

She'd tricked him.

She'd drugged him.

She'd kidnapped him.

Not alone, but with the help of that fuzzy-headed Irma to whom he'd been kind for weeks—overpaying her for naught more than bathing and gossiping.

"You are too large to carry," Irma explained in that raspy voice Jared had come to associate with her quick and gentle hands whilst she washed him each week at the brothel. "Move forward, ah say, so we can close the doors. The ceremony will be over soon, and you can be on yer way."

There will be no ceremony, he wanted to shout. Saliva oozed around the gag and leaked off his chin.

His vision swam, and the woman—the one holding the dagger to his back—kept going in and out of focus. She seemed more well kept than the other harlots—downright attractive, to tell the truth.

He tried to make out her features, but his vision bounced and blurred, disallowing him to discern her features.

His hatred burned hotter, coming up in his throat. He would have spit on her if his mouth had not been stuffed with wool.

The spinning in his head made it difficult to remain upright, and he had to concentrate to keep from falling over.

The doors slammed behind him, an ominous sound in the midst of the church. His bound arms burned and he strained against the ropes until they cut into his wrists.

Forcing a breath in through his nostrils, he blinked to keep himself upright. What had they drugged him with? His tongue felt thick and heavy as he pushed it against the woolen gag stuffed inside his mouth.

"Who are you?" he mumbled, but his question sounded like garbled muck, unintelligible.

The comely one looked nervously at her companion. "Irma, this is—"

Irma shrugged. "Right. So 'e's not so docile as I expected. We'll jes finish the marriage and get you both free. 'e'll be all right then after we explains t'all. 'e's 'armless, ah tell you."

"I'm not sure—"

"Oh, jes 'urry up and marry 'im. See 'ere, Brother Giffard is ready. 'es even got a Bible, 'e does."

Raising his head, Jared stared at the tall, loose-limbed man clothed in a monk's brown robe. He stood barefoot by the altar, a few yards in front of Jared. He had hideously furry feet, tonsured hair, and brows that pulled in tight between his eyes so that long lines ran up his forehead.

"Mayhap we should not—" the monk started, but Irma cut him off with a snap of her fingers.

The dagger eased from Jared's back, and the pretty whore pointed it at the monk. Her arm was as straight and stable as royalty pronouncing judgment on a traitor. Haughty and imperious. "Begin."

Damn princess. Her dress was whore red, but of all things he was sure she was not some common harlot. But who?

It did not matter. Whoever she was, he'd take pleasure in ripping her pride from her, hold her down and force her to eat like a cur off the floor. He pumped his hands to stave off the numbness that crept into his fingers; he needed presence of body as well as mind to get free from the shrew's clutches.

The monk cleared his throat. "This is not quite orthodo—"

"Do it now, Giffard. I have no patience tonight," Princess Harlot said. "For certes, you can smooth over any issues we might have with the church. You know the bishop."

"But I'm unsure if this is legal—"

Irma stepped forward and whispered something in his ear. A blush crept from the neckline of his robe and trailed up his cheeks until even his earlobes glowed bright red.

Fingering his Bible, the monk cleared his throat and began mumbling in Latin. *"Vis accipere hic praesentem in tuam legitimam uxorem . . ."*

Of a truth, the man was blackmailed. As caught in this sham as Jared himself.

Thirst for justice coursed through Jared, eating at his stomach and burning coldly through his veins. He shook his head, trying to clear the vestiges of drug from his mind. The hemp ropes scraped and ate at his skin.

More dizziness. A wash of acid came up in his throat.

The church's interior swam in an opulent display of color. The huge space, dappled with stained-glass rainbows, monstrous columns, and gory religious paintings, felt like a crowded tomb. One complete with grim reapers and souls destined for hell.

Grunting, he fought the ropes, fought the bile, fought his spinning head. He rocked back and forth on his knees. His hair fanned around him.

Ignoring his fury, the monk officiating the unholy sacrament droned on. ". . . *iuxta ritum sanctae matris . . .*"

Heedlessly. Recklessly. Stupidly.

He should have been saying his last rites instead

of the marriage ceremony. Jared vowed to have justice if it was the last thing he did.

"Calm, man." Princess laid a delicate hand on his shoulder, petting him like an overanxious dog as his struggles threatened to topple him from his knees to his belly.

Anger, so thick that he could taste it even against the sourness of the woolen gag, pulsed in Jared's mouth. He swung his body, butting her arm forcefully away with his head.

The motion off-balanced him and he fell, landing hard on his stomach, prostate at the strumpet's feet.

She knelt at once, laid a palm against his forehead. Her fingers were warm, not reptilian, as he had imagined they would be. "Irma, we cannot do this."

"Bah. 'e'll be fine. 'e's jes in a bit o' a stir 'cause 'is pride kicked up. I know men. This one is quite tame."

Tame? He'd show her tame.

Forcing himself to roll onto his side, Jared squinted up at the two female faces gazing at him. Irma's eyes held little pity, but his bride-to-be's were wide. One tendril of glistening hair roped downward from beneath her cowl.

He stared at the distinctive strand of hair, wishing he could remove the covering and see more of it.

Gwyneth of Windrose? His angel of light?

A brick of betrayal dropped onto his chest. How could his Gwyneth, the one he had pined for, be this harpy before him?

He looked at her again. Her features came into clear view for the first time. Nay. This woman was older, with sharp, harsh features made all the more prominent by the heavy layer of lead paint, dark kohl, and rouge. She lacked the luster of the fresh girl he remembered.

Not Gwyneth, then.

This was a woman of the world. Not an innocent.

She offered a thin smile. He cringed as her perfectly white teeth appeared. They should have been fangs dripping with poison. But, for certes, even tied and humiliated as he was, he could tell she was a woman who rivaled the beauty of his Gwyneth.

The thought angered him. He wanted no whore to sully the memory of the girl he had gifted with his book.

His body reacted differently, and he felt shaming heat enter his groin.

This woman was a devil.

A harpy.

A temptress.

The host of Satan.

Her comeliness was that of a calculating mind—the sort that intoxicated men and turned them into blathering fools on purpose, just to bend them to her will. Her wide blue eyes bespoke innocence, but her hips, tiny waist, and perfectly sculpted breasts seemed made for pleasure.

At once, he wanted to both tup her and kill her.

"We mean you no harm, sir," she said softly with a wide smile. One that had obviously oft gotten what she wanted out of most men.

But he was not most men.

Rocking against the floor, he strained to rise, but his limbs would not obey him. Tension pulled across his shoulders and he knew he would sell his soul to spit at her, to humble her, to rip the smugness from her face.

The monk shuffled his hairy feet back and forth. "I fear the abbot will com—"

Princess snapped her fingers at him and he fell silent.

Strumpet.

"I'd like to pay you for your trouble," she said, turning back to Jared.

And I would like to pay you for yours as well, he thought grimly.

Candlelight glinted off her elaborate headdress as she leaned toward him. For a mad instant he wanted naught more than to hold her down, one hand on her body, one on her neck, and rip it from her so he could get a better look at his enemy. The thought of seeing her shamed and devoid of pride burned through him in a fierce wave. It would be pure pleasure to repay his own dishonor measure for measure. He wanted her to be unable to toss her comely head and tempt a man with her eyes to drink poison.

He struggled, fighting to get up.

"Lmmg!" he growled against the gag, his best effort at the words "let me go."

The women blinked at him impassively.

Stinging formed on the backs of his eyes born out of rage, of mortification, of helplessness. To be tricked and taken by two women! Girls! Not even burly girls. Small, inconsequential slips of womanhood. It was the ultimate degradation.

For a heart-stopping moment, the remembrance of lying amid rat droppings on a dungeon grated his brain.

He shook off the thought, refocusing on the present and determining to get free. A pox on all beautiful women. Better to have a mousy wallflower who would be grateful to cater to a husband's needs. A quiet woman. A peaceful life. That's what he wanted.

Instead . . .

"Come on. I'll help you rise." Princess Whore pulled on his arm, her fingers firm and tight against his bicep.

His chest burned as if a coil of snakes, frustrated with captivity, writhed therein.

He glanced down at her fingers. Lily hands. Perfect cuticles. Shaped nails. They trembled slightly.

A tingling formed on his neck.

This one, no matter her being at a brothel, was not a common harlot. Those hands belonged to a lady. A lady desperate for marriage. With that hair, it was possible that she was even a cousin of Gwyneth.

Snarling at her, he forced himself, with her help, back up to his knees. Lady or no, she would pay for her crimes done here.

Drawing in a deep breath to steady his mind, he cocked his head to one side allowing curiosity to cut a slight notch in his fury. He needed to think rationally. He needed a plan to get free, to look around the church and find some way to cut his bonds.

A man could not be forced to marry. What sort of woman would think so?

How would the union be consummated? The thought of getting hard while a blade bit into his neck was laughable.

The officiating clergyman stammered out a few words, then looked at him expectantly.

Jared's knees ached from the stone floor as he waited for the gaggle of nitwits to realize that, gagged, he could not say the vow even if he wanted to.

Light from the stained-glass windows flickered

over them, casting blue and green dots over her face and homespun cape. Silence reigned in the sanctuary.

The monk glanced from Princess to Irma to Jared and back to Princess. "He is, uh . . . gagged."

Brilliant. Perfectly bloody brilliant. Jared stifled the urge to roll his eyes at his captors.

"We . . . should, uh . . . release him." The monk's halting tone confirmed Jared's thinking that he was no more a willing participant of this ceremony than Jared was.

Too bad. He would still pay for his part here.

"Be a good boy and I'll take out the gag."

Boy? She'd just called him a *boy*!

In the pit of his belly, hot fury congealed into ice. His shoulders relaxed as his resolve hardened. Afore this scenario ended, she would call him master. He'd see her kneeling before him as he currently was before her.

But such things could not be accomplished by reckless rage; they needed calculated intent.

He nodded.

Her fingers touched the edges of the gag, then trailed around his cheeks and mussed the back of his hair as she sought the knot. Her scent was of lavender and innocence—a far cry from her actions. Like Gwyneth's. He shook off the thought.

One of her breasts grazed his nose and her body jerked, curved inward to further avoid the touch. A dark thought that she might find his touch repulsive or frightening edged into his mind. A tool he could use?

He leaned forward, closing the slight distance between them, and squarely laid his forehead against her chest and twisted his head back and forth.

Gasping, she ripped the rough wool from his mouth and stumbled back, her eyes wide.

"Ne'er fear, friend. 'e'll be gone soon," Irma announced and stepped forward to put a stabilizing hand on the princess.

The corners of Jared's lips stung, worn raw by the gag. Determining to keep his composure, to not spit on the woman before him, he focused on moving his jaw around a few times. He needed to be free from the bonds and it was in his best interest to do nothing that would cause them to bind him any tighter.

"Your name?" The sound came out as more of a rasp and he worked his tongue around in his mouth to get saliva flowing.

"Never mind that," Irma said briskly. "Introductions later." She turned to Giffard. "What next?"

The monk tapped his hairy feet up and down on the stones a few times. "Just the words, my lady."

"You cannot hide your name from me, *wife*." Jared spat out the word wife even though they were not fully married. Nor would they ever be.

A short sword, wielded by Irma, pushed into his back, deeper this time. Drawing blood. Liquid trickled down his spine and seeped into his homespun tunic.

He ducked to the side and flexed his shoulders in an attempt to get away afore it severed his spine.

"Say the vow," Irma demanded, her eyes alight with fervor. "We do not have all night." The mole on her chin quivered.

Princess flinched and bit her lower lip. "Irma?"

"Will be o'er soon. 'e's naught someone to show mercy to. We let 'im go now, and we're all cooked. Jes finish this up and be done with it. Remember wot ya did afore. 'Tis better than that. We're a-doing this for yer own good, we are."

The princess's skin paled.

The monk thumbed his Bible.

"Say the words, dog," Irma continued.

"Go to hell," Jared gritted out. Burning fury singed his resolve to remain calm. He struggled, straining against the rope to rise from his knees and fight.

"You'll marry 'er." Irma's hand cracked across his cheek.

The bloody bitch. "A pox on you, whore."

"An' you as well, dog."

"Irma! Cease!" The princess stepped between them. "Truly, sir, we mean you no harm. This was supposed to be good for the both of us. I have gold for you."

Gold.

Gold would allow him to build a falconry business after he cleared his name. He could train hawks and purchase a small cottage—live a quiet life of peace.

"How much gold?"

"Plenty of it. I just want to be legally wed. 'Tis a simple exchange between us, naught more. I'm terribly sorry about bringing you here as we did."

He blinked at her. "Who are you?"

Her lower lip trembled but no words came out. The ring on her finger glinted in the candle glow.

A dispassionate anger chilled Jared's veins. The instant he was free, he'd take it from her—take all her jewelry from her. Ne'er again would she be haughty and lofty.

With an effort, he controlled his features and waited.

"I'm the daughter of a nobleman, I need to get married. I heartily apologize for this inconvenience."

Inconvenience? She wanted them to marry, for heaven's sake. Was she a half-wit?

"We will release you—" she started.

"Nay. Marriage would be perfect," he said stonily. He would take gold, her lands, her everything. Marriage would give him the rest of his life to make her regret this day.

The damn princess seemed determined to see through the vows before untying him! Irritating. Vexing. Infuriating.

His palm itched to bury itself in her hair, drag her down to the church floor and take her as an act of sheer dominance, to prove to them both there would be only one master in the end.

"What is your name?" he demanded.

"Gwy—"

Irma clapped a hand over her mouth. "The less 'e knows the better. Marry 'im, get 'old of yer lands, and send 'im on 'is way. The marriage can be annulled."

Gwy?

Gwyneth?

Gwyneth of Windrose?

Nay.

Never.

He had considered that earlier and dismissed the thought.

Nay, 'twas not his Gwyneth—the girl he'd pined for, the girl he'd longed for, the girl whose lock of hair lay braided in his pouch.

He took in the haughty lift of her chin and square set of her shoulders. He remembered a fresh-faced girl of fifteen summers—not a gaudy temptress. The woman before him was certainly beautiful enough to be his Gwyneth, but she was worldly, covered with powder and rouge and a horrid headdress. It made no sense that a woman who had suitors aplenty would choose a man from a brothel.

"Who are you?" he demanded again.

"My name is . . . Gwendolyn."

She was lying. He was sure of it.

"Why did you choose me?" he asked, wanting to know more.

"Silence!" The monk glowered at all of them and started again in Latin.

Jared gritted his teeth, biting back the urge to interrupt the ceremony and demand answers. The last two months of searching for his brother's murderer had taught him the value of patience and pretending he was naught more than a poor peasant. He slumped to purposefully make himself smaller.

He peered at the feathered hat, wishing to rip it from her and release her hair. If he could see all of it and not just the one strand perhaps he could discern the truth and demand answers.

He pulled his wrists against the ropes and counted the tiles on the floor, knowing he needed to bide his time until he could break free, bind her with the ropes, and lead her straight to these lands that Irma alluded to and obtain control of them.

Whoever she was, he would take her gold. And take his revenge as well.

"I will," he said when Brother Giffard prompted him.

His bride cleared her throat delicately and faced him when the monk announced the end of the ceremony.

Jared tensed his thighs, getting ready to attack. He would tackle his wife first, pull her downward to the floor, then grab the right hand candlestick and knock the monk senseless. Irma, unarmed, would be dealt with as the events unfolded.

"'Tis done. Thank you for your cooperation," she said gently. She rounded behind him and he smelled the scent of lavender, felt the brushing of her body against his neck as she bent to grasp the knot of the ropes. Her mannerism, so soft and feminine, was at odds with her behavior, and all the more heinous because of it. "Truly I do not wish any harm on you."

"Not even sticking a dagger in my back?"

She pulled at the ropes and he felt them loosen. Wiggling his fingers, he turned his head to glimpse at the woman who was now his wife. The sharp thrill of coming victory bubbled in his chest.

The ropes surrounding his ankles slid to the marble tiles with a small slithering sound. His thighs tensed as she moved to release the ones from his wrists. Only a moment more. A moment more and he would be fully in control.

He rotated his ankles, left, right, then left again.

Impatient, he shook the rope off, leapt to his feet, and whirled to face his new bride, already imagining her neck stretched across the opening of the town's stocks and the helplessness she would feel at being thus contained.

She gasped, eyes going so wide he nearly laughed.

In one swift motion, he stepped close, knocked her headdress to the ground, and fisted his hand in her hair near her scalp. Red feathers scattered across the tiles. He pushed her forward so that she was bent in two. A position she might as well get accustomed to.

She screamed. The sound echoed over and over again through the church.

Out of the corner of his eye, he saw the monk slide forward. Not letting go of his captive's hair, he spun on his heels and grabbed the nearest candlestick just as he had rehearsed in his mind.

The long tapered candles rolled across the tiles, dripping wax as they went. With a grunt, he smashed the heavy gilded weapon atop the monk's head.

Giffard howled and went flying; his brown robe fluttered out like a butterfly. He landed near one of the candles, motionless.

Good.

The girl under his hand jerked back and forth, trying to wiggle her way free.

"Cease." He tightened his grip, pushing her farther downward.

Her body crumpled forward as expected. She didn't stop struggling, but she was small and easy to control; from this position he could lead her wherever he wished to take her—make her crawl on her hands and knees as she had done to him. That would be the first dent in her pride.

"Stop moving," he growled.

Her hair had come unpinned and its ends trailed on the tiles like a maid's mop. He stomped on it, anchoring her in place, wanting her to realize exactly how powerless she was, how stupid she had been. He wanted her to ask for mercy. To beg.

A tremble went through her body, and she screamed again. "Let go of me!"

"Get on your knees."

When she did not immediately comply, he pushed her slightly, so she was forced slowly to the floor.

"Cease!"

"So much haughtiness, Princess."

"How dare you! You—"

At that moment, a large gilded object came flying across the church. Jared flinched to one side, but was too late. A heavy Bible slammed him across the temple. The metal hinges scraped down his cheek.

Through blurry vision, he saw Irma standing by the alcove, an open trunk beside her, right before he sank wearily to the floor and his hand loosed its grip of his captive's hair.

Chapter 9

Gwyneth's mind raced in an attempt to come up with some sort of plan as she and Irma tugged and pushed the unconscious, blood-splattered form of her new husband out of the wheelbarrow's belly and onto a narrow cot. They stood in the midst of a one-room chamber that belonged to one of Irma's regulars who was currently not in residence. It was spartan, but clean with barren timber walls and a swept plank floor. Irma lit a tallow candle. Dark, acrid smoke tinged the air.

Jared's scalp wound was only a small gash but it seemed to have poured oceans of blood—first in squirts and then in oozing drops. A scarlet trail dripped onto the planks and his tunic was awash with sticky red liquid. Irma threw his staff down beside the bed with a loud clatter.

Heavens! What were they going to do with him?

He was supposed to be lame and docile!

Instead, releasing him had been like releasing a dragon.

His large body tumbled onto the mattress with a *whomp* and another shot of fear quivered through her.

She pressed her fingers down on his wound to stop the flow of blood. His head needed to be stitched. "What are we going to do?" she asked, aloud this time.

All the way here, down the darkened cobblestone streets, she'd been asking herself that question. They could not release him, they could not go to the authorities, they could not—

"Poison him," Irma answered drolly, interrupting her frenzied thoughts.

Sickness washed through her stomach. "Do not be morbid."

"Ah ain't. 'Tis the best option. We kill 'im off and dump 'im in the river nice and slow jes like we did afore."

Horrified at Irma's coldness, Gwyneth stared at her friend. "We're not committing murder!" It was on the tip of her tongue to say that she was no murderess, but the words died in her mouth. She had already killed one man.

Irma shrugged, the gesture telling. "Right. Well, that's wot you'd do if you had sense."

"We're not doing that."

"Shame the Bible didn't brain 'im. You reckon Giffard got the blood cleaned up afore anyone showed up at the church?"

"Surely he did."

Giffard had helped them get Jared into the wheelbarrow and had shooed them away hastily, undoubtedly concerned about his own safety more than theirs.

She surveyed the man on the mattress, trying to discern what to do with him. She had to think logically, take it one moment at a time. Surely they would figure out something. She could go to Adele, get some help. Perhaps even send a note to Papa in Italy.

And tell her family what? That she'd captured a man out of a brothel and forced him to marry her? She nearly groaned. What a stupid, addle-headed plan this all had been.

Moving forward, she decided she would just secure him firmly to the bed, find something to stop the bleeding, and then give herself time to pace the floor and figure out what to do. Mayhap she could organize the cupboards. Straightening things always cleared her head.

With quick motions, she secured his wrists and ankles to the legs of the bed, then stepped back to survey her work. His body was so long and his shoulders so wide that he hung off the sides of the narrow cot.

Tied like a gift from hell.

Blood, some dried, some still red and sticky, covered his tunic.

"We need to get him cleaned up," she said to Irma, who had been busy pulling the curtains and lighting a fire in the small hearth. "Find some rags, stop the bleeding. If we can find a needle, I'll stitch the wound."

Irma shrugged. "Suit yourself. The blood ain't bothering 'im. It's slowed down to a trickle."

"We can't leave him thus. He needs to be sewn."

"Ah ain't ne'er sewn nobody in me life."

"Well, I have. You can help me clean him."

"Ah bathes 'im every week," Irma protested.

"Exactly."

"Nay. Absolutely not. We need to get rid of him,

not be cleaning 'im up like we're takin' 'im to visit the queen."

Irritated with Irma, Gwyneth surveyed the man. "How could you bathe him every week and not have known he was so strong! Look at his body. I've never seen so many muscles."

Irma clucked her tongue. "'e 'ad a staff. Asides, one man's like the next. Big lumberin' jackasses the whole lot of 'em."

"You won't help me?"

"Hmph. Ah say we poison 'im and be done with it. All ah gots to do is go back to the brothel and get a stash of—"

"Nay!"

"Yer jes being impractical. You can't stay married to a man like that, and if yer family finds out, you'll be ruined."

Gwyneth wrung her hands into her skirt. *Think, girl, think.* "We have to tell my family."

"Tell 'em wot? That you kidnapped a man, married 'im, and now 'ave 'im tied to a bed in a chamber near a church?" Irma scoffed. "That new overlord o' yers, Montgomery, 'll 'ave yer 'ead for it."

"Not if"—Gwyneth paced the small room twice; it was only a few steps from one end of it to the other—"we tell them he was the one who did the kidnapping."

Irma cocked her head to one side. "Wot's the difference betwixt that and us poisoning 'im? Lord Montgomery will 'ave 'im be'eaded if you do that, yes 'e will."

A rope of tension tightened Gwyneth's spine, pulling a hard knot in her shoulders and leaving a string of stiffness running from her lower back all the way up her neck. Sinking into a slat-backed chair, she buried her head in her hands. "What was I thinking?"

"There, there." Irma slid beside her, patting her on the shoulder. "I'll jes 'ead to the brothel and get the nightshade."

Gwyneth sat upright so quickly she nearly toppled over the chair. Irma jumped back with a yelp.

"We're not murdering him!"

A sour look, as if she'd just eaten a lemon, crossed Irma's features. "Why not? You did it afore."

"'Tis not the same! He's innocent!"

"No, he ain't. We jes didn't see 'im do whatever it was 'e did. One man's pretty much like the rest."

"You were the one who told me this one was different!"

"Well." Irma looked uncomfortable. "Ah suppose ah was wrong." There was an awkward silence, then Irma flounced to the door. "Will return with the nightshade," she said on her way out.

"Wait!"

The door banged closed in answer.

Gwyneth stared at it wondering if she should run after her friend or not. Slowly, she turned back to the man on the mattress.

Blood and dirt smeared across his face from his thick, dark hair to his goatee. His head lolled to one side.

A tendril of guilt swirled through her, but she pushed it aside. There was no call for him to act as he had in the church! They would have released him and, once she was in proper control of her dower lands, sent him on his way with enough gold to make his life comfortable. He was a peasant! A falconer! What she offered was far above his station. He should have been grateful! All he had to do was cooperate for a few weeks and he would have enough gold to set up a falconry business of his own. Instead he'd acted like a madman.

That thought sent her earlier panic somersaulting through her again. One moment at a time, she told her frazzled mind. Just one moment at a time.

Taking a deep breath, she rummaged around the room for items to dress his gash. Keeping her hands busy tending his wound would surely be better than standing around wringing her hands wondering what she was going to do with him.

The chamber was tiny, but she found it was quite clean and reasonably well stocked with supplies. No dust or cobwebs marred the corners, which pleased her sense of order and soothed her mind in a small measure.

A pitcher of water sat on a counter by the wall, and a cupboard by the window contained strips of cloth, needles, thread, and other basic living supplies in an organized fashion. The neatness brought a sense of rationality to her brain. At least someone had good housekeeping skills.

She gathered what she needed and returned to the man—her husband—tied to the cot. Husband! What a strange word. A strange word for an absolute stranger.

For the hundredth time since the scene in the church, she silently berated herself for the idiocy of this plan. How had she ever thought this was a good idea?

Undoubtedly, they would have to get the marriage annulled. Surely it would easily be declared illegal. Surely. But . . . what if her new husband didn't cooperate?

Shuddering, she set aside that thought, leaned over Jared, and forced herself to observe him with cold detachment.

She would sew up his wound and, once he awoke, they would converse civilly, come to an understanding. Surely she could make him understand how her plan could benefit them both. If not, the marriage would be annulled and they would put this horrible night behind them.

She poured water from a clay pitcher into a basin, removed the wig, and washed the white powder and kohl from her face. She would face him as plainly and straightforward as she could manage.

Feeling more levelheaded after thinking the matter through, she pressed a cloth to the gash and held it there for a few moments. When it did not stop oozing, she wiped the area around it clean as best she could, threaded a needle, and made quick tiny stitches down the length of the wound.

He moaned a few times but did not awaken.

She surveyed her work carefully, very gently pulling his skin this way and that to verify that it would hold. There would be a scar, but not much of one—her stitches were tiny and even. Her prized embroidery work had allowed her to earn gold to bribe the jailors. Brother Giffard used his position as a traveling monk to help her secretly sell sleeves to ladies of the king's court.

Her mother would be proud. Satisfied, she dipped her cloth into a bowl of water to wash off the rest of him.

The water turned from clear to red as she wrung out the rag over and over again. Slowly, Jared's features were revealed.

A small white scar beneath his left eye felt lumpy beneath her fingers and his raven hair was silky and thick. He had a slight widow's peak and a well-trimmed mustache and goatee.

She stopped her ministrations to stare at him.

Mercy, he was beautiful—especially for a peasant. Glossy black hair, high cheekbones, generous lips, and an almost aristocratic nose. Enthralled, she ran her fingers across his features. His chin was too pointed and his brows too winged. The two slight feminine features in an otherwise uncompromisingly masculine face fascinated her.

She'd never seen a man quite like him before. His breathing was deep and long and she wondered if she should wake him. With her finger, she drew a line across his cheek, brushed strands of his hair aside, and turned his face up so she could study it.

A shot of heat curled in her belly and for a fleeting moment she wished she could keep him here, like this, tied for her own pleasure. A man of her own. A husband she could totally control.

Guilt curled through her at the sinful idea. What a wicked thought!

Carefully, she turned his face from side to side, inspecting him.

At once, she blinked.

The monk?

The young monk?

Disbelief shot through her; she took a firmer hold on his chin and peered closer.

'Twas definitely him. The man who had given her the book with the dragon cover. The book she carried even now tucked in her bosom. He was older, harder—a crease had formed between his brows. She smoothed it down with her fingers and wondered what had happened to him.

"Of all things," she whispered, completely mystified and not knowing what to make of it.

How could he be here? Evidently he had not entered the monastery after all. Why?

Curious and intrigued, she slowly trailed her fingers down the column of his neck and loosened the ties of his tunic. She told herself that she needed to bathe him, that she needed to get all the blood off of him, but in her heart, she knew she lied to herself. He had been the one man she had felt a connection to all those years ago. The small book he had given her was pressed against her bosom, carried as it had been for three years. The dragon's tail had lost flecks of its gilding because she'd thumbed through the pages so often.

She pushed Jared's tunic upward, and sucked in a breath at the thick muscular ridges of his stomach. Heavens! It was so very different than her own soft, rounded white belly. He was tan, hard, chiseled.

Without thinking, she laid her palm fully across his midriff. Heat seeped from his body to her fingers. A wave of dizziness passed over her, and she snatched her hand quickly back.

Fanning herself with one hand, she reached for the cloth. She would attend her Christian duty of cleansing his wounds. He was not hers to keep no matter the beauty of his body. He was dangerous. Unpredictable. Had he not proved that in the church?

Asides, she had no interest in the carnal nature of man—such brought naught but pain on a woman.

She ran the wet cloth across the valleys and hills of

his torso and allowed her fingers to linger across his skin. So much tantalizing masculinity.

'Twas hard to believe that he was desexed, but Irma had been clear that his manhood never hardened.

She pushed the tunic farther aside, but it stuck to his skin where some blood had dried. She reached to unbind his wrists to remove it, but her hands hesitated on the ropes.

In the church, he had forced her to her knees all too quickly. Best to leave him bound until they came to some sort of an agreement.

She fetched a knife and sawed up the front of his garment and then down the sleeves. 'Twas ruined anyway; she would send Irma to find another.

The pieces of cloth dropped onto the floor in a heap and Gwyneth's eyes widened as she took in the expanse of his chest. Clothed, he had seemed large, but unclad he was more than merely large. Powerful. Enormous.

Mentally she counted the handbreadths across his shoulders. Wide. He was so bloody wide.

She wondered if instead of waking him, she should force more of the sleeping draught down his throat. If he were to get free, God only knew what he would do. Sliding her hand into her hair, she rubbed her scalp in the place where he had gripped her hair, the anchor point he'd used to force her to the floor so easily. Of a truth, the battle betwixt them could not be fought with physical force. Thank God he was unmanned and would be unable to consummate the marriage. Mayhap that was why he had been going into the monastery.

His naked chest rose and fell with deep, even breathing. She dipped her cloth back into the water, deciding to finish bathing him while she better formulated a plan to win him over to her way of thinking. She would be kind to him, smile at him, bend his mind to her will. She had plenty of practice doing that to men.

Back and forth the rag moved across his skin.

After a few moments, she stopped and stared at him. He was tied securely and completely helpless. She didn't have to charm him—he was hers to use as she wanted!

A thrill of sheer female power went through her.

How very fascinating!

All her life she'd been under a man's thumb in one way or another—first her father, then (now that her father was in exile) Lord Montgomery. All her life, she had manipulated, wheedled, and coaxed men to do her bidding. And here was a man she did not have to do that with. He was hers for the taking—to do with what she willed. She could undress him, wash him. *Kiss him.*

Kiss him?

Where had that thought come from?

Nay, she would not kiss him.

But she would look her fill until he awoke—ogle him as men ogled women. 'Twould be sheer joy to strike a blow for all women and leer at a man rather than the other way around.

He was, after all, until the marriage was annulled, her husband. Guilt swirled inside her, but she ignored it: He had agreed to the wedding fair and square, and he was the one who had broken his promise.

Fascinated by the opportunity to explore a man, she ran her finger lightly over his stomach. In doing so, her wrist gently grazed the area just below where his hose and braies met.

That area twitched, seemed to lift of its own accord.

Unable to tear her gaze away, her eyes widened. It twitched again.

Had Irma been wrong?

Curious, she touched the cloth near his groin. A swelling formed beneath her fingertips.

She gasped; a sinful thrill spiraled through her.

Quickly she pulled her hand back and set it in her lap. After a short time, the swelling subsided.

Irma had told her he had no manly desires! He was unable to perform the sexual act.

She kept looking at the area, but it made no more movement. Mayhap she had imagined the whole thing. Surely she had.

A few moments passed, then tentatively she leaned forward to shyly observe the area. Nothing. Naught. No movement at all. But what would happen if she touched it again?

A streak of dark desire went through her.

She shouldn't. 'Twas wicked! Horrible!

She glanced at his face. He still slept. There was no one here but her. No one would ever know.

Slowly, she eased her fingers forward and pushed at the thing beneath his linen braies.

It wiggled.

Curious, she leaned away and waited.

The lump settled, but not before she got a better look at the shape.

Eyes wide, she poked at it. This time it became higher, thicker, harder. Covering her mouth with her palm, she giggled. Irma had been totally wrong.

Tamping down a wayward tendril of guilt, she

reached forward again when it had once again sunk to oblivion. This time, she squeezed it—even beneath his linen garment she could tell it was cylindrical and fleshy. It hardened beneath her fingers and she laughed aloud.

What fun, wicked pleasure to toy with a man's body! They were such stupid, half-witted creatures that even in sleep they had no control over their own parts.

His eyes opened, locking with hers.

Her delighted giggle died on her lips, and she drew her hand back as if she'd been slapped.

He had the most intense eyes she'd ever seen. Intermingled shades of dark and light green agate caught in candle glow. They looked almost inhuman, as if they belonged to a thing dredged up from hell itself.

Not the eyes of a half-witted cretin at all.

Chapter 10

Jared's eyes drew into angry slits as he glared at the woman who circled over him like a buzzard. The screeching giggles that had escaped her maw pierced his head even more sharply than the Bible's hinges had done. She'd been stroking him, playing with him, toying with him.

Heat, a consuming rage, flowed up his spine, and flushed across his face until her figure took on a red, hazy cast and her features were fuzzy. He struggled to get free.

"Peace, sir."

His arms and legs ached from being fastened to the bed, his back felt stiff, and his temples pulsed with sharp pain. Worse, his cock throbbed.

"You will pay for this!" He fiercely worked the ropes that held his wrists against the frame to loosen the bonds. The bed bounced and clanked against the floor planks.

She jumped back. "Prithee, sir." Her skin paled and she wrung her hands in her skirt. The nervous gestures did little to appease his fury. To be humiliated as he had been was unimaginable. And yet, here he was.

The ropes held. With effort, he contained his wrath. "Release me now and it will go easier for you."

Silence.

An infuriating, long silence.

At last, she took a deep breath and shook her head slightly—as if to shake off her unease the same as a dog would quiver away water. She squared her shoulders, patted her hair, and looked him fully in the eye.

He blinked, trying to bring her features into focus, but the drug and the slam on the head made his vision blurry. Her image bounced.

"I have gold to pay you with," she said. "You have only to cooperate—"

"Do you think that what you've done to me can be appeased with something as vulgar as mere gold?"

She blanched. "Of a truth, we meant you no harm."

"I am not a toy to be played with." He lifted his head, straining against the ropes. Perhaps he could flip the bed onto one side and somehow crawl free. "Untie me, wench."

She swiveled her head toward the door. The motion made her hair glisten in the candle's glow. It was loose and swung freely down her back, a river of silver and gold. Even with his bouncing vision, the mass skimmed her body's curves in a way that framed her perfectly.

He glowered at her, wishing he could wipe his eyes, rub away the blurriness.

"Truly, sir, this has been a terrible mistake."

He snarled, frustrated that he could not rise from the cot, grasp her by the shoulders, and shake her.

"Please, we must talk. I can give you gold—a lot of

gold—and send you on your way," she explained. "'Twill be a transaction that is good for both of us."

His vision was bouncing less now and he blinked, wanting to get it under control. At that moment, the door swung open and Irma scrambled inside. Water dripped all over the floor planks. A puddle formed at her feet. She wore the same garish outfit she'd had on at the church, but it was muddied and rain-splattered.

Rouge reddened the whore's cheeks—obviously reapplied. She'd probably serviced a client or two as well since bringing him here. Disgusting.

He twisted toward the woman he'd married and sized her up as best he could with blurry eyes: The whore's garment she had worn in the brothel was gone and in its stead was a well-made gown, blue silk, with meticulously stitched embroidery around the dagged sleeves and square bodice. Her back was toward him and the long length of her luxurious hair snaked down her spine.

Dear God.

Betrayal hissed through him, sharp and cutting. Earlier he had suspected it was Gwyneth of Windrose. Yesterday, he would have been glad to be married to the woman he had dreamed about for so long.

A sickening wave went through him and for an instant he wished that his vision was still clouded and unstable.

Gwyneth.

Gwyneth of Windrose.

His Gwyneth.

No other woman could own that hair. It perfectly matched.the lock he carried in his pouch as a token to all that was good and right in the world—that there was still hope no matter how dark life seemed.

Pride fled him and he yowled in outrage. He bucked against his bonds. Rage boiled inside him.

"Faith, sir!" Gwyneth said, jumping back.

Still straining against the ropes, he scrutinized the brazenly manipulative woman he'd married. She had washed her face and no longer wore the Jezebel enhancements of a whore. Of a truth, she looked as pure and fresh as any court virgin—twice as attractive as she had before. A queen. A goddess among mortals. The thought tweaked his abhorrence of her. Her beauty came from the devil himself.

There was such a marked difference between the two women—one regal, one common—that he wondered at their friendship.

Irma crossed the chamber with heavy, unladylike steps, a woman on a mission. "Boat leaves soon. The jailor said we can exchange 'im for that girl Elizabeth and that kills two birds with one stone, it does."

Gwyneth stared at her friend, her hand clenched to her heart.

"It's either that or the nightshade." Irma held up a clay jar.

Nightshade! They intended to poison him?

Gwyneth did not move.

"'e can't stay 'ere. We shouldn't even be 'ere at all, you know. And the man said 'e had to be cleaned up and ready to sell. They wouldn't take 'im if 'e was all mangy like."

Jared shook against the bedframe; his wrists strained against the ropes.

Irma thumbed the mole on her chin.

"Nay," Gwyneth said, "there is a better way."

"Ain't no better way." Irma sidled across the chamber and began digging through the cupboard. "We gots to be rid of 'im. The boat or the poison. Where's the wine to mix this nightshade with?"

The harridans! Jared lurched and fought against his bonds. The bed jumped up and down, clanging heavily against the planks. "Let me go!"

Gwyneth jumped back.

"Silence him!" Clay jars clanked together as Irma dug faster through the cabinets. "Damn it all to the bloody devil! No wine!" Turning abruptly, she scurried to the door like the mangy rat she was. "I'll pop over to the brothel. Calm him afore someone 'ears 'im."

"Wait!" Gwyneth called, but the door slammed closed after Irma.

Curse it to the seven hells. With a grunt, Jared bucked his body off the mattress, nearly toppling the bed onto its side. He had to get free! The bed came away from the wall and bounced into the midst of the chamber, upsetting the slat-backed chair Gwyneth had been sitting in earlier.

Smoke from the hearth swirled in the air, a dark, fretful mist. The ropes cut into his wrists, painful as wasp stings. The frame thunked and bumped on the floor. It humped across the planks this way and that.

Still the bonds held.

Dammit!

To be at the mercy of women was surely the worst sort of hell!

His new wife reached toward him. "Cease! You will harm yourself."

"Untie me, wife!" His voice was scratchy.

Arms akimbo, she stared down at him as if he were

a child to correct. "We did not mean to cause you any harm or distress. You are being unreasonable."

"Unreasonable!" The skin around his wrists and ankles burned. His pride demanded revenge. And his groin, blast it all, still throbbed, overheated from her earlier touch as if that part of himself cared not a whit that he was bound for her pleasure.

She lifted her chin regally. "If you would just calm down, we could talk."

Haughty, haughty wench.

He stopped flailing on the mattresss. His pride yowled, but there was no help for it. The hemp would not break, and so long as he was tied, she remained in power.

"That's better," she crooned.

Gritting his teeth at her condescending tone, he forced his voice to be calm and spoke to her as if she were a half-wit. "I would like to be released so we can converse in a *reasonable* manner." As if one could have a reasonable conversation with a woman who kidnapped him from a brothel, forced him to marry her, and now intended to poison him or send him away on some ship.

'Twas one more *reason* a man should never, ever trust a woman—he'd been kind to Irma and this was how she repaid him. He'd thought of Gwyneth as some sort of paragon and she was as vile as the rest.

The temptress approached, ran her fingertip across his shoulder. His member sprang to life again as if eager for her touch. Curse it all!

"Do not touch me," he gritted out. A deep sense of fury born of shame and hurt slid through him as he realized he could do naught to stop her if she wished to fondle his groin and laugh again as she did afore.

Undaunted, she gave a small smile and pressed her palm against his shoulder. She knew! Knew her effect on him. Heartless.

Rain pounded down outside on the door, and he concentrated on it. Anything to keep his mind off the beauty before him.

Discreetly, he felt around the parts of the bed frame that he could reach to find any sharp corners or nails that could aid him in cutting the ropes.

He grappled for a sense of control.

"Sir, prithee, hear me out." She drew herself up in a haughty stance—one likely that she had oft used to get men to do her bidding. Her tone of voice was seductive. "I will make this worthwhile for you. I can give you gold and you can go free on your way."

In that moment he realized what it was that she wanted. She wanted to swipe away her crime with no punishment, to use his name on a marriage document and send him away. She did not wish to poison him nor did she want to go along with Irma's plans to set him on a ship. She merely wished him to go away, to leave her life and pretend she had not degraded him, harmed him. She wanted to do whatever she wished, treat him as less than a man and suffer no consequences for her actions.

Outrageous!

Resolve moved through him that she would get her comeuppance. She was the one who had insisted on this marriage and so married they would remain. There would be no ship, no poison, and there would be *no* annulment.

They had only to consummate the union to achieve permanence. Her best friend was a harlot, she had been comfortable in the whorehouse, and she'd been toying with his cock—laughing at it—when he had awoken: Of a truth, she was no virgin. And—his body was more than ready.

When he gained his freedom, she would simply belong to him, to do with as he pleased. To punish for the rest of her life. And that was that.

Taking a breath, he focused on getting free from his bonds. He could tell the rope was frayed, had began to come unraveled. Surely it was only one more stroke. One more rip.

He watched her walk across the chamber, back straight, shoulders rigid. Her hair, a curtain of shimmering satin, cascaded down her back and skimmed the tops of her thighs. Everything about her bespoke privilege and haughty imperiousness. She swiveled, looked over a shoulder at him. Of a truth, she was glorious. A seductress who was used to having her way with men, of laughing at them, trifling with them, bending them to her own devices.

The need to take, to conquer, pulsed through his mind as strong as the throbbing sensation in his groin.

She set the clay jar of poison in the cupboard.

Gathering his strength, he strained against the ropes, pulled, heaved. Agony ripped through his wrists; his biceps bulged; his stomach muscles quivered with exertion. More. More. He felt one strand snap. The moments dragged.

She walked back and forth several more times, her slippers quiet against the planks.

Another strand popped and still another.

Ripping himself free with a mighty heave, he let out a savage cry of triumph and sat up all at once. Success sang through his veins. He lurched off the bed, and hurtled toward his prize.

She shrieked and jumped back. Her hair flailed around her, the waves bouncing this way and that, but he was on her in two steps.

In a quick movement, he grabbed her by her shoulders, strong-armed her to the bed, and flipped her unceremoniously onto the mattress.

Breath whooshed from her lungs with a satisfying *oomph*. Her eyes went wide—two round moons—and conquest swam through his body like a raging river. She was his. All his. This time he would stay on guard. There would not be a repeat of what had happened in the church.

Her body sank onto the bed beneath him, warm and female.

A primal throbbing need to take and conquer coursed through his veins, scorching him, demanding restitution for his pride, to repay her for the indignity done to his body.

"You are mine," he rasped, the words a battle cry from deep inside him. Slowly he began scrunching up her skirt.

Gwyneth gasped, unsure what to do or what to think as Jared's big body crashed down atop hers, sinking her downward into the cot. He was huge, massive.

Stunned, she pushed against him, but it was like trying to move a catapult by oneself.

"What think you of this, wife?" His breath was warm and sweet, and his voice low and husky but the word "wife" was a sneer.

Her heart raced; she squirmed to get free. The

bare skin of his torso was warm against her bodice and he felt so very male. "Cease!"

He forced her arms above her head and transferred both of her wrists to one hand.

Panic lurched into her throat. She wiggled, bucked, writhed, but still he held her. "Let me go! Stop!" she yelled, befuddled with the sudden change in situation—the overturning of power.

"Be still, wife. You are mine now, to take as *I* please. You had no issue exploring my body at will. And now I will do the same to yours."

Her breath squeezed from her lungs. She turned her head to one side, anxiety climbing into her throat now that she no longer had control of the situation.

She wiggled beneath him, as caught as an insect in a web. "Get off me!"

"Nay."

The word was spoken softly, calmly, but with so much resolve he could have been shouting.

A shiver went through her.

She could feel his huge hand rasping against the tender skin of her thighs. His fingertips grazed her, hot and commanding. Heat flooded her face. Is this how he had felt? Helpless? Vulnerable?

"Cease!"

"Nay."

His palm slid up her thigh and cupped the area where her legs met together. His hand felt warm, firm, but not harsh. A bolt of sensation scattered through her body. A primal streak of alarm shot through her veins.

Holy Mary. Not like this! Not with her skirts flipped upward, tupped like a common doxy. But the creaminess between her legs seemed to laugh at her, to mock her. Only minutes before she *had* desired him, had wanted naught more than to couple with him.

But union should be on her terms, not his. Clearly, this man was unsuitable for such a goal and if the marriage was consummated, she'd never be rid of him.

"Please." The word came out a little strangled.

"Was this not what you wanted?" he said, his voice still soft but with a core of strength about it. Power. Utter power. "To have a man inside you."

"Nay," she denied. But she had. She had wanted him. She'd wanted to feel how his manroot would fit inside her.

A controlled anger gleamed in his eyes. She could feel the fierceness rolling off of him in waves, as if his wrath was a tangible thing. "You think men are toys to play with, do you not? Is that not what you are used to—men falling all over themselves to do your bidding?"

Gwyneth blinked. "Nay—"

"No more." He came off of her all at once. With a hard yank, he pulled her up to a sitting position, and flipped her onto her stomach. Reaching an arm beneath her, he fiercely tugged her up onto her knees so that she hung by her belly over his forearm. The sheets on the cot had the indentation of their bodies impressed into them.

She wiggled back and forth trying to buck off the man behind her. "This is not—"

"Shush." With an ease of casual indifference, he tossed her skirt fully over her shoulder. The blue silk hung in a ripple by her side. A loud rent echoed across the cottage and chilly air caressed her bare bottom. Her undergarments were flung aside.

Growling, he pulled her hard against the thick bulge

of his manhood and bent over her, his mouth near her ear. Like a savage, he sank his teeth into the tender skin of her neck. Chills slid down her overheated body and a small sting of pain lanced her flesh.

He did not break the skin, but held her as a lion would dominate his mate. For all his fearsomeness, she realized he was in complete control of himself. Her world spun as the joint emotions of fear and desire raged through her like a storm.

The fear she understood. But the heady dose of desire terrified her.

Her underarms stung, and the remembrance of how he'd held her at the church, of how he'd pumped the cot around the room using only his body weight shivered through her. He was strong. Powerful. He could hurt her, maybe even kill her if he took her roughly.

Yet there was nothing rough in his firm touch save the teeth sinking into her neck.

Frantically, she forced herself to think, desperate to find a way to appease him and send him on his way with a bag of gold. To consummate the marriage was unthinkable. This was a man she could not control.

"There is no need for this," she started, using a voice she hoped bespoke calmness and rationality. "I wanted—"

"—me tied and helpless while you did your worst. So you could run your hands over my body, feel my cock, laugh at me, then either poison me or toss me on a boat out of your way. You wanted to use me."

The skin on her neck felt hot and tingly where his mouth had been. A wave of guilt stormed through her. "I didn't mean to laugh—"

"Nay? I felt your hands move over me; I thought it was a dream until I woke to find a buzzard staring down at me squeezing my groin with her claws."

His words mortified her. Did he know of how she'd lingered over his shoulders, dipped her fingers across the ridges of his stomach, taken guilty pleasure in exploring his body? And he thought of her as a buzzard? An ugly, awkward creature.

Shaking her head at the humiliating memory, she twisted and tried to look over her shoulder at him. "Please! We must get the marriage annulled. If you rape me—"

"It is not rape for a man to copulate with his wife." The words sounded ominous, as if the whole body of the law and the church stood behind them.

She swallowed, realizing at once exactly how powerless she was, at what she'd brought on herself.

"Asides, I'm not so blind as to not notice the pleasure you took in exploring my body—"

Prickles spread across her cheeks. She'd felt warm, overheated as she'd touched him.

"You lingered over my arms, ran your fingers across my shoulders."

She wriggled to one side, tried to push her skirt back down, tried to buck him off of her. His forearm dug into her stomach and he leaned his body so that he was pressed against her, his thighs on hers, his groin against her naked buttocks, his torso against her back. His free hand slid beneath her so that his arm lay across her upper chest just beneath her collarbones and anchored her firmly against his body so she could not move.

A disconcerting spin of desire curled through her.

Her shoulders tensed, and nervousness churned in her belly. She could not want him. Not like this.

"Get off me."

"I do not think so, my captive bird. 'Twas you who started this, who thought you could drug a man, humiliate him, and suffer no consequences."

Damn male pride! "You are a peasant and I intended to pay you well! Get off of me and go about your way, falconer. My overlord will see you killed for daring to lay a hand on me, a noblewoman."

He guffawed. "I am your husband, woman, your lord and master, your family now. You are mine to command." He pressed against the soft area betwixt her legs, not quite entering her, but disallowing her any doubt of what would soon occur.

"Nay!" No matter her body's foolhardy attraction to him, she could not be married to a man such as him. He was too masculine, too much the conquerer. She needed a man she could control. If the marriage was consummated—

She gasped as she was pushed forward on the bed, her buttocks high in the air and her face pressed to the mattress. "Cease!" The linen sheet scraped her shoulder as she tried to scramble forward.

In one strong stroke, he plunged into her.

A scream ripped from her throat as a streak of pain shot through her sex.

He stilled. Perfectly still. As if his whole being had suddenly turned into granite. He didn't release her, but he didn't move either.

"Bloody hell."

A confusing mix of heat and fear stormed through her. Why had she touched him at all? Again, she tried to wiggle away, but he held her firm.

"I should have let you bleed to death," she snarled. "Or poisoned you as Irma suggested."

She felt a quiver go through him.

"You were a virgin!" It sounded like an accusation.

Fury pounded through her veins. "Of course I'm a virgin, half-wit. I'm of noble blood."

He growled at the insult, but she was beyond caring, beyond concern. Anger and pain had taken over her mind. She willed her body to fight, but she found she no longer had the will to do so.

Tension rose.

His hand slipped from beneath her shoulder, and his body eased away from her.

Slowly, he began to slide out of her. "You were in a whorehouse. I awoke to find you stroking my body and fondling me. There was no reason for me to believe you were yet untouched, *wife.*" He sounded angry.

She tucked her chin and braced herself for whatever unknown thing would happen next.

A shudder moved through him; she felt his thighs quiver and then their bodies were detached from each other. She felt sticky, open.

Stiffly, she fell onto her side on the cot, her legs curled up. She tried to push her skirt down, but her fingers seemed too puny to grasp the velvet strongly enough to accomplish her task. Her chest ached, a sensation that seemed to rise from her gut.

The mattress sank as Jared lay down beside her, propped up on one elbow, and touched her shoulder lightly.

Too distraught to move, she did not resist his touch. Her body felt oddly detached from her brain and she began to shiver uncontrollably as she realized her life had just been changed for the worse forever.

Chapter 11

Heart pounding, Gwyneth watched Jared, his large shoulders tight, push to a sitting position as she tried to gather her scattered thoughts. Wetness leaked from her sex, the area between her legs stung, and an odd scent permeated the air.

His demeanor had totally changed. Gone was the fierce and terrifying brute who had sunk his teeth into her and tried to dominate her like a beast, but her pulse still beat so strongly in her neck that she could feel the vein thumping.

A wrinkle indented the area between Jared's stormy green eyes; they seemed to be filled with concern, perhaps even regret. His mustache emphasized the downward turn of his mouth.

A mouth that had just been lifted into a snarl.

Quakes shook her body and her teeth chattered. Her body felt bruised, violated. She didn't know whether to run or cry or scream or some combination of those things, and her brain seemed too paralyzed to do any of them. If only he would leave, disappear like morning mist. But he was too cold, too intense to vaporize thus—no sunshine would ever penetrate his darkness to burn him away.

Jared blew out a breath. His thumb and middle finger made tiny circles around each other and she wondered if he'd hold her down again with his hands. The gesture seemed innocuous and at odds with the fierceness she'd seen in him just moments earlier.

She tried to rise, to get her muddled mind to figure out what to do next, but her body felt slow and thick as slime. What a horrible thing to be a woman, the weaker vessel, unable to fight, to be taken like an animal.

And the consequences of the coupling—a marriage in truth, an annulment impossible—were the worst of it all.

Her fingers skimmed the indentions that his teeth had made.

"I'll clean you up," Jared said after a moment. Placing a hand on her shoulder, he pushed off the thin cot, hitched up his hose, and retied them in place.

The world seemed disjointed. The quivers she felt on the inside seemed to grow instead of diminish. Her body was cold, frigid, like she was freezing from the inside out. How did Irma deal with such nauseating activity every night?

Lifting her head, she stared at the door. If only she could scurry from the bed, run from the chamber, run back to her home. Run away from the horrible choice of husband that she had made. None of the men Papa had chosen for her were as bad as what she had done to herself.

Feebly, she tried to swing her legs over the side of

the cot, but her limbs felt leaden and would not obey her command to rise and flee.

He returned shortly with the cloth she had used on him earlier. The irony was not lost on her. She had been a fool to think she could explore his body and pay no consequences for her actions.

The cot let out a squeak as Jared sat on the edge, his hip a whisper away. A measure of disgust sent stiff tension through her shoulders.

Nay.

Not disgust, she realized with sickening loathing for herself. Disgust would have sent her scrambling away, wanting to slay him as she had done to the brute who had debased Irma all those years ago. But she didn't feel disgust for his body being so near her at all, not even after what had just occurred between them.

The thought washed a fresh wave of shivers over her.

She had protested the consummation because she wished for a husband who would easily cow to her wishes. She had protested the manner he had taken her because it frightened her.

But her body had been well and fully alive with *desire*, not disgust, for him.

'Twas a betrayal of the worst sort—her mind longing for one thing while her body desired another.

Only minutes before he had sunk his rod inside her she had wanted him, lusted for him, been wet for him. Confusing, conflicting emotions that played through her like a gypsy band with unsynchronized instruments.

Dismayed, she wanted to rail at herself for her failure, to rail at God for the injustice done to women—

for always being the ones who were taken instead of the ones who took. She tried to focus her mind on the timber walls, on the droplets of rain that streamed through the cracks. If she could get her thoughts together, she could figure out what to do.

The shivering continued; her legs drew up and her body curled into a ball of its own accord. She wanted to cry, to release the powerlessness and humiliation she felt. How could she feel any sensation at all for him after what had just occurred?

Jared touched her thigh.

Her breath hitched as she realized her skirt was still wadded up around her torso. She reached to yank it down, to cover her exposed parts, but he caught her wrist and pressed her hand down.

A streak of panic climbed into her throat. She pushed at his hand.

"Peace, girl. We will not repeat what just happened right now."

Right now? But in the future? Now that the union was consummated, would he expect more marital rights? Men wanted heirs.

The thought of being humbled night after night in such a fashion terrified her. She could not fathom such a horrid thing.

The tight, hard muscles of his ridged stomach danced as he twisted his torso, pushed her onto her back, and gently tugged her legs apart. Realizing that fighting him physically was utterly pointless, Gwyneth remained still.

Humiliated by the indignity of her body, she squeezed both her eyes and her legs together.

"Relax, girl."

Despite herself, his voice soothed her, but she

turned her head aside, covered her ears with her palms. She did not wish to be soothed by this man who had made her feel vulnerable and despoiled. Who confused her in both body and mind.

Rough linen rasped her skin as he ran the wet cloth up her thigh. Red stains, in swirling hues that ranged from crimson to scarlet, smeared her legs and leaked into the sheet. The rag slid over the hump of her pubic mound.

Sensations rocked her.

Startled, terrified, vexed by her body's betrayal, she opened her eyes a slit. If only she could say a spell and make him disappear.

His hand, so large and blunt, traced the edges of folds, sliding very gently into the creases of her sex. He did not push her legs apart, though. He simply lingered, cleaning her, caressing her.

Long, slow moments passed. All brutality was gone and he seemed to take infinite care. 'Twas as if a different man altogether touched her—a tender lover.

Of their own accord, her knees softened slightly, allowing him access, allowing him to wipe blood from her bruised core. *Stupid fool.* She berated herself for such weakness. For such lunacy.

His head was bent over his task, his silky dark hair falling like a curtain of midnight. The hair on his scalp parted in a messy zigzagged manner. His mustache and goatee were only a shadow. His invasion was the worst sort: a gentle one.

Disgusted with herself for her passivity, for allowing him to touch her so intimately, for even entertaining the thought that this brutish man could ever be a tender lover to anyone, she dug her fingernails deeply into her palms, gouging them inward to feel the pain in sharp remembrance of how his teeth had felt on her neck.

The rag ran lightly over the sensitive folds between her legs—it was clear that he was taking great care to be extremely gentle, as if her sex were a prized, fragile vessel.

She set her jaw, determined to find some way to get the situation back under control, stop being so perplexed. She fisted her hands tighter until her knuckles went white and she felt a nail pierce the skin. The pain seemed to bring her more to her senses, give her will back to her.

Jared wadded the cloth into a ball and tossed it onto the floor. It landed with a wet splat.

"Y-y-you can go," she said, then stopped and cleared her throat, determined to sound stronger, not so squeaky. "I will send you gold." Yes, that was it. Even though the marriage was fully consummated, she would treat the union like a business contract. As if they were exchanging money for sheep.

He smoothed her skirt down over her legs. His green eyes were intense but he absently did that little circling motion with his thumb and middle finger again. "I'm not leaving."

"We can still get the marriage annulled." She felt better now that she was talking, so she sat up on the cot.

"'Tis too late for that."

"There is no reason for you to stay," she reasoned. "No one has seen us."

Talking aloud made her feel less wrapped up in her vulnerabilities and more in control of her own faculties. She folded her arms, lifted her chin, and forced herself to think logically. She was a strong woman;

she would survive this. Naught had happened to her that had not happened to countless wives all over the earth throughout history.

But I was to be the exception, her emotions seemed to wail, threatening to run away with her. *I was supposed to pick a man whom I could have sway over.*

"Please go now," she continued, her voice steadier than it had been. She pointed at the door. "Irma will be here. If you come to the brothel, I'll make sure you are paid well." That's it, she instructed herself, he was naught more than a stud horse who had gotten out of control. Now it was time to put him back in his place.

"Nay." His hand slid down her arm in a gesture that was possessive and alarming.

She shook herself off, pushing away her previous humiliation in a huff, just as Irma had done all those years afore. "Of course you are leaving. You are dismissed."

"Dismissed?" A dangerous glint formed in his eyes and he reminded her of a dragon again. Perhaps that was why he carried a staff with one carved into the top.

She took a breath. He was no dragon, merely a peasant, a lowlife falconer, a stupid mistake. She would simply have to undo the wedding knot the way she did when her stitches became tangled on the piece of embroidery—cut the threads, pull them loose, and toss them away.

"Time for you to go. Best you hurry afore my family finds out what you have done."

"What *I've* done."

Wickedly, she licked her lips. "Kidnapped me—"

The dark gaze that crossed his face was so intense

that for an instant, she faltered, then cleared her throat and continued. He needed to see how precarious his position was. How he could not treat a daughter of Windrose in such a fashion and get away with it. "—forced me to marry you."

"Forced you!" Jared stood so fast that the cot jiggled. Heat radiated off his bare skin.

Taking advantage of the momentary distance between their bodies, Gwyneth leapt to her feet. The small knife she had used to bandage his wound lay nearby and she lunged for it. Her hand closed around the hilt and she brought the weapon up in a wide swinging arc.

"Faith!" Jared jumped back as the blade sank into the flesh of his arm. His eyes went wide.

Ha!

Lifting her skirts, she whirled for the door and broke into a run. She would run all the way back to Windrose if needs be. No peasant barbarian would own her. Ever.

Footsteps thumped behind her.

Her heart raced. She reached the door, flung it open. Rain splashed onto her face.

Jared's hand closed on her wrist.

Nay!

Her body spun in a lurch and landed with a thunk against the solid wall of his chest.

She screamed and fought blindly against the arms that surrounded her. "Leave be! You have no rights to me!"

"But I do."

Jared tried to pull the screaming, wiggling girl into his arms before she hurt herself. Guilt spun through him like a wild, fierce wind. No matter the ease at which he had been able to enter her—at how moist her quim had been—he should not have pushed her to consummate the marriage. He was a bastard, a lowlife.

"Let go of me!" she screamed, kicking at his legs. Her face reddened with exertion as he moved deftly to one side and she kicked the air instead.

"Be calm, lady wife."

At the word "wife," she set out screaming again.

Unsure of the best way to soothe her, he released her. "Peace, girl."

She wrenched away from him. With a bang, she flung the door open and raced out into the night.

Jared took a deep breath, fighting the instinct to snatch her back. As much as he wished to lay the blame at her feet, give in to the thought that she had brought this on herself by stealing him from a brothel, he could not blame her for being terrified of him.

Her footsteps, soft because of her satin slippers, sounded on the cobbled streets. The candle glow filtering into the air from the windows lit the path, but the air was gloomy.

A wolf howled in the distance. She was running toward the docks, toward The Bald Cock, and it was the two-legged wolves that concerned him.

He could not leave her to fend off any attackers alone. When she calmed, they could talk about the right course of action. A marriage could not be so easily undone. She belonged to him now. He tied his breeks and slung his cloak over his shoulders.

At a distance, he followed.

* * *

Panting, Gwyneth rounded another corner and pulled the dank, damp air into her aching lungs. Shadows and moonlight shifted on the walls and cobblestones. The smell of sewage and rotting fish hung in the air. She grasped the knife's hilt in case Jared followed and she needed to defend herself.

She glanced over her shoulder but saw no sign of Jared. Thank the saints. She knew the streets in this part of the town—had traveled this way many times, but never at this hour of night. It was not far from The Bald Cock. She slowed her pace and kept to the shadows to avoid looking out of place and attracting attention. She wasn't wearing the shabby cloak that she normally wore and she knew her silver-and-gold hair would stand out like a beacon.

The brothel's back door was just ahead. Once she was safe inside, she would figure out what to do. Her breath sighed from her lungs. She'd made it. Mass every day for a week, she vowed. Twice a day.

Stuffing the knife into her bodice, she went the final distance.

A noise sounded to one side as her fingertips touched the door. A man leapt from behind a pile of rotting garbage.

She gasped as he unfolded, revealing a tall, thin body. Heavens! Hastily, she grasped the handle of the brothel's back door.

"Lady Gwyneth?" the man said, his voice kind, singsonglike. Someone here knew her name? She'd never been recognized in the past, but always before she had worn her shabby cloak, kept her hair covered and her face hidden.

She pulled open the door, eager to reach Irma, but the man stepped quickly forward and pushed it shut.

"Not so fast, Lady Gwyneth." The voice remained a singsong.

Her heart pounded, and the stench of dung and ale bit her nostrils—the smell of evil, of a rottenness that went even deeper than the man's unwashed body. Gagging, she yanked on the door and kicked it, but the man pressed forward and held it shut, disallowing her entrance.

"Irma!" she called desperately. "Help!"

"Shhh, woman. We have matters to discuss."

Quivering, Gwyneth backed away, hoping to lure him from the door so she could bolt forward into the whorehouse as soon as his attention shifted.

His looming shadow followed her and she was forced farther away toward the wall at the other end of the alleyway. "You're even prettier than they say," he said, smiling. Three of his front teeth were missing. "Maybe a kiss—"

"Get back," she commanded. "People are expecting me." Her voice sounded much calmer than she felt. *Never show fear.*

Beneath his cowl, he grinned, showing his missing teeth again. "You want to be nicey-nice to me, woman. I know about the murder. I know somebody who is looking for the green boots. They have been asking questions."

Her eyes widened and she lunged again for the door. This time, he grasped her arm in a hard, twisting grip. She yelped.

"Let go!"

"I require only a little payment—" His breath was fetid.

She yanked as hard as she could. "Irma! Irma!"

"Shush, woman."

"Leave be!" Her voice rose in pitch and she flailed her fists at him.

His grip tightened and he hustled her away from the brothel's entrance.

She snatched the knife from her bodice. "Back off!"

His hand came up, then cracked sharply against her cheek. "Silence."

She staggered at the force of the blow but gripped the knife tighter and swung around on him. The blade caught only air. Curses!

Grabbing her by the shoulders, he threw her to the ground.

Pain shot through her hip. "Oof." Heart racing, she scooted back on her buttocks, desperate to get away. The look in his eyes—as dark as his stench— terrified her.

His tunic flapped as he dove atop her, sliding them both into the filth. He smelled like stale ale.

She gagged.

"Where's your purse?" His hand dove into her bodice, mauling her breasts.

Screaming, she kicked as hard as she could and prayed for Irma or one of the other whores to hear her. "Help!"

Oh, Mother Mary!

With a hard yank, the man grabbed her hand and twisted it painfully upward.

"Aagh!"

"Shush, bitch."

Sharp pain lanced the pinky of her right hand. She opened her mouth to scream again, but the man kicked her in the side.

"No more screaming or I'll break it."

Oh, Saints. Oh, Mary. Her underarms stung, and

she shook so hard that her teeth clattered together. Terrified, Gwyneth held her throbbing finger, drew her body into a tight ball, and squeezed her eyes closed as panic overtook her and she waited to die. The man's fetid stench contaminated the air.

Abruptly, the scent left and a loud thunk sounded several feet away. Her eyes popped open. Jared stood over her like a dark rescuing angel, his form bathed in moonlight.

Relief poured through her.

The attacker scrambled to his feet, drew into a defensive stance. "We were just having a little talk," he said in that singsong voice. "Get her to tell you about—"

Jared lunged forward and slammed the man across the head with his staff.

The attacker fell onto the ground with a thunk.

Gwyneth shuddered, her mind going back to the man she'd hit with a stick in the forest.

Jared stared at the unmoving body as if to determine if further force was needed, then he turned toward her, his brows drawn into a deep frown. A beam of moonlight slashed across his goatee and lit one half of his face.

Although he had saved her life, there was still no love lost betwixt the two of them. Wary, she willed her legs to rise, knowing she should run, but her limbs felt numb, detached from her body. Uncooperative.

As if sensing her hesitation, Jared stooped down, still holding his engraved staff, and slid his arms beneath her bruised body. She felt herself being lifted from the grimy ground and pressed to his warm, wide chest.

"'Tis okay, girl. I have you now."

She knew she should resist, that everything that

had happened this night was terribly wrong, that there was too much between them for her to give in to the comfort of his body, but her arms snaked around his neck seemingly of their own accord. She buried her face in his shoulder. His scent was fresh, clean—sandalwood and spice—the smell of safety. Tears stung the backs of her eyes and then spilled down her cheeks.

"Peace, love, you are safe."

Love?

Her hand throbbed; her hip ached as well. Her body shook, and his demeanor of soft strength was too calming to resist. Inhaling deeply, she melted against him, sinking into the comfort that he offered.

Her mind screamed in protest. Jared was not a right match. He'd forced her! He was not a man she could control. He had done even worse to her than the man lying unmoving beside the wall, hadn't he?

Without a further glance at the man, Jared turned and carried her out of the alley.

Closing her eyes, too exhausted to fight, she surrendered. Tomorrow when her head was clear, when her body ached less, she would find a way out of the marriage and figure out what to do with Jared.

Chapter 12

Kidnapped him. Married him. Stabbed him. Would this woman's sins ne'er end?

A bright red blotch of blood spotted the linen bandage around his arm from where she had stabbed him earlier. His entire limb throbbed as he carried his sleeping wife toward his cave. Sleeping! As if her conscience was clear as an angel's.

Damp tendrils of hair stuck to her face and her lips were open in a soft pout. Part of him wanted to take her to the town stocks and see her get her come-uppance, but his heart tugged. She looked sweet, innocent—the Gwyneth he remembered—a far cry from the brazen temptress she'd been in the whore-house or the hellion who had forced him into the church on his hands and knees.

Rain drizzled upon them in a cold mist. He pulled his cape around her, wracking his brain to figure out what he would do with her.

Definitely he could not trust her, no matter how innocent she appeared while sleeping. And letting her go was out of the question: 'Twas obvious that she needed a protector. The woman had made one bad decision after the next and needed someone to rein her in.

Stepping over a fallen limb, he contemplated this. She snuggled even closer to his shoulder. Her forehead burrowed into his torso and her pink, bow-shaped mouth fell open in a soft sigh.

He would not let her go, not after what he had done to her. The sheet with her virgin blood was folded and tucked into his belt as further proof.

A virgin! Who would have ever guessed any semblance of purity could be found in such a woman?

Vexing. The woman was totally vexing. She was both naive and crafty at the same time. The way she was now, no one would ever think she was capable of drugging a man and forcing him to marry her.

Likely her family would be looking for her; he needed to find the damn monk to prove they were truly married so there would be no question whatsoever that he was her lord.

Above, an owl hooted. Frogs chirped. No moon shone. The wind kicked up. Rain blew.

Once his hawk was tended, he would make plans for what to do with his *wife*. It seemed that she had not recognized him at all. He pushed aside a small twinge of longing. He had thought of her daily for three years and she had not thought of him at all.

But he would have to continue in disguise at least until his name was cleared. If she learned that he had escaped from prison, she would turn him in.

"Well, Gwyneth of Windrose," Jared said, shifting her in his arms so his limb did not throb as much, "you are a package of trouble." And as attractive as she had been three years ago.

Gwyneth of Windrose. What an irony. What a mystery. What was she doing at a brothel? Why had she stolen him? How had she and Irma become friends?

So many questions.

In answer, her head lolled to one side. How on earth did she manage to sleep?

"You claimed to have plenty of gold. Why have you never married? A woman such as you would have plenty of suitors." He asked the questions aloud, musing to himself, and not actually expecting an answer.

The rain had mostly cleared by the time they arrived at the cave. His legs ached, his back ached, his arms throbbed.

And still the woman slept.

The hawk watched her with yellow eyes and gave him a sound of displeasure as they entered. She fluttered on her perch; she had been waiting too long.

"I know, friend," he crooned. "'Twas not in my plans to get married last evening or to be gone nearly so long."

Using the glimmer of moonlight that streamed in the cave's entrance, he laid Gwyneth atop the pallet of wool blankets that he had been using as a bed. She twisted, wiggled into the covers, and then curled onto one side—as peaceful as a baby.

Frowning down at her, Jared rolled his shoulders and stretched his arms upward, nearly touching the cavern's rock ceiling.

Aeliana ruffled in an obvious attempt to snare his attention. She eyed Gwyneth suspiciously, clearly jealous of another female being with him.

Jared smiled, glad of the hawk's irritation. Had she

been angry rather than jealous, he would have been concerned that she might take flight and never return when they next went hunting.

"In the morn, I'll take you hunting."

Aeliana made an annoyed sound as if to suggest 'twas past time already.

"Peace, Aeliana," he crooned, and sank to his knees beside his sleeping wife, intending to get a few hours of sleep. Mayhap somewhere in his dreams he would discover the answer for what to do with her.

Her body was warm, soft, and entirely too tempting as he stretched out beside her on the pallet.

A curl of her hair wound across his forearm. In the dark, the color was muted, but he knew what it looked like: a glimmering treasure chest of gold and silver, just like the tendril that was tucked in his pouch. He picked it up and rubbed it betwixt his thumb and forefinger, then held it to his nose and inhaled deeply. Just as he had done time and again in the prison. The scent, that of lavender, was as seductive and tantalizing as the silky feel.

He had frightened her earlier—indeed had intended to do so—and the way she now trustingly curled against him heightened his guilt of what had occurred between them. Somehow he would right his wrongs, make it up to her. He wouldn't let her go, but like his hawk, he would make her come to understand that life with him was better than life without him. It made him doubly eager to find Rafe's murderer so that he could clear his name.

He closed his eyes and drew her into his arms. A hard lump pressed against him where her bosom should have been. Puzzled, he glanced downward and noticed something poking from the top of her bosom. With the easy movement of a thief, he stole it from the top of her gown.

A book.

Nay, *the* book!

The book he had given her three years ago. He had spent hours carving and crafting the thin wooden cover for it.

Amazement washed over him as he ran his hand across the tiny bumpy scales of carved dragon and then flipped through the pages. Why had she carried it? What did it mean? He turned to shake her awake, to demand answers.

"Search the cave!"

"There, my lord!"

Hooves beat the ground, snapping twigs and crunching leaves just outside the entrance.

Jared snapped to a sitting position, tucked the small book inside his pouch and grasped his staff. His fingers found the familiar place where the dragon's tail wrapped around the wood.

Aeliana cried out and Gwyneth lurched awake, a confused and dazed look in her eyes.

"Where am—"

"Shh," he admonished, touching his finger lightly to her lips. From the sounds, he guessed that there were at least four or five men and he needed all the advantage he could muster.

"Wha—"

He clamped his palm over her mouth.

Gwyneth shuddered as Jared's hand pressed her lips into her teeth. Yesterday's nightmarish events flooded her mind. She tried to sit up, to scramble backward, to gain some sense of control.

A hand landed on her shoulder, pinioning her to

the hard stone floor and effectively stopping her struggles. The light coming in from the front of the cavern was dim. Shadows danced on the walls, monstrously large and terrifying.

Her heart pounded. Not a nightmare, but Hades.

She had landed in the underworld, the realm of a devil with silky dark hair and piercing green eyes. Terrifying. He loomed over her, tall and strong. He wore black breeks and a black tunic. She remembered how easily he had controlled her body before. Lurching upward, she strained to get away.

Nay!" she yelled. She pushed him back and screamed.

"Gwyneth?" a voice called.

Her family?

Horses, men shouting, the thundering of voices and hooves sounded in the forest just outside the cave. Trees rustled. She spun toward the noise.

A small party of men appeared just a stone's throw from the entrance. The dawn light illuminated them. Montgomery and several of his knights!

She gave a shout of joy. Never in her life had she been thrilled to see her brother-in-law, but his arrival meant that the current situation would be handled. Relief poured through her.

Montgomery sat atop a large black warhorse, his blue eyes flashing. She wished her sisters were also here, but she did not see them among the riders.

"Montgomery! Over here!" Kicking hard against Jared, she scrambled to her feet to race toward her brother-in-law.

Jared's hand closed around her shoulders afore she could make a step. He tugged her so that her back landed against his chest. "Not so fast, lady wife."

Stopping, she turned her head, squared her shoulders, and stared down at him even though he was nearly a head taller than her. Too much was at stake; too many women depended on her. Their marriage would have to be annulled. "I thank you for saving my life, but release me or you will regret it."

Jared's fingers tightened, indenting her skin.

"What the hell are you doing here, Gwyneth?" Montgomery boomed.

"Let me go," she demanded.

"Nay."

"You leave me no choice," she whispered. Tamping down her guilt, Gwyneth pointed at Jared and called to her brother-in-law, who sat regally atop a tall black mount. "Arrest this man!"

Incredulous, Jared gaped at his wife, who was now flapping her arms frantically in the air. Of all the faithless, underhanded things!

"I've been kidnapped!" she called.

The lying little wench. And he had felt tender toward her only moments earlier!

"God save us from female treachery," he muttered. Drawing the dagger from his belt, he buried his hand in her hair and set the blade against her neck. Her pulse pounded, making her alabaster skin jump.

"Help me!" she yelled. "This man is holding me captive!"

"Silence," he gritted out, wanting to kick himself for ever feeling any softness toward her. Long ago he had learned that women were faithless and untrustworthy—especially those who were clever or beautiful—and Gwyneth of Windrose was both.

"Explain yourself!" the tall warrior on the black warhorse demanded.

"I've been stolen!" Gwyneth interjected.

"'Tis untrue, my lord," Jared started, intending to talk his way out of the situation.

"He—"

He clamped his hand over her mouth and pressed the blade threateningly against her skin.

Gwyneth closed her lips. But he could still see the gleam of victory shining in her eyes as she stared at the riders. Without the monk to verify his story, he knew he looked guilty despite this scenario being all her fault. His original instinct to take her straight to the town stocks had been right on target. Once he had dealt with the riders, he would follow his initial plan to make her his personal servant for the rest of her life.

"The woman captured me from—"

The leader guffawed. "Of all the beef-witted excuses. Get away from her."

The rising sun, orange and round, glinted off their horses' flanks. There were four in all: the tall leader who wore a hood, a shorter man with silver spurs, one who appeared to be his squire, and Irma, who rode behind the squire.

Irma! Another betraying woman. The harlot rode very stiffly, bouncing like a rigid plank and looking somewhat terrified, as if she might tumble from her mount at any moment. Her toes were curled, her yellow scarf hung askew, and Jared suspected that she'd never been atop a horse afore.

Except for Irma, all were heavily armed with swords and daggers. One even carried a crossbow.

They crowded toward the cave's entrance.

Gwyneth tried to bite his fingers.

Jared clamped his hand harder over her mouth

and yanked her close to him so he could use her as a hostage.

Her cry died in her throat and a shudder ran through her. Good.

He sized up the men. Fighting three at once, especially one as large as the leader, would be difficult, but he had done such afore.

Tautness formed under Jared's shoulder blades.

"I know how this looks, my lord. Allow me to explain."

Gwyneth squirmed, trying to wriggle his palm from her mouth.

"Be still. You will not get away with this," he whispered into her hair. Lavender and innocence assailed his nostrils.

A pox on women! Was there nothing about them that was truthful and honest? She should have smelled like something as rotted as her conscience, but even her scent was deceptive.

"Away from her," one of the men called, drawing a long, wicked-looking knife.

"Harm her, and you will die."

Jared braced his legs wide apart, readying himself for battle as he tilted her head farther to one side. "The woman is mine. Do not come closer."

"Jared?" the leader asked, a baffled tone coming into his voice. His hood slid off his head, revealing the dark features and brilliant cobalt eyes of James Vaughn.

James?

Jared blinked, not believing his eyes.

In their younger, wilder days, the two of them had ridden the high seas together. Jared had been fighting the demon of Colette's memory and he suspected James was fighting something as well. Both of them had been too drunk to get around to telling their stories to each other, but there had been an instant connection between the two men.

"James? What the devil?" He didn't release Gwyneth. Likely this was some new womanly trick of hers. Had James been in love with her? Her beauty was such that she had only to toss her pretty head and men would be willing to race to their deaths for her.

"Jared!" James called.

Gwyneth shuddered. Wide-eyed, she glanced from one man to the other. Not a trick then, perhaps. She seemed genuinely surprised that the two of them knew each other.

Unsure of his old friend's relationship with her, Jared braced himself. She was his and he would not release her.

The other two looked back and forth at each other, clearly unsure what to make of this new development. Jared did not know what to make of it either.

"What are you doing here?" James urged his majestic black stallion forward. He didn't smile.

"I could ask you the same," called Jared, trying to assess their relationship. Was there longing in Montgomery's eyes? Jealousy? If he took the knife from Gwyneth's neck, would his friend embrace him or kill him on the spot? He could not tell.

"I'm here to"—he gazed from Gwyneth to Jared and back again with a hard stare—"rescue my sister-in-law from her own folly."

"My new wife, Gwyneth, is your sister-in-law?" Of all the bedlamite things. He pushed aside the sharp sense of relief that Gwyneth and James were not betrothed.

"Aye." James let out a bark of laughter. His horse twitched its tail restlessly. "You married *Gwyneth*?"

The mocking way he asked sent a shot of indignation through Jared. "Aye."

James's gaze raked over Gwyneth. "What evil deed did you do to deserve *that* punishment?"

Unbidden, anger washed over Jared—the same as he had felt years ago when Rafe had been disrespectful to her. He released her mouth and glared at his former friend.

James pointed at Gwyneth. "No man in his right mind would want *her* for a wife."

"I have had dozens of offers for marriage," Gwyneth said defensively.

"And you've spurned all of them," James said, placing one hand on his hip while holding the reins with the other.

She lifted her chin, but pinkness tinged her cheeks. Embarrassment?

"I want her as a wife," Jared interjected, coming inexplicably to Gwyneth's defense before James could make another mocking laugh.

James looked pointedly at the knife that Jared held at Gwyneth's neck. "So you kidnapped her?"

"I want no husband at all!" Gwyneth said afore Jared could answer the charge. He felt her quiver against his chest. "Release me."

James gave Gwyneth a scornful glance. "No matter my personal feelings, I am here to protect my sister-in-law. Step away from her."

Jared felt her body sag against him as she let out a sigh of relief.

"Best to do as he says." The smirk was back in her voice.

So much for defending her, he thought sourly. Women were a treacherous lot, to be sure.

He gazed from his old friend to his wife and tightened his grip on the knife. The need to conquer snapped through him like a whip.

"The woman is mine," he growled. "She wanted me so much that she stole me from The Bald Cock."

Mortification poured through Gwyneth, and her palm itched to cover his mouth—only she could not move so long as he held a knife to her throat. Her neck ached from Jared's hold, and her body felt stiff from yesterday's events.

"I didn't want you. I want no man."

"You did not mind sleeping near me last night."

One of Montgomery's men moved forward. Finally. At last they would stop their gawking and see to getting her free from this situation.

She cringed as she felt Jared's hand tighten on the dagger at her neck. She wrapped her hands around his wrist. The crisp hair on his forearm tickled her palms. Her little finger throbbed from where the attacker had twisted it in the alley yesterday. The man Jared had rescued her from.

"Do not be beef-witted," she hissed. "If you kill me, you will never get away from here alive."

In answer, Jared turned both of their bodies until his back was fully protected by the wall of the keep and she was spun around to face him. The hard, flat blade of the knife pressed against her back and his hand fisted in her hair.

Gooseflesh popped up on her legs. "Cease!"

His green eyes flashed and her head was forced

back at an angle that made it difficult to swallow. Giving a warning look at Irma and James, forbidding them to move forward, his lips crashed down on hers. Claiming her.

"Wha—" she tried to say, but his mouth dominated hers in a punishing bid for possession. The world swirled under her feet as her reality tilted. He wanted to kiss her?

She tensed, then willed herself to relax as she realized he would do naught to harm her. The instant she softened, so did Jared. His lips became tender against hers, gentle even. Deep inside, low in her belly, sensation stirred. A wanting.

Of its own accord, her body seemed to press closer to him, enjoying the feeling of being his. As if she knew by some primal instinct that he didn't intend to hurt her.

She jumped back, startled by her emotions, startled by her own actions. Jared didn't stop her from pushing slightly away from him, though his fist still held in her long hair.

Blushing furiously, angry with herself for responding at all to Jared's kiss—how could she!—she faced her brother-in-law. Montgomery was scrutinizing her with a disapproving look. She unfocused her eyes, too mortified to even glance at Irma. Irma didn't kiss men. Ever.

Jared laughed.

He knew! Knew she had been affected by his lips. The dagger was slack in his hand, no longer pressing against her back, and she realized it had been a show, a proof that she belonged to him.

Faith, how could her body betray her thus?

"I hate you," she hissed.

"For certes," he said drolly. "And you are still mine. As wife or hostage."

Horrified, she turned to Montgomery, wishing she could somehow run and hide. She tried to bring her hands up to hide her stinging, swollen lips from the damning gazes of the small crowd, but Jared forced her hands downward, caught like a bug on a string. How could she have surrendered to a kiss? Had she no wits at all? She didn't even like the man!

"You chose me," Jared reminded her.

Irked at his high-handed arrogance, she longed to reach for the dagger, to try to turn it against him.

The fire in Montgomery's blue eyes bespoke ill tiding. As if he was ready to slay them both. "The harlot"—he pointed at Irma—"says that you stole my sister-in-law from a brothel."

"'Tis true," Gwyneth rushed out before Jared could speak. "I went to visit my friend and this man kidnapped me."

Jared's green eyes flashed at the lie. "The two women drugged me—"

At that moment another man rode forward, this one with a foppish hat and long, pointed shoes. Unlike Irma, he was a good rider. A long, thin sword hung at his belt.

"Release my bride!" he yelled. "That woman is *my* wife."

Chapter 13

"Ivan?" Gwyneth gasped.

She knew him vaguely but had not seen him in years. He was the younger son of a wealthy lord who had holdings in the north. In her rare dealings with him, she had thought him to be prissy and silly, but his list of victories in dueling and on the tournament field was well known. He was quick and skilled with a sword and the bards often sang of his accomplishments.

"The woman is mine." Ivan pointed boldly at her.

Not another man laying claim on her!

"The documents were signed." He slanted a glare at Montgomery and pulled at the feather on his cap.

Behind her, she felt Jared tense. Heat from his body filtered through her gown.

Quickly, she sized up Ivan, trying to fathom how to twist this new situation to her advantage. He was lean and not nearly as thick as Jared, but he had square shoulders and hardness in his limbs. He rode skillfully, he and his horse moving as one.

Jared's hand tightened on the knife

In contrast to his frilly clothing, Ivan's face was alight with fierce determination.

"Gwyneth, fair Gwyneth, I will rescue you from this beast who has taken you from my arms."

Taken you from my arms? Until this moment she had had no idea whom it was she was to be married to. She barely remembered him!

Jared growled, a primal and barbaric sound. His arm tightened around her rib cage. She could feel every intake and exhale of his breath.

Still . . . she needed a champion—'twas obvious that Montgomery would not help her—and here God provided her with one. Surely 'twas divine intervention.

Hope sprang inside her. She would be relieved of one man at a time. After Jared was soundly defeated, then she would find a way to get rid of Ivan. Simple as that.

"My beauteous love," he rambled on, "you are even more wondrous than I remembered." He gazed at her with moon-faced puppy love.

She resisted the urge to roll her eyes at his ridiculous fodder. What idiocy. Mayhap Jared was the lesser of two evils after all.

"My Gwyneth—"

"Nay," Jared said quietly, "The woman is mine. She forced me to marry her, and we will stay married." The firm resolve in his voice sent a shiver of foreboding up Gwyneth's spine. 'Twas as if he planned some horrible life of shame for her.

A knot formed under her shoulder blades. She had no choice but to use Ivan. "I will be free of you," she breathed. No matter what she had to do.

Evening sunlight glinted off the hilt of Ivan's blade,

reassuring her that despite his foppish manner, he was equipped to fight.

Once Jared was sent away, the marriage would be annulled and she would live a life of independence and freedom. Elizabeth could be rescued. And Elfreda. Her women would be safe.

"Ivan—"

Jared's arm tightened around her ribs, but the knife did not bite into her.

"Go away, boy," Jared said, his voice a challenge. "We were married at the church near the hatter's shop. Find the monk if you need proof, but see here." He reached inside his pouch and produced the ripped sheet with the dark stain of blood on it.

"Nay!" Gwyneth tried to pull away from him. "The wedding was illegal. I was forced. The church will not honor it."

Lifting a brow, Montgomery turned to Irma. "Well?"

"I spoke truth, my lord. Jared kidnapped Gwyneth from the brothel." Irma clutched her yellow shawl around her shoulders with white knuckles, but when she spoke her voice was calm, as if spinning tales came second nature to her.

"The brothel?" Ivan echoed, an incredulous look on his face. His long pointed shoes stirred up leaves as he turned this way and that to look at different people.

"The harlot lies," Jared asserted. "Ask her why Gwyneth was at the brothel."

Gwyneth sucked in a breath. No noblewoman would set foot in a whorehouse, much less go there as often as she did. If Ivan spurned her, Montgomery would have a reason to leave her here with Jared.

For the rest of her life.

Quickly, she put on a slight pout and licked her lips in a way she knew looked both innocent and seductive. As expected, Ivan's gaze rested on her mouth. It was too easy.

"I was merely walking . . ." She rolled one of her shoulders slightly in a discreet but suggestive manner.

"Stop wiggling," Jared said in a low voice, then louder: "No decent woman would go for a casual walk in that area of town. Especially not without an escort. She is guilty."

"I was bringing a potion to the sick child of a woman who cannot afford to go to the apothecary herself," Gwyneth finished. She put on a pleading, innocent look for good measure. Most "sins" such as being alone in the wrong area could be forgiven if a child was involved and she was acting altruistically. It was a story Irma and she had planned for times such as this and she *had* visited the sick and brought medicine to families in the area. That part at least was not a lie. "Asides, I was not alone. Brother Giffard, a man of God, was with me."

Jared's nostrils flared. The muscles of his thighs tensed.

She turned her face to Ivan's so that she didn't have to look at him. So it would be easier to lie.

Ivan beamed at her, clearly taken in by her assertions. She tamped down her guilt at allowing him to think that she was some sort of virtuous woman. That she wasn't just using him.

"Jared attacked us, forced us into the church, and threatened the monk to marry us without banns being read. The wedding is not valid."

Jared growled. "You lying little hoyden," he gritted

out. He turned to Montgomery. "Surely you do not believe this woman's lies."

Montgomery had a look of scorn on his face. His hands flexed on the reins as if he were planning to wheel the black stallion around and ride home without her. Saints! Somehow she had to get him to take her back to Windrose, to her home. Despite the lack of banns, the court would see the marriage as valid if Jared was with her for any length of time.

Ivan pushed his feathered cap off his forehead and glowered at Jared. "I demand you release my bride."

"Your bride no longer." Jared's arm was a steel band around her body and she could feel the steady thumping of his heart against her own.

Ivan puffed his chest out in a way that reminded her of a peacock and faced Montgomery. "Make him release her. We have signed a contract."

It seemed that even the frogs had stopped chirping. Jared's hawk was also silent. Montgomery didn't take her part, but he didn't make any sign of sending his men in to attack Jared, either.

Ivan urged his horse forward. The long points of his shoes wobbled.

Gwyneth trained her face to appear innocent and not show any sign of victory, but in her heart she felt relief that she would have a champion after all.

Montgomery held up a hand, halting Ivan's progress. "If you speak the truth, Gwyneth, then how does the harlot know so much about you?"

Gwyneth's heart lurched. She struggled to maintain her composure as her mind raced for an answer or plausible explanation. She had no way of knowing what Irma had told him, so anything she said could show her dishonesty.

She glanced at Irma, who was watching the happenings, fiddling with her skirt, and clearly debating if she should turn and run.

Gwyneth gave her a pleading look.

"Me lord," Irma said, taking a deep breath and adjusting her yellow shawl, "me lady Gwyneth 'as been a noble mother of mercy to the most wretched of souls. She brings apples and toys to the children and medicine and comfort to the elderly. All who know 'er love 'er as if she were Saint Mary 'erself. She is the most kind'earted of beings, unsullied by the grief of this world or the places where such must walk to visit those under her care. Amy, Tatum, and Maude all would 'ave died if it 'ad not been for 'er loving kindness and mercy. Now this child she brought potion to yester—"

Gwyneth coughed. If Irma kept spinning tale after tale, trying to sound fancy, 'twould be obvious that the two of them were making things up on the spot.

Through lashes lowered to give the impression of modesty, she saw that Ivan was eating Irma's words as if they were manna from heaven. Jared, on the other hand, looked furious. His eyes had darkened from green to nearly black and a tight tic formed in his jaw.

"My lady," Ivan breathed, "thou art as kind and gracious as thou art lovely to behold . . ." He turned to Montgomery. "I insist you do something, my lord."

Montgomery glowered at him. "I *plan* to do *something*. I plan to head home to Windrose. It is obvious the newlywed couple have a few issues to work out."

"You can't just leave me here!" Gwyneth cried, her voice rising in pitch. She sought to escape from Jared's arms, but he held her tight.

"You got yourself into this," said Montgomery with a shrug.

"It seems my wife has no respect for authority." Jared gave her a small shake as if to belabor the point.

"If you can teach her aught, old friend, 'twill be a blessing for us all," Montgomery drawled. "Come, Ivan, leave them. If we go now, we can be home afore it is too late. My own wife was quite angry that I would not allow her to ride with us, and I must soothe and comfort her."

Irked, Gwyneth pulled forward but was held in place by Jared's arms. "My sister will be furious!"

Montgomery shot her a look. "Bah. I'll tell her that 'tis clear that her nitwitted sister has rejected the husband we chose for her and picked a man from a brothel. Whatever you get from Jared, you deserve. Mayhap your new husband can teach you respect."

"You can tell your wife that I will not harm Gwyneth so long as she obeys me," Jared said. "Mayhap that will comfort her."

Obey him!

"Fair enough." Montgomery pulled his horse's reins to turn it toward Windrose. "'Tis all any man should expect of his wife."

Gwyneth gasped as her brother-in-law and his knights remounted and turned toward the trees. They couldn't mean to just leave her here—bound to a falconer, her life in his hand. She knew Montgomery disliked her, but they were family!

He motioned for Ivan to come with him. "Truly, Ivan, 'tis done, they are wed, and she is not worth bloodying your sword over."

Something had to be done!

Ivan's enormous blue sleeves poofed out like a frustrated bluejay. "Nay! She was my promised bride."

Jared guffawed. "We are married by her demand and here is proof of the consummation." He waved the bloodied sheet like some sort of victory flag.

"You beast!" How could she have kissed him?

"Silence, wife. This is between men."

"Men ever use women for their own purposes," she hissed.

"Come, Ivan." Montgomery snapped the reins and his horse started walking into the forest.

"I will send help," Irma mouthed at Gwyneth. She wrenched free and took off running.

"Irma!" Montgomery said but did not chase her.

Jared began tugging Gwyneth back into the cave. "Go home, boy. The woman is mine already."

As if she were no more than chattel.

Ivan hesitated. He glanced from Montgomery to Jared.

Faith! He was her only hope. Firmly setting aside her guilt at using him without any plan of following through on marrying him either, she drew herself up to an imperious stature. She had to do this for the women who depended on her. "Ivan, he kidnapped me last night. You must help me."

Jared stiffened. "Careful, wife."

Montgomery rolled his eyes.

"Please," she said, gracefully licking her lips. "I can make you happy—"

With a yell, as if her encouragement was all he needed, Ivan brandished his sword and charged forward.

Chapter 14

Gwyneth's body lurched, pushed to one side as Jared crouched, dagger held in front of him in a defensive fighting stance.

Ivan's horse barreled toward them.

"Mercy," Gwyneth breathed as Ivan's sword crashed down upon Jared, so close that she was unsure if he was trying to rescue her or kill them both.

In a blur of motion, Jared stepped in front, shielding her with his body. He parried the blow as best he could with the dagger. His body rocked backward, but his arm held.

Her eyes widened at the sheer strength of his limb. He faced Ivan, who was already swinging his sword in another attack.

The unfairness of Ivan's dueling tactic seemed at odds with his earlier words, which had been pretty and cordial and courtly. Crouching, she scrambled backward out of the way. Her back thumped on the damp wall. The sweat on the horse's flank assailed her nostrils. The beast's eyes rolled, and it seemed ready to panic, but 'twas as if an uncontrolled battle lust had overtaken Ivan and he was heedless of his mount. No wonder the bards sang of his numerous victories on the tournament field. He had skill and innate quickness.

"Mayhap you could make yourself a set of braies with that needle sword," Ivan taunted as he plowed forward. Hooves thudded on the stone and the sword came down again.

Jared fell this time, beaten back and now in the smaller section of the cave. The hawk fluttered her wings frantically and strained against the tether of her perch, then, with a snap, broke free and flew from the cave.

Ivan leaped off his mount in a powerful movement that was at odds with his eccentric, prissy style of dress.

His stallion, startled from being set free so quickly, tossed its head and brushed past her body, knocking her backward.

Gwyneth took a step to catch her balance, but her slipper caught in the hem of her dress. Arms wheeling, she fell. A hoof landed near her hand, missing her by a thread's width.

"Gwyneth! Get back!"

Not Ivan's voice. Jared.

Jared scrambled forward so that his own body squeezed between her and the horse.

Ivan advanced recklessly, a menacing expression on his face. He seemed to have completely forgotten that she was present as he bore down on Jared.

The cave walls closed in around her. The morning sun glinted off Ivan's sword. Jared's dark hair swirled as he quickly scooped up his staff from where it had fallen earlier.

Heart thrumming, Gwyneth tried to find an opening so she could crawl from the cave.

Ivan's reckless fighting style was a sharp contrast to Jared's unfailing patience. Mayhap she should have kept silent rather than encouraging Ivan.

She slid back until she could go no farther.

Ivan lunged.

Jared's staff came up this time for the parry. The wood creaked but held and Jared stepped to one side.

Carrying both the dagger and staff, he rounded on Ivan and ran lightly backward.

The move puzzled her because it temporarily put him at a disadvantage. Ivan wheeled around blindly, nearly whacking her in the head with his sword.

Gwyneth jumped back, suddenly understanding that Jared's move was to draw the battle away from her, to protect *her.*

Guilt settled in her chest. She tried to shake it off, to think of the ladies in the prison she needed to save and all the reasons she must get rid of Jared, even lie or cheat to do so, but the unfairness, like the sharp stench of a bog, pricked her.

She looked from one man to the other. Jared was calm, in control, but deadly intent gleamed in Ivan's eyes. Dread coursed through her as she realized this would be no friendly tournament competition where the loser would come away with naught more than a few bruises and a chink out of his pride. Blood spill would be the outcome here.

Jared might die.

His death would be on her conscience forever, the same as if she had murdered him herself.

For all his sins against her, Jared had been forced

into the marriage. He might not be totally innocent, but he did not deserve death.

"Wait!" She lifted her hands trying to ward off the fight between them. Somehow she had to stop them.

"Too late for that, lady wife." Jared's shoulders tightened. Overhead, the hawk circled, waiting, watching. "You have prompted yet another man into doing your bidding and now we will finish this."

"Aye!" Ivan echoed. "The victor claims the woman."

"Nay!" She scurried from the cave, ready to race between them. "Cease! I am not a prize to be fought over!"

"Do not fear, my lady," Ivan called, not even looking at her. "I will slay the beast for you and you will forever be rid of him."

Montgomery and his knights formed a ring around them, preventing her from getting close. She pushed, but they closed the ring tighter so that she could not pass.

"Stay where you are, lady wife, while I take care of this boy of yours!"

She elbowed Montgomery, but he did not budge.

Jared and Ivan were now circling each other, both down in a fighting stance. Jared held his staff with two hands in front of his body and Ivan brandished his sword above his head. The engraved scales of the dragon that was carved into the wood were clearly visible.

Large hands grasped her and hauled her out of the way. She squirmed, thinking for an instant that Jared was in two places at once, then realized that she was being rooted in place by Montgomery.

"Best to obey your husband," he said grimly. His eyes, a flashing cobalt blue, snapped with anger despite the dry tone of his voice. Splotches of mud splattered his tunic, proof that he had been out all night scouring the land looking for her.

She struggled, trying to move forward, but he half dragged, half carried her several yards away. He was as tall as Jared, and just as impossible to control.

"Leave be!"

"Bah! You can watch the unfolding of your folly from here. Mayhap it will teach you a lesson in proper behavior and decorum."

Helpless, she trained her gaze back on the fight. Her heart pounded.

Montgomery's men laughed and cast bets.

Jared and Ivan circled each other, each crouched, thighs flexed and their guard up.

"I will win your hand from this barbarian, my lady," Ivan called chivalrously. But he never looked at her, not even for an instant. 'Twas as if his words were merely for show. Like his clothing. And inside he was of an altogether different nature.

There was a sickening thunk, and Ivan crumpled to one side. The dagger stuck out of his shoulder and blood oozed from his tunic.

One knight whistled and cheered from atop his horse, but another man had dismounted to get a closer look.

"Heavens!" She squirmed, trying to get away from Montgomery.

Jared leapt forward, both hands on his staff, one near the tail of the engraved dragon. He was quick and powerful, but unhurried: grace rather than force. He twisted the staff this way and that—up to his shoulder, down to his waist, from one side to the next.

She'd never seen anything like it afore in her life. 'Twas as if he moved by magic in some sort of strange exotic dance.

The men circled each other. Attack. Counterattack. Attack. Counterattack.

The sword and the staff came up, then at the very last second, when Gwyneth thought they would smash together, Jared twisted his torso and brought the end of the staff farthest away from Ivan in a quick arc. It caught Ivan's hand in a hard whack and his sword dropped to the ground. Ivan yelped and dove for it, but Jared snatched the weapon from the ground.

The men took in a collective breath. One gave a shout of approval. Gwyneth would have clutched her chest if she had been free to do so.

Montgomery held her by the shoulders but paid no heed to what she was doing.

Jared lunged toward Ivan, clearly the victor. He flashed her a look that sent a shiver down her spine.

Nay! Nay! Nay!

Jared's dagger headed straight to Ivan's chest. "Yield."

The points of Ivan's shoes flopped; he tripped over his own feet and fell into the dirt. His outlandish clothing proved to be his downfall. He scrambled backward on his arse, redfaced and panting, toward the outer edge of the circle of men.

Jared advanced, blade lifted.

One of the men surrounding them laughed and gave a small clap. "Look at the young pup!"

"A fool in foolish shoes!"

"Beat by a man with a stick."

"Never seen anybody move like that."

Ivan shielded his face with his hands as Jared leapt atop him.

Seeing that the fight was finished, Montgomery let go of her and moved closer to his men.

Wheeling on her heels, Gwyneth slid a few steps away, hoping to sneak to the horses before anyone saw her. She had to reach Irma, get to the brothel, and come up with a plan. The past two days had been a disaster. She slid two more steps. Then two more. No one looked her direction. Twigs snapped but the men were so intense on the drama between Jared and Ivan they paid no attention to her.

Her legs quivered, but she willed herself to be patient, to not walk too quickly.

The squire's horse, a medium-sized mare, was close to her. His attention was fixed on the fight. She closed the distance, her mind racing with hope, latched onto the mare's neck, and swung quickly atop its back.

Not daring to glance back, she walked the horse through the forest—slowly at first, and then, as she was more and more assured that she wasn't being followed, urged the horse faster. She had no clear idea of where she was heading. Her heart beat so hard it pounded in her ears as she raced for freedom.

Within a few moments, she entered the edges of the city. Early morning sun beat down on the closed shutters of houses and shops. Only a few people were moving about—a tinker toting his wares, a cart filled with hay, a few walkers, a carpenter with a bag of tools, but mostly the streets were quiet. Still no sight of Jared. Ha! Surely she could hide somewhere within and then pick her way back to Windrose—find Irma and her sister. She had been attacked before because she had not hidden herself very well, but this time she would be more cautious. Somehow she would find a way out of this situation.

"Gwyneth! Wife!" Jared's voice boomed behind her.

Heavens!

She sped her mount into a gallop, passing the cart of hay. Hooves thudded on the cobblestones. Cold prickles went up and down her legs.

She glanced behind her. Jared raced toward her on Montgomery's steed. Even from this distance, the fury coming off of him was palpable. Determination shone in his eyes.

Oh, sweet saints.

"Hurry! Hurry!" She urged the mare, kicking its flanks frantically with her heels.

Jared was on her within seconds, his large hands reaching across her body, grabbing for her reins.

"Nay!"

He drew her horse up short and with one hand he dragged her from her mount.

She squirmed and kicked. "Get away!"

"Cease, girl. You'll make both—"

She screamed as she saw the ground speed upward. At the last moment, Jared twisted his body so that she was cushioned. His back thumped hard against the ground and breath fled her lungs as she landed against him.

She scrambled to her feet, intending to run, but he snatched her wrist afore she could take a step. Yanking her in his wake, he snatched the reins of both of the horses.

"Help!"

The tinker turned her direction.

"Silence, wife!" Jared's chest heaved in great panting breaths.

The man looked back and forth at the two of them.

Jared gave the man a furious glare. "Pardon, sir. My wife is in need of discipline. Just move along."

"Your wife, you say?"

"Aye."

"The marriage was forced—" Gwyneth started, but before she could explain, Montgomery clattered down the cobbled street on the third horse and pulled up short.

The tinker snatched his cap from his head and gave a polite nod. "Lord Montgomery."

"G'day," Montgomery said. "Just move along. These two have just been wed and have a few issues to work out."

The man nodded.

Gwyneth smarted.

As far as men were concerned, a husband had every right to expect his wife to be in subjection to him.

"Sorry to bother you, sir," Jared said cheerfully. His lips turned upward into a jaunty smile. "I'll just take care of my *wife* now."

"Nay!" she said, but the man nodded at Jared and James. How bloody unfair!

"Looks like you've got enough trouble." The tinker snatched the handles of his cart and began pushing it down the road. Pans and knives and silver hair-combs jangled.

Legs apart, hands on hips, Montgomery faced Jared. "Jared, I fully release Gwyneth to your care. Best of luck with the training. Consider my stallion a wedding gift. I will take the other horse back to my men."

Gwyneth gasped. "You can't just leave me here with him."

"Sure, I can." Montgomery handed the reins of his own horse to Jared. He took the reins of the horse that she had ridden in her escape attempt and rode away.

"But he kidnapped me!" she exclaimed to his back.

She saw her brother-in-law shrug. The ogre! How on earth could her sister have any love for him?

"Silence your lies, Gwyneth," Jared gritted out, "else I'll gag you."

In an upstairs window, a shutter snapped open and a woman with a sleeping cap peered out into the street.

"Please!" she called to the woman above them, who closed the shutter as quickly as she had opened it. No help there.

A young lad carrying firewood glanced her direction.

Perhaps she could use him.

She shook her hair and pointed at Jared. "This man stole me."

The lad gaped at her. A familiar male reaction. Good.

Squeezing her arm, Jared yanked her close to him.

She squirmed but it was like trying to fight iron chains.

Fury flowed off of him. "Cease, *now,* woman." He swung them both onto his mount and wheeled the horse around into a gallop.

Chapter 15

A pox on women!

Frustration yanked the brittle strings of Jared's patience as he pulled Gwyneth close, clamped his hand over her mouth, and debated the best course of action to take her in hand. He needed to establish himself as her lord once and for all.

She wiggled and squirmed, but fortunately James's horse was very well trained and Gwyneth was small. Her hips ground against his crotch, making that part of him swell uncomfortably. What was it about this infuriating woman that made his body react so strongly?

But in his heart, he knew. She was fiery, intelligent, brazen, a challenge. The way she had manipulated and used Ivan was infuriating beyond measure, but her cleverness was something to be admired. As much as he hated to admit it, she fascinated him. Just as she had the first time he'd seen her.

Her pretty face and seductive mannerism made men do foolish things. At the brothel, all she had done was blink her beautiful sky-colored eyes at him, and he had fallen straight into her deceitful web. Just as Ivan had done.

So long as she preyed on the idiocy of men to take up her cause, she was a bloody menace to peace and order and civility. He had no doubt that if he had not sped away on the horse, one of the men would have changed their mind about helping her. Keeping her in line was imperative.

She shook her head back and forth against his palm as they trotted down the cobblestones to the edge of the city. A blacksmith's hammer rang in the air one street over.

"If you swear not to make a spectacle, I'll release you," he said.

She nodded quickly. Her long braid bobbed.

Slowly, he lifted his hand from her mouth.

She worked her jaw back and forth a few times, but said naught. Good. Subdued at last.

They passed more houses, more shops. A young burly-looking lad carried a heavy canvas sack up the street. His boots marched on the cobblestones in a hard clomping rhythm and a dagger was tucked in his belt.

Gwyneth caught his eyes and, afore Jared realized her purpose, tilted away from him, fluffed her hair, and batted her eyes brazenly at the boy. "Lad! Lad!"

The faithless vixen! Furious, Jared spurred the horse into a gallop afore the boy could react.

Gwyneth gasped as the horse rounded a corner and her cheek bumped against Jared. Anxiety filled her chest at the brooding look on his face. His tunic was damp with sweat and she could practically smell his anger. Worst of all, she felt alone. So very alone. Ivan was defeated. Her family had abandoned her.

The houses and shops blurred past as Jared rushed the horse at a breakneck pace.

The pensive look of darkness on his face made her shiver and double her determination to find someone to help her.

Clanging sounded. Hot, sooty air swirled around them and she realized they had reached the blacksmith's shop, which was several streets over. The smithy, a gray-bearded man who appeared to be about half a century old, stood beside the forge, banging out a horseshoe.

He was shirtless, had red skin and large biceps, and wore a leather apron. Pausing in his work, he put his hammer down beside the anvil.

She gave him her best smile, hoping to find a friend, but he did not so much as glance at her.

"Welcome, my lord," he said as if she weren't squirming furiously on Jared's lap or his hand wasn't clamped over her mouth. Foreboding clouded her mind like a dark, dangerous fog. "Is there aught you need?"

"Have you a scold's bridle? My wife is in desperate need of one."

A brank? Coldness tingled down Gwyneth's spine. "Nay—" She tried to speak, but Jared's fingers tightened around her mouth.

The blacksmith's eyes lit up. "I 'ave one here, my lord. One of my best pieces. Took me hours to fashion it." The leather apron rustled as he hurried over to one of the shelves. His chest seemed to puff out.

"Perfect."

Gwyneth felt her legs go liquid as Jared slid off the

horse and dragged her with him. He surveyed the wooden shelves. Hammers, rasps, files, pincers, and various other instruments for making wire, armor, chain, nails, and swords littered the shop.

He turned and looked at her calmly. Too calmly. "I am going to release your mouth. If you make so much as a squeak, I will take you straight to the town's stocks and leave you there instead of something as mild as a scold's bridle." He paused dramatically.

Sweat beaded in the small of her back. She wiggled, desperation sliding through her. Memories of being publicly humiliated by her father bit her thoughts. Her mind raced for a solution. Perhaps she could seduce him, get him to stop.

"Oft an untrained hawk needs a hood," he said mildly.

Oh, God. She was in hell. Jared was a madman.

But he was not observing her with the light of insanity. His eyes were sharp, perceptive—as if he were noticing and measuring her every reaction so he could tailor his punishment, make it worse if he so desired. She was used to men looking at her, but none had ever scrutinized her as Jared did. It seemed that he could see past her skull and into her mind.

Nay. Into her soul. As if he knew of every bad thing she'd ever done, every flirtatious, manipulative deed she had ever made.

His eyes condemned her.

It was to rescue people who were hurting, she wanted to proclaim in her defense. But, of course, he would never know about Elizabeth, Blythe, or Elfreda and the other women at the prison.

Her legs quivered, her fingers trembled—reactions she needed to hide from Jared's keen eyes. If he knew such things, he would take pleasure in them, use them to control her.

She lifted her chin, determined not to let him see the panic she was fighting. Long ago, Irma had shown her how to stand proudly, to disallow the thoughts of others from affecting her.

She tried to catch the smithy's eye, hoping to gain some sort of sympathy, but the man gazed lovingly at his own craftsmanship.

Sunlight gleamed off the brank as the blacksmith lifted it smugly into the air. It was a small metal cage with a collar, a nose hole, and a tongue depressor.

She blanched, looked away.

"Beautiful piece, I say. See 'ere, four flat bars and a knot on top. Made it just so to fit o'er a woman's head, I did. The piece here"—he pointed to the loop at the bottom—"goes right into 'er mouth to hold down 'er forward tongue. Ye won't 'ave to be aworrying about 'er being a scold anymore, I tell you."

The man's voice had a weird high-pitched lilt that seemed at odds with his brawny arms and chest. He sounded practically gleeful.

Shuddering, she inched backward.

"Perfect," said Jared, swiveling toward Gwyneth. His dark hair fell across one eye. "Let's see how your hood fits."

She shook her head, frantically looking for a place to run and hide, frantically trying to come up with a plan to persuade him from his purpose. She opened her mouth to speak.

"The stocks," he said coldly.

She bit her tongue and pleaded with him with her eyes.

No sympathy shone in his face. His jaw was hard, set.

She turned to one side.

"There is no value in running, wife. You cannot hope to get far."

A tremble ran through her. He was quick and agile on his feet. She had no chance of getting away. Her best defense lay in a complete pretense that the punishment he planned was ineffective because it did not bother her in the least. Then she would seduce him into believing that it was safe for him to trust her. Mayhap she could poison him.

Her heart pounded as Jared took her by the shoulders, steered her inside the blacksmith's shop, and forced her to sit on a stool. Resolutely, she vowed not to show fear. Absolutely no fear. Somehow she would get through this and he would never know how her stomach felt sick and her palms clammy. She chewed the inside of her cheeks to keep herself from crying out, to keep from begging.

He motioned the smithy to him and took hold of the brank. "Let's see how it fits."

Oh, heavens. Her body lurched, and a sharp pain shot under her shoulder blades. Sweat beaded her upper lip. Quickly, she licked it away, not wanting Jared to notice.

She craned her neck to see if Montgomery had followed them. Surely he would not have abandoned her if he had known Jared planned to display her in a scold's bridle. Somehow she had to send a missive to her sisters, tell them how horrid her new husband was.

Several of the town's inhabitants had gathered outside the blacksmith's shop. A woman being paraded about in a brank was high amusement. They were whispering and craning their necks to discover who it was. She searched the crowd, determined to find someone to come to her aid.

To the left she saw Anna, a woman whose husband she had charmed out of a few pence. Gold she had used to rescue Theresa, a young silver-haired girl of about sixteen summers.

The woman looked positively gleeful.

Gwyneth stood. She did not deserve this.

Jared gently pushed her back down with one hand on her shoulder.

The metal cage sank onto her head, pulling at her hair. The flat iron pieces—one in the back, one in the front, and one on each side—encircled her head.

"Nay!" she cried, unable to contain herself, and the metal tongue loop slid into her mouth and shut off her cry. The lock snapped behind her head with a resounding click. She squeezed her eyes shut, wanting to run, wanting to fight, but knowing any physical effort would be futile.

Anna gave a little titter, reached forward boldly, and gave her hair a yank.

Gwyneth felt her brain go fuzzy; the edges of darkness crept into her vision. She sucked in a deep breath to keep from fainting. That would be the ultimate humiliation.

The blacksmith puffed out his chest. "See. Perfect fit."

"Aaaah," she mumbled, unable to say anything else.

Nay.

Nay.

Nay.

She glowered at Jared.

What beasts men were!

His gaze fought with hers. He was monstrous! Horrible! She would poison him!

"Stand up."

The crowd gathered closer. One man elbowed another next to him. "Now there's a good 'usband, I say. Must keep a woman under control."

"Oh, she'll fight him," answered a peasant maid from the crowd. "Look at her eyes."

"He'll win, no doubt."

"Oh yeah?"

"Yeah."

Gwyneth ground her teeth against the metal tongue depressor. Through the bars of the head cage she could see them all staring at her, condemning her.

Mortification heated her cheeks.

Jared hoisted her to her feet. He took hold of the leather leash attached to the brank and tugged her forward.

The crowd parted for Jared as he led her from the blacksmith's shop. One woman boldly reached up and touched the metal cage as she passed.

"'Tis Gwyneth of Windrose!" she exclaimed.

Another woman gasped. "Gwyneth?"

"Aye!" echoed Anna. "About time that someone gagged the bitch."

"She's pretty but evil."

"A hellion."

Bitch? Evil? Hellion? Gwyneth longed to cover her ears so she would not have to listen to the calls and jeers and comments that were even more horrible than the cage on her head. She had married Jared so she could take care of unfortunate and mistreated women—women not unlike some of the ones here! Disgusting. All of them.

As they walked, she searched the crowd, looking for someone with kind eyes, someone with sympathy to her cause. If only she could start a rebellion, rally people to her cause.

"The woman is a witch, I tell you. Once she looked at me son and from that day on, he was no longer interested in other women. He even writes her poetry though she pays no attention to him at all."

Glaring at the woman, Gwyneth lifted her chin. How dare they judge her! They knew naught of her life! A curse on them all!

Defiantly, she threw back her shoulders, even knowing the effect was ruined with her head in a cage and her tongue held down. She glanced frantically around the crowd to catch the eye of a man who would champion her.

She would not let them see her crushed. Somehow she would find a way out of this and come out better in the end.

Somehow.

She cast a dark glare at Jared. The man would rue the day he had treated her thus. Her mind worked furiously. She would transform herself, make herself the most congenial, fantastic wife he'd ever known. She had the skills to make him fall in love with her if she set her mind to it. Once she had accomplished that, she would leave him cold and heartbroken, have him tossed into prison to rot for the rest of his miserable life.

He would be sorry he ever dared to cross her.

Chapter 16

The instant Gwyneth lifted her chin in haughty indignation, guilt blew through Jared like a fierce north wind.

He gritted his teeth. How could she make him feel guilty when he was the one who had been wronged! A scold's bridle was a minimal, non-painful punishment and far lighter than she deserved.

But guilt swirled round and round inside him, intensifying with each droplet of sweat beading on her skin, each throbbing pulse of her heart in her neck. 'Twas clear it was taking all her courage to keep from panicking, to keep from falling onto the ground crying. The experience for her was far, far worse than he had intended.

His fingers flexed and released as he fought the urge to take the damn thing off of her.

But if he took the cage off so soon, she would undoubtedly go back to her old ways of trying to find a man to fight for her—a lifetime of that would be intolerable.

Damn. This was supposed to have been a simple

display to assure his position, get her to cease all attempts of encouraging men to champion her. He did not wish to do any damage to her womanly sensitivity.

"Can you see her?" a woman tittered.

"Always been a bitch."

Pearls of perspiration trickled down her neck.

His fingers itched to wipe them away.

Damn. Damn. Damn.

Conflicted about what to do, he held on to the leash that was attached to the scold's bridle.

A short woman in a linen cap shuffled forward and craned her neck to see around two stocky men who had axes slung at their hips. "Let me see," she snickered.

"Evil vixen."

"Stole me son's 'eart."

"Ruined my marriage."

Forcing himself to ignore all thoughts of sympathy for his wife, Jared passed through the crowd. So many had gathered. So many who might know him. He tried to imitate the demeanor of a wronged nobleman. He could not afford for anyone to recognize him as Jared the monk or Jared the prisoner. Clearing his name was imperative.

A woman from the crowd tittered.

"She deserves it, she does!"

He glowered at her, disliking the way she thrilled in Gwyneth's humiliation.

Gwyneth's brows were furrowed, her shoulders rigid. She shuddered stiffly and he resisted the instinct to put his arm around her shoulders and protect her.

Protect her from what?

From himself?

Bloody hell.

The woman did not deserve protection. She'd tried to murder him. She'd stabbed him. She'd nearly gotten both of them killed.

If he showed weakness about his decision to force her past the crowd wearing the bridle, Gwyneth would see him as weak-willed. She'd use his compassion and twist it to her advantage. A man would step forward to champion her, endangering his life and hers, and dooming her champion to certain death.

The brawny man at the edge of the crowd fingered the hilt of his axe. Light glinted off the blade.

Taking the horse by the reins and his wife by the leash, Jared led them away from the gawkers. He would release her as soon as they were away from the crowd.

Two women laughed aloud, clearly delighted.

One man swayed forward as if to step in the path.

He gave the man a quelling glare before she could look at him with pleading eyes. God willing, the iron brank would teach his wife a sharp lesson so that she would no longer attempt to manipulate young men into rebelling against him. Then he would never have to do this again. Ever.

The walk was too slow. Exceedingly slow. But he could not quicken his pace for fear that she might trip. With every step, guilt hammered his heart.

At last they made it through the city's gates. As soon as he could, Jared led her off the road into the trees and away from the snickers and whispers. Privacy at last.

"Sit," he said, indicating a fallen log.

She obeyed, flouncing down atop it like a queen despite the cage on her head. Clearly she had regained her composure despite her near panic earlier.

Amazing. Her regality was so much a part of her that even when she'd been soundly defeated her shoulders didn't slump. Her bravery made him feel small. As if he was the one who had been vanquished.

He forced himself to take a breath and not rush to take off the scold's bridle—he did not want her to know of the guilt he was furiously tamping down. If he was a smart man, he'd leave it on her all night. He could not afford to be weak now, not when gaining any measure of peace between them relied on establishing dominance.

His hope of them building a life together lay in her understanding that he would tolerate no more insolence. Once that was established, he could allow her more freedom.

Slowly, he traced his finger around the collar of the brank. A slight redness marred her skin, but there were no cuts or indentures. She would have no marks or bruises. Good.

He had so many questions about her. Why had she been at the brothel? How had she met Irma? Why had she forced the marriage? Such a gulf between them. Circling her with measured steps, he contemplated exactly where to start with his questions, where to start with her training. Like a hawk, she needed to understand that life would be better with him than without.

"It will do you no good to scream or run. There is no one here. Do you understand?"

The pulse at her throat pounded in hard, quick bursts as he reached behind her, making him want to gather her in his arms and soothe away her fears and worries.

She stared past him into the trees, and he wondered

if she was trying not to quiver or if she was searching for someone to help her.

"I will unlock the brank on the condition that you answer all my questions."

Slowly, she nodded, but her eyes gleamed with indignation.

Good. He wanted to tame her, not break her spirit.

Watching her closely to verify that she did not intend to leap from the log and run into the forest, he reached behind her neck to unlock the brank. The metal slid against her hair. Strands of her long, shiny locks were caught in two of the rivets. He stopped and carefully unwound them so that they would not pull against her scalp, then he dropped the apparatus into her lap.

Judging from the reactions she had just shown, fear would be a better deterrent than any actual force against her.

She rubbed her face and worked her jaw back and forth but said naught. Her shoulders were square, her chin lifted. Her hammering pulse and fidgety fingers belied her bravado.

The sunlight filtering through the canopy caught her hair, making it shimmer. Glorious. Despite it all, she was the most gorgeous woman he'd ever seen. Her alabaster skin, clear blue eyes, and striking features were like those of an angel. Feylike and ethereal. Her hair cascaded from her scalp to her hips as if it were a waterfall made of a mixture of sunshine and moonlight. A man could drown there.

"Tempting other men to challenge my authority was foolish," he said, trailing a finger along the edge of her neck to press on the beating artery.

"I—"

"You will not speak without permission." He made his tone sharp, harsh. It would likely do him a world of good to never allow her to speak again, but he was too curious to give such an order. "Because you used your voice to tempt a man to challenge me, you will be required to remain silent save to answer my questions. Consider it part of your new duty."

Her fingers tightened into fists, evidence that she was bursting to speak, to rant at him.

"If you find this too difficult on your own . . ." He picked the scold's bridle from off of her lap, and twirled it in his hands as if to refasten it on her head.

Alarm replaced anger in her eyes.

He hated this. But he had no choice but to establish the line of authority between them.

She glared at him but snapped her mouth closed.

Good. He noticed her knuckles were white. Fright? Outrage?

Likely both.

"Look at me."

Her eyes flicked to his. The blue had darkened to the color of storm clouds, and her jaw hardened. The moments stretched as he waited to test her, to see what her reaction would be to his instructions that she remain silent.

She opened her mouth as if to speak.

He quirked a brow.

Slowly this time, she closed her lips; whatever words she intended remained unspoken.

"Very good."

Her eyes flashed with haughty resentment. That she was not defeated and had regained some of her arrogance inexplicably pleased him.

She lowered her eyes and chin before looking back

up at him, a gesture of salute that she had given over
to his authority. He wondered what that mild act
must have cost her. He knew the action was merely a
ploy; she did not feel subdued at all and would soon
be up to her old ways of manipulation and charm,
but at least she was a decent actress.

"Very, very good." He ran his hand around her ear
and across her cheek. She flinched but did not resist
his touch.

"Why were you at the brothel?"

She stared at the ground.

Holding the metal cage with one hand and taking
her chin between his thumb and forefinger with the
other, he tilted her face up to his.

"I did not give you permission to take your gaze off
of me," he said evenly.

Anger flashed in the blue depths of her eyes. Good.
Anger he could deal with.

She licked her lips, her little pink tongue darting
out against the luscious pad of her lower lip.

Unbidden, his groin tightened. He released her
chin quickly. He did not want to feel any emotion for
her at all except that of victory. Not guilt and certainly not lust. Guilt made commanders weak and
sexual relationships complicated matters.

He had no choice but to act with levelheaded mas-
tery. She was a hawk to train.

Gwyneth glared at the man in front of her, resisting
the urge to leap from the log and yank patches of
hair from his goatee. Pain shot through her palms as
her fingernails dug into her flesh. Her emotions

mixed together in a slurry of outrage, indignation, and fear.

The comments of those who had gathered to watch her humiliation jumbled one after the other in her brain.

Useless bitch.

Horrible woman.

Evil vixen.

They aren't true, they aren't true, she tried to soothe herself, but in her mind, she was fifteen again and running from the snide girls at the feast. *You are smart, brave, useful, a grand lady, your mother would be proud,* she told herself, using the words that Irma had told her hundreds of times, but she wanted to crawl under the log rather than sit upon it. Crawl beneath it and curl into a ball and hide her face from the world.

"I was at the brothel because I went to visit my friend Irma," she said simply. Even to her own ears, her voice sounded defeated. Dulled.

She smoothed a wrinkle in her skirt and flitted her hand through her hair, trying to find some sense of normality, some part of herself that was still Gwyneth of Windrose, the prized beauty of the land, the girl who stared men down at prisons, charmed people into doing her bidding, and felt no fear, the persona that she and Irma had so carefully constructed.

She tried to think of something intellectual to say that would lay a foundation for Jared to be ensnared in her web, but the jeers of the crowd had ripped away her façade and she felt shaken and vulnerable.

"How is it that you and Irma became friends?"

Those women depend on you, luv, she heard Irma say. *No feeling sorry for yourself. Chin up.*

No feeling sorry for yourself.

No feeling sorry for yourself.

"I know our friendship is unusual," she hedged.

Jared tucked a thumb into his belt. "Quite."

A throbbing headache pounded in her temples and exhaustion numbed her limbs. Life had become so complicated. She could not run, she could not fight. Since Montgomery had blessed the marriage and Jared had caused such a display in front of the townsfolk, an annulment was impossible.

In her mind, she could see Elizabeth's form slumped against the dirty prison wall. Her eyes, a dark mossy green, always looked so mournful and hollow.

Gwyneth clutched her chest. As troublesome as it was to admit, her extraordinary looks and position as heiress set her apart—made her uniquely suited for her purpose. She would not abandon what she had started. She alone had been able to do what Irma and the other wenches at the whorehouse had been unable to accomplish.

She *would* find a solution—find some way to manipulate Jared into behaving according to her wishes. Perhaps if she could comb her hair and change her clothing she would feel stronger, less self-conscious.

"Tell me," Jared pressed. His midnight hair fell across his forehead and his tall body loomed over her. "Clearly your family did not know of the friendship."

She shivered at the dark tone in his voice.

He had small wrinkles around his eyes as if at one point he had lived a life of joy but all such thought of such was gone now. He was simply dark, mysterious.

Think, girl, think.

Chin up. No feeling sorry for yourself.

If he learned of how she went weekly to the brothel, how she bribed the guards at the prison, or how she had murdered a man, he would do more than lead her through the town wearing a scold's bridle.

He could have her thrown into prison or tried as a witch or cast into an asylum. His winged brows took on a demonic tilt and she could imagine metal prods of the brank pushing into her mouth, holding down her tongue as he carted her off to jail. Sweat trickled from her brow.

"Why did you not become a monk?" she asked, wanting to change the subject.

His shoulders tensed. "God had other plans. Why are you friends with Irma?"

She scrutinized his face, trying to discern the best way to appease his questions.

Why, why, why had she ever believed Irma knew anything about men? She would never trust her friend's judgment again.

"What do you plan to do with me?"

"I suppose that depends on you," he said mildly. Reaching upward, he snapped a twig off a low-hanging branch.

"What does that mean?"

"It means that you will cease running from me, stop changing the subject, and answer my questions."

"Right."

Never in her life had a man had so much power over her. Usually men fell worshipfully at her feet. Jared seemed to analyze her every move. Of all the things she had ever imagined, this marriage was the worst possible nightmare.

No feeling sorry for yourself, no feeling sorry for yourself, she chanted silently. What was done was done. She would work with the present rather than the past. She would find a way to control him.

"As you wish, my lord," she said steadily, taking a breath.

In the brothel, she had been able to talk him into drinking drugged ale. She saw the looks he gave her. He was not immune to her, and she could use that to her advantage. If only she had a haircomb and could put herself in order!

"Your respect is welcomed, but I do not like repeating my questions." Jared's mustache emphasized his frown. He rubbed his hands on his breeks in a slow motion, as if he were trying to do something, anything to hang onto his patience.

The question? The man vexed her! Gwyneth's mind raced in a tumble of words and events and images as she tried to figure out what he had asked her last—the last thing she wanted was to further incite his fury. First he had asked why she was in the brothel, then—

"I met Irma when I was a girl," she said, suddenly remembering what they had been discussing. "We have been friends ever since." She would give him as much information as she could without telling about the murder.

"How does a whore become friends with the noble Gwyneth of Windrose, who is also known as the beauty of the land, the maid with the glittering hair?"

Squirming under his disapproving gaze, she soothed her hair self-consciously, wishing she could hide it under a wimple.

He was the image of austere masculine beauty—

angular features and wide shoulders. In contrast with her tangled hair, his straight, dark locks were smooth and unruffled. He wore a black tunic of homespun fabric and plain brown leather boots. His clothing was common, but the man was not. His countenance bespoke intellect and contained power—a man very different from the ones who fell mindlessly at her feet.

Perhaps if she could bathe, untangle her hair, change her garments, and get some sleep she could find some of her confidence again.

"I met Irma while I was out walking one day." She lowered her voice, adopted a low, husky tone.

Jared worked his jaw back and forth. He watched her so keenly she thought her skin might burn under his gaze.

"You are hiding something."

She ran her hand through her hair again. "Of course I am not."

If only she could rise, walk about. What was it about this man that made her feel so on edge—as if her skin wasn't quite large enough for her body and she could hide nothing from him?

"You are. Tell me."

The murder she had committed flooded into her mind in a rush. Desperately, she tried to push the memory aside afore the guilt and horror of the act was written on her face. But the earthy scent of the forest, the copper stench of blood, and the freshness of the river were as clear to her senses as if she were back in the forest near her home and holding a limb to bash in a man's head. In her mind, she could see her victim swirling down into the depths of the water.

Her fingers curled around the brank's bars, her knuckles turning white. The cage was heavy in her lap and the metal dented the fabric of her gown. Surely it was better to wear it than to tell the story of murdering a man.

"I, uh, need privacy," she said.

Strong male hands landed on the log with a loud whomp.

She jumped. Puffs of dust sprang into the air. Terror streaked through her.

Jared lowered his face until their noses nearly touched.

That she had ever thought him capable of any tenderness seemed foolish now. The brank pressed between them, hard and heavy against her lap.

"Do not toy with me, Gwyneth."

Her bladder cramped.

"I-I-I wasn't." At least not anymore. She really did need to make water now.

"Do. Not. Test. My. Patience. Wife." Every word was punctuated as if it were a declaration all to itself. Worse, he spoke softly, which made his polite, clipped tone even more intense. Her father shouted and ranted, but this man had no need to do such.

Heart pounding, she stared at him, at his passionate green eyes, and waited for him to strike her across the face with one of his huge paws.

She wouldn't plead, she wouldn't beg.

He moved slightly back, and she flinched. His hand lifted.

Unable to watch, she closed her eyes. Shivers ran through her and she cringed, awaiting the blow.

Her life had become hell.

Worse than hell.

The life of a married woman.

His palm landed on her cheek, but not harshly as

she had imagined. She flinched, but there was no crack in the air, no feel of pain, nothing as she expected. The fingers were as soft as a butterfly's wing brushing her skin.

"I do not beat women."

Her eyes flew open.

"Not that you don't deserve it," he added gruffly with a long-suffering exhalation. "And you might not want to test that resolve. You vex my patience sorely, so I suggest that you answer my questions."

Absently, her fingers fiddled with the bridle's collar, and she flicked a nail across the knob on the top of it.

"Right." She cleared her throat, her mind racing for a way to tell him part of the story while leaving out other parts.

Jared moved away from her as if to get himself back under control.

Realizing that she was gripping the iron bars of the brank so tightly that her fingers were going numb, she released them and composed herself. She had faced down men before; this would be no different. She tried to remember all that Irma had taught her about men—how to get just the right mixture of boldness and shyness.

"When I was a girl, I left a certain feast—" She squared her shoulders. The memory of him giving her the book tickled her mind and she did not want him to know how she'd carried it with her all these years. Even without checking, she knew it was gone from her bodice—had likely fallen out in the scuffle.

He tilted her chin up. "So you recognized me after all?"

If only she could cover her face, not let him see the

emotions that bubbled to the surface. "Why did you not enter the monastery?"

A deep frown line formed between his brows. "'Tis a story for another day. Tell me about meeting Irma."

"I met Irma while I was out walking." That was close enough to the truth. "We have been friends ever since." She ended with a note of finality in her voice so that he would ask no more.

He leaned forward and ran his thumb down the side of her neck.

Her toes turned cold as if all her blood was needed to keep her neck from turning aside, from turning her eyes toward the trees, away from Jared and his piercing eyes.

A leaf swirled downward. Heavens, if only she could get up and run.

She shook herself. Nay. She would fear him no longer. She had seen his reaction to her when she licked her lips earlier, and she would use it to her advantage.

No common falconer would be her master.

Chapter 17

She was lying. Stalling. There was some secret that she absolutely did not want him to know. Her eyes shifted and her lily-white hands fidgeted in her skirt.

Curiosity piqued, Jared determined to find out what made her so nervous.

But time was short. His attempt to keep her quiet had rebounded on him. He had not expected such a crowd to gather when he put the brank on her.

If he was recognized, it would only be a matter of time before he would be put back in prison unless he found the real murderer. He gripped his staff as the familiar feeling of outrage at the injustice done to him floated to the surface. The scars on his legs demanded revenge.

They should get to his cave and gather his belongings as soon as possible—get away from the townfolk and head to the protection of her castle.

Gwyneth scooted forward, the bark scraping the blue silk of her dress.

Suspecting that she intended to leap from the log, he neared her, touched her cheek.

She shivered, and he feared that she would panic like an untrained hawk if he did not allow her room to move about.

"Come, Gwyneth." He held out his hand, palm up. "We will see to Aeliana and you can tell me your story on the way."

Moments later, he settled her before him on the horse and headed for the cave. Her body was warm—soft and altogether too feminine for comfort. Despite the events of the past two days, her hair smelled of lavender and she seemed to have no qualms about being near him. She relaxed against him the same as she had yesterday, adding to his discomfiture.

"Why did the two of you become friends?" he prompted when they had gone a short distance and Gwyneth was not forthcoming with any answers.

He felt her cringe as if she did not wish to discuss this topic. "We are close to the same age," she said.

Jared tightened his arms around her, wishing he could squeeze answers out of her, but he tamped down his impatience. He had frightened her enough and now needed to work on building trust between them so they could forge a life together.

"Why did you leave the feast? I gave you the book and you ran out."

A deep flush began to creep up her neck. Interesting. He touched her neck. She shivered.

The horse picked its way through the trees. Jared found the thin trail that led by the river in the direction they needed to go. Water bubbled over rocks nearby.

"I left the feast because—" She paused, toying with the ends of her hair.

"Go on."

"'Twas a long time ago," she hedged.

Their bodies swayed with the rhythm of the horse's hooves and he could feel the gooseflesh on her arms. Instinctively, he pressed her close to him.

Gwyneth took a deep breath.

In her mind, she was back at the feast. Somehow that day, long forgotten, had been layered over this one.

She remembered the stares of the women, remembered the boasting of her father, of how Brenna had made breastlike statues of the pink salmon.

The hurt swelled in her chest and she felt her pride slip away. Any moment she might break apart and begin to cry. If Jared laughed, it would crush her. She twirled a lock of her hair round and round her hand.

While the reasons for leaving the feast were not nearly so dangerous as confessing her crimes, emotionally it put her even more on edge. She did not wish to tell this man of her issues with her family, or how she had been despised, hated by the women, and how the men leered at her. Of the memories that the brank had stormed into her mind.

She lifted her chin, wishing she could blink her eyes and make Jared disappear. He did not. But he did not press her to answer either.

She turned her face aside to count the branches on the passing trees. One. Two. Three. Four. Five. Six. Surely they would reach the cave soon. Then she would come up with a plan to be rid of him.

Jared said naught. His patience was even more disconcerting than his anger.

Seven. Eight.

The silence was punctuated by the horse's hooves crunching across leaves and it grew heavier with each step as if one of them should say something. Anything.

Nine.

"I remember the look in your eyes that day. You were hurt," he said at last, so softly it startled her.

"The"—she twisted so that she could give him a sideways frown—"minstrels. The bloody minstrels would not be quiet."

"You left the feast because the music was bad?"

"Not exactly."

He held the reins with one hand and traced the back of his fingers down her arm with the other. A disconcerting trail of heat followed in their wake.

She stiffened, facing forward again in a tight line. "I mean, yes, exactly, that was the reason."

"No, it is not, Gwyneth. The truth." His arm wrapped around her upper arm. Possessive. As if to say that all of her, even her private thoughts, belonged to him.

She drew in a breath to quell her racing emotions. Birds twittered and frogs chirped beside the river.

"Tell me." His voice was strong, smooth, seductive. Compelling.

"The women were mean to me," she blurted before she could stop herself. Her face felt hot. What a nitwitted reason.

"I see."

She blinked, disconcerted by his calm acceptance of her explanation.

Though he still held her firmly, his arms seemed to relax.

Even her ears felt hot now. She should be accustomed to gossip, not be some awkward child who cared about the petty remarks made by silly girls. And, yet, inside her, punctuated by today's parade

while wearing a brank, she once again felt like a
gangly adolescent.

Shaking off her unease, she squared her shoulders
boldly. She was that girl no longer. She was Gwyneth
of Windrose and she would act thus. Men lusted after
her. Women were jealous. She had practiced and
studied and learned the art of seduction so that she
could twist things to her advantage. Right the wrongs
and injustice in a world controlled by men. She had
a duty to the imprisoned women.

No feeling sorry for yourself. No feeling sorry for yourself.

Her heart was untouchable. It had to be. She
would bend Jared to her will as she did other men.

The cave was just ahead. Two large oaks partially
concealed the entrance of it.

Jared drew the horse to a halt and swung down. His
hands spanned her waist, warm and large, and he
helped her down.

Their eyes clashed as she slid down his body. She
licked her lips. His gaze moved to her tongue and she
saw tension from across his shoulders.

Ah. Something she was familiar with. A reaction
she could use to steer the conversation back to a safe
subject.

Carefully, she drew her finger down her neck in a
practiced gesture. *Men find female necks erotic*, or so
Irma's lessons had gone.

A flash of heat lit his green eyes. Their bodies were
close enough that she felt the slight swell betwixt his
legs, but he looked at her as if she'd just grown a
horn out the top of her head. "Why are you trying to
seduce me?"

"To distract you from your questions," she said
boldly, seeing no reason to hide her thoughts.

His body stiffened so quickly that he pushed back. His fingers touched her chin, lifted it. "Gwyneth of Windrose, how did you become so efficient at seduction that men do your bidding for only a glance?"

"I have seduced no man."

"But you have—"

"I was a virgin when we married," she protested.

"Because it suits your purpose to pit one man against another."

Indignation flashed inside her. "You have no concept of the lot of women—of the unfairne—"

"You were going to tell me the story of yourself and Irma," he interjected, cutting her off.

So, back to that! She licked her lips, determined to distract him from his inquiry, but inside she felt more like a petulant girl than a temptress.

He was stoic. Unaffected.

She stretched languidly, awaiting the familiar male reaction, for the signs that he was distracted from his questions.

Naught. No reaction at all. As if he did not even notice. She could have been a tree stump.

Annoyed, she lifted her chin. "I disliked the music, the women were mean, the men leered at me, and I wanted to walk alone," she said sharply.

"Men still leer at you. You twist it now to your advantage and welcome their stares so that you can control the situation. Just as you promoted Ivan to fight for you and you tried to control this conversation by licking your lips to distract me."

For a split second, the judgment in his voice felt as if he'd ripped away every shred of pride she had and stuck a knife in her gut.

She coughed to hide her reaction and flicked

her hand in what she hoped looked frivolous and carefree. And innocent. As if she had no idea what he was talking about. Her hair bounced.

"Then you stretched your body and moved it pleasantly against me."

Heat climbed up her neck.

Untouchable.

She needed to be untouchable.

Like ice.

She hardened her jaw. Irma had spent many hours teaching her to walk, to flip her hair just so, to place her hand just there—practicing so she could get what she wanted.

Nay, what she needed!

What he said was true, but how else was a woman to survive in a world where men held all the power? He had no right to judge her.

"I was young, unused to the stares of others. It was intended that I was to be married, so I thought to run from the relationship."

"Run?" He slid his finger down her sleeve and toyed with the delicate little roses on the embroidered trim around her wrist. No doubt he could see and feel her pulse pounding. She took a step back, but he followed her, stalking her every move.

"You gave me that book and I thought I might learn how to read—be more than just a pawn in men's games."

His finger pads against her skin disconcerted her. The sensation was soft and rough at the same time. She was used to touching men—sometimes on the arm, sometimes on the shoulder—but never did they dare to touch her.

"So is it normal for you to run from suitors?"

She took another step away from him. "Apparently so."

"Ah."

His body was too large, too close, and it seemed as though he could see into her brain.

She shifted slightly away from him, from the fingers that grazed her skin and made her feel even more undressed than his eyes did.

"How many times have you been scheduled to be married?"

She clamped her lips. Her private matters were none of his concern.

A throbbing pain began on her left temple; she pressed it with her palm, thinking desperately of how to change the subject, to gain control of the conversation.

She squirmed to get free, but that brought her into even more intimate contact with his body. Unbidden, her nipples tightened, betrayed her.

He grinned. Grinned! The blackheart!

"What are you laughing at?"

"I only wish to keep your overwhelming desire for me in mind for the future."

"My overwhelm—" Outraged, she lifted her chin.

He looked pointedly at her swollen nipples with a wolfish grin. "'Tis obvious you want me."

"I do not."

His gaze flicked back to her face. "So, how many offers of marriage have you had?"

Her temple throbbed harder as he switched from one subject to the next with lightning speed. What an irksome man.

"Several." She rubbed her forehead. "I do not wish to speak of this."

"But I do." There was a long pause. "So, how many offers?"

"'Tis not your concern."

"Four?" he pressed.

Heavens! The numbers ran into the double digits. A shaming amount.

Why on earth did he want to know this? Something about his judgmental gaze made her feel as if she'd somehow shown up naked for Mass.

She shuffled her feet, drawing a figure eight in the leaves with her toe.

"Seven?"

She squirmed, then wanted to kick herself for doing so. What right did he have to condemn her! Facing him squarely, she asked, "Why are you no longer a monk? Did they kick you out of the monastery for asking questions which were none of your concern?"

A glimmer of pain touched his eyes and then was gone. He shrugged. "It was not the life for me."

"I see," she said, trying to match his tone of condemning judgment.

"Have you had nine offers of marriage?"

A pox on him and his bloody questions.

"I have not counted them." But she had. Twenty-six offers of marriage and she had managed to manipulate her way out of each of them. So, why did this man's assessment of it bother her so? He was a man like all others. Nay, he was even worse: a monk who had repudiated his vows, been found unworthy of God.

Never care about a man's opinion, Irma had instructed. *They are mindless dolts who care only about their fleshly desires.*

But, although 'twas obvious that Jared desired her,

he did not seem particularly inclined to act on that. He appeared to be in complete control of himself.

She flipped her hair over her shoulder in an effort to distract him, get him to lose some of that iron control.

His mustache twitched downward as he gave her a look of searing disapproval. As if he were an abbot rather than a man who had been tossed out of a monastery.

Mercy. Other men tripped over their feet when she so much as looked at them for too long, but it seemed that Jared scorned her attention.

Nay. Not scorned. He noticed her as much as other men, but he did not stammer or blush. She twisted a strand of her hair round and round in her fingers and flipped it again.

"If you keep doing that, you might hurt your neck." She frowned at him.

His legs were braced apart and wide shoulders bespoke power and control. He stroked his goatee, running his thumb back and forth across his chin. She recalled how he had been the only man to look at her face rather than her cleavage all those years ago at the feast. He looked at her as if he were more interested in actually knowing something about her than any flirtations she did.

"Eleven?"

She tried to nod, but he must have caught the look in her eyes, for he seemed to peer directly into her brain and she knew he would know if she lied.

"More?"

It had been years since anyone made her feel awkward.

He tapped his chin, his long fingers ruffling his goatee.

Her patience snapped. "Twenty-six!" She should be proud of her conquests, but somehow he made her feel ashamed, embarrassed of them. In her mind, she saw the dejected, hurt looks men had given—of how she'd flirted with each of them, batted her eyes, flipped her hair, but turned them down with a flat no. She hadn't wanted to hurt them, but in her heart she knew she had. Some had given her baubles, some scarves, other small favors. These she always kept, sold them and used the coins to buy more women out of prison. She had reasoned that she had good motivation to use the men—after all, it was generally a man's fault that the women were imprisoned in the first place.

Jared gave a low whistle. "Twenty-six offers of marriage and you stole a man from a brothel to gain a husband."

That, too, had been a sacrifice for her women, but Jared would not care about such things. She crossed her arms over her chest. "Do not remind me."

Abruptly, his hand covered hers and pressed it to the flat bars of the brank. A not-so-subtle warning. "Watch your tone. I am not one of the men you toy with and toss away heedlessly. You belong completely and wholly to me, and you *will* speak respectfully."

She swallowed past her pride. "Grant pardon, my lord."

"Did you and Irma poison any of them?"

She slid her foot against the cave's rock. "Nay."

"So I was the only one offered that possibility?"

A shame that she had not allowed Irma to follow through. She smiled sweetly. "Best to watch your food."

His hand tightened atop hers. "Best to watch your tongue."

She lifted her chin but kept her voice level. "Yes, my lord."

Their gazes locked.

"We must go soon."

She glanced around at the walls of the cavern. "Why are you living in a cave?"

"To keep people from finding me." His shoulders hunched forward.

A wave of apprehension swirled over her. Something dark lurked just beneath his skin. Something frightening. What sort of man had she bound herself to?

"Who is looking for you?"

He opened his mouth to speak, then, apparently changing his mind, closed it. Her heart iced as she gazed into his green eyes.

He was an enigma. A stranger who now owned her.

"What do you mean that people are looking for yo—"

His hand sliced through the air, cutting her off.

The sound of hooves crunched leaves. His shoulders tightened.

"We must go."

Chapter 18

The sun drooped in the sky the same as Gwyneth's shoulders drooped on her body as they headed for her dower lands. Jared's chest had been in close contact with her back for what had seemed like hours. In every moment of that time she had felt his every flinch, his every breath, his every motion. His scent—the enticing smell of outdoors and leather—toyed with her senses.

Most of the day, Jared had plied her with question after question about Irma and the brothel, and she was tired from fending them off.

Aeliana flew overhead, following them, and Gwyneth envied her freedom to fly.

The horse, too, was exhausted. It swayed rather than walked, and reminded her of a large, sluggish boat with torn sails.

She wriggled to one side, wanting to lurch from the slow-paced mount and hide in the woods from her captor. The skin beneath Jared's large hand tingled and her slight wiggle pressed his fingers even closer to the curve of her breasts.

The sun sank and the treetops glowed purple. Her eyes felt gritty, and she longed for a bed.

In typical manner, Jared seemed to be in no hurry to rush along and Gwyneth found herself torn between resentment at their slow pace and fascination that a man could be so patient with a horse.

Her father would sometimes beat his mount so hard with a crop that hair would fly off its haunches.

Spying a patch of green grass, the stallion veered to one side. Jared gently led it back to the middle of the road, disallowing their mount from stopping, but he did not prod the horse to speed up.

"'Twould be faster if we walked," Gwyneth groused with another resentful look at Aeliana's freedom to soar. At this pace, nightfall would be upon them afore they reached her castle.

"You wish to walk?" Jared asked.

She shifted slightly. The movement brought his hands even more into awareness, of how his long fingers and wide palms grazed her ribs. Masculine hands.

The heat radiating from him was oppressive, and once again she cursed her bad choice of husband.

Husband. Lord. Master.

Irritation flamed into anger at each familiar turn, at each bend of the road that brought them that much closer to her dower lands. Jared should have been long gone, not bringing her like a prisoner to her own properties.

Her properties. Not his.

She had visions of her people taking one look at her exhausted face and rallying into a war band to rid themselves of the intruder. She took deep breaths to relax, but the nearness of his body grated on her nerves.

Dismayed, she resigned herself to the agonizing ride, looked forlornly at the passing hedgerows, and tried to think up a plan to get herself out of this current predicament. Could she send a missive to Adele? Get Irma to bring poison? Consult Brother Giffard?

The turrets of her keep could be seen now, and hope sprang in her heart as it always did when she saw her lands. Soon she would see the small but neat castle, the green lawn, the whitewashed walls. It was a perfect place for her to build a shelter where women could come for help. All she had to do was be able to manage and control the land in her own right— something that had eluded her for years.

Jared's heat pressed against her back, reminding her that her latest attempt at gaining control was not going as she had planned at all.

More hedgerows passed.

A foul stench wafted their direction as they passed another bend in the road and her small castle was just ahead.

She covered her nose and mouth. Flies swarmed the area. Garbage clogged the flow of fresh river water into the moat and an oily brown scum floated on the surface of the dark waters of the moat.

Appalled, she sat up on the horse to better scrutinize the area, a perplexed frown worrying her brow. She had not been here in nearly two years, but her estate, small as it was, had always been kept in pristine condition.

The evening sun's light reflected a murky orange off the scum-crusted water.

Horrified, she peered at what she could see of her keep.

Crumbling walls. Rotting roof. Dead grass.

She nearly choked. Her precious inheritance, her key to an independent life and would-be home for women, was in ruin?

"Sweet holy Mary." She had been told that her lands were in order! The last time she had seen them, she had overseen a new coat of lime on the walls and the keep had sparkled in the sunlight.

Anger coursed through her in a long, flat wave—at last giving her some energy.

Swiveling her head to better glare at her captor, she addressed Jared sharply. "Stop the horse and dismount."

"Nay."

Her shoulders knotted.

For a moment her eyes clouded and the vision of the rundown buildings went fuzzy. She should have been here to take care of things instead of leaving it in the care of men!

"Not much of a keep, lady wife," Jared drawled. "From what you said afore, I had expected something grander."

Grander. It *had* been grander last time she had been here.

She stiffened, made to lurch from her mount, but Jared's arm around her rib cage prevented the action.

"Let me down," she demanded again, determined to discover exactly what had happened. She would go straight to the steward.

Jared's breath whispered against her neck as he pressed her closer to his body. Barbarian!

Sharp pain pierced her palm; her nails dug into the tender pads of her skin.

She shook out her hands, wishing she could shake off being his captive just as easily. She longed to leap off the horse, race to the keep, and exact answers. She craned her neck this way and that, taking in the dilapidated outbuildings and ill-kept grounds. Whole walls had been knocked down. Vines grew in a tangle over the cistern.

Horror pitted in her stomach. It was like a graveyard.

The oddest part of it all was the silence. The utter silence. No workman's hammer. No seamstress's gossip. No children playing or dogs barking or chickens clucking.

Where was everyone? Had the keep been raided and everyone dead? Surely she would have gotten a message . . .

On the heels of horror and apprehension, guilt weighed down her chest. The missives she had received on her properties had indicated that all was well. She'd been betrayed! Lied to.

She should have come here and determined the state of the estate herself! The events of this past year: her father's exile, her sister's marriage, being forced by the king to be under Montgomery's control had kept them all busy and on edge for months.

"Please," she hissed. "I would like to see about my people."

They rode farther into the bailey across the patches of overgrown grass. The horse's slow pace made her feel as though she would jump out of her skin.

"You will stay with me," Jared said.

She gritted her teeth. 'Twas so unfair the places of men and women—that men should have control.

"I am not going anywhere," she reasoned—indeed, where would she go? "I only wish to see about my lands."

"Lands sorely neglected for quite some time. A few more moments will not matter."

Men had allowed her castle to deteriorate: The sludge-filled moat, the pockmarked walls, and the crumbling roof were the fault of her brother, her father, and Montgomery. Men who had only their own interests at heart and took no care for the people at all. They had let the land sink into such turmoil! And then lied to her about it!

A woman wearing a dirty muffin cap and wrinkled apron appeared in a doorway at the top of the stone steps that led into the great hall.

Squinting, Gwyneth recognized her as Kaitlyn, one of the senior maids responsible for the running of the keep when the lady of the manor was not in residence.

"Kaitlyn."

She looked thinner, harder. Older. Her face had more lines on her forehead and her lips seemed to turn down in a permanent frown.

"What happened? Where is everyone?"

With a shrug, the woman gave a questioning look at Jared.

"Where is my steward?" Gwyneth pointed at the dilapidated walls. "What has happened to my keep? Where is—"

In his unhurried pace, Jared's hands became firm on her rib cage, cutting off the rest of her questions.

"I am the lady's husband, good woman," Jared interjected before Gwyneth could gather her wits to finish her sentence.

"I see, my lord." Kaitlyn bobbed her head, taking in Gwyneth's disheveled hair and the stains and rips marring the blue silk of her dress with a dispassionate gaze. If she was shocked or upset, it did not show on her wrinkled face. As if she'd faced so many horrors that one more—a small one such as the lady of the keep being disheveled—was naught but a petty grievance.

"The larders are nigh empty, milady, milord. Winter is coming. Irvine died. So did Thomas. Starved for lack of milk. My breasts have no more life in them."

More weight fell on Gwyneth's chest until the guilt threatened to consume her. "Children died?"

The woman's mouth drew into a flat line as if sheer stubbornness was all that had kept her alive. "Aye."

Evidently she was not surprised by her arrival because she no longer cared.

Gwyneth pushed her hair behind her shoulders. "Kaitlyn, you must tell me what has occurred." It made her sick to think of hearing all the details, but she must know.

"Aye," echoed Jared. She felt his body stiffen behind her, saw his hands tighten on the reins.

The woman fisted her wrinkled hands at her sides. "Little Edward, Mary's son, caught the ague and wheezed himself to death. We had no medicine."

Her chest squeezed. Somehow she should have prevented this. She should have come to her keep to see how they were faring for herself. She could have protected them, helped them.

"Are you here to help us, milady? Or are you here to take the rest? We have the barest of items in the pantry, the wine has been stolen, the—"

Out of the corner of her eye, she saw Jared's jaw harden. She could practically feel his condemnation of her.

Gwyneth cleared her throat, stopping the woman

midstream. To regain her people's trust, she would have to show leadership. She didn't need a list of what was missing, but what was still here. They needed food for the winter and enough firewood to keep warm. The walls and roof needed repaired. The pantries needed organized and the items counted.

"Where is the steward?" she asked, determined to get a sense of what supplies they had and what they would need, of how many servants were at the keep and how many depended on her to fill their bellies.

The woman gave her a withering glare, her face becoming even more prunelike. "The steward, 'e ran off, milady. Took the meats and the last of the apples. Your father did not pay him."

Curse her father! How dare he be so obsessed with his rebellion against the king that he had paid no attention to his tenants and servants.

"Has anyone been here to check on the estate?" Jared stepped forward.

The woman turned sharply toward him and Gwyneth felt herself being dismissed as a viable person to look to for leadership. "Nay, milord. Not these past months. Not even after the raids began."

Raids. Starving children. Gwyneth's chest ached; she wanted to bury her face in her hands and weep. How could she have allowed this to happen? She had spent so much time and energy helping women in prison and none on her people—had assumed that they had been cared for.

"The knights left and we had none to protect us," Kaitlyn continued.

Gwyneth gritted her teeth to hold back tears. She needed to be strong and put things back together. The stench from the clogged moat wafted toward them with a puff of breeze. From here, garbage and sewage could be seen floating atop the disgusting water. She resisted the urge to cover her nose. She would breathe what her people breathed. Together they would set things aright.

"Did Montgomery offer no protection when he was given the place as overlord?" she asked. It had only been a few months, but surely enough time to do something. Her brother-in-law, ogre that he was, had done well in taking over the other lands; she had to give him credit for that.

Kaitlyn's sharp intake of breath answered her question. "My daughters and I hide in the woods or the cellar when the marauders come. We've gotten quite good at hiding the food. The youngest, Abigail, wasn't fast enough. She"—again the woman's accusing eyes—"we found her in the woods, her body savaged. We could not stop the blood from betwixt her legs . . ."

Gwyneth winced, remembering the pain in her woman's place that the terrifying violation had caused. For that to have happened to an eight-year-old was beyond evil. Vile.

"We had no priest to bury her properly—"

"When did this occur?" Jared swung off the horse, pulling Gwyneth with him.

"Two months past."

Hand on hip, he looked sharply around at the gate and walls as if to discern who might hide behind them. "Who attacked? From whence?"

His tone, dark and strong, gave Gwyneth pause. 'Twas as if he was remembering some evil event from the past.

Dark circles shadowed the woman's eyes. "I know not, milord."

"We will see to the child's proper burial," Gwyneth promised. "Have the rights said by a priest. I am most sorry for your loss." Her words seemed hollow, inadequate. The blank expression on Kaitlyn's wrinkled face echoed the thought, and Gwyneth wondered if perhaps she should have said naught, should have allowed the woman her grief instead of pretending she could wipe it away with a decent burial and a lame apology.

"The raiders will be punished," Jared interjected. Despite his common garments, he stood like a knight.

'Twas almost like he cared.

"Have you any food to eat?" he continued.

"We have a little, milord. Turnip broth. Three chickens. Six onions."

"Turnip broth! That is all?" The shabby walls of the keep seemed to shake at the vehemence of his voice—as if a few more tiles would fall from the roof.

Kaitlyn shrugged, turned her face to one side inviting him to look around and see for himself what desperate state they were in. "We have two cheeses left. Three loaves. A bag of apples."

Jared tapped his walking stick once, twice, then pointed at the doorway the woman had emerged from. "Go fetch water. And find someone who knows about hawks," he finished with a glance toward Aeliana, who had perched on one corner of the hearth's chimney.

Not waiting for Gwyneth's compliance, he turned, stalked up the stone steps to the keep's door, and flung it open. He carried his staff like a shield. The

engraved dragon on the wood could have been alive.
Its red eye flashed in the sun.

She followed along behind him, tripping at his
pace and frowning at his back. He did not even know
these people, and had been tricked into being lord
here. He was a stranger. A peasant. An unwilling
bridegroom.

But he was not acting like a peasant. He said the
right things, did the right things—like the lord of
the keep. Gwyneth worried her lower lip. Irma had
assured her that he was naught more than a falconer,
but then Irma had also assured her that he was impotent and that was far from the truth. Plus there was
the mystery of why he had not entered the monastery
or why people were searching for him.

So much she did not know about him.

If he turned out to be a nobleman, she would be
stuck with him for life. A wash of acid lurched into
her throat and she fought a wave of nausea.

She determined to gain control of the situation.
"Let me loose, Jared. I need to see to my people."

"Your people need a real leader."

"Release me. I am mistress here."

"And I am lord."

She placed her hands on her hips. He certainly was
not acting like a peasant.

"Enough. We go hunting. Together."

Chapter 19

"Hunting?" She crossed her arms and faced him squarely. "I have not even checked on the kitchens yet."

"Later." He retrieved a thick leather glove from his pack, then instructed a servant to take the remaining items to the master's chambers and handed the horse's reins to a young lad.

"Your people are hungry, and we will not rest until they are fed."

"I thank *you* for bringing food for my people, but *I* know naught about hunting," she reasoned. "I will stay here and check on the pantries."

"You will remain by my side at all times."

"But I must attend my duties."

"Your new duty is to attend me. I will not leave you here to start a rebellion."

"But—"

"Come, wife."

She tapped her foot, not budging. He was correct that the castlefolk needed to be fed—and she planned to do just that—by checking the pantries and kitchen and setting things in order. She would braid her hair, find a plain kirtle to wear, and work alongside the maids to get matters organized. A lady had duties!

"If we must go together, then the hunting can be done in the morning. There are things here to take care of."

"Nay. We go now. Aeliana has been patient enough, and your people need food."

"Kaitlyn explained that there was cheese and apples for the evening sup. We will see to the larders and tomorrow we will all get a fresh start." Perhaps she could even have a bath.

"Come, lady wife."

She did not move. "Nay. Go without me."

"Absolutely not."

When he did not move either, she realized that he intended to simply stand there and wait. For all eternity if he had to.

Obstinate man.

"Fine." She glowered at him; the blue silk of her gown rustled as she stepped forward. Dizziness washed over her, and she reached for something to steady herself. Jared's arm extended. The muscles danced beneath her fingers. Heavens, she was tired.

She could not remember ever feeling this exhausted or discouraged in her life. She rubbed her temples and noted that her hands were smeared with dirt.

She half expected him to curse at her as she regained her balance, but instead he waited, not restlessly as most men would, but with a sort of endless patience. That of a master falconer.

She did not speak the words aloud, but she found herself grateful that he did not shame her in front of her people by forcing her to move too quickly.

'Twas as if her attempt at compliance was enough to satisfy him.

For certes, she would have fallen on her face.

Wondering at his patience and too tired to fight, she followed, annoyed that she had to cling to his arm for balance. Her legs and back ached; shooting pain ran up her spine in a line from her ankles to her neck. It was madness for him to insist they go back out when they had barely arrived and the keep was in such a state of despair.

Hours passed. Dark shadows shifted on the walls of the bedchamber as Gwyneth listened carefully to the sound of Jared's breathing and wondered if she could make it to the door before he awoke.

Stomach churning, she debated on a course of action.

How had she gotten into the bed? She had no recollection.

They had returned late from the hunt—she mostly stumbling—and fallen directly to sleep in one of the chairs by the hearth. She stared at one of the corner posts on the large four-poster bed of the master's chambers, wondering how she had gotten from the chair to the bed. She still wore her blue silk gown—now even more wrinkled than it had been. She had not braided her hair for sleeping as was her habit, and it tangled around her.

But at least her people had been fed fresh meat.

For that she had, despite her annoyance at Jared's high-handedness, been grateful.

Jared's back was turned toward her—how odd to be sharing space with a man!—and his hand tucked beneath his cheek, his glossy hair falling over his fore-head. His hair was slightly damp as if he had bathed and the ends skimmed his wide, tanned shoulders. He looked . . . beautiful and her fingers itched to touch him, to trace a nail down his shoulder blade. Beautiful? What a miserable thought. No doubt as soon as he awoke he would be ordering her about.

For the rest of her life.

The ghastly thought spurred her into action.

Slowly she circled one of her ankles. He did not know his way around the castle, so surely if she was able to get out the chamber door she could work her way through the labyrinth of hallways to the back exit of the keep. Then she could make her way through the woods to the city, and make it to the brothel.

She must talk to Irma and come up with a plan. To-gether they would defeat him.

Jared's chest rose and fell in a deep, even rhythm.

Heart pounding, she sat up carefully. A thin ray of moonlight slipped around the oiled-hide window covers and illuminated portions of the chamber. The curtains of the bed swung like heavy ghosts.

Silently, easily, she slid her legs around to the side of the bed. Jared did not move.

A shiver caressed her spine as her toes reached the cold floor. She bumped her elbow on the small table that sat near the bed and still he did not awaken.

She smiled. Mayhap this would be easier than she thought.

From the tales she had heard, most warriors slept lightly like herself. Only soft breathing came from the bed.

Fumbling in the dark, she found a candle and flint on the table, but did not strike it.

With quiet steps she tiptoed across the floor, holding her hands out in front of her to maneuver around any furniture or other items. Her hand touched her cape, which was folded on top of one of the trunks against the wall.

Aeliana let out a loud cry.

Blast! Gwyneth twisted toward the bed, straining her ears to hear Jared's breathing. No snores sounded this time.

The hawk ruffled and cried out again.

"Shh. Shh," she soothed.

"Aeliana? Gwyneth?"

Jared was awake!

She snatched her hand away from the cape and licked her dry lips. "Here, my lord."

"What are you doing?"

Her heart pounded and she glided a step away from her cloak, the damning evidence that she was trying to escape.

"I head to the garderobe."

Aeliana cried out again as if the hawk understood every word and was protesting her lie.

"'Tis okay, pretty bird," he cooed softly. "All is well."

Pretty bird? She'd like to stuff it with apples and roast it over the fire.

Clutching her hand to her chest, she willed her heart to calm.

"Why are you over there when the garderobe is that direction?"

She wished she could see his face, but she could only make out a thin outline of him on the bed.

"If you attempt escape I will lock you in our chamber."

Think, girl, think, she instructed herself, her mind racing for a plausible excuse. "I did not wish to disturb your sleep and lit no candle. I jumped when your hawk frightened me." *Blasted bird.*

Jared rose from the bed and she could see him slightly better. His outline was as magnificent as a Greek god. His head swiveled toward the door and back to her, evidently debating if she spoke truth or not.

A beam of moonlight illuminated his bare hip. The tight muscles of his buttocks flexed and released as he moved forward.

His fingers closed around her wrist. "The truth, Gwyneth."

She did not answer. Nor did she fight his hold. Her legs tensed.

"'Tis too late for leaving. You are my wife now."

"But you do not really wish to be married."

"Nevertheless. 'Tis clear you are incapable of taking care of yourself."

"Incapable!"

"Someone has to feed you and your people. You were nearly killed last night."

"But I was not."

"Because of me."

She clamped her lips tightly, resenting that she owed him thanks.

"The keep also bears proof that you need a master."

"I am not a slave!"

He waved his hand dismissively at her hot words. "Lord of the keep then."

"You are a peasant, not a nobleman!"

He shrugged. "But a man. Not a woman." The moonlight danced across his wide shoulders. "And you need a man to care for the lands."

"Men are the reason the keep looks thus."

"I doubt that. 'Tis your lands after all."

"I have not been here!"

"Exactly."

"Come back to bed." He tugged her toward the mattress, forcing her to take a step.

She wiggled her fingers, trying to get away.

His fingers tightened, pressing against the pulse that was pounding at her wrist, and he gave a small tug toward the bed.

In her mind she felt herself being pulled over to the mattress. She remembered how he had pushed her down before.

Terror streaked through her, banding her chest in a tight squeeze.

The wrinkled linen sheet blurred before her eyes and in her mind she saw the cot in the chamber with its bloodstains. A battlefield. One where she was the vanquished.

She grimaced, anticipating the feel of his large hands scrunching up her dress, of the way he would grasp her beneath the stomach, force her knees—

"Nay!" Her foot connected with his shin and he gripped her all the tighter, squeezing her in a crushing grip.

He didn't lift her skirts and for a moment she was confused.

She squirmed, frantic to get away.

"Be still, wench."

Something in his voice caused her to stop struggling. It was lower than it had been earlier, more dangerous.

Panting, she looked at him. They had not moved toward the bed at all, but were still in the midst of the chamber.

She blinked.

His hair that had been so silky and smooth earlier stuck out around his head as if rats had run through it. Likely her own matched it in form.

"I'm not going to hurt you." His shoulders looked hard with tension, as if it was by sheer force of will that he didn't rope her legs together and beat her senseless. "But I'm not going to let you go either. Submit to your new lot in life as my wife and 'twill be easier for you."

Submit? The very word brought a lurch of anger into her chest. Never would she submit. She'd seen what submission brought to women. The stench of the prison came to mind. Submitting to a man could bring about the worst possible life.

"Relax, Gwyneth." His hands on her shoulders were warm, comforting. The fingers made gentle little circles on her skin.

Unbidden, a tendril of heat formed low in her belly.

"You are safe here with me, Gwyneth."

"Safe!" The word came out a half-choked cry. "You have taken my freedom from me." She glanced at the wrinkles marring her gown—it seemed that her entire life had been wadded up.

"Nay, wife, I have only taken my rightful place as your lord."

"Rightful place! 'Tis my castle, not yours."

"You forced the marriage, not I. Let us talk about this, lady wife. Mayhap we can find some common ground betwixt us." His arms closed around her

Panic rose in her throat, but his arms were comforting, not harsh. His scent was that of musk and sandalwood. Interesting and masculine. If he was embarrassed about being naked, he did not show it.

Inwardly, she wanted to scream. She should not find him interesting! He was annoying. Frustrating.

"You are frightened." He leaned down, further invading her space, and brushed a gentle kiss against her neck.

A kiss!

She shivered, pulled back, not wanting to respond, but the heat that had formed in her belly flamed higher. As if her body had a mind that was not hers at all.

She whimpered, caught between wanting to press forward into his heat and wanting to run from the room.

"Shhh," he whispered soothingly. His calm, controlled demeanor gave her confidence that whatever he had in mind, it would not be a repeat of their horrendous wedding night.

Gently, he reached down. His hand slid down her leg to beneath her knees. As if she weighed no more than one of her embroidery hoops, he picked her up and carried her to the bed.

She stiffened, her body as unyielding as a rock.

Moonlight set the plane of his face in patterns of shadow and light. Interest mixed with concern shone in his green eyes.

One hair on his goatee was ruffled and she resisted the urge to smooth it down and put it back in place.

The mattress sank beneath her body and the bedropes creaked as they sat on the bed. Maneuvering her as he willed, he turned her until her back faced him.

Gently, his hand buried in her hair.

"Wha—"

"Shhh," he admonished. "When we returned last

night you fell asleep in yonder chair by the hearth and I carried you to bed. Your hair looks a fright and still has leaves in it."

Her hair? He was concerned about how her *hair* looked?

"Let me . . ." Gently he pulled out a few twigs and started his hand through her hair. His fingers caught in a tangle.

She squeezed her eyes shut, expecting his large male hands to pull her hair in a smarting sting or pull out a knife and hack out the knot. Instead, he stopped, held the strand of hair carefully, and unwound the delicate strands one by one.

Her mouth felt dry. Too dry. For an instant she understood why Aeliana trusted him, why he was different than other hawkers. Despite all that had occurred between them, there was a deep kindness in him. He had fed her people, been kind to a tired horse, carried her to bed, saved her life . . .

A curl of panic swelled in her belly. Trusting a man was dangerous. She glanced at the latch on the oaken door.

"Shh," he soothed. "There has been enough strife between us. Perhaps we could have a new beginning."

The mattress wiggled as she twisted on the bed so that she could look directly at him. His bare torso—wide and muscled—came into view. "I do not want a beginning, but to end this relationship!"

"In time you will come to trust me and enjoy my ownership of you."

"Ownership!" she cried, outraged, and glared at him.

His green eyes sparkled and he grinned.

"You are teasing me," she accused.

Winking at her, he kissed her knuckles.

Before she could stop herself, she snatched one of

the pillows and smacked him across the chest with it.
Feathers flew.

A deep line formed on his forehead and his eyes
widened.

Oh, sweet Mother Mary! She tensed her legs, intending to jump from the bed and run to the door.

Then he laughed. A rich, dark sound that filled the
chamber. It was the most musical sound she'd ever
heard. Such a far cry from the serious, brooding man
she knew he was.

Startled, she hit him again. Feathers flew around
the chamber.

He laughed harder and wiggled his brows up and
down. "Peace, girl. I surrender! No need to attack me
with pillows."

A giggle of laughter rose in her throat. She clamped
her lips tightly closed against it. He was the enemy, not
someone to share a moment of joviality with.

Taking her by the shoulders, he slowly guided her
body back around so that her back was to him. "Now
be still and I will dress your hair."

Dress her hair?

Shoulders stiff, chin lifted, she remained perfectly
still, silently vowing to herself that she would not be
seduced by his laughter, not by his gentleness. She
knew how strong he was, how dominant, how much
he intended to control her and her lands. She would
not be taken in as Irma had been by his façade.

For long, slow moments, neither of them spoke.
But in her mind she could still hear his laughter
echoing around the chamber. The sound was so dark,
so rich, so intoxicating that a girl could get lost in it.
Lose all sense of responsibility. Resisting the urge to

cover her ears with her hands, she gripped the linen bedsheet and twisted it back and forth.

His fingers twined in and out through her hair.

She took a deep breath and forced her eyes to remain straight ahead on the swinging bed curtain in front of her. It only brought her more into awareness of the sensation of his hands against her scalp. He touched her hair with the care of handling fine silk. Many maids had dressed and combed her hair, but none had ever done so with the reverence and concern he had. Not once did he pull her scalp or snap a strand.

Out of the corner of her eye, she could see the thick muscles of his naked thigh. A whiff of soap—lavender scented—touched her nostrils. He must have used it when he had bathed himself. The soft floral scent contrasted with his hard masculinity.

A quiver went through her body as she felt herself sinking down into his enchanting ministrations. The chamber around them, all the issues between them seemed to fade until she could see and hear and smell and sense only Jared.

One strand at a time, he untangled the mass, then took a comb and ran it down the length as if he were handling the king's treasure. With deft fingers, as if it were the most natural thing in the world, he divided it into three sections and braided down the length.

She closed her eyes, wishing somehow she could block him out, but the sensations only intensified.

This was all wrong.

This was all right.

Chapter 20

Long rays of morning light streamed across the dusty chamber. Gwyneth squinted at Jared's long body stretched across the bed. He had combed and braided her hair last night! He had *only* combed and braided her hair last night. Of all the vexing things.

His eyes opened and locked with hers.

Disconcerted, she blinked, unsure what to say. The future was never safe for women, but it seemed more dangerous than ever now.

"Get dressed," he said without preamble. "We go hunting."

"We just went hunting yestereve."

"'Tis something to be done daily."

Surely he wasn't expecting her to go tramping through the woods with him and the bird every single day. "There is no reason for me to go with you."

Jared swung his legs over the edge of the bed and leisurely made his way across the chamber. "Ha. You will remain by my side."

"But I need to see to the kitchens, the larders, the repairs, and the castle's accounting."

"Do not play coy with me, Gwyneth. If I leave you here, you will gather every able-bodied male you can gather, form a rebellion, and I'll never get any peace."

"I will no—"

"You will." He stooped beside a trunk beneath one of the windows, opened it, and rooted around inside.

Gwyneth cringed, feeling invaded, the same as she had last night when his hands had intimately touched her hair and scalp.

He lifted a worn kirtle from the trunk and tossed it onto the bed beside her. "You will have no more need for fancy houppelandes. Put this on."

So, already back to ordering her around. She tapped her fingers on the bedsheet.

Likely politeness and charm would gain her more ground than sourness until she was able to reach Irma and her sisters. If she could soften him, then she would at least be able to move about the castle unhindered.

She painted a smile on her face. "Yes, my lord."

He looked at her as if he could see right through her pretense.

Quickly, she quit the bed and yanked on a plain homespun kirtle without complaint. "Ready, my lord."

He quirked a brow.

She smiled her best smile and fluffed her hair. Since she was stuck with him for the time being, today she would convince him that she needed to take her right-ful place as lady of the keep.

She would charm him into trusting her. With luck, she would be able to leave the keep freely at night within the week so that she could get to Irma. She busied herself with her morning routine of washing her face and combing her hair.

He sat on one of the chairs by the hearth and pulled on his boots. For a moment, she could not stop staring at his lips and thinking of the way he had kissed her neck last night. They had been generous and soft against her neck, she had not fought him, and she wondered why he had not required anything more of her.

Instead he had braided her hair.

She looked at him carefully, her mind ticking with ideas about the best way to go about winning him over to trusting her.

He latched the boots' buckles and crossed one ankle over the opposite knee.

She would seduce him. Make him believe she was the most congenial, interesting, wifeliest of women. Then she could go about her duties unhindered and not have to clomp about the woods pinned to his side.

She ran her hand over her braid, feeling the even plaits that he had made. "Nearly ready, my lord."

He gave her a quick nod of approval and set both feet on the ground. One victory.

Tilting her head to the side, she peered into the looking glass. The kirtle, homespun and brown, was shapeless and unattractive. It did not show her curves the way her fancy gowns did at all. She considered this for a moment.

'Twas freeing to not be wearing a fancy houppelande—to not have her breasts hanging out or her lacing so tight that she could not breathe. But, on the other hand, it would be more difficult to win Jared's affection and trust dressed so plainly.

It felt odd to not have the book tucked into her bosom, but it made no sense for her to miss it.

Aeliana ruffled as Jared approached her and turned her yellow eyes on both of them.

Gwyneth smoothed down her skirts. She needed to know more about the hawk so that the bird would not alert Jared when she left the chamber at night.

Satisfied that she could make some progress this day, she smiled at her husband.

If Jared noticed her new vigor or found her enthusiasm unusual or her clothing unflattering, he did not comment on it. A comfortable silence filled the room, which was odd considering how much had happened between the two of them in such a short amount of time.

But last night they had slept in the same bed and his body had been enticing rather than frightening. He had not tried to jump on her or force her and she'd been lulled into sleep by the rise and fall of his chest. Perhaps she could make the best of things.

Jared finished dressing and made his way over to his hawk. He set Aeliana on his gloved hand and spoke to her in soft, soothing tones, almost as if he was singing her a song.

He took his staff, pouch, and various gear used for hawking, to get himself and Aeliana ready for the hunt.

After a few moments, Jared motioned for her to follow and they walked down the keep's steps and across the barren bailey toward the edge of the woods. They passed an abandoned garden overgrown with weeds. Several dilapidated outbuildings stood along the outer walls.

The air was cool and crisp. A light fog gathered

around the shrubs and curled in thin white wisps like fragile ghosts.

Jared's hand was steady as he carried the hawk on his leather glove. He moved in a smooth, gliding walk. Aeliana and he seemed to have an understanding, as if this routine was, to them, as normal as breathing.

The gentleness he had with the hawk fascinated Gwyneth. "Aren't most hawks hooded?"

"Aye. But Aeliana is not most hawks. She kept me alive at a time when I could not feed myself."

"When was that?"

His staff made soft taps on the ground. "I was . . . placed wrongfully in prison a few years ago—"

Her heart lurched. "Prison?"

"—and she brought me pigeons," he continued, not answering her question. "Most hawks would have left their owners, but not my Aeliana. She cared for me as well as though she was my keeper rather than the other way around."

No wonder their bond seemed so strong.

"But why were you imprisoned? I thought you were to be a monk."

"A misunderstanding." Jared turned slightly and scanned the area. A giant hawthorn tree and two oaks stood just ahead and many shrubs squatted along the ground. It was clear that he was finished with explaining what he meant.

"What sort of misunderstanding? Is that why people were looking for you?"

"Shush. Time to hunt, not talk." Jared's fingers tightened on his staff, squeezing against the engraved dragon. "No talking unless spoken to."

So they were back to that. Hmph. So much for

the comfortable silence. Time to stop enjoying the morning and start analyzing and planning out how to work this relationship to her advantage. She wondered what he had been in prison for. So much she did not know about her new husband.

They reached the edges of the forest a short while later. The hawk's yellow eyes seemed to drink in the scene like a starved man at a feast. Jared flicked his hand and tossed her into the air. Her black and brown wings opened in a graceful spread and she flew overhead, following them.

With his staff, Jared began to flush out prey from the bushes. The red eyes on the carved dragon flashed this way and that. At once a rabbit ran out, its brown body scampering to and fro away from them. The hawk followed it, then swooped down in a blur.

Gwyneth gasped and leaned back to watch. Before, she had been too exhausted to pay much attention to the hunt, but this time she found the chase exhilarating.

The rabbit squeaked as Aeliana caught it in her talons and lifted it into the air. For a moment, she wondered if the bird would fly off with its prey, but instead she returned to Jared.

Jared, obviously pleased that Aeliana had caught something on the first run, cooed softly to the bird.

"That is—"

"Silence."

As the morning progressed, more and more frustration built inside Gwyneth at Jared's insistence that she remain silent.

She longed to talk, to ask questions so that she could learn more about him and the hawk.

She twitched her hair, trying to get his attention,

but he only stuffed the prey into a canvas bag, gave Aeliana something from a pouch at his belt, and set about flogging the bushes again.

Maybe she should feign tripping, give him an excuse to speak with her and break his code of silence.

The trail widened and plenty of tree roots lined the ground—a ready excuse. Dragging her toes across one of them, she stumbled to get Jared's attention. He reached a hand out to steady her. She waited expectantly, but he nodded and turned back to hitting the bushes with his staff. The scent of wood and grass hung in the air. Glossy green leaves floated upward and a steady *whack, whack, whack* rent the air.

Devil take it. How could he say naught all morning long?

"Jare—"

He cut her off with a wave of his hand.

Frustrated, she followed along, trying to pick up more clues on how man and hawk worked together. He had fed the bird something from his pouch but the hawk ate it so quickly that she was unsure what it was. Raw meat, likely.

Perhaps she could sneak some from the kitchens to placate Aeliana when she woke up during the night.

A flock of birds lifted into the air and the hawk swooped again.

Another animal was caught, stuffed into the bag.

Whack, whack, whack. More leaves. More thrashing of the bushes.

More flights. Each time Aeliana returned without the least hesitation. What was Jared's secret? How did he get the hawk to trust him so much? All she needed was some small bit of knowledge that she could use to be able to leave her chamber without upsetting it.

That way she could make it to the brothel, speak with Irma, and send a missive to her sisters. Rescuing Elizabeth, the one who could not speak, weighted heavily on her chest as well. So much rode on her success.

Tapping her foot, she contemplated her options. He had not taken the bait when she'd feigned tripping.

What about—without overthinking the action, she stood on tiptoes and kissed him on the cheek as he was stuffing the next rabbit into the canvas container.

His whole body reacted with a jerk. Dropping the bag with a thunk, he grasped her hard by the shoulders; she gasped.

"What was that for?" A harsh line formed between his eyes.

She smiled inwardly. "I needed to ask you something."

The look on his face was incredulous, like he'd just been bitten by a poisonous spider and was waiting to die. "You kissed me so you could ask me something?"

"You told me to not speak unless spoken to."

Above them, Aeliana made a noise, obviously eager to get on with the hunt.

Jared glanced upward.

"I would like permission to speak as long as I do so respectfully," she rushed. She hadn't intended to be so graceless, but it might be the only chance she would get at asking.

Frowning, he released her shoulders. "Nay."

Devil take it!

Gathering her courage, she leaned forward and kissed him soundly on the lips. If once had worked . . .

The forest spun as she was pushed backward until rough bark scraped against her back.

In one quick motion, Jared snatched her wrists
and pinioned them above her head. From chest to
thigh, his heat seeped into her body, filtering through
her kirtle.

"What are you about, Gwyneth?"

A memory of their coupling flitted into her mind,
but she shoved it from her thoughts. If Jared intended to hurt her or force her into her wifely duties
he would have done so while they were in bed together, not out in the forest like an animal. She had
naught to fear physically from him except having to
wear the brank again. She shivered. That was bad
enough.

His eyes had taken on a stormy green. "Why did
you kiss me—does it have something to do with you
getting up in the night?"

Curses!

She licked her lips, wanting to formulate her
answer carefully to appease his suspicion. "I only had
to use the garderobe last night," she said slowly.

He waited, as if expecting her to say more.

Aeliana circled above them.

Jared's falconer's patience agitated Gwyneth.
'Twould be easier if he railed at her, demanded answers. This waiting, this patience from a man was
bizarre. Her father had gone on long rants whenever
she'd broken one of his rules; he never actually asked
for explanation. She had learned to wheedle her
way around it, but never by straightforward speech.

She bit her lower lip. The way he looked at her as
if he could see inside her made her long to tell him
things, confess secrets that he did not need to know.
'Twas as if somehow he had cast a spell on her that
compelled her to speak the truth.

Truth! What use was that to a woman? Every time she'd told the truth, it had been used against her later.

"I would like to talk to relieve the boredom of the day, my lord."

"Boredom of the day?" He glanced at the sun, which was barely creeping over the horizon. Yellow and orange tinged the sky. "The day has not yet begun."

"'Tis my favorite time of day," she said with what she hoped was a convincing smile. She made her voice as husky and feminine as she could manage. Most men responded to that by pure instinct. "I will not cause you any trouble, I swear it. I would only like leave to speak at will so long as I am respectful."

His brows drew together again and he seemed to be debating.

"I am . . . curious about hawking, my lord," she said, tossing him bait. 'Twas clear he loved his sport.

"About hawking?" He looked mystified, stunned even.

"Aye." She blinked. Shouldn't he at least move his jaw around or develop a tic or something? His stillness, his patience was just plain odd.

Aeliana made another noise.

"You may speak," Jared drawled, "for a price."

"A price?" She frowned. "You have already taken over my dower lands." *And my virginity. Although you agreed to take only a trunk of gold.*

"Another kiss."

Another kiss? A thrill of victory slid through her. She could definitely use this to her advantage.

Tilting her head to one side to better scrutinize his handsome face, she pondered this.

"A kiss would be fair, Jared," she whispered, purposefully using his Christian name to create a sense of intimacy between them.

For an instant he looked somewhat startled in the male way she was familiar with: His nostrils flared and his eyes dilated slightly.

Victory! She clenched her teeth together to keep from smiling. If she tweaked his pride in any way, she might be back at the beginning of this conversation.

He leaned forward, his lips brushing her skin. The touch was surprisingly gentle considering how captive he held her body. Her hands, still held above her head, relaxed.

His mouth lingered on hers. There was no bruising demand for domination, just a slow, gentle conquest. Her body slackened as lips touched lips, breath touched breath.

Heat pooled between her thighs.

His tongue licked the seam of her lips and tightness formed in her belly. For an instant the world stood still as he tasted her mouth. He did not hurry and she felt herself slowly being sucked under his spell. Birds chirped their morning songs and the brush rustled in the slight breeze.

His groin pressed against the softness betwixt her legs and she felt his manhood swell.

She gasped as the memory of Irma being pulled down in the woods crashed unbidden into her mind. Her shoulders went rigid, and Jared's hands on her wrists felt suddenly tight even though she could easily move her fingers. Darkness clawed its way up her throat.

Immediately Jared broke the kiss.

"What's wrong?" He looked back at the trail. "Did you see something?"

Images of the man pumping his manroot into her friend crashed on her mind. Her legs tensed. A small squeak came out of her throat.

He released her hands and put space between their bodies. "Did I frighten you? It wasn't my intention— I mean, at first it was, but then—" He stopped, and pointed to a fallen log a few feet away from them. "We should sit for a moment."

She blinked to clear her head, to clear the past and deal with the present. Taking her hand, he led her to the log. The bark snagged the cloth as she straightened out her skirts.

"Are you well?"

"Aye."

His knuckles brushed her cheek. "Surely you know I have no intention of forcing you. 'Twas only a kiss we shared."

"Yes, my lord."

Guilt crossed his face. "I had not intended to bring back memories of our wedding night. Truly, things do not have to be thus between us. We could have a new beginning."

The wedding night had not been on her mind, but she said naught to correct him.

"I thought we could court each other."

Why was he being kind? "Court? We are married already."

"'Twas only a thought."

She scooted away from him. A little rip tore in her skirt. She didn't like this new consideration he was showing. Easier to think of him as an uncontrolled brute, not someone capable of any patience or consideration. Certainly not someone worth *courting*.

"Come on," he said, taking her hand and lifting her to her feet as if they were guests at a feast, not tramping through the forest to hunt for tonight's supper. "We need to finish the hunt so the servants will have meat tonight."

She disliked the idea of depending on him, but, given the current state of the keep, Jared's provision would be heartily welcomed.

He hoisted his prey bag and headed into the forest again.

"How did you begin hawking?" she asked.

Jared's wide shoulders shrugged in an easy motion. The comfortable effortlessness he had in his body reminded her of Irma. It contrasted sharply with her nervous stiffness.

"I was raised by a hawker."

"Raised? He was not your father?"

"Could have been. I do not know. He treated me well."

"Were you an orphan?"

"Likely some would say that."

She slowed her pace, watching him, wanting to know more, to understand where this stranger she married came from. "I do not understand. Was your mother there?"

His body seemed to tense all at once. "My mother did not want me."

She stopped. From his tall boots to his straight hair, she took in his towering form. Despite the issues between the two of them, he was a handsome, well-built man. He was kind to animals—cared passionately for his hawk—and had compassion on people.

"Your mother would have been proud of you, I'm sure."

"My mother was too busy parading about in frilly jewels to have much regard for her bastard son."

The words were spoken without guile, but bitterness came through in his voice all the same. Her heart inexplicably went out to him. She touched his forearm.

He flinched and stared down at her fingers. Her sapphire ring glittered and her skin was soft and white in contrast to his rough homespun garment. "My mother's hands were well kept like yours."

Her mouth rounded into an "oh." Without overthinking it, she placed her hand firmly on his chest and gazed up at him. "Your mother *should* have been proud of you, Jared, even if she wasn't." The words fell out of her lips before she could stop them.

His hand topped hers and pressed it farther into his torso.

"You are"—she glanced upward at Aeliana—"good with birds."

His shoulders relaxed by a small fraction. "I like the thrill of the hunt. A falconer and his bird develop a relationship that is different from that of having a dog or some other pet."

It was a different side of him that somehow made him seem more real, more human. Not at all the dunderhead she had thought him to be when they were at the brothel or the brute she had witnessed at the church.

How odd to relate to a man in such a manner. Almost as a friend.

"I know many falconers lose their birds. I suppose a hawk is different from a dog because she can fly free at any time," she said, trying to concentrate on the conversation and not the confusing jumble of emotions he made her feel.

Aeliana, Gwyneth noted, had perched on a limb above them. The hawk lifted into flight again when Jared began walking.

"One must make her realize that her life is better with you than without you." Turning abruptly, he winked at her. Winked! "Not unlike a wife."

She lifted her chin. "I do not wish to be *trained.*"

"Peace, wife. I was just beginning to enjoy the hunt." Trained? Courted? The man made her daft.

She wanted to grouse at him but knew that doing so would not win her the favor from him that she needed. If they could forge some sort of cordial relationship, then mayhap he would allow her to tend to her duties at the keep and she would be able to see about the ladies in the prison.

The morning fled as Jared told of how Aeliana had been with him her whole life and how they had bonded in an uncanny way. Once the conversation started, they shared a pleasant morning. He passionately shared information on hawk training. The tension between them eased and Gwyneth was reluctant to return to the keep.

She indicated the prey bag. "The hunt was productive this morning."

Jared's chest puffed out. His body bent backward as he shielded his eyes with his hand and gazed up at the bird with unabashed admiration. "My Aeliana is a wonderful hunter. Never had a bird like her before."

That he took such pride in his hawk intrigued Gwyneth.

"Is it possible for me to hold her as you do on your wrist?"

"Perhaps. I do not have another glove today but on the morrow I will bring one."

Gwyneth smiled. This would be easier than she'd thought.

She would bend Jared to her will and he would help her attend to her people. She would gain Aeliana's trust enough to be able to sneak out of the keep at night. If she were able to go about her duties, mayhap life would not be so bad after all. She would get to the prison and see Elizabeth and the others to safety.

Jared might be a problem, but she could work around him. As she did with all other men.

Chapter 21

She'd kissed him to get his attention and talk him into allowing her to speak! Of all the outrageous, conniving things.

Worse: It had worked.

He had received a missive from someone who knew something about Rafe's green boots. He should be combing the town looking for ways to clear his name afore he was discovered, not kissing his wife and instructing her on the finer points of falconry. And certainly not talking about his mother.

Gwyneth had claimed that his mother should be proud of him. His chest ached at the thought. His mother cared about parties and gowns and jewels. Not about the child she'd given birth to.

Leaves crunched as they walked back toward the keep.

His new wife was making him daft. Her scent, her soft steps, the rustle of her skirt, all called to him. The consummation, disaster that it had been, did not count at all. And sleeping beside her last night—holding her, kissing her, combing her hair, touching her softly but not forcing himself on her—had been a test of extreme measure.

She lifted her hand to shield her eyes from the morning sun and squinted up at the hawk. The way she paid attention to Aeliana, gazed at her in admiration, intrigued him. Likely it was some ruse, but it certainly didn't seem faked. In his experience, beautiful women were interested in ribbons and jewels and fancy hairstyles, not in something as practical and useful as hunting.

She twisted and stretched backward, further following the flight of the hawk. The curve of her waist and the swell of her hips made his groin tighten. Even wearing a plain kirtle, she was stunning. Her high cheekbones and wide blue eyes set her face apart from other women's. Her luscious body would tempt a monk.

Last night the way her hand had curled on his chest and her hair had fanned across his shoulder had made his body feel frighteningly alive. Hungry.

Of all things, Gwyneth was a temptress. Even in the plain brown kirtle.

Nay.

Especially in the plain brown kirtle.

He took a tight grip on his staff, vowing to not allow her to push him into doing or saying anything he would later regret. They needed to get going. He would head into town—hours later than he had planned—and look for clues for finding Rafe's murderer. His disguise in plain sight would not last long. Soon the authorities would be after him.

He tamped down the surge of rage at the unfairness he had suffered. Of how the scars on his legs still burned.

Gwyneth walked slightly behind him, and he could only see her out of the corner of his eye, but it didn't help. He could hear the way her hips swayed within her dress.

She distracted him as no woman ever had done. His thoughts strayed all too often to her legs or her neck or her hair.

It would be good to remember the traitorous nature of women—of how they pretended one thing while planning another—just as she had with her kiss. He had already told her too much and if she put the pieces together, she would turn him in herself.

Aeliana rode on his shoulder, his skin protected by the leather padding he always wore, and he carried the bag with the bird's prey inside.

He dropped the day's kill off at the kitchens. A flurry of excitement by the cook and servants set pots banging and fires burning. He found a young lad to take Aeliana, grabbed a white linen cloth from a peg, then headed back out to the bailey.

"Where are we going?" Gwyneth asked as they walked under the portcullis and onto the road away from the keep.

For his own peace of mind and to keep himself from blathering out any more about himself, he considered taking back his approval for her to speak. He blew out a breath. She had given him no reason to do so and the thought bit into his sense of fairness.

"To the village," he said, knowing it would not truly answer her question.

He handed her the cloth. "I wish you to wear this."

"This?" She unfolded the linen, her brows drawing together.

"To cover your hair while we travel." Avoiding all

public attention would be best. The hurly-burly with the brank had shown what a spectacle a beautiful woman like Gwyneth was to the townspeople.

"Oh." A keen look lit in her eyes. "Should I have retrieved my basket? Some spices for the meat would make the stew taste better. Perhaps we could stop at the—"

"Nay."

Her look of anticipation dropped away. "As you wish, my lord." She folded the linen deftly and tied it around her head like a scarf, completely covering her treasure of silver-gold hair.

Her outright acceptance of his decision irritated him even more than if she had verbally sparred with him.

He slid a sideways glance her direction, taking in the soft creaminess of her skin, the blue of her eyes, the pink bow of her mouth. She was a manipulative siren, not a compliant, congenial helpmate. For her to pretend to be interested in something as mundane and housewifery as spices for the kitchen made him suspicious. Undoubtedly, she wished to purchase herbs that would render a man dead, not make him a tasty meal.

Mayhap he should lock her in a tower or send her to a nunnery instead of keeping her by his side all the day long. That is, of a certain, what an intelligent man would do.

He gave her a harsh look. She smiled sweetly in return, looking like a misunderstood angel in her white linen hair cloth and modest attire. Blast it all. 'Twould be better if she dressed like the vixen that she was.

A cart loaded with turnips rumbled down the

cobbled street toward them. It slowed as it passed; the jaws of the two men in the front dropped as they took note of Gwyneth.

"'allo, there, lovely lady—"

Not attention already!

Jared stiffened, and he gave them both fierce glares until they sped up again.

He reached to adjust her scarf so that more of her forehead was covered.

She blinked and pulled slightly back when his hands touched her face. "What are you—"

"Shush."

A line formed betwixt her brows, but she did not finish her question or fight him as he tucked a wayward strand of hair beneath her covering. Perhaps he should insist she mask her face as well. He could not very easily ask covert questions about Rafe with everyone staring at his wife.

"Do not speak with any other men," he instructed.

"I didn't!"

"I do not want you causing another public hurly-burly."

"I wasn't! You were the one who—"

"I do not want men challenging my rights as your lord."

"They weren't!"

He glowered at her.

"I had naught to do with the men looking at me."

"Do not dress in ways that attract attention."

She glanced down at her plain kirtle and blinked a few times.

"The lady of the keep should dress in a respectable manner so that men do not leer at her."

She laid a hand gently on his shoulder and looked

up at him. Her blue eyes were guileless. Likely she had practiced for hours to be able to give just that look to a man. "If you dislike my clothing, my lord, I will wear whatever pleases you."

Why was she being so bloody congenial? He knew she was doing it apurpose. Likely to drive him daft. Or get him to trust her so that she could get away with murder.

He shrugged her hand away.

"Which of my garments displeases you? I will have the maids burn it when we return to the keep."

He looked her up and down. Her plain dress elegantly swept her curves.

"Is it the brown kirtle?"

"Nay!"

"The yellow shift?"

"Nay!"

"My wimple?"

"Nay!"

"Then?"

Her clothing was perfectly respectable. Modest. Plain, even. Furthermore, except for one sapphire ring, she wore no jewelry nor any kohl or rouge as the harlots or the ladies of the queen's court were inclined to do. Her natural brilliance set her apart from other women, not any outlandish behavior on her part.

His ravings about her clothing were unfair even to his own ears.

"What you are wearing is acceptable," he groused and marched farther down the street, picking up the pace for both of them.

"As you wish, my lord."

As you wish, my lord. Why did the woman have to be

so bloody vexing! "Do not pretend softness when you feel none for me," he growled.

She lowered her eyes and bowed her head. "Aye, my lord."

He huffed. Why did she not snap at him? Of a truth, her prickliness had been easier to deal with than her submissiveness. When she was fighting him, he could justify himself, but he had no weapons against a woman being soft and adaptable. Even Aeliana seemed to welcome Gwyneth's presence this morning. Traitorous bird.

Shops lined the streets and a flurry of motion went on around them. Children ran back and forth kicking sticks. Vendors plied their wares in the streets, pushing carts and holding up everything from cooking pots to embroidered sleeves. Several men gazed at Gwyneth, but Jared grasped her arm and none called out to her.

He rubbed his thigh, feeling the bumpy scar that ran from his knee to his groin. If he was recognized, he would be thrown back into prison. Bloody nuisance to have a beautiful wife who attracted attention just by walking down the path.

He pulled his hood up so that his face was in shadows and felt a surge of outrage. He was innocent, by God! He should not have to hide while the killer was free to roam.

She looked at one shop longingly, but Jared shook his head and pulled her forward through the crowded street.

He needed to stop thinking about his wife and find out what the man knew about his brother's boots.

But even now he could feel the skin of her lips on his. His groin tightened as the taste of the sweet nectar of her mouth lingered unbidden in his mind. If he thought he could trust her to not gather poisonous plants or rally every man on the grounds into taking up arms against him, he'd send her back to the keep to do something, anything besides keeping her tightly by his side. 'Twas excruciating.

"Hey! Hey, pretty girl! Look at me, pretty girl!" a street performer called to her as he did a handstand. "Leave your lord and be my bride, pretty girl. I'll stand on my head for you."

Even knowing the man's contemptible and outrageous speech was just part of his act, Jared latched on to Gwyneth's upper arm and marched her past him like a prisoner.

Blast! She wore a plain dress and a hair covering, and she was *still* the most brazenly gorgeous, exotic female he'd ever seen. What to do with her vexed him.

If she wasn't kept under tight rein, heaven only knew what might happen. Rebellion? Treachery? An uprising? 'Twas no wonder Montgomery was so glad to be rid of her.

"Are we in a hurry, my lord?" she asked after a few moments. He noted that she was panting trying to keep up with him and he slowed the pace somewhat.

"Nay," he said.

"Where are we going?" She looked around, taking in a nearby baker's shop that had a rack of fresh pies in the window. The warm scent of apples and cinnamon hung in the air.

They had reached the cobbler's shop: Jared's destination. Ignoring her inquiry, he pushed open the door, glad to be able to not delve further into this conversation.

At that moment a small street urchin came barreling up to them. "Lady Gwyn! Lady Gwyn!"

Jared grabbed Gwyneth to get her out of the way before she could scream.

Too late, they were both pushed back by the force of the child projecting itself at her. Filthy hair, skinny legs, and a grime-splattered tunic was all he could make out as the child plowed straight into Gwyneth, smearing dirt all over her kirtle. He wasn't sure if it was male or female.

He cringed, fully expecting Gwyneth to give the child a dressing down for ruining her kirtle.

The memory of running across the castle lawn, with open arms, came sharply into his mind. He was four years old and the falconer he lived with had confessed to him that morning that the lady of the keep was his real mother. She had been gorgeous that day— arrayed in a rich velvet houppelande with an ermine collar. He'd wanted to hug her, be held in her arms the way that Rafe was. As he approached, she'd turned to one side. He kept running toward her. "Mama," he'd said. His body jerked as he remembered the way she'd cuffed him. "Don't call me that. Don't ever call me that. Go back to that dirty falconer."

Jared shook himself. He was no longer a child.

"Kiera!" Gwyneth stooped and picked the child up, completely heedless of the dirt.

Kiera? Gwyneth knew the urchin? The grime-coated girl looked to be about six and had fuzzy brown hair that was caked with mud. The stench rolling off her was biting.

Another memory, this one of Gwyneth holding a child on her hip at the faire and how he'd wanted her as a wife to fill her with his own heirs floated unbidden into his mind.

"Mama said you got married," said the child, her small hands burying in Gwyneth's luminous mane of hair.

"Aye." Gwyneth nodded. "Where have you been? You are filthy."

"Farmer Matthew let me feed his pigs."

"Did you have to wallow in their muck?"

Jared wiped his hand over his nose to diminish the stench.

"I was hungry. 'e said 'e would give me a scone." The girl plucked at Gwyneth's wimple, smearing more mud on the white cloth. "Why are you wearing this?" she asked.

Gwyneth spared a quick glance at Jared. "My new lord wishes it of me."

"Mama says all men are lumbering jackasses."

"Well." Gwyneth looked distinctly uncomfortable. "Um."

"Look what me gots for you, Lady Gwyn." The girl reached into her tunic and pulled out a set of carved bone buttons.

"That's wonderful, Kiera. Did Farmer Matthew give those to you?"

"Oh, no, Lady Gwyn, me gots it from the vendor over yon." She pointed down the street at a tinker pushing a cart piled with all manner of goods—cooking pots, feathers, hats, tools.

A furrow formed on Gwyneth's brow. "You bought buttons for me?"

"I sees ya coming up the street a bit ago, Lady Gwyn, so I sneaks in real nice and easy and"—the girl leaned close to Gwyneth and whispered something in her ear.

Jared cocked a brow as Gwyneth's face paled. Of a truth, the child had just confessed she had stolen the baubles.

"Kiera." Gwyneth set the child down and gave her a stern look. "You mustn't steal buttons."

"But I gots them for you. Why did you not bring a haircomb to me like you promised, Lady Gwyn?"

"It . . . it just was not possible right now."

"Why nots?" Kiera wiped her nose with the back of her hand.

Gwyneth looked from the child to Jared and back again.

"Oh." The urchin backed up and put her hands on her hips. "Ye thinks yer too good for us now that yer married. Mama always said that would 'appen." At once, Jared realized where he'd seen that look before. This was Irma's daughter. Her frizzy hair and big brown eyes gave her away.

"Nay, Kiera, 'tis not like that at all."

"But ye don'ts come see us anymore. Mama said we's count on you. And you didn't bring me a comb even though you promised!"

Gwyneth looked at Jared.

"You won't be going to the brothel, wife." He could scarcely walk down the street without men trying to steal her away from him.

Kiera glared at Jared, her little jaw jutting out.

"You should bathe," he said. "You stink."

"Mama used to bathe you—" Kiera started.

"Mayhap your mother would let you come see me," Gwyneth said brightly, obviously trying desperately to change the subject.

"She won'ts. She says nobles are bad peoples."

Jared could see the pain dance across Gwyneth's face.

"We have to be going now, Kiera," he said firmly. The sooner he cut off this unhealthy relationship, the better. His wife would no longer be cavorting with harlots and their children. Irma had been part of the scheme to kidnap him. If Jared didn't need to avoid the authorities, he would have her brought before the judge and thrown into prison.

"Asides, Mama's taken with fever."

"With fever?" Gwyneth clasped Kiera by her shoulder. A look of concern crossed her face. "What fever?"

"She's in bed." Kiera turned to Jared. He noted that she had the same large brown eyes, the same jut of her jaw, and the same boldness as her mother, Irma, did. "I wants to show Lady Gwyn me new doll." She took Gwyneth's clean, lily-white hand in her dirty one. "Come, Lady Gwyn."

Jared stepped forward and placed his hand on Gwyneth's shoulder. "Time to go. I have people I must speak with."

"I-I'm sorry, Kiera."

A wash of anger clouded the child's face. She glared up at Jared, yanked her hand out of Gwyneth's, and shook her finger at him. "Mama was right. Big lumbering jackasses, every last one of 'em." Whirling, she fled down the street.

Chapter 22

"Heave! Ho!"

Frustration worked through Gwyneth's body as she shielded her eyes from the glow of the morning sun. Men lined up on the banks of the moat and pulled carriage wheels, branches, waterlogged fabric, rotted carcasses, and other garbage from the green, slimy water. A cloud of flies buzzed the area and waves of stench wafted into the air.

Five days had dragged by with Jared insisting that she follow him around night and day like a puppy. She was useless here, watching the men. She needed to be in the great hall supervising the maids, overseeing the meals, making new tapestries for the walls.

Elizabeth's wide green eyes slid into her thoughts. She wondered if the child was still sitting by the filthy prison wall hugging herself or if she had gotten free. If only she could bring the girl here—give her skills to work. Teach her to communicate.

Aeliana's talons tightened around the leather glove on Gwyneth's hand as she flexed and released her fingers.

She looked longingly at the keep, then turned to watch the progress. With luck the river would be undammed and fresh water would flow through the moat by noon.

Jared, unlike any lord she knew, did not stand idly by watching the servants. He was stripped to the waist and pulling in tandem with the other men. Broad shoulders tapered to a narrow waist and sweat trickled down the curve of his spine. But it was not his bronze, godlike body that fascinated her: For the past week, he had been designing and building a contraption with a series of pulleys to make the lifting easier. That he was a man of intellect and not mere brawn fascinated her.

The book he had given her tickled her mind and she wondered what had happened to it. It had been with her on the wedding night, but she had not seen it since Jared had rescued her from the man who had attacked her behind the brothel. Likely it had fallen from her bosom into the alleyway.

A wave of sadness hit her that she had never learned to read. Her time had been spent making and selling embroidery and taking care of Windrose. She shook her head; the women at the prison needed her and the sacrifice she had made—using her time to get enough money to be able to rescue them—was worthwhile. Perhaps it was a foolish dream and her father had been correct that teaching women to read was a worthless waste of resources.

"Heave!" Jared boomed and what appeared to be a wagon lifted from the clogged moat. Slime dripped from the wood.

The burden was too heavy for the number of men and it sank back into the green, murky water.

Jared called men to him and dusted an area on the ground. He knelt and drew in the dirt, making lines that went this way and that. The leather of his breeks tightened against his buttocks.

She licked her lips.

A few moments later, the workers changed the pulley system slightly and tried again. This time the cart came dragging out of the water.

Despite her best plans to stay unaffected, Gwyneth's admiration for Jared rose with every bit of progress that was made. His chest lifted and fell in mighty gasps as they dragged the cart away from the moat and into a large pile to dry. Later, a fire would be started and whatever could not be salvaged would be burned.

Jared's eyes flashed in the sun like green agate as he turned toward her. He lifted one arm in greeting. A ripple of muscle danced.

She touched her hair, remembering how gently he had braided it yesternight. Her scalp had tingled with pleasure at his careful ministrations.

Logs lifted, unclogging the inflow of fresh water from the nearby river. A rushing stream flowed into the moat, at first mingling with the dirty water and then pushing it through.

Hope sprang inside Gwyneth. As vexing as it was to be forced to spend every minute of the day and night at Jared's side at least her lands would be made useful again. Hopefully soon she would be able to resume her work in the prisons.

"Thank you, my lord," she said a short while later as he approached her. "Both your care for my land and your cleverness in making that device is appreciated."

"Our land," he corrected as he always did when she made personal claim.

"Perhaps I should see about the keep in *our* castle," she said pointedly. "The shelves need organized."

"Nay. You will stay with me. I want no rebellion."

"I want to clean the kitchens, not start a rebellion!"

He rinsed himself off in a barrel of clean water and donned his tunic. "The kitchens are being taken care of by Kaitlyn."

"Kaitlyn has not—"

"Enough on this, lady wife. This subject has been discussed and my answer is no."

What a stubborn, obstinate man! Placing her hand on her hip, she opened her mouth to speak, but he cut her off with a wave of his hand toward their chamber.

"Shall I get the brank?"

She gritted her teeth. "Nay, my lord."

"Good." He turned, obviously expecting her to follow. Hmph. "'Tis time for the morning hunt so that we will have meat later."

Frustrated, she resisted the urge to stamp her foot and did not budge from the spot.

He twisted back toward her, taking in her scowl with a grin and a wink. The same wink he had given her years ago when he'd gifted her with the book. "Asides, I have something for you."

"Something for me?" What on earth could he possibly give her? "I am sure you have naught that I want."

"Oh, but I do, Gwyneth. Come on . . . admit that spending every moment with me has not been *all* bad."

"It has been nigh a week and I cannot even use the privy without your permission!"

He grinned. "But I've never denied you."

She rolled her eyes but fell in step beside him. Just as she did every day.

"I only want to see to my duties."

"Your only duty is to attend me."

Irksome. Utterly irksome. "If we must live together, then I do not see why I cannot—"

"Silence, wife. Or we go back for the scold's bridle."

She clamped her lips and squared her shoulders. If only she could talk to Irma and come up with a plan!

They followed the river to the south through the forest near the edge of the wall.

Despite their row, companionable silence yawned between them as they walked. Aeliana took flight and circled overhead. No matter how much she wished to be at the keep organizing the household, Gwyneth found the time that they spent hunting each day magical. The issues between them faded as they watched Aeliana catch prey.

The suspicion in the bird's yellow eyes had lessened. She no longer ruffled when Gwyneth came near. Today she had practiced soothing the hawk by singing a soft song to her the same as Jared did.

Several rabbits were caught, but instead of heading farther into the trees, Jared drew Gwyneth over to a shady place beneath a giant oak.

He reached into his tunic and brought out the book with the carved dragon cover.

She blinked. "Where did you get that?"

"You had it in your bodice the night I carried you back to the cave."

"I thought I had lost it."

She reached for it, but he held it away. The fabric of his tunic strained against his shoulders. "First, tell me why you carried it with you."

She placed one hand on her hip. "What do you mean?"

"I doubt you were teaching the harlots how to read."

Unbidden, she felt her cheeks heat. The book had been her constant companion for years. She still did not know how to read, but it had represented hope to her all the same that someday she would have a place for women and control her own lands, her own life, and her own destiny. Every time she glanced at the dragon on the cover she'd felt new courage.

She looked at the sharp planes of his face—at the precision of his jaw and the sheer masculinity of his goatee and mustache. Her dreams seemed silly and foolish in the harsh light of reality.

"Of course I did not carry it around," she denied, not wanting him to know how often she'd flipped through it, thinking of how he had winked at her. How he'd been the only man to give her a gift that honored her intellect rather than her beauty.

"The binding is worn and the pages have been softened through wear." He took her chin and tilted her face up. "Why do you lie when the truth would be simpler?"

"Simpler for men, mayhap."

"Why would you carry around a book that a stranger gave you?"

She shrugged and turned aside to peer into the branches of a nearby oak. "I liked the pretty cover."

"You lie. Again." His eyes seemed to discern things she would rather keep hidden. "Did you ever learn to read?"

"Women have no use for reading," she said bitterly.

His hand splayed across her cheek, then traced down her neck. The book pressed between their bodies.

"I can teach you."

She shivered as heat curled low in her belly.

"You want . . . to teach me to read?" Jared was the oddest man she had ever known. They had spent night and day together. Every night after he had combed and braided her hair, he had held her in his arms on the bed. Not once had he attempted to force himself on her and she found herself relaxing more and more whenever he touched her. Now he was offering this?

His hand closed around hers. "Aside from hawking, I can think of no better way to spend the day than reading." Intelligence sparkled in his green eyes.

Carefully, he opened the pages of the book. It fell open to a small drawing of a young knight at court—her favorite.

Curiosity won over her pride. "What does it say?"

The corners of his mouth lifted. *"Some said that women all love riches best, While some said honor, others jolly zest, Some rich array; some said delights in bed, And many said to be a widow wed."*

She leaned closer, intrigued.

His face touched hers; his goatee brushed her cheek. "I told you years ago that 'twas about the place of women." He flipped to a different page, took her finger, and ran it under the words as he read: *"How she was young and fair in all her charms, In utter joy he took her in his arms; His heart was bathing in a bath of bliss, A thousand kisses he began to kiss, And she obeyed in each and every way, Whatever was his pleasure or his play."*

She snatched her hand back but could not ignore the fluttering in her core. "You are trying to seduce me," she accused.

"Is it working?"

She drew her long braid over her shoulder. It dangled into her lap and pooled on the fabric of her gown. "Maybe."

His shoulder rubbed hers. Body heat filtered through his tunic and she was all too aware of his clean, masculine scent. "Why did you marry me, Gwyneth?"

"What do you mean?"

"Evidently you were running from something."

"I had wanted to control my own lands."

"Why? A husband would be an asset."

The casualness of the morning had relaxed her. For an instant she contemplated telling him about her embroidery work and the women at the prison and the reason she had not had time to learn how to read.

Jared thumbed the book's spine. Her scalp tingled in response—as if it already longed for nightfall when he would braid her hair. "You might like this passage as well":

> *What women most desire is sovereignty*
> *Over their husbands or the ones they love,*
> *To have the mastery, to be above.*

Her brows drew together as she tried to fathom the workings of his mind.

At that moment a scream sounded. Jared and Gwyneth both jumped as a young lad wearing too-short breeches and a worn tunic ran out of the woods, snatched Jared's bag of prey, and took off running. His bare feet crunched against leaves.

William! 'Twas William from The Bald Cock. A harlot's son. What in heaven's name was he doing here?

"Ho!" Jared leapt up and ran after the boy.

When he was a stone's throw away, the bushes rustled behind her. "Psst! Lady Gwyn! Lady Gwyn!"

She whirled and recognized Emma—another of the children from the brothel. She had long red curls and a toothless grin. "What—"

"Shh"—the girl brought a finger to her lips—"Irma sent us. Come soon. 'Tis desperate."

"What is wrong?"

William let out a howl—a signal?—and Emma turned on her heels and disappeared into the forest.

A few moments later, Jared came back to her, his chest heaving from the short run. He carried the bag of prey.

"Strangest thing. The boy threw it at me before I even got close to catching him."

"Odd," Gwyneth echoed. She twirled her fingers around her braid, drawing the strands between her fingers. She looked at the leafy bush where Emma had just been. Should she tell Jared?

The exchange with Kiera when they had gone into the village crashed in her mind. Jared had been adamant that she was no longer allowed to speak with whores' children or ever visit the brothel again. As pleasant as this morning had been, Jared could not be trusted. If he knew of the connection, he might be tempted to go after William and have him brought up on charges of stealing. She tapped her foot nervously on the ground.

Come soon, Emma had said. *'Tis desperate.*

What did the message mean? Had something happened to Irma?

She held up the small book. "I would like to learn more. If you would not mind teaching me . . ."

Jared's torso twisted and his tunic pulled tight across his shoulders as he looked from the forest to her and back again. "Right." Slowly, he opened the book.

Chapter 23

Irma. Irma. Irma.

Her friend's name pounded in Gwyneth's brain as she looked around from her seat on the dais. *Come soon. 'Tis desperate.* Her mind and heart ached to be able to go to the brothel.

If only she could have asked Emma and William more questions.

Her hands fidgeted. Every speck of dirt came sharply into view and she wanted to move about and calm her nerves.

She had cleaned and organized the master's solar and all the trunks in their chamber, but had been able to do naught here. All day Jared had explained letters and sound and words to her. She was thrilled with her new ability to read small words but he had not allowed any reprieve from his presence to do her work.

The lack of tapestries sent drafts of chilly air whispering through the crumbling mortar of the bricks.

Cobwebs hung in the corners and filth caked the mantel of the hearth. An unholy stench rose from the rushes as scruffy mongrels rooted for the rotting remainders of past meals.

Gwyneth rubbed her nose, wishing she had brought a sprig of lavender to hold. If only she had her embroidery hoop so that she could still her fidgeting fingers and be useful!

Her fingers twitched to grab a broom, to wipe down the walls, to tear down the shabby curtains and send them to the laundress for washing. If the children were sent to pluck fresh herbs, if three or four maids swept out the rushes, if they all worked together, the great hall would be in working order by midnight. Perhaps then her mind would be tranquil enough to solve the dilemma about how to get around Jared so that she could check on Irma.

The sound of laughter, loud boasting, and bustling servants rose and fell around her as the evening meal of roasted game and a simple vegetable stew was cleared away in a haphazard fashion.

Jared, sitting next to her on the dais with his long legs stretched out and his body relaxed, talked amicably to the man next to him about repairing the ropes on the portcullis.

She drummed her fingers on the table, frustrated that he forced her to sit idly by his side rather than direct the maids in clearing the trestle tables. The serving wenches were practically tripping over each other.

Without thinking, she reached for the frayed hem of his tunic.

Startled, he swiveled toward her.

"If I had a needle—"

"Likely you would poke it in my eye."

She stood to her feet. "If we must be married, I'd like to be a wife, Jared!"

His eyes darkened and his hand closed atop hers, squeezing in warning and pulling her back to her seat. He leaned close to her ear. "I will not tolerate disrespect from you in front of the servants."

"You have no right to keep me pinned like a bug to your side!"

"But I do. You will speak civilly or wear the brank."

Lifting her chin, she clamped her mouth closed.

With her eating dagger, she pushed the last of the bland, tasteless mush around on the bread trencher they had been sharing. The cooks had used no spices—something else that needed correcting. The flavorless meal served in the dirty hall was a loud testimony to her failures as lady of the keep.

She recalled the way Kiera had jutted out her six-year-old jaw, shaken her grimy little finger at him, and called him a lumbering jackass. If the scold's bridle did not loom as a threat, she would jump up and do the same right this moment.

The thought of Kiera sent more worry into Gwyneth's mind. Kiera had said her mama had a fever. Sometimes whores got fevers and died. She wished she would have asked Kiera if her mother had pain in her stomach or felt burning when she used the privy, but 'twould be unlikely that the child would know such things unless she'd overheard one of the other whores talking. Somehow she had to get to the brothel to see about her. Mayhap she could take her some mercury or find a physician to treat her. Was that what Emma and William's message was about?

Her shoulders slumped as if a lead weight pressed

atop them. Irma. Kiera. Elizabeth. The castlefolk. The harlots. The imprisoned women. So many to care for. And no authority to do what needed to be done.

Something pricked Gwyneth's ankles; she jumped and slapped at it. Looking down into the dirty rushes, she saw black spots hopping. Fleas!

Heavens, something had to be done about cleanliness.

Jared took another gulp of ale from his tankard, apparently unfazed by the filth in the great hall.

One of the dogs by the hearth scratched its neck vigorously.

Gwyneth gritted her teeth. "The dogs are scratching, my lord."

He gave her a look that indicated he thought she might be addle-headed. "Dogs scratch," he said and turned back to the man he had been speaking with.

"There are also cobwebs in the corners, my lord."

He picked up his tankard. "Spiders spin."

"I know spiders spin," she said tightly, straining to keep her voice respectful although she wanted to grab him by his goatee and force his head this way and that to look at the mess and dirt and disorganization. "The hearth is dusty."

His gaze slid to the hearth, which was caked with ash. Couldn't he see the shabby state of the hall?

He shrugged and knifed another piece of meat. "We have food. That is what matters."

"I thank thee for sending rabbits to me mother for food," the man next to Jared said, regaining his attention.

Faith!

"And for sending pigeons to my family as well, my lord," another man said.

"And to mine!" said another.

"And mine!"

"A toast!" From one of the lower tables, a workman wearing a shabby brown tunic and torn hose stood to his feet and lifted his goblet high into the air. "To our new lord!"

"To Jared!"

"And his hawk!"

"Huzzah!"

Sullenly, Gwyneth raised her goblet. At least he had done well by her people. "To my new husband," she said blandly. *Who forces me to follow him around like a dog and disallows me from my duties, my friends, and my responsibilities.*

She shuffled her slippers in the rushes and studied her husband as she scratched at her flea bites.

He wore a faded tunic with a ragged hem—peasant clothing—yet he stood out as a clear leader. His straight black hair was combed back from his face and held in place by a leather band. His fingers were wrapped casually around his tankard and there was ease in his shoulders. For all his faults, he was a handsome man.

A pretty maid batted her lashes at him as she poured more ale into his drinking vessel. Gwyneth glowered at her and the girl sashayed away.

Jared, she noted, didn't follow the sway of the girl's hips, but instead took Gwyneth's hand and drew a light circle on her palm. Unbidden, tingles went up her arm.

Her thoughts lingered on the meticulous care he used every night in braiding her hair. 'Twas odd that he never insisted on more. Sometimes he would kiss her neck, but never once did he insist on any marital relations.

As if, as Irma had said, he had no interest in the act of copulation.

He lifted his cup in a toast, and turned his attention to the people, but he did not let go of her hand. The action was possessive but not frightening.

Was he not attracted to her?

He had accepted her kiss in the woods readily enough.

Forsooth, the man vexed her. She had always been able to read men, but Jared was an enigma.

He tilted his head to one side, putting his profile in sharp relief. Despite herself, she enjoyed him holding her hand.

A man in peasant garb drew near. "The carpenters have arrived to repair the back gate, my lord."

"Very well." Jared pointed to the kitchen. "Send them to Kaitlyn to prepare sleeping arrangements for them."

Kaitlyn to prepare the sleeping arrangements! "My lord—" Jared squeezed her hand, an obvious warning to keep still and not to interfere.

Argh!

She tapped her chin.

"God willing," Jared said to a small group who had come up to him, "the storehouses will be full and we will have enough for the winter."

"Hear, hear!"

"Hear, hear!"

Another cheer went up in the great hall.

Various workmen, peasants, servants, and maids crowded into the hall, bumping into each other randomly and toasting Jared. Kaitlyn's wrinkled face gazed up at him as if he was a savior. A toothless workman smiled at her, his eyes alight with joy.

Despite the cobwebs and dirty rushes, he *had* fed her people and done a fair job with organizing the repairs. He had even sold the horse that Montgomery had given them to buy supplies.

"My lord," she said, after the toasting and cheering had subsided and the castlefolk had resettled onto their benches. "There is a small matter I would like to discuss with you." She put on a cheerful smile.

"Aye?" He flicked a crumb off the table with his thumbnail.

"But first I wish to tell you that I, too, am grateful for the fare you have provided for my people."

"Our people," he corrected.

"The castlefolk needed strong leadership and you have provided—"

"What do you want, Gwyneth?" he growled.

She bit her lip. Her praise must have been too exuberant. In her experience with flattering men to charm them into doing as she wished, she had learned that no amount of admiration was too much. But Jared wasn't most men.

She took a breath, deciding to forge ahead anyway. "I would like to see Irma."

Jared looked at her with the same intense look he had given when he'd forced information about how she had met Irma. His body was both relaxed and on guard. His fingers flexed on his tankard.

Taking a breath, she willed herself not to squirm or look away.

"You will have naught to do with the brothel. 'Tis not respectable. I said such when we were in the town."

Gwyneth huffed a breath and twisted her hands into her skirt. "But—"

"Enough." He set his goblet down with quiet authority. "There will be no more cavorting with harlots."

She opened her mouth to argue.

One of his dark, winged brows raised and she knew that forthcoming next would be a threat about wearing the brank.

The feel of the metal holding down her tongue in the blacksmith's shop bit the forefront of her mind.

A curse on him! "As you wish, my lord."

Damn the man. She took a breath and cleared her brow.

A man wearing a workman's belt with a hammer attached hurried up to Jared with several scrolls beneath his arm. "The plans for repairs on the outbuildings, my lord." He dumped the pile onto the trestle table in front of them.

She caught one scroll and unrolled it.

Jared tucked a lock of his straight, dark hair behind one of his ears as he bent over the parchments. His wide shoulders rounded and his brow furrowed as he pointed at the keep's drawings. "Nay, not here. The tables for the supplies should go along this wall."

Despite her dismay over his refusal to allow her to see Irma, warmth rose in her heart toward him. The way he had taken charge of the repairs was honorable.

She signaled one of the serving wenches to refill his goblet.

Jared looked slightly startled by her action. His long fingers pulled at the edge of his mustache. "Gramercy, wife."

She contemplated matters. She had kissed him and

he had allowed her to talk. Perhaps if she seduced him he would release her from having to walk around with him day and night. Then she could make her way to find out the meaning of Irma's message.

She tilted her chin down and blinked flirtatiously at him. If he became enamored with her . . .

His eyes widened, then he turned away, giving her his back as he discussed the repairs with the workmen.

Frowning at his shoulders, she vowed to come up with a better seduction plan. Difficult! That's what the man was! Why did he not act as other men did? She had thought him to be a simple peasant and he was anything but.

Inwardly, she chided herself that she had anticipated touching him again.

She studied the parchments, wondering if she should offer advice on the outbuilding plans. The men seemed too lost in conversation to pay her much heed even when she inched forward. As if she were invisible.

A serving wench haphazardly piled bread trenchers and carried them back into the kitchen. She nearly ran over another maid who strained under an over-stacked platter. The second woman staggered and then tripped. Bread, meats, and scraps flew into the rushes.

Barking, the dogs surrounding the hearth leapt to their feet and scrambled for it.

"Cease!" the woman tried to shoo the dogs away while the other maid scurried into the pack.

Heavens, the servants needed supervision so they could come and go from the kitchens without running into each other.

Through lowered lashes, she glanced at Jared.

Organizing and cleaning the keep wasn't the same as checking on Irma or getting Elizabeth out of prison, but it would still be more useful than sitting here doing naught. If he did not allow her to leave his side, she would summon the maids to her and direct them from there. She would take care of one issue at a time.

She motioned to the maid who was attempting to fight off the dogs. "Hither, to me."

Wringing her hands, the woman approached. She wore a wrinkled apron and it looked like it had been months since her wimple had been washed.

"Yes, my lady?"

"Who is in charge of the kitchens and the cleaning?"

"Elton is the cook, my lady."

"And the cleaning?"

The woman looked stumped. Well. That explained the condition of the rushes. "Go and tell Elton, Kaitlyn, and the other serving wenches to attend me," Gwyneth instructed. "Some changes will be made."

At once Jared looked up at her, and frowned. She tensed, expecting him to dismiss her order, but one of the maids stepped forward.

"You called, my lady?" the woman asked.

Before Jared could instruct otherwise, Gwyneth smiled at the woman and sized her up. She was young, short, solid, and had strong arms. A good fit for shoveling out the hearth and carrying buckets of ashes to the garden.

"Fetch pails and a shovel. There is much work to do in this great hall."

"Have you work for me as well, miss?" another servant sidled up next to them.

This one was tall and willowy, with long, thin arms.

"Aye. The curtains need to be taken down and tended to. No longer will we live in filth. As my lord has said, we must get ready for the coming winter." She shot a charming smile at Jared, hoping that honoring his authority would somehow appease any conflict that had arisen by her taking charge of the organizing of the hall.

Fortunately, Jared had returned to the plans to rebuild the keep.

Gwyneth let out a breath, feeling stronger and more confident in her abilities. With or without Jared, she would be able to accomplish what needed to be done.

Tonight she would check on Irma.

She signaled a maid to refill Jared's tankard.

Chapter 24

Gwyneth contemplated her options as she and Jared climbed the stairs toward their chamber later that evening. If she was going to check on Irma then she needed to sneak past Aeliana and she needed Jared to not be suspicious if he awoke. She couldn't very well hop on top of him like a desperate harlot, but perhaps she could bargain with him.

"You've done well," Jared said as they turned one of the tight corners in the steep, narrow stairwell. Candles glowed in the sconces. "You have skill in knowing which servant is best for each task."

Startled by his praise, Gwyneth paused, her hand clutching the oak railing. The wood was smooth against her palm, worn from years of use.

"The great hall looked presentable by the end of the evening."

No one had ever praised her for any womanly skills except for that feast where her father had embarrassed her by announcing the width of her hips and size of her breasts. "Gramercy, my lord, I feel that it is best to keep the servants occupied in their proper positions."

"Very good."

Jared continued walking toward their chamber. She followed, watching the lazy roll of his hips and shoulders. When she had tried to flatter him, he looked at her with disdain, but now he praised her for domestic organization. Odd.

"I could do so much more if I were free to roa—"

"Nay. Absolutely not."

Lifting her chin, she vowed to gain her freedom. He had not drunk nearly as much ale as she would have liked although she had made certain the serving maids kept his goblet full.

The door to the bedchamber opened with a creak as he ushered her inside. The wide-toothed wood comb atop her dressing table caught her attention.

Her belly fluttered as she thought of how his hands felt on her skin when he braided her hair. Tonight she would seduce *him.*

Aeliana rested on her usual perch. She turned her head as they entered but Jared spoke softly to her and she did not make any noise. Gwyneth memorized the calming words and tone so that she could copy them when she stole from the room.

A tub of steaming water sat in the middle of the room. Several cloths, linen towels, and a cake of soap lay on the floor beside it.

Jared's body jerked before coming to total stillness. "Did you order this brought here?"

She licked her lips. "Aye."

Stroking his goatee, he gazed from the bathing tub to Gwyneth.

"'Tis for you," she said, lowering her voice to a husky whisper.

He propped a hand on his belt. "What do you want, wife?"

"I enjoy the way you braid my hair in the evenings." She separated a strand of hair from the rest of the mass and twirled it round and round her fingers. His gaze followed its path. Good. "I thank you for taking care of the repairs on the roof and taking responsibility as lord," she said, watching his reactions carefully so that she would not be too profuse in her speech. "I thought perhaps I could begin to act as lady of the keep in other ways as well."

"So you had water brought to our chamber?"

"Irma said you came to the brothel to bathe every few days and I thought . . ." She allowed her voice to trail off. "'Tis a wife's duty."

"You are offering to bathe me?"

She sauntered over to her dressing table and leisurely finger-combed through her hair. "Only if you wish me to."

His agate eyes sparkled. "'Tis a fascinating proposition."

She bowed her head to avoid any sign of victory that might be written on her face.

He didn't readily agree as most men likely would, but he removed his mantle and laid it across one of the trunks.

"Perhaps I should undress you," she pressed.

His brows slammed together. "Gwyneth, what do you really want?"

To go to the prison. To not be watched so closely. To set up a school for women. "I'd like to be free to organize the kitchens and the serving maids. The whole castle—not just the great hall—needs to be cleaned."

"I see." His voice took on a stern note.

If only he wasn't so suspicious of everything she did!

"I thought perhaps you could trust me a little . . ."

"Trust you? The woman who drugged me in a brothel and forced me at swordpoint to marry her. Perhaps you wish me naked so that you can better see the vein in my throat."

"I thought—"

"Nay. You may *not* wander about the keep as you will. Likely I'd end up with poison in my stew."

Curses! This wasn't working at all!

She splayed her hand across her cheek as if she were blushing. Perhaps if he thought her request was merely a cover-up for something more primal. "Irma seemed to indicate that you enjoyed your baths."

Despite his suspicions, interest sparked in his eyes. Ha! He wasn't so unaffected by her as he pretended!

She tossed her hair slightly forward to hide her smile.

"I will"—she paused, unsure of the exact game they played or how far she should push her advantage— "help you with your boots if you like."

The lines around his mouth tightened. "How very wifely," he remarked, but she was uncertain if it was a compliment.

"Perhaps you could sit here." She glided to one side and patted the three-legged stool. Even though he had said nay to her initial request, if he began to understand that it was good for him to allow her to be in charge of some matters, surely she would be granted more leeway.

A dark look formed on his brow as if he did not trust her for a second, but he strode over, kinglike, and sat. For all his arrogance, she could not help but admire the width of his shoulders, the fluidity of his motion. 'Twas odd that he had faked a limp when they first met.

As slowly as she could manage so that she could drag out the moment and force him to focus his full attention on her, she sank down before him and began to unlatch his boots.

The interest in his eyes blazed. His hands were relaxed on his knees. The left one made little circles with the thumb and middle finger.

She slid one boot off his foot, then the other. The crisp hair of his muscled calves grazed her palm. A sharp intake of breath sounded from him.

Victory!

The man was *not* immune to her. He was *not* so different than other men. That realization slid through her like a bolt of power.

Wiggling her hips with measured slowness she rose and untied his tunic. The pulse quickened in his throat, and his left hand twitched faster. She tugged the garment over his head.

Heavens, his torso was magnificent. Wide shoulders. Trim waist. She ran one finger down the dips and crevices of his stomach, admiring the maleness of his body.

He sucked in another breath and another wave of power went through her. Heat spiraled up her spine. If she could affect him, she could control him. If she could control him, she could be a mistress. If she could be mistress, she could control the keep, save her women, see about Irma and effect changes in the world.

Irma was right: honor was for men; women had much better ways.

The warmth of his body filtered into her fingers as her hand lingered on his chest. So very different from her. So large. So interesting.

Slowly she trailed her fingers downward to the laces of his breeks. The pulse thumped in his throat and she smiled. Victory again!

Latching onto that thought, she peeled his breeks down his long legs.

He lifted his hips to assist her with the undressing as if offering himself to her. A pleasurable display.

His member sprang free. She stifled a gasp. The color enticed her—tan with a blue vein—and it reminded her of an elegant, elaborate tapestry.

A trickle of perspiration worked its way down her spine sending a heated chill through her body.

Without a word, he rose and walked to the tub. If he was self-conscious in any way, he did not show it.

She wiped her hands on her thighs, wanting to be as unaffected as he was by his nudity, but her belly fluttered as the muscles of his hips and buttocks clenched and released.

Flicking her braid over her shoulder, she unfolded a washing rag.

A bead of sweat wet her brow. She wiped it away, wondering how it was that she was perspiring. Ne'er before had a man made her feel so uneasy when she set about to charm him. But, then, she reasoned to herself, all other men she'd been around wore clothing.

He sank into the tub, bending his legs so that he fit. Silver tendrils of steam wafted upward.

Moving forward, she determined to make him think of her as a wife, an equal, not a puppy to be by his side all the day long.

Asides, she reasoned, his body would be a joy to touch.

Dipping her hands into the water, she wet the cloth and the cake of soap.

He leaned forward with a sigh as she ran the rag across his shoulders. Oh, but his body was wondrous. For luxurious moments, she bathed him, enjoying his maleness. Not once did he reach for her, just as Irma had said.

A green tinge of jealousy bit her as she thought of her friend running her hands over this man's body.

Jealousy? Quickly she pushed the thought aside. Irma despised all men and—she glanced downward— she had been quite clear that Jared had never been aroused when she had bathed him.

An insane sense of pride flowed through her that Jared's member was stiff and long tonight.

What a stupid thought, she chided herself.

But—she peeked through lowered lashes—and wondered if she dared to touch it. Could she run the rag downward, pretend 'twas an accident?

And what if he rose from the tub and took her again like a beast?

She considered this and realized she had not been concerned about such.

He had been in complete control of himself. He had fed her people. He'd spoken to her kindly. He'd combed her hair. He'd backed away when she'd shown the slightest amount of fear.

All this past week, he had been teaching her to read.

Moisture trickled down the tanned skin of his

shoulders. He sat very still, knees bent in the small tub. His member bobbed in the water, large and mesmerizing, but not terrifying.

She made a few more swipes with the rag, then squeezed the water from it. The room felt overly warm. She needed to get up, walk around, get some air.

He stood and water ran down his torso in thick rivulets. His chest was wide, breathtaking, and she found it difficult to do aught more than stare at him. Despite her earlier vow to pretend indifference, she sucked in a breath.

His manroot, slightly purplish, stood at attention. It was thick and long, and she recalled how it had felt when he had slammed it inside her. Unbidden, a tremble started up her spine and her stomach clenched. She took slow, deep breaths to keep herself stable.

"I would ask you to be gentle with me, my lord. I swear I will not fight you."

Silence filled the bedchamber as if he was contemplating her words. As if he had not even been considering copulation although his body was truly awake and ready.

"You need not fear me, Gwyneth. I require your respect, but I am not interested in your degradation. I think despite our beginnings that somehow we will forge a reasonable relationship."

A reasonable relationship. The promise was more than she expected, but how could a relationship with a man ever be reasonable?

"I do not believe that is possible."

"Why not?"

"Most men are . . ." Her voice trailed off as she thought of the various men she knew. They didn't take responsibility for their families, cheated on their wives, seemed ready to rut with any female who would spread her legs or pay them any attention.

"I am not 'most' men."

She blinked at his assertion. The way he'd insisted on hunting for meat for the peasants and been responsible for her people had impressed her. "Of a truth," she murmured.

"We will take things slowly. You will enjoy it."

A lick of heat caressed her sex. "Enjoy it?"

One corner of his mustache lifted in a tantalizing half smile.

She *had* been enjoying touching him. But 'twas time to bargain. "I thought that perhaps you would allow me to go about my duties."

He laughed.

Laughed!

She propped a hand on her hip as annoyance rose up her cheeks. "I cannot imagine what you are laughing at."

"For a woman who frequents whorehouses and dresses to provoke men, you certainly know very little."

"There is naught pleasant about the act of copulation. You've proven that to me already," she retorted, lifting her chin.

Something flashed in his eyes. As if she'd just thrown down a challenge.

"What about the kiss we shared in the woods? I think you should surrender to feelings of pleasure rather than power, Gwyneth."

Surrender? Pleasure?

"Copulation for women is about duty."

"Oh?"

She touched his face with her fingertips. "But I am ready."

Like a snake striking, he snatched her hand. "Why do you want to do this?"

"I was trying to seduce you so I would not have to spend every bloody minute of the day by your side," she blurted out, then wanted to kick herself for the confession.

'Twould be much better if he was hauling her to bed like a beast—that is what a woman expected. The calm mannerism he used to talk of pleasure and enjoyment flustered her. Usually with men, it was they who blushed and stammered and blurted out ridiculous confessions.

With a firm hold, he held her hand away from her side so that she was fully exposed to him. His gaze raked down her body. She fisted her hands to keep from shivering but was unable to stop butterflies from forming in her belly. He wasn't just looking at her as if he saw beneath her clothing, but as though he saw something deeper, darker—all the way to that secret part that wished to surrender to desire and belong fully to a man.

Fully to *him.*

She hated feeling vulnerable and out of control. And she definitely didn't want to feel pleasure from him . . . did she?

He released her.

"Truly, we should not discuss this anymore." She swiped the washing cloth off the floor and folded it neatly.

"But I think we should." His voice, low and husky, sent heat spiraling through her.

She imagined his hand roving over her skin. The

thought was not nearly as unpleasant as she would have liked it to be.

"You enjoy how it feels when I comb your hair."

Not wanting to look at him, to experience how exposed he made her feel, she darted her gaze to the mantel. It was clean and bare—cold. She had dusted it this morning, and nothing decorated the surface to make it inviting or homelike. She took a step toward it to wipe it off again just to verify that no dust remained.

"Nay," he said, "'tis not time to clean the chamber, but time to—"

She whirled.

"—clean yourself." He indicated the tub as he reached for a linen towel and dried himself.

Breath seemed hard to draw as she realized that he intended for her to be undressed for him the way he had been undressed for her. Somehow the power had shifted again, and she felt uneasy.

"You did say you wished to please me, to seduce me, yes? So that you might take your place as lady of the keep."

Her heart pounded hard and fast; her chest quivered. But, he was offering her a bargain. Just the bargain she had wanted.

"You need to get used to being naked in front of me."

She gasped. "Naked in front of you? There is no need for that. The church says—"

"Do you wish to walk freely about the keep or not, Gwyneth? Surely there is some compensation for me for such a boon."

She shot him a glower, but he only laughed.

"And I find it pleasurable for you to be naked," he continued, completely ignoring her objections.

Irritation at his high-handedness flicked over her. "I offered to do my marital duty," she huffed.

"We'll see to that later," he promised darkly.

This seduction was not going at all as she had envisioned and she wondered how on earth Irma managed to keep so many men begging at her knees.

Tamping down the urge to resist, to race around the room and adjust any items that were out of place from the exact location she had left them in this morning, she reached for the bodice of her gown. She had wished to show him she could be a wife in truth, and she would not lose her nerve now.

Her kirtle fell in a heap at her feet. Quickly, she stepped into the tub, eager to cover herself with something, anything. She did not glance up at him; she did not wish to see his reaction. He was just sitting there, watching her, and likely trying to find something else to say or do to make her nervous.

"Not so low in the water, wife, I enjoy seeing your—"

Crumpling up the washcloth in one hand, she flung it at him. It landed with a soggy splat against the mattress.

Aeliana ruffled.

Jared's eyes flashed with dark amusement.

Curses! How did he vex her such that she lost control of her temper? It was not like her at all to throw items.

"Pick it up," he said softly.

"You mean, get out of the tub?"

"I do not know any other way for you to do such," he drawled as if she were a simpleton.

"I'm naked."

He shrugged. "Excellent."

"Hand me a towel."

"Nay. Absolutely not."

His mustache twitched with mirth. "But I'll allow you to go about the keep unhindered . . ."

Moments ticked by as a silent battle of wills clashed in the room.

Ire rose inside her. How dare he sit there demanding her to parade around in exchange for a simple freedom that all wives should have! 'Twas barbaric.

One corner of his mouth lifted into a half smile. He was enjoying this. The rogue.

"Fine!" Thumping her hands down hard on the sides of the wooden tub, she lifted herself upward. If he wanted her to walk around naked, she would do so. Mayhap it would make him stammer, act the imbecile as so many men did when they saw a leg or arm exposed.

Determined, she rose and stalked toward him, fully aware of how most men responded to her.

An inferno blazed in his eyes, but he did not stammer or reach for her. In fact, he sat perfectly still, very much in control, and if she had not known that he harbored lust for her, she would not have believed it.

Deftly, she reached down and picked up the cloth. Past caring what he would do, she stuck out her chest and held the cloth out to him, wanting a reaction. This calm, controlled, domineering exterior was intolerable. Irksome. Even his wild, beastlike self had been better than this.

"Satisfied?" she sneered.

"Mind your tongue." His eyes flicked to the scold's bridle on the table beside the bed.

So they were back to that. Blast it all.

In a deft swirl, she spun on her heels, stalked to the table, and picked up the brank. With a heave, she lunged it into his lap, sank to her knees at his feet, and glowered defiantly at him. "Do your worst, barbarian. I won't fight you."

He blinked at her, clearly startled, then his hand raised and cupped her chin. The gesture was gentle, tender even.

A tremble shuddered through Gwyneth's body. Of all things she had expected him to do, that was not one of them. She pulled back.

His hand caressed her back, not controlling, but comforting.

She frowned up at him.

He tossed the brank across the room. It landed on the floor planks with a clank, then rolled several more feet.

He leaned down so that his lips tickled the fine hair on her ear. Heat licked her core.

"W-what are you doing?"

"My worst."

Chapter 25

Run, a voice beckoned in her mind as Jared's lips softly slid over her ear and warmth flooded her body. For all her lessons from Irma, she had no clear idea of what she was doing. His breath sent tingles of heat down her spine. Gooseflesh popped out on her arms. She pulled back, wanting to put space betwixt them, to think straight, assess the situation, properly plan a course of action.

Unlike before, Jared's arm tightened around her back in a cagelike grip.

She gasped, the feeling of being trapped rising in her throat.

"There is unfinished business here, wife."

She forced a deep breath into her lungs, determined to remain calm. Surely seduction could be organized the same as managing the kitchens.

"You're trembling."

He wasn't supposed to notice!

"Fear or desire?" he asked.

"I'm"—water dripped from her long hair and trickled down her thighs in soft slithers as she became all too aware that she was unclad—"chilly," she lied.

His teeth grazed her ear. "Do not lie to me, Gwyneth."

"I-I'm not," she stammered.

He did not contradict her lame reply but instead trailed his tongue down her neck.

A shiver went through her, her nipples peaked, and a bead of sweat dripped down her temple.

"I—" She struggled to think of something to answer, to put distance between them, but no words came to her mind. She should have wrapped herself in a towel! Then, at least, he would not be able to clearly see her reaction to him.

She turned toward the garderobe, thinking that perhaps she could hide inside. He drew her close. Their bare torsos touched, skin grazed against skin. White-hot sensation speared her.

Somehow her plans of seducing him into allowing her freedom had been turned against her—she was acting the part of blushing bride, a nervous ninny, not a victorious vixen.

"There is no reason to be uneasy."

She lifted her chin. "I'm not uneasy."

He nibbled her ear. "Liar."

"I'm not lying."

His hands slid down her body, leaving trails of sensation in their wake. "Speak the truth."

One hand cupped her beneath her knees and the other wrapped around her shoulder, then, at once, she was lifted and placed onto the mattress.

His biceps, the size of small trees, danced as he braced his arms on either side of her torso and leaned forward.

A shudder ran through her as she realized how fully at his mercy she was. Her breath hitched in her throat.

He was strong and had lifted her as if she weighed only as much as a handful of leaves. How could she have thought even for an instant that she felt any desire for him whatsoever? Of course all she felt was fear!

But she didn't.

She felt safe.

"You're trying to frighten me apurpose!"

"Is it working?"

"Nay!"

A slow, knowing smile lifted one corner of his mouth. "If 'tis not fear you feel, it must be desire."

"Of course I'm afraid. Terrified."

"Nay, you are not." His voice was low, calm. Knowledgeable. Too knowledgeable.

Embarrassed at her response to him, she resisted the urge to cover her breasts and quim with her arms. Could he see the trails of heat that still lingered from where his tongue had been?

"Speak truth rather than cover it with female lies and manipulation, Gwyneth."

"I am not manipulat—"

"To make a marriage, there must be honesty between us."

Honesty? With a man? Impossible.

"Fine," she huffed, frustrated with the turn in conversation, with how the situation had escaped from her control, with how vexed he made her feel. "I do not wish to be married to you. How's that for honesty?"

She pushed her shoulders back as if she were a

soldier going to battle. "I'm ready for the act. Desire runs rampantly through my veins for you." The sooner they started, the sooner the deed would be finished. "I'm ready to earn my freedom to walk about the castle."

His intense gaze slid casually down her body. "You are as stiff as yon hearth poker." He made no move to bring their bodies closer together.

"Nevertheless."

To distract herself from her turbulent, confusing emotions, she began making lists of things she would do if Jared ever allowed her to manage the keep. Organizing always relaxed her.

Clean the great hall, change the rushes, sweep the cobwebs, and organize the pantries.

Jared's palm cupped her shoulder, and she squeezed her eyes shut. *Clean the hearths. Wipe the tables.*

"Relax, wife."

Her eyes popped open. "You cannot command me to relax," she said tightly. "I won't fight you."

"I am not interested in tupping an iron slab."

"Then get off of me!"

"I thought you wanted to seduce me."

She glowered at him. "I have changed my mind."

"But I haven't changed mine about wanting to be seduced."

Faith, the man irritated her.

"I only wanted to seduce you because the servants run over each other and it looks as though the rushes have not been changed in two years." And she needed to see what was wrong with Irma. Her voice sounded defeated even to her own ears.

"Gwyneth, the feelings you are having do not have anything to do with the servants."

She swallowed. It would be easy to claim he did not know what he was talking about, but he would likely only see through her lie. "I did not start out thinking that I would want to couple again, but—" Heat crept up her cheeks and she turned her face away, not wanting to see the victory in his intense eyes.

His fingers lifted to her cheek and he ran his knuckles from her hairline to her chin.

She flinched, not sure what to make of the gentle movement.

"I am truly sorry about what happened on our wedding night."

Sorry? His words hung in the air. Unexpected. His voice was rough, like something scraped his throat, and she wondered if he had ever apologized before.

"'Twill ne'er be thus again, I swear. The desire you felt earlier—I can make it grow so that there will be only pleasure between us. Of a truth, I have felt so much guilt I could scarcely live with myself."

She tilted her head back. A haunted look lurked in his eyes.

Guilt?

He felt guilt over his treatment of her?

"I'm so sorry, Gwyneth. Let us start over."

That a man would feel remorse over the act of copulation intrigued her. All she knew of men was they cared little for the feelings of women around such matters. Their lusts were self-centered, selfish, and self-seeking.

During war they raped at will and during peacetime they preyed upon women in the forests and alleys. Even supposedly "good" men satisfied their base desires at stench-filled brothels. From what she knew, naught mattered to them save their own greedy lust.

But since their wedding night, he'd shown no interest in copulation.

Was his restraint the result of *guilt*?

"This marriage is not what either of us intended," he said, "but, truly, we should try to make it as amicable as we can."

There was a very long pause.

"I can't seem to think straight when I'm around you, Gwyneth. Your skin, your voice, the way you walk . . . You leave me breathless and I was afraid I would spend the rest of my life tormented with wanting to touch you and afraid of frightening you. Your desire to seduce me tonight was a welcome relief."

Warmth spread inside her chest.

"I made you something."

"Something for me?"

His shoulders hunched slightly and he looked . . . vulnerable. Picking up his leather pouch, he untied its string. "I think I've wanted you since I first saw you at the faire."

She sat up slightly.

"Close your eyes."

She hesitated, unsure what he was about.

"Trust me, Gwyneth."

Trust him? There was so much between them. But she closed her eyes.

"Now hold out your hand."

She opened her eyes. "This is a trick?"

"Nay. Go on. Close your eyes and hold out your hand."

Taking a deep breath, she complied.

The *click* of wood and something was dropped into her palm.

She blinked. An exquisitely carved wooden bracelet. She lifted it into the air.

It was made of a smoothly sanded ring of wood that was about an inch thick and had carved words in its surface. It had a small red rock embedded on one side. Squinting, she tried to make out the words.

"Her price"—she turned the bracelet to read the rest of it—*"is far above"*—cocking her head to one side, she sounded out the next word just as Jared had taught her—*"r-r-ru-bies."* Amazed, she read it again. "Her price is far above rubies."

"'Tis from the Bible," Jared said. "The next part says, *The heart of her husband doth safely trust in her, so that he shall have no need of spoil,* but there was not enough room for me to carve that."

Trust? There had been naught but mistrust between them.

Clutching it to her chest, she blinked at him. "You carved this for me?"

"Aye." He tugged his goatee. A gesture of nervousness? Was he afraid that she would reject the gift?

"It's . . . lovely." She slid it onto her wrist, spinning the wood round and round.

"It's not a ruby."

She ran her fingers over the wood. "It's the eye from your dragon staff!"

"Aye." The edge of vulnerability had crept into his voice again. His shoulders stiffened.

She touched his cheek, her fingers brushing against his goatee. Her heart felt as though it would burst in her chest. Men gave her jewels—diamonds, emeralds, and rubies. But no one had ever taken the time, had the patience, to make her something from his own hand.

"An amicable marriage would be nice," she said at last. But the words were inadequate. He left her breathless.

"If you will let me, I can give you pleasure to erase the memory of our wedding night," he offered. "I would like to have a real marriage."

Warmth spread through her. Her body felt tight as a bowman's string. "Are you so arrogant in your skills as a lover?"

He laughed. Laughed? "Skill with one woman in bed proves little on the next." He traced his fingers down her arm. "Some women might find this pleasurable but some might not."

Gooseflesh popped on her skin.

"Or perhaps it could be that you like this better." He began kneading her arm from her shoulder to her wrist.

Little sparkles of delight followed his fingers.

"Or mayhap this." Taking her hand in his, he encircled each of her fingers one by one from base to tip in a spiraling motion. The soft caress was so luxurious and unexpected that, unbidden, a mewl escaped her lips.

He smiled, and his eyes lit with interest. "So this then," he said, retracing the path his fingers had taken.

Tingling filtered through her body and she stared at their intertwined fingers. In sharp contrast to hers, his hands were wide and tanned with long, blunt fingers. Rough calluses on the palms and tips proved that, unlike herself, he had done manual labor.

She tried to recall how he had flipped her on her

stomach, dragged her to her knees, and prodded her roughly with his member, but the memory had faded. If she had not experienced it, she would not have even thought that such violence was possible for this impossibly patient man.

Over and over again his fingers traced up and down hers. Slowly. As if they had all the time in the world. As if there were no conflicts between them. As if Irma had not sent a desperate message.

For an instant, she wished it could truly be thus between them—that it was indeed possible for them to have an amicable relationship.

Not letting go of her hand, he sank back onto the mattress, a pillow propping up his head. "When you are ready, I would like you to climb atop me."

Climb atop him?

Her eyes widened.

"I do not wish to climb atop you!" But the idea bounced around in her mind. What would it be like to take rather than be taken? She had enjoyed exploring his body.

He laughed gently and drew her hand to his mouth and kissed her fingers. "When you are ready. I recall you enjoyed exploring my body very much when I was tied to the bed."

Her cheeks heated that she had just been thinking of the same thing.

"I recall how you had been wet when I touched you."

She wanted to jump from atop the bed and crawl beneath it.

"Mayhap first you could show me the techniques that Irma taught you concerning the seduction of men."

She nearly choked. Without thinking, she placed her hand across his mouth to silence him.

He grinned. Grinned?

"You are smiling!" she accused.

"Is holding a man's mouth shut part of the seduction plan?" he rumbled against her palm.

She snatched her hand back. "Of course not."

His wide shoulders quaked.

"You find this humorous?"

"Of a truth," he said, smiling unrepentantly. "Tying men to the bed, holding their mouths shut with your hands—perfect seduction technique, I think."

Her brows drew together. "You're teasing me."

"Come, Gwyneth, admit it . . . I'm not completely an ogre."

"Well." She cocked her head to one side. "Not *completely,* perhaps."

"So about those seduction techniques . . ."

Somehow the tension in the room had dissipated. Her shoulders relaxed and a tendril of excitement swirled into her belly.

Bending down, she kissed his neck. "Do you like this?" She kissed his cheek. "Or this?" she asked, echoing his earlier words.

Sparks blazed in his green eyes, igniting an echoing fire inside her core.

Reaching up, she ran her fingers into his hair. The place on his scalp where she had stitched him after the wedding snagged her palm. He winced.

Carefully, she inspected the wound, nearly completely healed. "Does it hurt?"

"You could kiss it," he whispered.

She brushed her lips against his scalp, inhaling the musky scent of his skin. He was delicious. Intoxicating.

She gazed down at his long body. Scars crisscrossed his legs including a long, bumpy one that ran from his groin to his knee.

"What happened?" She ran her finger down its length.

He inhaled. "A story for another time. Come, girl, I want you."

Closing her eyes, she swung her leg over his body so that she straddled him. How magnificent to be riding atop a man!

She gazed down at him through lowered lashes. His manroot jutted into the air. Lightly, she ran the tip of her finger over it. A hiss of breath sounded from his parted lips. Unable to stop herself, she laughed, enjoying having him at her command.

"Careful, girl."

But the warning in his voice did not stop her. Wrapping her palm around his member, she lifted on her knees and guided it toward her quim.

"Wait." Jared stuck two fingers in his mouth, then pressed them between her thighs.

Gwyneth shivered and gasped. He made small, gentle circles around the folds of her sex. A trickle of sweat ran down her spine and her thighs quivered. Arching her back, she surrendered to sensation, to the feel of his fingers. Tension built inside her core.

"I want—"

He lifted his hips and guided himself inside her.

Startled, she gazed down at where their bodies were connected, at where his cock impaled her. Desire flooded her limbs.

Slowly she began to rock back and forth. Back and

forth. She kneaded his shoulders and sank down
upon him, then lifted and bounced up and down.
Amazingly marvelous. Every shift of her body produced a new sensation and she wanted to explore
them all. Fast, slow, back and forth, up and down.

Pressure built inside her quim. She closed her eyes,
curled her toes—wanting, longing for something she
did not understand. "Jared," she whispered as the
sensation of eruption burst inside her. She shivered
and collapsed atop him, feeling shattered.

His eyes were closed and his hands fisted in the
bedsheet. His hips thrust upward, pushing his
manroot deep inside her. He cried out and she
caught the sound in her mouth and pressed her
tongue inside to tangle with his. She wanted him.
All of him.

Gwyneth lay awake for long, languid hours feign-
ing sleep. Moisture seeped between her legs and she
felt pleasure. Pure pleasure.

His arm wrapped around her waist and a calm
peace settled over them, as if their spirits had somehow melded together. The bracelet on her wrist
made her smile as she spun it round and round.

Her price is far above rubies. No one had ever thought
of her as being more precious than rubies. And he'd
given her the red rock from the dragon's eye.

She wanted to belong to him forever.

When she was assured that he slept, she lifted up
slightly. She did not wish to leave the comfort of
Jared's arms, but she was determined to see about
Irma. She had made friends with Aeliana so she would

be able to leave without arousing the bird. After what had happened between them, if Jared awoke and she was gone, he would not suspect.

Assured by this thought, she quietly swung her legs over the side of the bed.

Chapter 26

A damp, cold cloak woven of fog and midnight bore down on Gwyneth's shoulders as she made her way toward The Bald Cock.

Sneaking away from the keep had been easier than she'd expected but her heart still pounded. Aeliana hadn't even ruffled her feathers when she left and true to form, Jared slept like the dead.

In her hand, she clutched a short knife she'd taken from the kitchen.

Swirls of white mist floated in the inky darkness as if ghoulish forms from the spirit world guided her way down the path into the city. She scurried from tree to bush to shrub, guided by the sparse rays coming from the quarter moon.

Her thoughts went to how Jared's hands had felt on her skin just hours ago, how his manhood had felt buried inside her, how his legs had been entangled, bare buttocks on display, in the linens as she had stolen from the solar and set about on this mission. What would he do if he awoke and found her missing from the keep?

The newfound peace betwixt them would be shattered.

Mentally, she shook herself; she would concern herself with Jared later. She twisted the bracelet on her wrist. *Her price is far above rubies.*

Every few steps, she looked back over her shoulder and gazed this way and that. Naught but huts, shop buildings, empty wagons, and a few sleeping chickens. And the creepy feeling that someone, something was out there. Watching her.

The houses grew closer and closer together, some of them made of wood and stone, others constructed of mere sticks or even hay. Two chemises hung on a line, blowing like eerie ghosts. The road changed from dirt to cobble.

She breathed a hearty sigh of relief as she pushed open the back door of the brothel and stepped inside a short while later. The usual smells of sweat, grease, and copulation hung heavy in the air. Putting her hand to her nose, she took a few steps into the sloppy kitchen.

The door leading to the main hall of the whorehouse swung open with a loud bang and Irma rushed through. Her hair, always frizzy, looked even more frazzled than usual. Her chest heaved and her eyes looked wild. Red stains marred her cheeks.

"Irma!" Gwyneth ran to her friend and embraced her. Clammy sweat poured through her dress. "What is wrong?"

"M-m-my daughter! They have taken her." Irma quivered as if an icy wind blew through her.

"Kiera?" Coldness seeped into Gwyneth's bones.

"A-a-aye."

Gwyneth hugged Irma tightly, her alarm growing. Ne'er had she seen Irma so shaken.

"Taken her where?"

"The magistrate came. There was something about stolen buttons and then they took 'er to the prison." Tears leaked off Irma's chin.

Buttons? The ones Kiera had given her when Jared and she were together?

Gwyneth willed her hands to not tremble.

"T-the boat leaves tonight!" Irma was panting hard, panicked. "They will not let me 'ave 'er. I do not know what to do. I thought you 'ad abandoned me."

"Oh, Irma!" Guilt rose like bile in her throat. "I could never abandon you. Jared would not allow me to leave his side."

Kohl blended with tears. Black smears streamed down Irma's cheeks.

Gwyneth steered her to the tankards and poured watery ale into one. She did not have time to worry over her own emotions. "Drink. Then talk. We will get Kiera free." Somehow.

"Oh, Gwyneth," Irma wailed, "what am I to do? I do not 'ave the coin to see 'er released. They are demanding a 'igh ransom. I know not why."

Worry furrowed Gwyneth's brow. She had no coins and she could not return to the keep. "We need only to focus on a plan," she said more calmly than she felt.

Irma dug into her bosom and pulled out a small, ragged pouch. "Take this, Gwyneth. I've been working as 'ard on me back as I can."

Sickness washed up inside Gwyneth's throat. "Kiera said you had a fever."

"I gots no time for fevers. I gots to get me daughter from the prison."

"Heavens." Gwyneth took the pouch with trembling fingers. The two pearl buttons on her sleeves twinkled. "Get me a knife and help me cut these off. Mayhap it will be enough to bribe the guard if I fancy myself up and distract him." She yanked her mother's sapphire ring from her hand. "I'll offer this as well. I need to borrow one of your gowns."

She fidgeted with the wooden bracelet, glad that it was made of wood and common rocks. She did not think she could bear to part with it.

They rushed to Irma's bedchamber. Gwyneth changed garments and Irma quickly painted Gwyneth's face with lead powder and kohl. She added a patch under her eye.

A knock sounded and one of the wenches opened the door a crack. "That man who comes for a bath is asking for you, Irma."

Irma's rouged lips rounded into a silent "oh."

Through the crack in the door, Gwyneth saw Jared standing in the midst of the brothel, staff in hand. Shock filtered through her body and for a moment she was frozen and unable to move. "Heavens, Irma! Jared's here."

Panic lurched into her throat as she frantically cast her gaze around the room, taking in the narrow bed, a chair, a table, a chest, and a small window. "I think he might have seen me. What should I do?"

Irma raced to the door and threw the bolt. "You must go. Quickly!"

"How?" Gwyneth rushed to the window, scrambled onto the chair, and gazed down into the mud- and garbage-splattered alleyway.

Her heart dropped into her stomach. There was a small ledge outside and then from there it was a long ways to the ground. "I can't jump. 'Tis too far."

"The bedsheets! Grab the bedsheets!"

Gwyneth jumped off the chair and hurried to the bed, pulling away the sheets. Yellowish stains dotted the linen, some still fresh. Bile rose in her throat. Somehow she had to straighten the matter with Kiera and then come back for Irma. Her friend could not remain a harlot for life.

Pounding sounded on the door. Mercy!

"Gwyneth!" Jared bellowed. His voice sounded like thunder—something that came from an angry pagan god rather than a mere man. "I know you are in there!"

She tied the sheet clumsily around the table's leg and threw it out the window.

The pounding on the door increased. The shutters on the window rattled.

"Gwyneth!"

Taking a deep breath, she pushed through the opening and shimmied her way down. She cringed when her hand touched something wet and sticky on the sheet.

A rip and the linen tore loose. She landed with a hard *thunk*. "Ooof."

Ignoring the pain in her right leg, she scrambled to her feet and took off running, her slippers slapping against the cobblestones.

She cut through an alleyway.

"Wife!" She heard Jared's voice behind her. "Face your comeuppance!" He must have kicked through Irma's door and was yelling for her out the window. She pumped her legs harder. If he caught her, no doubt he'd haul her straight to the authorities. Have her tried as a witch. He would never forgive her for tricking him as she had done.

When she reached the dock near the prison, she paused and leaned against a dirty wall, clutching her chest. The realization that she was fully and completely alone pulled at her as she tried to fathom what to do next.

Get Kiera.

Find some way to explain things to Jared.

A man wearing a filthy cloak lurched down the alleyway. He carried a tankard of ale.

Straightening, she trotted in the other direction.

"Hey, woman! Hey, woman!" The man stumbled toward her. "'ow much for a quick tup in the bum?"

Gwyneth shuddered and silently vowed to go to Mass every day for a year if God would see her through this night.

The prison was an ugly, squat building with no decoration to lighten its dreary walls. It was made of crumbling brick. Its tiny windows were like the eyes of a giant squatting spider dredged up from hell itself. The eerie feeling of evil and death always threatened to choke her as she looked up at it.

Tamping down her unease, she made her way to the front and tugged at her tresses to better arrange them.

Was the kohl that Irma had applied running down her face?

She gave herself a good shake. She was here. She had done this many times afore. She could do it again. She did not have time to waste.

Holy Mother, she muttered as she always did when

she rounded this corner of the building, *I ask for your blessing.*

Taking a breath, she composed herself and stuck out her bosom. The harlot's garment revealed more than any of her kirtles or even her houppelandes. One more breath upward and her nipples might pop free. The book Jared had given her was tucked into her bodice. Its spine could be seen when she glanced downward. He might hate her, but the small book gave her comfort. It seemed normal. An anchor. As if nothing had changed and this exchange tonight would be routine.

She pulled out the pouch that contained her ring, the few gold coins Irma had given her, and the buttons they had cut from her sleeves.

The guard with the bull neck and one earlobe longer than the other stood in the darkened doorway. She said a silent prayer of thanks. He had been friendly with her the last time.

His eyes widened as she approached. "Lady Gwyneth."

She smiled and ran her hand over her hair.

His gaze went to her revealing clothing. Nay, to her cleavage.

She set her jaw so that she wouldn't grimace. Blinking, she tossed her hair over one eye in a gesture she knew most men responded to.

He licked his lips.

'Twas always thus. Men who leered. Men who stumbled over their feet. Men who wanted to tup her. Of a truth, over the past days when she had been so linked at Jared's side, the reprieve from such attention had been a relief. His presence kept them all at bay.

"You have a girl here. Brown eyes. Curly hair. Her name is Kiera."

His gaze snapped back to her face, taking in her long locks and overdone eyes. She itched to wad her hair into a simple bun, but she forced her hands to remain at her sides.

Do not show fear. Do not show fear.

She twisted her fingers around one strand of hair, playing with it coyly, then proffered her bribe.

He palmed the jewels and coins in an easy stroke.

Victory! Thank God.

"This way."

The scent of dirty hay and rat piss lingered acidly in the air as she followed him down the hallway. The keys hanging from a heavy ring on his belt jangled as he swaggered down the narrow aisle. He was a slope-foreheaded brute with keen eyes and a thick stomach. 'Twas doubtful that he had proper authority to release the girl. But no matter. A woman called out to her, but she did not turn.

Get Kiera and get out. The stench worsened as they moved into the bowels of the prison. She longed for her handkerchief and she took short, quick breaths to keep from vomiting. The guard's torch made eerie shadows on the slime dripping from the walls.

Her stomach churned.

Prisoners on either side of the narrow, dim walkway held grime-crusted fingers out to her, wafting even more of the stench her direction. If only she had thought to bring a sprig of lavender!

"Hey, lady! Hey, lady!" one called in a harsh voice. Their voices blended as a roar, and she caught only bits and snippets of what they were saying: "Help us, lady—We don't belong here—I'm not supposed to be in here—It was a mistake—I can pay you well—If you'll just help me—Get a note to my brother—to my father—Help me—please—please, lady, please . . ."

She clutched her chest.

Kiera was too young, too innocent to be in a hell-hole such as this.

Forcing herself to ignore the pleas of the women, to ignore the smell and filth, Gwyneth gazed forward and trudged behind the guard.

"This one, lady." The guard stopped, pointed to a pitch-black cell to the left, and unlatched the door. It swung outward with a creak.

The stench was even worse inside the cell, that of decay and death. Gwyneth held her nose, willing her stomach not to lurch. Fleas hopped up her slippers, nibbling her ankles as she slipped inside. She squinted into the darkness.

The guard lifted his torch.

Kiera huddled in the corner, covered with a shabby, rat-bitten blanket. Muck covered her from head to toe and the lower half of her skirt had been ripped away in one section as if perhaps she'd tried to fend off an attacker. Purple bruises laced her arms and the section of her exposed calf.

Elizabeth, the mute dark-haired child, lay on the ground next to her, sprawled beside the wall. Her straight black hair fanned across the dirty floor, its ends in Kiera's lap as if the two children had hugged each other to sleep.

Gwyneth's stomach fell. "Oh, mercy."

The two girls did not move.

Her vision blurred as she knelt. "Kiera? Elizabeth?"

Kiera's eyes fluttered open, sending a ray of hope shooting through Gwyneth.

The guard cleared his throat. "Time is short."

Desperation overtook Gwyneth, and she shook her harder. "You must awaken. Arise. Come with me." She struggled to lift the girl into her arms.

Kiera moaned and her eyes rolled back into her head.

"We have to get you out of here." She shooed away a rat that ventured out of the mildewed hay. Using all her strength, Gwyneth straightened, holding the child.

Elizabeth shuttered awake. She touched the hem of Gwyneth's skirt and looked up at her with pleading green eyes.

"You comin' or not, lady?" The guard shifted back and forth on his stubby legs, squishing the rotting hay that was strewn around on the floor.

"You could help me," Gwyneth snapped. The muck under her slippers made her footing precarious.

He shrugged and turned on his heel. "Best you hurry, 'ere the door slam shut on both of ye."

Elizabeth tugged Gwyneth's skirt again.

Mercy. Reaching down, Gwyneth grasped Elizabeth by the hand and lifted her to her feet. "I'm taking this one too," she said with a glare at the guard.

"Ye did *not* pay for that one."

Gwyneth's feet slid this way and that on the grimy floor, scattering hay, fleas, and vermin as she sought to rise. Rats squeaked and scurried into the next cell.

With a heave, Gwyneth got Kiera's arm up over her shoulder and kept hold of Elizabeth's hand. She nearly gagged at the stench coming off of the girl's body. Oozing red sores covered her face. Her fingers looked pale and her body, almost skeleton-like. But her grip was surprisingly strong, giving Gwyneth the edge of hope she needed to keep pushing, to keep striving, to keep walking.

Heart pounding, Gwyneth trudged forward carrying Kiera and holding Elizabeth's hand.

"Ye didn't pay for that one, lady," the guard said again.

"Step aside." She panted with exertion, knees buckling, but she latched on tightly to both children. She would get them out of this hellhole if it were the last thing on earth that she did.

The guard wiggled the iron door back and forth as if considering. It let out a menacing creak.

Kiera moaned and Elizabeth clutched Gwyneth's hand in a death grip.

"I will bring more coin next time. Step aside."

He gave her a nonrepentant grin but let them pass. The louse. The useless imbecile. Once profitability was restored on her lands and she had more power and influence, she'd somehow have position taken. She could speak with those in charge, write demands. For now she needed to get the girls to safety and think of some way to explain it all to Jared.

Her legs ached as she half carried, half dragged the two girls out of the cell.

A few moments later, the guard showed them out through a back door of the prison and they found themselves in dawning sunlight. Pink and orange tinged the sky and the scent of murky water stung Gwyneth's nostrils. They were near the river—where, no doubt, ships hauled many of the prison's inhabitants to their new lives.

They made their way out into the city's cobbled streets. Her heart sank with every step. Kiera kept slipping, her eyes and head rolling back in pain. Elizabeth's bare feet sloshed in puddles of garbage.

The long walk to the prison had been taxing and Gwyneth's legs, shoulders, and back already shook from trying to hold Kiera. With every step the girl seemed to become more and more limp.

They needed a physician. *A priest,* whispered a dark voice. Nay. Somehow they would make it. They had to.

"Child, I'm so sorry. I should have been here sooner." A curse on Jared for being so hardheaded.

Dawn bounced off the cobblestones and spread dull light over the nearly deserted town. Their breath made little puffs of white clouds that misted around them as they walked. Dampness hung in the air and the fog, thinner than before, swirled around their legs.

Here and there a few of the townsfolk stirred. Candles flickered. Shuffling could be heard inside the huts and buildings.

At that moment a man barreled out of the mist from an alleyway. His hand shot out and latched onto her arm in a tight, painful grip. She screamed, losing her hold on Kiera.

Chapter 27

The fingers squeezed Gwyneth's arm and pulled her away from Kiera, who went sliding downward, unable to support herself. She grasped for her in a desperate bid as their attacker came fully out into the street. Elizabeth scrambled backward.

The jailor! He stared at them with a scowl, his piggish eyes overly bright. "Not one word, woman. You have something I want."

Gwyneth whirled on him, and stood up to her full height. "You have your payment," she said, "begone with you."

"Ye did not pay for the other child."

He pulled her tight against himself, his stench—that of unchecked lust and evil—eclipsed Kiera's unwashed one.

In a sudden burst of strength, Kiera pulled at the arm latched onto Gwyneth's. "Let Lady Gwyn go!"

He backhanded her and she crashed to the cobblestones. The wound on her cheek opened and blood squirted onto her filthy dress.

Gwyneth screamed. She tried to knee him in the groin and break free.

The man latched his hand even tighter around Gwyneth and moved his hips from side to side, protecting his crotch from her blows. "Peace, lady. 'Twill only take a minute."

Elizabeth ran at the man and bit him on the thigh. "Ouch!"

Picking her up, he threw her across the alleyway. Garbage scattered as she hit the ground.

"Elizabeth!"

He grinned.

Dear God.

"You animal!"

Elizabeth scrambled over to Kiera and hugged her.

Hands fisted, Gwyneth glared at their attacker. "Leave them alone."

"Gold. Give me gold."

Mercy. If she had had a trunk full, she would have gladly handed it over. "I gave you what I had."

"Lying bitch! I've seen you. I know who you are." He leaned in closer to her. She nearly gagged.

"Take it out in flesh," a voice came from a mangy-looking rat lying in a cesspool in the alley. "I ain' had no entertainment like this in nigh a decade."

Bile rose in her throat.

Kiera squirmed. Blood streaked from her nose and dripped off her chin.

Gwyneth reached for her, to yank them all to safety, but the man grabbed her by the arms. She screamed and kicked.

He began scrunching up her skirt.

At that moment, a dark figure rounded the corner of the alleyway—another torturer set on watching her humiliation. He looked like a specter or perhaps even a demon conjured from hell. She shuddered. Had her prayers begun to work in the reverse these days?

"Let. Her. Go."

Jared! Her heart leapt at the sound of Jared's deep voice. He carried his staff so it glinted in the moonlight. His eyes shone with intensity, but for once, she was grateful for the vengeful gleam she saw in them. He looked like a savior and for a moment she wanted to run to him, crying, grateful that he had come to save them.

Seeing him gave her the strength to yank free from the beast holding her arm. Quickly, she scooted away, rushed to the two girls, and knelt beside them.

The blood from Kiera's nose smudged across Gwyneth's bodice as she tried to lift her. The girl's grip was weaker and lacked the fortitude that it had when they were back at the jail. Elizabeth grunted and tried to help.

The guard eyed Jared's staff and laughed. He pulled a saw-bladed knife from inside his tunic.

"Nay!" gasped Gwyneth.

With a lunge, Jared leapt forward, heedless, reckless, racing straight for the bull-like jailor.

The fleeting image of a striking cobra passed through her mind as if Jared was purely animal, primal—not something born of man or civilization.

He let out a primal sound as his staff connected with the jailor's bull-like neck. The man fell with a squelchy thunk.

The jailor's eyes widened. He had not even had a chance to fully grip the hilt of his own knife. The man jumped to his feet and tossed a dark look at Gwyneth. "You will pay for this, woman." He whirled on his heels and ran. His footsteps rang on the cobblestones and faded.

Clutching her chest, Gwyneth turned to Jared.

Not a trace of sweat beaded his brow. His chest rose and fell in even, unlabored breaths. As if he was not affected at all.

"Are you well?"

She shivered.

"We have to go before the night watchmen or the authorities find us," Jared said, his voice low and undisturbed. As if 'twas common for him to fight with a man afore breaking his fast.

When she didn't move or speak, he bent and touched her arm. "Can you rise?"

Her body felt as though someone had filled it from toe to neck with granite. Elizabeth wound her skinny body in Gwyneth's skirt.

Kiera made a strangled noise. Her mouth moved up and down and she gasped for breath. A deep gurgling sound issued from her throat.

"Kiera?"

The child's eyes rolled back.

Terror slipped through Gywneth's soul. "Kiera? Kiera!"

The girl gurgled again and her hand slipped into the cesspool floor of the alleyway.

Dead.

"Nay!" Gwyneth gasped, gathering her young friend into her arms. "Nay!"

A shallow breath came from Kiera's lips. Not dead then.

Gwyneth shook Kiera's body, trying to rouse her. "Wake up, Kiera! Wake up!"

Jared knelt beside her.

Clutching the girl, Gwyneth rocked back and forth.

Jared ripped a strip from the hem of his tunic. He swabbed blood from Kiera's face and arms and inspected her carefully.

"She needs to be stitched," he said, gently taking the girl into his arms. "Come, Gwyneth. We must leave." He glanced back at the opening of the alleyway. "If the townsfolk catch us here, we'll be charged with illegal jailbreak."

At that moment, a window creaked open above them. Two maids chattered, complaining about the morning's work.

Jared yanked Gwyneth and Elizabeth to his side, pressing them against the wall so that they would be out of sight of whoever was above.

With a heave, the contents of a chamber pot were launched into the alley. The filth landed in the already disgusting puddles and splashed over them.

Gwyneth's stomach lurched, this onslaught being the final straw in the morning's events. With a gag, her stomach launched into a series of dry heaves.

"Who be there?" The maid in the upper window stuck farther out the window, looking downward, her head swiveling back and forth.

Jared pushed them into the shadows. His fresh, musky scent almost eclipsed the filth and stench. She quivered in his arms, too weak to resist hanging onto the strength that he offered. She covered her mouth to hold herself back from making gagging noises, but her stomach wouldn't stop heaving.

"Come on," Jared whispered into her hair. With a tug, he half led, half carried her down the dank alleyway away from the voices above.

Elizabeth followed. He smoothed Kiera's hair down and cradled her against his chest. "Let's get home."

Gwyneth stumbled forward, ignoring the aching, throbbing agony in her legs. Her knees and thighs shook with effort, but she willed them to hold up her body. Quietly, she fell into step with him and headed back toward the keep as if following him was the most natural thing in the world to do.

Chapter 28

They had saved Kiera and Elizabeth! Despite it all, they had made it home safely. With patient gentleness, Jared washed the child's limbs and held her still as Gwyneth sewed up the worst of the girl's wounds. Elizabeth watched from a chair in the corner. She had bathed and was wearing a fresh dress. She chewed on the damp ends of her straight, dark hair and gazed around the chamber with her intelligent moss green eyes.

Gwyneth soothed the sleeping girl's curls off her face and kissed her forehead, vowing to go straight to the chapel and offer prayers of gratitude.

In the past, she had had nowhere to take children except to the brothel, but now she had her lands. The two girls would grow up with tutors, with gowns. They would not be raised as whores or street orphans.

She rose, wanting to hug Jared, wanting to give him thanks for saving them, for carrying the child here. She slid her hand into his. "Oh, Jared, how can I ever—"

Controlled fury glowed in his eyes, stopping her sentence in midstream.

His fingers squeezed hers. "We go to the bedchamber." His tight jaw and the set of his shoulders told her that he fully expected her to dislike what he was about to do. He whirled, dragging her with him.

"What are you doing?"

He didn't answer.

They wended the steep spiral stairs that led to the master's solar, startling a guard on the way who leapt to his feet and stood at attention.

She stumbled on the stones as she tried to keep up with her husband's quick pace.

"Slow down!" she hissed, but he walked faster. He moved with crisp determination rather than his usual fluid grace.

"Shush, wife."

Her legs still ached from the long walk to the prison and the sprint away from it. "I cannot keep up with you," she panted.

His hand squeezed hers in a firm, almost painful grip. "Keep silent. I am barely holding on to my control without you provoking me."

The feel of the brank bit her memory, making the taste of metal well up in her mouth.

He marched her the rest of the way to their chamber. Trepidation churned in her stomach. Did he plan to tup her as he had before? To beat her? To pack her belongings and send her to a nunnery?

They passed another guard. She gave him a pleading look but he made no move to interfere. Had Jared established himself here so quickly?

She pulled against him to yank her hand free and

try to run. She might be able to make it to the back
entrance of the keep.

The door to their chamber slammed shut with a
loud crash. The room spun as he whirled her around.
She crashed against his chest and took a step back.

"Sit," he commanded, indicating the stool by her
lady's dressing table.

She sat.

"I can expla—" she started, but closed her mouth
when he raised a brow and stalked toward the scold's
bridle that sat on a small table near the bed.

Coldness trickled over her.

He picked up the metal mask, and turned it over
and over in his palms. She remembered the crowd
staring at her, taunting her as she had been forced to
wear it. A shudder quaked through her. She could
think of naught much worse than him plopping it
upon her head and parading her through the streets.
Gwyneth of Windrose, the beauty of the land, the re-
bellious uppity wife led about in disgrace. Some
would cheer the thought of seeing her so humbled.
The Ashworth sisters would likely carry the tale all
the way to London.

Jared sat the brank on the table with a clunk that
made her jump in her chair. He crossed the room,
dug through his supplies, and pulled out a knife and
a leather strop.

Merciful heavens. Did he plan to cut her throat?
She glanced at the door, willing it to open so that
she could run. She tensed her thighs and slid herself
forward on the dressing stool.

"You cannot make it to the door in time."

She sank back down, but anger cut through her
fear. "What are you doing?" she demanded.

"You lied to me. You seduced me. You betrayed me. You manipulated me." The blade swooshed against the leather strop, punctuating every sentence.

The sound grated on her nerves. "And for that you plan to kill me?"

"Nay."

She stared from the knife in his hand to his face and back again.

Her hands twisted into her skirt, wrinkling the fabric.

A dark shadow crossed over his cheeks and he stalked over until he stood behind her. Alarm ran up her spine and she glanced again toward the door. Heat from his thighs, from his body, wafted off of him. Leaning forward, he set the knife on the dressing table in a slow, deliberate show.

She gazed down at the shiny blade, wondering if she should attempt to pick it up. Was this some test?

His hands grazed the tops of her shoulders. There was no pressure on them, yet the weight felt as though an entire mountain pressed down on her body. A shiver ran through her. He seemed to be doing everything possible to set her on edge. And it was working.

"Do you want to reach for it?" he said very calmly.

She weighed her words carefully. "You saved Kiera's life today. I have no desire to harm you."

"Good."

Her brow furrowed and she turned her face toward him, trying to fathom what he was doing.

His jaw was set, determined. "You have spent your life knowing how to charm men. I did not realize what you got from your relationship with Irma until I saw you at the jail."

She grimaced.

"Irma taught you how to apply kohl to your eyes as you did tonight—to be attractive to men such as the jailor so they will allow you to bribe them with a blink of your eye."

It occurred to her that he was jealous.

"I saw you toss your hair, use it as a warrior would use a weapon."

"I did no—" The words died on her lips. It was true. She'd flipped it around for the jailor.

"But you did."

More than his words, his tone gave her pause. The solid strength, sense of resolve and determination frightened her. A flock of butterflies flittered in her belly.

She shivered as his hand touched her neck and wondered what she should do: run, stay, resist, submit?

He ran his fingers through her hair, his palms sliding up the scalp causing heat to form and pool through her body. "Your hair is beautiful, Gwyneth."

"Th-thank you," she said, but it did not sound like a compliment at all.

"The bards sing about it."

She felt his hand draw the mass upward and then fist in one side. A few strands pulled against her scalp.

"It's silky, seductive, tantalizing. I have enjoyed brushing it and braiding it each night for you. I took a piece when I gave you the book. Did you ever know?"

"Nay."

Long, tense moments passed. Apprehension tightened across her shoulders. His silence made her more nervous than any lecture had done. What sort of man stole a woman's hair?

He released her so suddenly that her entire body

jerked. He crossed the room in two strides and sat on the edge of the bed.

"Come and kneel in front of me. I intend for you never to be able to use your hair as a weapon again. Bring me the knife."

She gasped. "You plan to cut my hair?"

"Aye."

"This is a punishment?"

"Nay, this is what I must do to keep you safe. You cannot continue to put yourself in danger by leaving the keep in the middle of the night."

Anger flashed inside her. "If you would have given me leave to go during the day, I would have been perfectly safe. I've been there many times!"

"Men stare at you, want you. You are a bloody menace to yourself and others."

"I have been wearing plain kirtles and a headscarf."

"You were not wearing such at the jail."

"I do *not* want my hair cut."

"Nevertheless, bring me the knife."

The blade glinted on the dressing table. If he merely wished to cut her hair, he could easily have held her down and done so. But no. 'Twas not her hair he wanted, but her submission.

"You manipulated me with your kiss, fooling me into allowing you to talk so that you could ask questions about Aeliana. You learned to soothe her for the purpose of escaping while I slept. You seduced me last night to win my trust."

She licked her lips. All those things were true.

"I needed to rescue Kiera."

"—who is a thief—"

"—who is a little girl who would have been sold as a slave for a man's pleasure."

"Is that what happens to those women?"

She let out a breath and her shoulders slumped. "The pretty ones, the young ones are sold as slaves. Usually they are never heard of again, but every now and again one returns." Gwyneth closed her eyes, not wanting to think of the atrocities she'd seen, of the bruised bodies and broken spirits.

"Go on."

"The returned ones never lose the haunted look in their eyes. One girl, her name was Madeline, had cuts and scars striped up and down her limbs. On her belly were burn marks where they had held her down and branded her. Her nipples had been burned off—"

Jared's brow furrowed. "How often do you go to the prison?"

"The ship leaves every couple of months. I go every week to rescue who I can. Save for my mother's ring, which I gave away tonight, I have sold all of my jewelry. I worked each night to embroider sleeves and trim which Brother Giffard sold for me."

"The monk?"

"He travels into London frequently."

"I see." Jared stroked his goatee. "How do you learn about the women who are to be sold?"

"Through Irma. She keeps track. We have wanted for a long time to make a shelter for them here, but neither my father nor Montgomery would allow me to control my own dower lands."

"And that is why you kidnapped me?"

She nodded. What a disaster the marriage had been. "I was desperate. 'Twas a mad idea, but we thought you would be satisfied with a small amount of gold."

"I wasn't."

Her shoulders slumped. "I am truly sorry, Jared. I had not intended for it to be complicated for you."

"I forbid you from manipulating men to do your bidding anymore with your beauty."

Sighing, she picked up the knife and toyed with it. "What other choice do women have? We cannot fight like a man."

"I will go with you next time."

Her gaze snapped to his. "You will?"

"Yes."

Gwyneth looked at him, unable to speak. He would actually go with her?

"You speak truth?"

"I give my word on it."

Silence reined in the room. As if time had stopped. She toyed with the ends of her hair.

Of all things, she had not expected Jared to give over to her ideas about rescuing women. She searched his face. "Why?"

But in her heart, she already knew why. He took care of people—that is why he was here: to get gold for his family, only he'd been caught up in taking care of her people as well.

Dear God.

She loved him.

The thought hit her like a quarry had fallen atop her.

She loved him; her hair meant nothing to her. Oft it was more of a burden than a pleasure—especially when the minstrels sang of it or men acted like fools. If Irma would have let her, she would have cut the mass years ago.

Rising as gracefully as she could, she held the knife and walked to him. Silently, she handed him the blade and sank to her knees in front of him with her back turned the same as she did when he braided it. If he went with her, she had no use whatsoever for her long locks or any other ornamentation. She would be rid of the bards singing songs to her hair and of having to preen and flirt with men to get her way. And if this appeased him of his anger, 'twas an easy sacrifice.

She grasped the mass in her hand and held it up, an offering, gladly given in exchange for his presence at the prison. "Cut it."

His hands buried in her hair, tilting her head back so that it rested on his muscular thighs. She grimaced, expecting him to start hacking away.

Doubt crept into her mind. What if he did not go with her? Perhaps she had given in to Jared too easily. What would she look like bald?

She squeezed her eyes shut but did not attempt to move away.

He laid the knife down on the bed and divided her hair into sections. She felt it tug at her scalp and realized he had gathered it into a ponytail and was braiding it into a long plait just as he had done every evening.

She wondered at his reasoning and twisted to glance at him. He looked both pensive and determined, the edges of his mustache even more turned down than usual.

At once, she felt the edge of the knife against her neck and then a tug.

A quiet *whomp* sounded as he tossed the plait to the floor beside her. It looked like a thick, dead snake. She stared down at it, wondering at how such an item had made men so possessed that they sang songs about her.

Her neck felt oddly naked and vulnerable, and she reached her hand up to feel it. The ends of her newly cut hair, blunt and bristly, brushed against the back of her hand. It had been cut off at her nape.

He pushed her head back so that it rested atop his knees. She bit her lower lip, wondering what it was that he wished to do with her. Did he plan to cut more? To shave the rest as if she were a sheep?

Slowly he began massaging her temples, his fingers splaying across her temples and ears. He took hold of her earlobes between his thumb and forefinger and began to rub in the slowest of gestures.

Her eyelids fluttered closed. Warmth flushed over her skin. A line of heat ran from her forehead to her toes. Her toes curled.

For an instant, she wished she had strength to resist him. He had a way of plowing through her defenses, leaving her feeling naked and vulnerable like no other man had ever done.

She reached upward, tugging at her shortened locks self-consciously.

She should get ready for bed, straighten out the drawers in her dressing table, or clean cobwebs from the chamber's corners.

"Surrender." At first she thought the whispered command was only in her mind, but she felt the bristle of his beard against her cheek, felt his breath slide silkily over her skin.

A whimper escaped her throat.

His hands trailed down her neck to her newly exposed nape. She should get up, fling his hands away, tell him he had taken her hair already, he would not steal her dignity as well.

But she wanted, longed for, craved his touch. Of its own accord, her head leaned into him, pushing herself farther into his arms rather than pushing him away. With a sigh, she surrendered. She was his and he was hers.

Heat stirred deep in her core, and the area betwixt her legs tingled. She pressed her thighs together, trying to ease the tension, trying to bring a measure of peace to the craving she experienced.

"I want you." The words were spoken with husky heat, his green eyes smoldering.

"I—"

His lips claimed hers.

Chapter 29

Amazement washed over Jared like a flood. She'd given him her hair! Just like that. It was the last thing on earth he had expected. He had braced himself for her to collapse into tears or throw some sort of fit, not gracefully kneel at his feet and trust him.

He ran his hands through her shortened locks. At the beginning, he had planned to shear it all off so that she could never seduce another man with it again. That she would actually have allowed him to do so touched a long-frozen spot in his heart.

All women, but especially beautiful ones, were vain to the point of nonsense, but here, this woman—the most glorious one he had ever seen—had not even hesitated once she was assured that the women she wished to rescue would be safe. Clearly her concern was for others, not for herself.

He traced his fingers down her cheeks, exploring the smoothness of her skin, the delicate structure of her features. The ends of her shoulder-length hair tickled his wrists. He bent forward, wanting to kiss her, wanting to gather her in his arms and make love to her.

Make love?

The thought seemed to come out of nowhere. Tup, he corrected himself, but the words "make love" slid again across his mind as his lips touched hers.

A mewl of pleasure escaped her throat. Heat swelled in his groin. Her mouth was yielding, as hungry for his as his was for hers. He wanted her. More than he'd ever wanted a woman.

"Get up."

A look of confused rejection lit in her eyes, then she looked down at the floor planks and scooted away from him.

He reached for her, lifted her to her feet, turned her toward him, and encaged her in his arms. "I didn't mean for you to go away. I wanted you to be closer to me."

She tugged at her shortened locks and didn't quite meet his gaze, unlike the way she had always done so boldly in the past. Her vulnerability called to him and at once he regretted that he'd cut away her shield of hair. She didn't look any less attractive with it gone, but clearly she felt more exposed.

He splayed his hand across her cheek and ran his hand gently down her spine. "Though the bards compose ballads to it, 'tis not your hair I find attractive, Gwyneth, but your spirit. I had thought you were shallow, silly, and selfish, but I see you for who you are now—a woman with a brain and a heart."

Her mouth fell open, but no words came out.

Drawing her forward, he spread small kisses down her cheek and took delight when she relaxed against him. Her lavender scent intoxicated him.

"At first I thought you were a woman like others I have known—never to be trusted and after only their own gain, but tonight when I saw you walk into that jail . . . Gwyneth, you're so brave."

"Brave?" She wound her hands around his neck. "No one has ever called me brave."

"I saw what you did—you weren't there to seduce men, but to help those who could not help themselves."

A tear slid down her cheek. He thumbed it away, his heart nearly bursting with emotion. He wanted her to be his forever.

"I wanted to set matters aright. Those women suffer and have no place to go and no one to speak for them." .

"I'm sorry I did not hear you out about going to see Irma. I did not understand." He slid his finger down her neck. "I love you," he whispered.

Gwyneth lay in the afterglow of passion, her legs intertwined with Jared's and her head on a spot just beneath his right shoulder. Her hand trailed round and round on his chest. Her fingernail caught on a tiny mole on one side of his stomach—a tiny flaw in an otherwise perfect torso. The wooden bracelet he had carved for her twirled on her wrist. She drew a lazy circle around it with her finger. Of a truth, he was the most amazing man she'd ever known.

She let out a satisfied sigh, her heart nearly bursting with joy.

He appeared to be lost in thought, staring up at the folds of fabric that made up the bed's canopy and making those circles where his thumb and little finger twirled around each other.

"What are you thinking of?"

"Murder."

"Murder?" Startled, she propped herself up on one elbow, gazed at his enigmatic face to try to discern what he was feeling. "Did you kill someone?"

He turned toward her, jiggling the bed ropes. "No. But I was accused of it once."

"You were?"

"Aye."

"What happened?"

"There was bad blood between me and my brother. When he was found dead, I was the most likely suspect."

"What happened between the two of you?"

The tips of his mustache tugged downward. "There was a woman."

"And?" She ignored the tinge of jealousy that rose inside her.

"My brother and she were to be married. But I took her."

"Did you love her?"

Pain lurked in his eyes. "She was beautiful—nearly as beautiful as you—and I was taken by her smile and glittery clothing. Rafe always seemed to have everything—the land, the keep, our mother's love, so when she came to me, I didn't resist. I thought she wanted me the way I wanted her."

Gwyneth soothed the wrinkle that had formed between his brows, wishing she could iron out the past as easily. "She didn't?"

"She came to the mews where I was working with the falconers. She was dressed in a green surcoat with a yellow underdress. I remember the clothing because—" He rubbed his temple and ran a hand through his hair.

"And—"

"I killed her."

Gwyneth started. The mattress wiggled. "You murdered her?"

"Not just her, but our child as well."

Coldness seeped through Gwyneth.

"I should have refused her, should have walked away when she came to me, but I did not. I wanted her and I took what she offered. While we were in the throes of passion, Rafe and other men came upon us. We were caught in the very act. I tried to hide her, protect her, and"—he swallowed—"she accused me of rape."

"Accused you?" Gwyneth sat upright on the bed. "But you said that she sought you out."

"She did."

"That's outrageous!"

"Not unlike a certain woman who accused me of kidnapping her after she forced me to marry her," he said with a wry smile.

Gwyneth leaned back against the pillows, guilt weighing on her chest. "Truly, Jared, I am sorry. I had not intended for your life to be so complicated."

He took her hand and kissed her knuckles. "She was doing what she thought she must to protect herself—the same as you, I think. Perhaps I've judged her too harshly."

Gwyneth chewed on her lower lip, not sure what else to say.

"The men captured me, but I escaped, took a ship to nowhere."

"Oh."

"That's where I met James, your brother-in-law. Rafe believed her story and married her even though she was despoiled. Of a truth, though, he did not marry her for love. She was a wealthy woman. Later I learned she was pregnant with my child. The babe was too large for her and they both . . ." Jared took a deep breath and turned his vivid green gaze fully on her.

"It was not your fault that she or the babe died."

"If I would not have taken her—"

She touched his arm. "Jared, you did not murder her. Women sometimes pass in childbirth. 'Tis part of life."

He ran his hands through his hair. "Enough questions about me. Tell me about you. Have *you* ever murdered anyone?"

The question was asked lightly, a halfhearted attempt to change the subject but she cringed all the same.

Realizing belatedly that her jaw hung slack and guilt likely shone in her eyes, she cleared her throat and sank back onto his chest. He didn't know about the rapist and what Irma and she had done. "Of course not."

There was a long pause. Outside, a tree branch scraped against the keep's wall.

He stroked his goatee and stared at her in that way that ripped the veil from her thoughts. "Why are you lying?"

She softened her voice and patted his chest. "Do not be ridiculous. I could never kill someone."

"This from a woman who planned to ship me off

on a slave ship." He continued to look at her until Gwyneth squirmed beneath his scrutiny.

A tremble began in her shoulders and worked its way through her body as she was transported back in time to the murder. She could practically see the man's lifeless eyes staring up at her. His jaw had been bristled with a beard and he had an aristocratic nose. The man's eyes had widened when she'd walloped him over the head with the limb. His body had twisted in a sluggish half circle as he swirled downward into the water with his tunic full of rocks.

"Open the door!"

Gwyneth jumped as a cacophony of banging and clanking sounded in the hall outside their chamber.

"Wh—"

Bang! The door crashed open and Ivan, surrounded by a large band of armed knights, rushed into the chamber. Beside him was the jailor and a man whom Gwyneth recognized as one of the city's judges. Swords flashed in the air. Armor clanked. Men shouted.

Still naked, Jared leaped to his feet and grabbed his staff.

"Arrest her!" Ivan said, pointing at Gwyneth. *Oh, God.* Her sins had come to haunt her.

Boots clomped on the floor planks. They shoved Jared aside and rushed to her. Strong hands grasped her by her upper arms and dragged her from the bed.

"Cease!" Her head pounded as she was pulled to the center of the room. Chilly air blew on her skin. The bedsheet trailed behind her, slipping down her body.

Jared rushed forward and slammed his staff on

the head of one of the knights. Hoisting his sword, the man turned. Three others turned with him, cutting her and Jared off from each other. His staff was brought up again and then with a loud crack the wood snapped in half as it caught one knight's armor and splintered. He reached for his broken staff, but one of the knights kicked it away before he could reach it. It clattered across the planks and rolled near one of the trunks.

Swords pointed at Jared's bare chest and he was pushed against the wall.

Two men held her near the bed. "Jared!" She squirmed but could not break free.

"What is the meaning of this?" Jared demanded.

"Your lady wife is not at all the innocent she pretends to be." Ivan tugged sanctimoniously on his tunic. "She murdered your brother and threw his body in the river."

Oh, mercy.

All the men turned to look at her.

Gooseflesh popped up on her arms and legs and her nipples puckered with the cold air. She bowed her head. Her hair swung in front of her face, but it was no longer long enough to cover her naked body.

Ominous silence filled the room.

"By order of the court, Lady Gwyneth is under arrest and you are not to interfere," said the judge.

Sweet heavens.

"Get her a kirtle and take her now."

"Nay!" But her heart pounded and her mind raced. "Jared!"

Knights closed around her and the scent of sweat and eagerness of overexcited humans assailed her nostrils.

Across the room, Gwyneth saw Jared's brows slam together.

Her shoulders rounded and she crumpled inward. Her shortened hair bobbed.

"It was an accident!"

The men holding her squeezed her upper arms tighter.

"Tell them," Ivan continued. "Tell them how you filled his tunic up with rocks and sold his boots to buy jewelry. That does not happen by accident."

"Did you do that, Gwyneth?" Jared demanded.

She swallowed, not daring to look at him.

"There have been other men as well. She takes them from brothels to rob and sell. A coldhearted bitch."

"Nay—"

"You really sold his boots?"

She could feel Jared's gaze on her. "I—"

"Silence, witch!"

A thin woman with a sour, pinched expression slipped from around the soldiers. "She took my husband."

"And my son," said another woman who had also been hidden by the men. "He gave her gold and we never saw him again."

Oh, God.

"That's not tr—"

"I said silence!" Ivan roared.

The pinpoint of a dagger pricked her skin.

"Take her," Ivan said to the men, pointing toward the door.

The magistrate turned to Jared. "An apology, my lord, for the time spent in prison. Now that we have the real murderess, all should be taken care of."

"Jared! Surely you do not believe—"

"Was the murder of my brother what you were hiding from me?"

Gwyneth shivered.

"The truth for once, *wife*."

"How many other men have you tricked as you did me?"

Pain knifed her chest.

"Did you kill my brother or not?"

Unable to meet his damning gaze, she closed her eyes and lowered her head. Tears slipped down her cheeks.

"Tell me."

"I-I-I—"

Jared's hands balled into fists. "Of all the bloody things. You *did* murder a man. And let another suffer for your sins."

"But—"

He turned away from her. "When will I ever learn women cannot be trusted!"

Ivan tugged at the lace poking from the ends of his sleeves. "Take her now."

Gwyneth struggled against the hands binding her. She longed to break free, run to Jared and beg him to understand. Surely then he would enfold her in his strong, gentle embrace.

Jared's legs were braced apart. He held his staff steady. He did not move forward to protect her as he always had afore.

"Jared?"

No answer.

"Jared?"

A gown was thrown over her head and then a hood blocked her vision.

Chapter 30

Still naked, legs braced apart, Jared stared at the swirling knots in the closed oak door of the solar, afraid he would break in half if he moved. Agony burst in his chest. The men had filed out, taking Gwyneth with them.

He had trusted her, believed in her.

The knowledge that she had murdered his brother felt like he'd just swallowed a large stone. One that lay so heavy against his lungs he could scarcely breathe. He could still smell the stench of rat piss and rotting hay, still feel how the manacles had bit into his wrists and ankles.

Scars laced his legs—the result of being dragged across the rough-hewn stone floor of the prison.

Wearily Jared sank to the floor beside the bed, laid his head in his hands, and rubbed his temples. The witnesses had said that she had used other men as well and he had seen how she charmed them for her own gain.

Memories of how she'd made him crawl across church tiles and forced the marriage bit into his mind. Then she had accused him of kidnapping her. Later, she'd seduced him for her own purposes as well.

And, yet, he'd come to trust her anyway. What a fool he'd been.

Aeliana fluttered. Jared raised his head and set his hand down on the floor to rise. The rope of hair tickled his palm. He lurched as if Gwyneth were still here and had touched him with her fingers.

Taking a deep breath, he stared at the long silver-gold lock. It curled across the floor like a glittering snake, reflecting light from the candles that burned in the sconces.

What sort of woman allowed a man to crop all of her hair without so much of a whimper?

Slowly, he lifted the braid. It was soft and thick, much heavier than the piece he had taken with him to the prison. He held it up to his nose, the same as he had done so many times before. Lavender. Lavender and innocence.

Yet, it was her fault he had been in that dirty prison. Her fault he'd drank poisoned ale. She'd reduced him to naught.

Closing his eyes, he twirled it around his forearm, trying to discern what to do next. He could leave, get on a ship, and flee as he had done before—never let anyone close to him ever again.

But, of a truth, the people—his people—needed Aeliana's hunting talents to survive the winter. Somehow they had wormed their way into his heart.

The ends of the lock of hair brushed against the skin of his wrist, softly taunting him. *The people need you and you need Gwyneth,* it seemed to say.

The memory of how she had bent her head when

they took her came sharply to his mind. Without her glorious mass of hair, she'd been naked. Vulnerable. She had confessed to killing Rafe in cold blood, to filling his tunic with rocks and dumping him in the river, but he wanted her all the same.

Was she a witch or an innocent?

At that moment, Kiera and Elizabeth barged inside.

He snatched the bedsheet and wound it around his hips.

Brown hair frizzed around Kiera's elfin face and she wore a clean dress. In contrast to Kiera's curly locks, the other child had long, straight, dark hair. She was taller than Irma's daughter and her skinny arms poked out from too-short sleeves.

Kiera propped one hand on her hip and gazed at him with a look that was as forward as her mother's. "Where's Lady Gwyn?"

"She's not here." He looked into the girl's trusting eyes. In his mind, he saw the magistrate toss a kirtle over Gwyneth's naked body and a hood over her face. Agony lanced his chest. She was a murderess, but he loved her. He could not stop himself. And, just like Colette, she would steal pieces of his soul and sell them for her own gain if she let him.

Kiera took in the long strand of hair hanging from his fist. "You scalped her!"

"Nay," Jared started, "I—"

Kiera pointed at the braid. "That's her hair!" Tears welled in her eyes. "Why would you take it?"

Jared twisted the braid back and forth. Its lavender scent wafted upward. "'Tis complicated." An understatement. But impossible to explain to a child.

Hand on hip, Kiera shook her finger at him. "My

mama says that nobles are bad people, but Lady Gwyn isn't bad."

Jared remembered the way her mama and Gwyneth had tied him to a cot and sought to poison him. How he'd been dragged on his knees.

The dark-haired girl tugged Kiera's sleeve. "We should go."

"Aye," Jared agreed. "'Tis time to take you back to your mother." At the brothel.

Despite it all, his heart tugged. Gwyneth had wanted a better life for girls like this. She'd wanted to train them, give them skills. In only a few years, Kiera and the other one would be whores, the same as Irma. The only "skills" they would learn was how to open their legs several times a night.

He set his jaw.

The castlefolk were not his responsibility.

The women in prison were not his responsibility.

These girls were not his responsibility.

They would use him. Just as everyone he cared about did.

"We go to the brothel now," he asserted quickly. Best to be rid of the two children as soon as possible. "Wait outside until I am dressed."

Quickly he donned his boots and cloak, determined to drop both children off at the brothel with Irma. He would be rid of them, then take his hawk and leave England forever, wash his hands of marriage.

A few minutes later they made their way down the steps of the keep and into the bailey.

"My friend's name is Elizabeth," Kiera said as they walked past the newly cleaned moat. "She doesn't talk, but her name is carved on the wooden beads she wears. That's what Lady Gwyn told me."

"Wooden beads?" Coldness filtered through Jared's chest, but he kept trudging ahead, his eyes on the path. "What do you mean, child?"

"The beads—the necklace she wears."

Not slowing his pace, Jared glanced at the child. His brow furrowed. She had green eyes and straight dark hair. Could she be . . .

"Show me."

Kiera pulled her friend close, hugging her tightly by the shoulders. "You can't have them. You already took Lady Gywn's hair."

Jared stopped and glowered down at the defiant little girl. So much like her mother. So much like Gwyneth. "I'm not going to take them. I want to *see* them."

"Nay." Kiera turned to her friend. "Do not trust a man. Ever."

A tense moment passed. Elizabeth cocked her head to one side, looking up at Jared as if weighing out the matter for herself.

"I saved your life, little one. I mean you no harm." He held out his hand, palm up. A gesture of peace.

Abruptly, she nodded, pushed her cloak to the side and lifted the beads for him to see.

Jared's knees trembled as he stared at the wooden necklace hanging around her neck. The one he had carved for Colette. He had not put her given name on it, but her middle name: Elizabeth.

This was his child. Her eyes, her hair. He should have known.

Dear God. He reached for her, touched her cheek.

His legs shook and he could no longer hold himself up. Slowly he sank to his knees beside the little girl.

"What are you doing?" Kiera asked.

Blinking dazedly, he gathered both Kiera and Elizabeth into his arms. The two girls squirmed, but did not resist his open display of affection.

"Why are you crying?" Kiera asked.

"I-I-I'm not."

Elizabeth rubbed his cheek, her tiny finger coming away wet.

"Or maybe I am."

God had not abandoned him after all. Somehow, through some miracle, God had given him back his child. God and Gwyneth. His wonderful, impossible, glorious, defiant wife.

Quickly lifting one girl in each arm, he quickened their pace.

Kiera grabbed him around the neck. "Are we in a hurry?"

"Aye."

"Why?"

"Because I need answers."

Chapter 31

Gwyneth slid her fingers across the damp stone walls looking for a hold so that she could climb to the lone window above her in the prison cell. Dismal rays of light slid across the flea-infested rushes. A rat rooted in a pile of putrid garbage that rotted in one corner.

Defeated, she sank to the floor, heedless of her kirtle and cape—the only things she had been allowed to bring before guards had hauled her from her chamber and dragged her to this hellhole. She knew all too well the fate of imprisoned women: slavery.

She put her head in her hands and drew her knees up to her chest. Jared had been in a place such as this for three years. Her fault. All her fault. Had he felt this lonely and deserted? She recalled how his lips had flattened when he learned she was a murderess.

The flutter of wings sounded on the ledge above. She glanced up. A hawk's head poked through the bars, her yellow eyes gleaming in the dim light.

"Aeliana!" Hope sprang in Gwyneth's chest.

The hawk swooped through the bars holding a pigeon in its claws. With a thunk it was dropped at Gwyneth's feet. Just as Jared had described that the bird had done for him.

"Food!" one of the other prisoners said.

Quickly Gwyneth snatched the pigeon. A tiny rolled parchment was tied to its leg with a piece of twine. Puzzled, she untied it and pulled it open.

Bold, thick handwriting was scrawled across the missive.

Keep silent.

Jared?

She held the note to her heart, read it again, then held it back to her heart. Jared had not abandoned her after all!

But what did he mean, "keep silent"?

At that moment the cell's door clanged open. The guard, Jared, and Irma entered. A fierce scowl marred Jared's handsome face and his hand was latched around Irma's upper arm. He wore a black tunic and she was dressed in a scarlet dress. An angel of death and a lady of the night.

Gwyneth leapt to her feet. "Irma! Jared!"

Irma's hands were bound behind her back and she wore her yellow scarf around her head.

The town magistrate filed in after them. He wore a wide wine-colored cape and a white wig.

"I am innocent!" Irma exclaimed, wide-eyed. "Tell them, Gwyneth! Tell them!"

The parchment crackled in her hand. *Keep silent,* it said.

She gazed at Jared's face. His jaw was tight and his eyes guarded. There was no twitch, no wink, to tell her his thoughts.

Irma grabbed her shoulders. "You must help me! Please, Gwyneth."

Keep silent.

"Lady Gwyneth," the magistrate said. His wig hung irritatingly askew.

"This harlot is an accomplice to the murder of my brother." Jared pushed Irma into the cell. "Leave her here."

"We have come for your story, Lady Gwyneth. I know of your kindness to the poor and wish to release you. Noblewomen should not be in such a place as this."

Keep silent.

"If you are innocent, then speak, Lady Gwyneth." The magistrate puffed out his chest.

Keep silent.

"Gwyneth! Tell them! What is wrong with you?" Irma pleaded.

Gwyneth tried to catch Jared's gaze, tried to discern what to do. If she spoke up, she could go free. But the note. Could she trust him?

The judge tugged his misaligned wig so that it hung lopsided and askew the other direction.

Her mind raced.

You will no longer consort with whores. He had been furious that she and Irma had tricked him. He had locked her in a brank.

But her mind went to the way his arm had wrapped around Kiera and carried her gently from the jail. At how he had shown concern for her people.

"Well, Lady Gwyneth?" The magistrate propped his hands on his hips.

Gwyneth looked at the man's sweating face. Clearly he had his reputation at stake.

"See," said Jared, "it is as I said. Both Gwyneth and Irma are guilty."

Gwyneth wrung her hands. "There has been no trial."

Jared turned sharply to the judge. "You do not wish for your mistake of my imprisonment to be made public. It would be quite an embarrassment."

Gwyneth's heart lurched. If she said naught they would spend the rest of their life in prison. Did Jared have a plan?

Keep silent.

She considered all the times Jared had insisted that she keep silent, all the times that he had threatened her with the brank.

Was she a fool to trust him?

"Please, Gwyneth, please!" Irma raised her hands into a prayer position.

"You have only to speak for her and I will release her." The magistrate tapped his chin.

"She is guilty," said Jared.

Gwyneth looked from Jared's unsmiling face to Irma's pleading one to the judge's anxious one. Was she risking their lives on something as flimsy as fragile hope? What if Jared had sent the note to ensure her silence so that he could be rid of both of them? If only there was one instant of time where he let his guard down so she could be assured that she could trust him.

Naught.

He was an enigma. As always.

Her price is above rubies. He'd carved a bracelet for her with his own hands. Surely even tarnished rubies were too valuable to throw away.

Jared released Irma and thrust her toward Gwyneth.

The cell's door shut with a loud clang.

* * *

Irma leapt toward Gwyneth, hands outstretched like claws. "How dare you!"

The force of her friend's anger felt like a blow to her stomach. "Irma?"

Irma whirled quickly to the bars of the cell, grasped two in her hand, and peered down the hallway. "Ho! Come back here, you lumbering jackasses!" She rattled the bars back and forth. "I can make it worth your while, I can. We can make a bargain. I have skills . . ."

Gwyneth's heart sank. "Irma, no."

"Shut your piehole! We can get a larger cell if they know it's good for them."

Queasy sickness washed over Gwyneth. The idea of tupping prison guards in exchange for petty favors brought bile rushing into her throat.

Irma turned to Gwyneth and blinked. "With your looks, you'll be able to secure extra blankets for us when it gets cold."

"I will not—"

Irma rattled the cage again and hollered down the hall, "Come back, guard! I'll 'old her down while you cram it in 'er."

Saints.

"Irma, stop it!"

"Come later!" Irma waved her arms toward the guards. "She's of noble blood. Practically a virgin."

Gwyneth threw an arm around her friend and clamped a hand over her mouth. "Shush!"

Their eyes met. Dark wisdom rather than fear or desperation shone in Irma's gaze. Irma tugged Gwyneth close until her breath whispered against Gwyneth's ear. "We have a plan."

A plan? Heavens. It had been Irma's plan that had gotten them both here in the first place. If she had never stolen Jared and forced him to marry her . . .

"What do you mean?" Gwyneth whispered.

"Keep silent."

Keep silent? The same thing that had been written on the parchment. "I do not under—"

"Is there a problem in here?" One of the guards appeared at the cell's door and peered through the rusty bars. He wore a dingy tunic and worn breeches. A scar slashed down the side of his cheek.

"You betraying bitch!" Irma screamed and thrust Gwyneth away so hard that she staggered backward. "I refuse to share a cell with this woman."

Keep silent?

"Irma—"

The guard looked from Irma to Gwyneth. "Do you need something?"

"Nay." Irma flounced to the wall and sat beneath the lone window.

Keep silent?

Praying that she was making the right decision, Gwyneth shook her head.

The guard gave her a sly smile. "I will come for *you* later. The boat leaves tonight."

Hours later, Gwyneth paced back and forth, back and forth across the small cell. She had packed down the flea-infested rushes and was now wearing a path to the stone floor. Her fingers rubbed fretful circles on the tiny missive until a hole had torn in the parchment.

Her mind raced, one thought slithering over the next like a pit of angry snakes as she gazed at Irma, who was asleep against the damp stone wall.

Irma had said the same words that were on the parchment: *Keep silent.*

She had claimed that "we have a plan."

We?

Jared and she?

Her friend had refused to talk or even come near but as the hours passed and moonlight winked on and off through the window, Gwyneth wondered if she should shake her awake and demand answers.

Keep silent.

Why?

Had Jared tricked her friend the same as the two of them had tricked him and planned to leave both of them here?

Footsteps sounded against the flagstone. "That cell yonder. Take them all. Pay careful heed to the woman with the silver-gold hair. She will fetch a high price."

Price?

Her heart hammered. She scampered to the back wall and reached for the high window, wishing she were a spider so that she could climb the stones and escape.

"The boat is here. Take her quickly."

Two men stopped in front of the cell. A key rasped in the lock and the door clanged open.

"Come, woman."

Gwyneth's heart lurched into her throat. If Jared had a plan, why wasn't he here? Her gaze darted back and forth, measuring the distance to the door. Her legs tensed to run. "Nay!"

"This way, woman." A meaty hand gripped her upper arm in a painful grip. "Get the other one too."

Irma yelped as the other man kicked her awake. He wrenched her to her feet and pushed her forward.

Shoulders aching, Gwyneth pulled against the man's hold.

"Fight and we'll chain you. You'll have a better chance on the boat being unbound."

Holy Mary. Despair threatened to crush her chest. What a fool she was to have trusted Jared. He would be too late to save them.

"Nay!" Gwyneth shook her head. "I can pay you."

The man cuffed her across the cheek. "We'll get our payment. Move along."

Guards shuffled her and Irma into darkened streets. A light mist shrouded the moon and rained down on them. Coldness seeped through her bones. A glimmer of hope lit as she recalled how Jared had rescued her in the alleyway behind The Bald Cock. She looked this way and that at the passing shadows, hoping that she would see him.

Naught.

Nothing.

Tears stung her eyes. Jared would be too late to save them. If he was coming for her, surely he would have been here by now.

She touched her wooden bracelet. *Her price is above rubies.*

The scent of briny water wafted in the air as they neared the docks a short while later. Moonlight glimmered across the waters.

"There has been a mistake." Gwyneth's heart pounded. This could not be happening.

"Silence, woman, or you will be gagged."

Irma stared out at the harbor. Light gleamed off the tops of the gentle waves.

Wood clattered as they were forced down the gangplank and loaded onto a ship. Water lapped the edges of the ship.

Darkness and the stench of unwashed bodies nearly overpowered her as the two of them were hauled below deck and thrust into a chamber that was filled with bedraggled women. The stench of desperation hung in the air even stronger than the dirt and mildew and uncleanliness. Agony lanced her chest. These were the ones she had been unable to rescue. In the corner, she saw Blythe, her thin shawl still wrapped around her shoulders. Elfreda sat against the wall, eyes closed, face turned upward.

Gwyneth's eyes clouded as two fat drops blurred her vision. Unheeded tears trickled down her cheeks.

She wiped them away angrily as betrayal cut her heart. Jared had set this up to punish her. He had at last gotten his revenge against her—just as he had promised when they had married.

He had taken everything from her. Her castle, her freedom, her friend. She tugged at her shortened locks. Even her hair.

Her heart, a voice whispered inside.

The red stone in her wooden bracelet glimmered. He would not have given her that if he intended to abandon her, would he?

Torn inside, she bit the inside of her cheek to distract her thoughts. She could not think of it—she needed to formulate a plan to escape. Somehow she would find a way to free herself. And others. Just as she had done for years. Without Jared's or any man's help.

She felt the ship rock and sway beneath them. A woman lurched against her and pinched her cheek. "Fine white skin. Will your titties look as creamy when they strip ye naked and haul you to the block?"

Gwyneth cringed and closed her eyes. She bit the inside of her cheek until the copper taste of blood formed on her tongue.

"Maybe you'll get a rich master who won't expect much but a quick tup every now and again."

The breath left her lungs and dark spots danced before her eyes. Wrenching away from the woman, she fought her way to the locked oak door, which loomed more daunting than a fortress wall.

Mother Mary full of grace.

Nay.

Mary had abandoned her.

Panic rose. She pounded on the door with her fist, welcoming the pain that shot up her arm at the effort. "Let me out! Let us out!"

"They won't let the likes of you out of here."

She pounded harder, desperation clawing at her throat as she felt the ship sway, moving away from the dock. The note to keep silent had obviously been a trick.

Heedlessly, recklessly, she began to scream.

Another woman, this one with a toothless grin, laughed.

Chapter 32

Irma, who had been slumped against the far wall, leapt to her feet as a loud noise, like that of a cannon being fired, sounded and the entire ship rocked. It was dark in the chamber and Gwyneth wondered how many hours had passed. There were no windows to tell if it was dawn or still night. The stench of sweat and urine choked the air.

"Now, Gwyneth! Now! We've got to get the women out of 'ere." She ripped the yellow scarf off her head. A long flow of silverish gold hair cascaded downward and flowed to her waist. A wig.

"Wh—"

"No time to explain. We 'ad it made with your 'air. Give me your cloak and lead the women up the stairs and toward the back of the ship after I 'ead off the guards."

Before Gwyneth could speak, Irma had untied Gwyneth's cape and wound the yellow scarf around Gwyneth's head. Pulling the cape from Gwyneth, Irma pushed Gwyneth toward the crowd of women. "Hurry! Jared is coming!"

"But—" Gwyneth's emotions tumbled one over the next and her thoughts jumbled together.

Irma swirled Gwyneth's cape around her shoulders and pushed her way to the door.

"I don't underst—"

A key appeared in Irma's hand as if by magic. "Well, come on then. Don't just stand there with your mouth agape!"

"I don't—"

"Jared. It was hidden in me hem. No more time. Take the women! Go!"

Confusion melted into understanding. 'Twas another of Irma's outlandish plans. She grabbed her friend in a huge bear hug. "I thought you'd abandoned me."

"Never! You are my finest friend in all the world."

Renewed hope brought strength rushing through Gwyneth's limbs. She stood straighter, waved to the women, and began counting them.

"To me, women!" Irma called to the crowd as another cannon blast rocked the ship. She waved her arms in the air to get their attention. "Attend me!"

Dirty faces turned and stared at Gwyneth and Irma. Irma peered at Gwyneth expectantly too. She took a breath of the rotted air, then pushed her shoulders back. The two of them had gotten out of many situations together and this would be no different.

"To me, ladies! We have a plan to get all of you safely out of here." Gwyneth had no idea what the plan was, but she would be more believable if she did not tell them that. Irma had said to lead them up the steps and go to the back of the ship. She trusted her friend.

"Likely the guards outside the door will be some-

what distracted by the 'urly-burly above the deck,"
Irma said, adjusting the wig. The silver-gold hair
fanned around her. "I will race past them and lead
them on a chase. They know that if the officials find
a noblewoman 'ere that they will be taken to the
crown and put into prison to await trial. We suspect
that they 'ave orders to kill you."

"To kill *me*?"

"Aye—because you are of noble blood. Your testimony could get all of them 'anged. But if we get to
Jared, we can stop the whole slave trade. Take the
women."

"Jared did this?"

"He came to see me."

Gwyneth's hands trembled. "He didn't abandon me."

Irma touched her face, dark wisdom in her eyes.
"'e brought Kiera and Elizabeth to me at The Bald
Cock. I've never seen a man so wracked with guilt
about letting a woman be taken. I told 'im the whole
story with killing a man in the woods. 'e loves you."

Her heart pounded. "I love him too, Irma. He's—"

"Well, come on then. We have to get to 'im."

Joy leaping inside her, Gwyneth nodded and faced
the women who were staring up at her with grimy
faces and matted hair. Stopping the inhuman selling of souls had been her quest for three years. She
had done it one woman at a time, and the possibility of stopping it altogether sent a thrill of hope up
her spine.

"Someone has come to rescue us," she announced.
"Follow me closely, and all will be well."

Nervous whispers filled the chamber but Gwyneth
cut them off with a raised hand. "Silence." She nodded
at Irma and a look of trust passed between them.

Irma slid the key into the lock and opened the door a tiny crack. Loud shouting and the clomping of boots and cannons could be heard. The guards were not standing at the door but down at the end of the hallway. One was on the ladder and only his legs and feet could be seen. He seemed to be communicating to the other what was happening above.

"Once you get on the deck, lead the women to the stern of the ship," Irma whispered, leaning close to her friend. "I will distract the guards."

"But—"

"Whatever you do, keep covered and pretend that you are me. The other women are of no consequence to them, being commoners and whores, but if *you* are found here . . ."

Gwyneth's stomach churned with nerves. "Nay, 'tis too dangerous for you."

"I will be fine."

"Nay! Let me go!" Gwyneth held her friend's sleeve, but Irma swung open the door and clattered noisily into the hall. The guards turned.

"Hey!" one yelled.

Irma flipped the long silver wig behind her shoulders and took off running down the opposite direction.

"That's the noblewoman!"

"After her!"

Boots stomped as the men clattered past the open doorway and raced after Irma. The rest of the women stood wide-eyed. Carefully, she counted them again. Twenty. Twenty souls she could save. And Jared was waiting for her.

Heart thumping, Gwyneth waited until Irma and the two guards rounded a corner and then began motioning women out into the hall. "Shh," she admonished as she led them to the ladder and quickly climbed it. They were in the lower portion of the ship and there were a series of other ladders to climb. She set one woman who looked strong and healthy in the back of the line to alert them to any issues, then found another woman who could count and set her in charge of making sure that the group was accounted for. The sounds of the men fighting grew louder and louder.

At last, one by one, the women climbed out of the ship's dark hull. They squinted and covered their eyes in the dawn's bright, stinging light. The fresh scent of sea breeze mingled with the sulfuric stench of cannons.

On the bow of the ship, less than a stone's throw away, swords flashed in the air. Men shouted.

She craned her neck, searching for Jared's dark hair, for the staff that he always carried.

A screech sounded above and she glanced upward. Aeliana perched on the mast of the ship, her yellow eyes gazing at the men fighting on the deck.

Silently, Gwyneth said a prayer of thanksgiving. Jared had come for her, and the women would be safe.

"This way, ladies." Hope renewed, she began leading them toward the back to the ship just as Irma had instructed. The briny breeze lifted her shortened hair. The ship rocked and swayed. Seabirds cawed.

"By order of the king, this ship is under arrest!"

Gwyneth whirled as she heard the words being boomed out across the deck.

Jared stood, staff in hand, legs braced wide apart on the bow of the ship. Desire shot through her. He wore a solid black tunic and black breeches and was the most wonderful sight she had ever seen. Her legs tensed and she wanted to run to him, wrap her arms around him, and never let him go.

Montgomery and men dressed in garments depicting them as members of the king's guard stood beside him. Swords glinted, and the men who had taken her and Irma captive had their hands in the air in a gesture of surrender. She saw the jailor with the uneven earlobes. The judge was also in the crowd.

A breath of relief whooshed from her lungs. Another ship, one flying banners that she recognized as Montgomery's, was pulled alongside the ship that they were on.

"Jared!"

His head lifted at the sound of her voice. Their gaze caught and he hoisted his staff as if in greeting. The carved dragon looked majestic against the backdrop of the ship and sea. Wind lifted Jared's dark hair so that strands of it beat around his striking features. "Lady wife."

They stared at each other awkwardly and she realized she was still unsure where she stood with him. Irma had said that he loved her, but his dark face gave her pause.

"You must explain your experiences to the magistrate," Montgomery said.

Behind her, the women whispered among themselves.

Jared held out his hand, a gesture both tender and strong. "Come, Gwyneth. You are mine."

Her heart soared at his words. Lifting her skirts, she raced to him. Their bodies melded together as he lifted her in his arms and squeezed her tightly. Their hearts thumped against each other. He felt warm, so very warm, and she wanted to bury herself in his embrace.

Her fingers wound into his thick, straight locks. "I thought you had abandoned me."

His green eyes smoldered and his breath caressed her cheek. He touched the wooden bracelet on her arm. "Her price is far above rubies."

"I do not deser—"

Her protest was cut off as his lips crashed down on hers. Gwyneth felt herself being sucked into a storm of passion. Jared's tongue breached all her defenses and pushed past her lips to intertwine with her own. All the activity around them seemed to disappear until only heat and heartbeats remained.

Montgomery cleared his throat.

Gwyneth started. Jared released her slightly but his arms still curved around her waist possessively. They turned back to the circle of men and the ones they held captive.

"What is the meaning of this, Montgomery?" demanded the judge. His wig hung askew, just as it had before.

"These men planned to sell my wife as a slave." Jared pointed at the ruffians.

A barrel overturned on the deck and rolled toward them. Irma crashed through crates, rigging, and chains. The long silver-gold hair flowed behind her.

Burly men chased her, swords drawn. "Come back here, bitch!"

The magistrate puffed out his chest. "Arrest those men too!"

"Halt!" called one of the king's men, leaving the circle of the others.

"Wh—"

The men chasing Irma looked confused as they were stopped and hauled over to the rest of the group.

Irma stumbled to the edge of the deck and propped herself against the railing, panting. "At last."

"Explain!" demanded the judge.

"They planned to kill me because they thought I was Gwyneth of Windrose," panted Irma, indicating the long silver-and-gold wig. "They knew that she had information about the illegal slavery."

Seeing her opportunity, Gwyneth cleared her throat and stepped forward. She pointed to the women who huddled together at the back of the ship. Elfreda's eyes were wide like two round moons. "Many women have been sold into slavery to brutal masters. I have dedicated my life to freeing them."

The magistrate's hands twitched and his eyes shifted. He signaled his men to keep watch over the men being held prisoner and motioned at Gwyneth, Jared, Montgomery, and Irma. "Come. We have much to discuss."

The full moon beamed down on them as Gwyneth and Jared, hand in hand, climbed the steps to their home. She squeezed his palm, her heart filled nearly to bursting with the events that had happened this day.

"You saved all of them," she said, amazed. "And stopped the inhuman trade altogether." He had accomplished something she'd never thought possible. "I am not even sure how you managed to round up enough men in such a hurry."

He smiled at her, a warm glow in his agate eyes. "It wasn't difficult to make the magistrate nervous once

I threatened him with public exposure about my wrongful imprisonment. And James owed me a favor—he *is* the king's enforcer, after all."

"But you did it all for me."

"Of course." He raised her hand to his lips. His mustache tickled her skin as he kissed her palm. "It was very brave of you to face the prison."

She swallowed. "But, Jared . . . I . . . I was telling the truth. I really am a murderess."

He tugged her into his arms so that her head was tucked under his chin. "Irma explained it all."

"She said that you went to see her."

"I did. She told me about how Rafe had raped her in the woods. How you took a stick and bashed his head and then the two of you hid the body in the river."

"You aren't angry with me?"

"How could I be angry with you for acting for justice?"

She thought of the scars that crisscrossed his legs. "You spent three years in prison for a crime you did not commit—for something that I did."

"But I am alive."

Guilt weighted down her shoulders. "You have such scars."

"Perhaps if I would not have gone to jail, they would have arrested you and you would have been sold as the other women were." He pulled her close to him, embracing her as if she were the most precious thing in the world. "I could not live with myself if that would have happened. I'm glad I was in prison, because it kept you safe."

His patience and generosity touched her heart. He was so different than the other men she knew.

"And I found my daughter as well."

"Your daughter?"

"Elizabeth. She's mine. From Colette."

Gwyneth's brows drew together. "She is?"

"I will explain it all later. She had on the wooden necklace I had given to her mother."

"You gave her a necklace?"

Reaching down, he spun the bracelet on her wrist. "Colette thought my gift was beneath her."

"She was a fool, Jared."

Jared shrugged.

Gwyneth ran her finger down the length of his arm, admiring the way his muscles danced under her fingers. "The gift was not the necklace, my lord. The gift was the man who carved it."

His shoulders rounded and moisture gathered in his eyes.

She touched his cheek. "What is this?" She wiped away a wayward tear before it could fall. She touched it to her lips, tasting its saltiness.

"No one has ever called me a gift before," he said, his voice rough with emotion. "My own mother—"

Standing on tiptoes, she kissed his lips. His goatee tickled her skin. "—was a fool as well to not recognize what a treasure you are."

Candles glowed in the sconces as they traversed the hallway to their chamber. She turned her face to one side and batted her eyes flirtatiously at him. "I thought you were quite a gift when I had you tied to the cot."

Hunger gleamed in his eyes. The corners of his mouth lifted in a predatory, knowing smile.

They reached the door, but before it could be

opened, she stopped. She turned to Jared and ran her hands boldly up his chest. "There is something I would like to ask you."

"Aye?"

"Jared, my lord, will you marry me?"